FORT VENGEANCE AND SHADOW VALLEY

Two Full Length Western Novels

GORDON D. SHIRREFFS

WOLFPACK
PUBLISHING
— EST 2013 —

Fort Vengeance and Shadow Valley
Print Edition
© Copyright 2021 (As Revised) Gordon D. Shirreffs

Wolfpack Publishing
5130 S. Fort Apache Rd. 215-380
Las Vegas, NV 89148

wolfpackpublishing.com

eBook ISBN 978-1-63977-065-6
Paperback ISBN 978-1-63977-066-3

FORT VENGEANCE AND SHADOW VALLEY

FORT VENGEANCE

To my mother, Rose

FOREWORD

Fort Costain Arizona Territory, was built on a branch of the lonely San Ignacio. Don't look for it on the maps, for the War Department ordered it abandoned in 1890. The site is near a rutted gravel road which cuts off from the state highway which closely follows the old Butterfield Trail. Follow the gravel road for twenty miles until you see the only outstanding feature of the terrain, a gaunt pinnacle of rock which thrusts itself up from the barren soil like a warning finger. Beyond this pinnacle is another rutted trail that leads to the mesa where Fort Costain once was. The rock is called Intchi-dijin Rock by the Apaches, or Black Wind Rock by the whites. It too has a story.

Scattered through the ocotillo, mesquite and prickly pear on the mesa top you can still see low mounds of adobe, the old buildings of the post. Shards of pink and blue glass litter the hard earth, mingled with old horseshoes, rusty metal and corroded brass buttons. It is all that is left of Fort Costain, once an isolated outpost of the United States Army.

The hills about Fort Costain are quiet now, brooding beneath the bright sunlight and the starlit nights. Civilization has passed it by, but history remembers it in the dusty files of the War Department and in the yellowed newspaper clippings of the early seventies. It was listed as Fort Costain by the War Department. To the men who served there it had another name...*Fort Vengeance*.

CHAPTER ONE

The Abbott-Downing's swayed easily on its great leather thoroughbraces; sideways as the spinning wheels hit the chuckholes; yellow dust flowed through the open windows and sifted between the cracks, coating every thing inside.

Dan Fayes opened his eyes to look out at the hazy hills to the north. Somewhere in there was Fort Costain, his destination. The dust gritted between his teeth and abraded his throat, and he suddenly wanted the comfort and taste of a long nine. He slid his hand inside his coat, feeling for his cigar case. Then he looked at the young woman seated opposite him. Her scarf was tied across the lower part of her oval face. Her hazel eyes were steady, self-possessed.

She spoke through the fine scarf. "If you wish to smoke," she said, "please do. It can't be worse than this dust."

Dan smiled. "Thanks. The tobacco might cut the dust in my throat."

"I doubt it."

Dan took out a cigar and lit it. He snapped open the lid of his repeater watch. "Half after four. A long afternoon."

The big man seated beside the young woman looked up and nodded. "We'll be at Tres Cabezas home station within the hour."

Dan took his cigar from his mouth. "You know this country, Mister Manners?"

"I'm division inspector on this line."

"Tres Cabezas is my stop."

"Then you must be headed for Mesquite Wells?"

Dan shook his head. "Fort Costain."

The girl eyed Dan and then looked away.

Manners accepted a cigar from Dan. "You're army then?"

"Yes."

"I hope you're not assigned there, Fayes."

"How so?"

"Devilish place. Out on the devil's hind leg."

"I understand it isn't far from Mesquite Wells."

Manners laughed. "That isn't saying much. Begging your pardon, Miss Moore."

She looked at Manners. "No apology is necessary."

Dan leaned back. "You're from Mesquite Wells, Miss Moore?"

"I live near there with my father."

There was a veiled look of amusement in Manners' eyes. "There's no branch line to Mesquite Wells."

"I'll be picked up at Tres Cabezas," said Dan. "Perhaps you can ride with me, Miss Moore?"

"Thanks. We usually ride in army transportation from here to Mesquite Wells. My father does some contracting for Fort Costain."

The coach swayed around a curve. Manners pointed with his cigar. "Tres Cabezas."

Dan slid along the seat and looked through the billowing dust. A low rock structure showed on a knoll in front of a crescent-shaped area of rock. The hills were some miles north of the station. A triple-headed formation of rock showed dimly through the purple haze. Tres Cabezas. Three Heads. A damned lonely, forgotten speck of civilization on the Arizona landscape. Arizona hadn't changed much since his last tour of duty there in '59 and '60, thirteen years before.

Harriet Moore adjusted her scarf with a gloved hand.

She studied the lean planes of Dan's face. The well-trimmed blond mustache with the faintest trace of red in it; the wideset gray eyes. He was army all right. "U.S." probably was branded on his lean cavalryman's flank. An officer, like all the others at Fort Costain, yet somehow different.

The driver snapped his twelve-foot lash, and the six mules increased their pace. The greasy chuckle of the hubs rose in time to the steady clucking of the sandboxes.

Moore grinned. "Silver always comes into a station in style. Nobody to see him come in but hostlers and grease-boys, but he isn't one to miss a grand entry."

The coach swayed across a gravelly wash and hit the far side. It came to a brake-shrieking halt in front of the station. "Ho, greasers!" yelled Silver.

The unkempt hostlers trotted out the relief team as the Mexican grease-boy slaked the hot axles. The shotgun messenger opened the coach door. "Tres Cabezas," he said.

Dan dropped to the ground after Miss Moore. He winced as his left leg came back to life. Unless he kept moving the Minie ball wound stiffened a little. He took his gun case from the coach. Manners said, "I owe you a drink for the cigar," and sauntered toward the station.

Miss Moore drew the scarf from her face. She would have been classed as a little better than plain in the fashionable society of New York or Washington. In Arizona Territory, still a man's world in '73, she caught every male eye.

"I'll enjoy your company to Mesquite Wells," said Dan. "Perhaps you'll tell me about the country?"

"There isn't much to tell. The mines are dying out. Cattlemen are trying to get a foothold. Most of the Apaches are uncomfortable on their reservations. Some of the *broncos* try to incite the reservation bucks into going to war."

They passed the thick, bolt-studded door and entered the big low common room. A zinc-topped bar stretched along one wall. A lanky trooper leaned against it, holding a whisky glass in his hand. He glanced casually at Dan and with interest at Harriet. "Hello, Harriet," he said.

She smiled. "Corporal Tanner! What are you doing here?"

He grinned. "I wish I had come to meet you. I'm lookin' for Sergeant Haley."

"Why?"

He downed his drink. "Old Mike went over the hill last week.

"I don't believe it!"

Tanner shrugged. "You can take my word for it. Old Mike got a bellyful of Fort Costain. We've had four desertions so far this month. Twenty-two since the first of the year. Two suicides. It's worse than when you were last here, Harriet. Maybe you ought to marry me and leave here. My old man says I can have his farm in Iowa."

"What about that girl in Tucson, Bob?"

Tanner grinned. "You think I'd look at *her* if you was to let me court *you?*"

Manners went behind the bar and got a bottle and glasses. "Come on, Fayes," he said.

Dan eyed the bottle. *Surely one or two wouldn't hurt.*

Manners filled the glasses, eying Harriet as she passed into the hallway. "Nice filly. Too damned bad about her."

Tanner turned slowly. "What was that you said?"

"Too damned bad about her."

Tanner hitched up his trousers. He was slightly drunk. "You watch what you say! You hear?"

Manners smiled. "No offense, Corporal. What I meant was that it's too bad she has to stay at her father's place."

Dan took his glass. "Where's that?"

Manners relit his cigar. "Jim Moore has the hog ranch on the road between Mesquite Wells and Fort Costain, just over the post boundary line. Saloon. General store. Freight yard. Unofficial officers' club."

"Harriet is a lady," said Tanner.

Manners eyed him. "I didn't say she wasn't."

Dan sipped his liquor. The fire of it swept through him. The same old spark that usually ignited a roaring holocaust in him. It was his first drink since the interview with

General Sherman in Washington. He had broken his promise.

Manners downed a second drink. "Well, I'll be on my way. As it is, it'll be after dark when we reach Calabasas swing station. I'll see you, Fayes."

Tanner eyed Dan. "You headin' for Mesquite Wells?"

"Fort Costain."

Tanner's reddened eyes narrowed. "You ain't no fresh fish," he said. "You an officer?"

"Yes. Major Fayes."

Tanner straightened up a little. "I'm sorry, sir. I was just cuttin' the dust."

Benny wiped the zinc. "I coulda told you he was an officer, Tanner."

Dan hesitated. The noncom was on duty, tracking down a deserter, and therefore should have let the forty-rod strictly alone. Still, Dan had not officially taken over command of his new post. He removed his cigar from his mouth. "I'd go easy, Corporal," he said.

"Yes, sir."

"Where's my room?" asked Dan of the bartender.

"Down the hallway. Last one on the right. Ain't fancy, but we don't often get stopovers here."

Dan picked up his luggage and went out. He heard Tanner's unsteady voice behind him at the bar: "After he's at Costain for a while he won't worry none about me havin' a few drinks. Not after he sees how them *officers* swill day in and day out."

Dan continued down the corridor to the room at the end.

He dumped his luggage and dropped on the dusty cot. The liquor was working within him as it always did.

Dan puffed at his cigar. This was his last chance to stay in the service. The Benzine Board was lopping off excess and inefficient officers right and left, stripping high rankers from the shrinking Regular Army. The Congressional appropriation of 1869 had cut down the regular infantry regiments from forty-five to twenty-five. The cavalry had been increased for frontier duty, and many first-class doughboy officers had transferred to the mounted arm.

The words of General Cump Sherman seemed to come to Dan on the desert wind. "You're about due for the Benzine Board, Fayes. Your record was spotless. You were a colonel of volunteers at twenty-three. But since Appomattox, it has been one continuous round of drinking, women, and gambling while on your inspection tours. Luckily you still have many friends in the service. They have prevailed on me to give you another chance. I'm assigning you to Fort Costain, Arizona Territory. It's a rotten mess. Don't thank me, Dan. Your results will save, or *lose,* your commission. If you fail...well...send in your resignation before you get your orders to appear before the Benzine Board. It will be easier on all of us."

Dan closed his eyes. The damned insatiable craving for liquor had started the last year of the war. Before that time, he had had his share of bottle courage, but then it had been a war of movement. The fighting at Spotsylvania Court House, in the Mule Shoe area, had shifted the balance from a love of action and excitement to that of a matter of holding on to the last shreds of courage for decency's sake.

Fighting with his regiment, part of the battle-wise Sixth Corps, he had been struck in the left thigh by a Minie ball. The hours that had followed, lying in a rain-filled ditch, tinted red by flowing blood, listening to the groans and shrieks of the wounded, had somehow cracked the citadel walls of his inner spirit. That rainy night a nameless enemy had gained control. From then on, through the remainder of the war, he had leaned heavily on the glass crutch.

The bottle had been his aid and comfort when his leg ached intolerably, and when the wartime memories came back to gibber and drool at him in the night. He had requested a transfer back to the cavalry, his original arm, after Appomattox, pleading the wound which made it difficult to march. Surprisingly enough he had been dropped no lower than major, with duty as a cavalry inspector. Slowly but steadily liquor had saddled him and tightened the cinch.

Then it had slipped a spade bit into his mouth to make its control of him complete and sure.

Dan's duties had carried him from the Texas-Mexican border, where yellowlegs had watched the ambitions of Maximilian, through the Indian Territory up to Forts Laramie, Fetterman, and Kearney, then down through Colorado and New Mexico to Forts Union, Craig, and Bliss. Liquor flowed like water at post affairs. Old comrades from West Point and the war helped him along his wet road. Then there were the nights spent in raw frontier towns where there was no amusement except hurdy-gurdy girls and saloons.

Dan opened his eyes and watched a centipede crawl across the windowsill. *Had it really been eight years?* He had spent the last year in Washington, preparing reports and recommendations, bidding farewell to discharged officers who had served their country in time of war and peace and who now had been callously thrown back into the mad civilian struggle for money, most of them by training ill-equipped for the fight. Over seven hundred and fifty of them had been cast adrift.

Dan dozed uneasily for a time and then got up to wash. The sun had died, and he lit a candle lantern. He eyed himself critically in the cracked mirror. The gray eyes were darkly shadowed. The reddish-blond hair had lost the shine of youth. His hard hands gripped the sides of the washstand. This time he had to make good. He would never be able to face himself in a mirror again if he didn't. It had always been his dream to end his life in service harness. If he failed, he might as well be dead; for a man without a dream was truly dead.

CHAPTER TWO

T he common room was lit by a big hanging Rochester harp lamp. The yellow pool of light flooded the table set with chipped graniteware for two. The greasy odor of cooking filled the station. Miss Moore was already seated, still wearing her gray traveling costume. Benny bustled into the room from the kitchen, bearing a loaded tray. "Mex strawberries, sowbelly and jamoka," he said apologetically. "Our fresh supplies ain't come in yet."

Corporal Tanner was nowhere in sight. "We'll be dining alone," said Harriet.

"Quite cozy," said Dan.

"You've been west before this time?"

"My first assignment was as a shavetail at old Fort Buchanan near Sonoita Creek."

"That is now Fort Crittenden."

"Then I served at Fort Grant at the base of the Pinalenos most of the time."

"So you know the Apache?"

Her tone caused Dan to look up quickly. "Yes. Why do you ask?"

"Last year there was a great deal of trouble in the Tonto Basin."

"I understood the Apaches in this area were living quietly on their reservations."

She raised her head. "They've never really been quiet. The Tucson Ring has been working overtime to stir them up."

"The Tucson Ring?"

She nodded. "Grafters, rustlers, dishonest contractors and frontier riffraff. Their plan is to keep the Apaches restless so that the War Department will be forced to keep troops here. Crooked politicians and contractors cheat the government on hay, lumber, and other supplies. The settlements near the posts profit from the soldier trade."

"You seem to be well informed, Miss Moore."

She nodded. "I've heard my father and his business friends speak of it many times."

"Has your father been long in business out here?"

She flushed a little. "Since after the war. He was with Carleton's California Column in 1862 when it came through here. Later he was stationed at Fort Bowie in Apache Pass. He took his discharge out here and sent for me after my mother died."

"Do you like living near Mesquite Wells?" The instant he saw the look in her eyes Dan regretted his question.

"As long as you are going to Fort Costain, Major Fayes, you might as well know the truth. My father runs a combination general store and saloon with a small freighting business as well. The place is known far and wide as Moore's Hog Ranch."

"Running a saloon is no dishonor, Miss Moore, as long as it is run with decency."

She stood up. "To *some* people it is a dishonor. People who do not have my father's decency." She left the common room and walked outside.

Dan finished his meal and followed her. She stood by the high-walled corral, watching the fine paring of the moon as it rose above the eastern heights. The light sharply accentuated the angular peaks.

"There is nothing more beautiful than the desert at night," he said.

She nodded. "I'm glad you said that. So many officers think otherwise."

"May I smoke?"

"I like the odor of good tobacco." She turned and leaned back against the wall. "Smoking must be a great solace."

He lit up, the flare of the lucifer showing his lean tanned face. "It is."

"I often wonder if women would be accepted in society if they took up smoking."

"Not cigars, I hope."

She laughed. "No."

The moon rose higher, flooding the desert with silvery light, marking the desert growths with sharp shadows. "Are you a brevet major?" she asked.

"No."

She eyed him. "Then you will be relieving Captain Ellis Morgan. He's C.O. of A Company. Costain is a three-company post, you know."

He nodded. "How long has Morgan been in command?"

"Three months. He succeeded Major Dunphy."

"What happened to Dunphy?"

She seemed surprised. "You don't know? Of course, you wouldn't. It was hushed up." She became curiously quiet.

"I'd like to know," he said. "You might as well tell me. I'll find out when I get there in any case."

"Yes," she said quietly. She turned and placed her slim hands behind her back. "Jim drank a great deal. It had a terrible hold on him. His officers and men laughed behind his back. It didn't help Jim any. *He knew*. There was a terrible fear in him. He had a fine war record under Wilson." She looked away. "But the guerrilla warfare of the Apaches was too much for him. He sought his courage in the bottle. Apparently, he didn't find enough there. One night he shot himself."

Dan took his cigar from his mouth. Her words had struck home like the smash of the Minie ball which had wounded him. "You seem to know a lot about Jim Dunphy," he said quietly.

Her steady eyes held his. "Yes. You see...we were engaged to be married."

In the silence that followed a coyote gave tongue out in the wastes.

Dan relit his cigar. "I'm sorry I talked you into telling me about it."

She shrugged. "You would have found out. Don't condemn Jim too harshly. Some men follow a walk of life for which they are fitted. Others try to follow a way of life for which they are *not* fitted yet lack the courage to leave it. Jim was one of those. There was too much pride in him to let him resign."

"It isn't an easy thing to do, Miss Moore."

"Perhaps there are times when it takes more courage to turn back than to go ahead."

He touched the puckered bullet hole beneath the left trouser leg. In that last bloody charge at the Mule Shoe, he had been afraid. Other officers had turned back, with fear etched on their white faces, but Dan had gone on into the leaden sleet, rallying his men. He had paid the price.

A far greater price than an occasional twinge in his left leg.

She paced back and forth. "Dad sent me to Albuquerque to stay with his sister after Jim died. For a long time, I did not want to come back and then I knew I had to."

"Why are you confiding in me, Miss Moore?"

She stopped and looked up into his shadowy face. "I don't really know. Perhaps because you are going to take Jim's place. Good night, Major Fayes." She turned and walked quickly into the station.

Dan loosened his collar and let the dry desert wind seep down beneath his shirt. The light went on in her room, the next one to his. His secret had always been his own. It wasn't any longer. She knew.

The cold rain slanted down, puddling in the greasy mud of the tangled woods about Spotsylvania Courthouse. The leaves dripped and the pools of' lead-colored water were dimpled by the drops. Dead and wounded of both sides were scattered thickly, half-sunken in the mud. There was a steady groaning, almost inhuman in sound, broken now and then by an agonized scream. A foul smell hung in the wet air. A miasma of blood, powder smoke, sour clothing and death.

The rain was fine and steady, now and then illuminated by ghostly fingers of lightning. A dead man lay five feet from Dan, his twisted fingers gripping his bloody undershirt. A muddy footprint showed on his bluish face. Somewhere in the night a Union band played a polka, more like a dirge in the saturated darkness. The last of the staggering, wild-eyed Union assault troops had long disappeared into the night, leaving a bloody debris of dead and wounded to mark their attack.

The wind swept through the dripping woods, bowing the trees like the heads of keening women. A figure moved through the soaked brush, bending now and then over a body. The man knelt beside a young Union officer. A flash of lightning showed the gleam of the knife and the severed finger in the man's hand, with a ring still on it. The ghoul wore Union blue.

Dan shifted, feeling for his Colt. It was gone, lost in the thick mud. His sword lay shattered at his feet. Dan rolled to one side, gritting his teeth at the spasm of pain which shot through his shattered left leg. He felt in his pocket, drawing out a stubby Southern swivel-barreled derringer, souvenir of Antietam. He cocked it, hoping to God it was not too wet to fire.

The ghoul came close. He stopped at Dan's feet and then reached out with a muddy hand. Dan fired up at the dim face. The lightning flashed, revealing the jagged cut of the mouth as the soft slug smashed home under the bearded chin. The ghoul pitched forward across Dan's body. Warm blood dripped down on Dan's face.

Muskets popped from the shattered Rebel breastworks as the shot alerted the defenders. The limp body jerked as the slugs drove home in it. More blood ran down on Dan's face. He screamed as it blinded him. Again, and again.

Dan sat bolt upright. Cold sweat soaked his undershirt. He smashed his back against the adobe wall behind him, clawing for his service forty-five. Then sanity came slowly back to him. He saw the white-plastered walls of the little room and the dappled moonlight on his bed.

Dan's hands shook as he wiped the sweat from his face. It had been almost a year since he had had that particular nightmare. He dropped his legs over the side of the bed and held his face in his hands. What was it Harriet Moore had said? *Perhaps it takes more courage to go back than to go ahead.*

CHAPTER THREE

The morning wind scrabbled at the thick walls of the station. A crissal thrasher gave voice somewhere out in the mesquite. Dan opened his eyes. After his nightmare he had lain awake for hours, wishing for a drink. Now he arose and splashed water on his face and dressed swiftly. Out on the sunlit desert, a thread of smoke floated up from a distant peak, raveled by the fresh wind. Dan swung his gun belt about his lean hips and settled it. He slipped a double-barreled derringer into his coat pocket. At the bottom of one of his bags was the little swivel-barreled derringer he had found at Antietam. He never saw it without thinking of that rain-soaked night at the Mule Shoe, yet he could not bring himself to get rid of it.

Harriet Moore was at the table when he entered the common room. She smiled. "Good morning. You slept well?"

"Yes," he lied.

The steady hazel eyes held his for a moment and then she looked away. Dan sat down and filled a cup with steaming black coffee. He wondered if she had heard him during the night.

Benny entered the room. "Mush and sowbelly. The hens ain't layin' this mornin'," he said with a grin.

While they ate, they heard the popping of a whip out in

the desert, followed by the steady thud of hoofs and the rolling of swift wheels. A hostler looked in through the doorway. "The Dougherty from Fort Costain is here," he called out.

The vehicle ground to a halt outside of the station. A dusty trooper entered the room. "Major Fayes here?" he asked.

Dan stood up. "Yes."

"Trooper Samuel Booth. Dougherty driver."

"My luggage is in the end room. Bring Miss Moore's as well from the room next to it."

"Yes, sir?" Booth glanced at Harriet. His homely face broke into a grin. "Miss Harriet! I heard you was coming home."

"I arrived last night, Sam."

"Your Paw will sure be tickled."

Dan paid the tab and went outside, lighting a cigar. He walked toward the Dougherty. A civilian leaned against it, his face shaded by a battered Kossuth hat. He gave Dan a sketchy salute. "Gila Barnes," he said, "government scout."

"Major Fayes."

"You don't remember me?"

"By God!" said Dan, "you were at Fort Grant with me in '6o!"

Barnes grinned. "Yeh. You was a shavetail then. Nantan Eclatten."

Dan laughed as he recalled the name given to him by friendly Pinalenos. Nantan Eclatten. Raw Virgin Lieutenant. The name had persisted even after rough fighting against the elusive Intchi-dijin, Black Wind, a pure quill *bronco* of the Tontos. Dan gripped the scout's hard hand. "I'd have thought that by now you would have been long gone to the House Of Spirits."

Barnes shifted his chew of spit-or-drown. "Oh, they tried a few times. My mother always said I'd come to no good."

Dan looked past the scout at the thin tendril of smoke against the clear sky. "Did you see that smoke, Gila?"

Gila nodded. He spat accurately at a gecko lizard, splattering the fine scales with brown juice. "We been seein' 'em for three days."

"What's up?"

"Only smoke so far." Gila wiped his stained beard. "Don't yuh remember, Dan?"

Dan grinned. "Sudden puff means strange party on plains below. Rapid puffs means travelers well-armed and numerous. Steady smoke for some time means to collect scattered bands at some predesignated point with hostile intention if practicable. What's going on, Gila?"

"*Quien sabe?* The Tontos have been restless but haven't broken loose. The Pinalenos are at peace."

"So?"

"The Chiricahuas may be up this far. Might even be a band of White Mountain 'Paches or wanderin' Mimbrenos from New Mexico."

"The road is safe?"

Gila shrugged. "Few roads in Arizona are ever really safe. We left the fort last night and camped out at Yellow Wash. Nothin' happened."

Harriet came from the station followed by Booth carrying the luggage. "Hello, Gila," she said with a smile, holding out her hand.

Gila wiped his hand on his greasy shirt. His craggy face broke into a wide grin. "Miss Harriet! Well, I'll be damned! Tickles me pink to see yuh."

"Is everything all right at the ranch?"

"Fair to middlin'. Your Paw is fine. Arm bothers him once in a while. Outside of that he's as healthy as a cub bear."

Booth rolled up the canvas boot cover and stowed away the luggage. Dan placed his cased rifle in the wagon. Gila helped the young woman in. Booth climbed into the driver's seat and took the ribbons. "All right, sir?" he asked.

"Roll it, Booth."

Booth slapped the reins on the dusty rumps of the wheel mules. The Dougherty rolled out onto the stage road and then turned onto the yellow ribbon of rutted track which trended north toward the low hills. The smoke was gone now.

The sun climbed higher, soaking the desert in yellow heat. The dust rose from hoofs and wheels. The ragged hills, bleached as white in places as dead men's bones, were stippled with brush. A dull haze was forming over the mountains. It was a dead land with the slender shoots of ocotillo showing above the high mescal plants. Chollas spread their fangs among beds of prickly pear. A lone saguaro raised long arms in supplication to the pitiless sky.

"Like traveling on the moon," said Dan to himself. Harriet turned. "That's the first thing you've said since we left Tres Cabezas."

Dan leaned back on the hard jump seat. "Silence always seems to be a part of the desert. It seems almost unholy to speak too loud."

"As in a church."

"In a way."

"Some church," said Gila over his shoulder. He slowly cut a fresh chew of spit-or-drown. "I always think of the desert like it was a cougar. Nice to look at, when you're at a distance. Close up you get the truth. The claws inside the velvet."

"You sound like a poet, Gila," said Harriet. "You've been reading again."

Gila stood the chew into his mouth and spoke thickly. "Oh, I didn't read that. A shavetail once said that to me years ago when we both got lost out here. No water. No trail."

Dan eyed Gila. "I remember," he said quietly.

Gila nodded. "It was you."

"Only I didn't say the desert was like a cougar. I said it was like a woman."

Gila turned. "Waal, I didn't want to say that in front of Harriet, Dan."

Harriet eyed Dan. "That sounds bitter."

He looked out across the harsh desert. "It was meant to be. At that time anyway."

"And now?"

He looked at her. "I'm not so sure it still isn't the truth."

She leaned back and studied the lean planes of his face. She had struck a responsive chord in him. A strange man. It *must* have been him screaming in the night.

Gila suddenly jerked his head and held up a hand.

Booth reined the team to a dusty halt. Dan looked out of a side window. High in the brassy sky was a drifting spot, like a scrap of charred paper. A revulsion formed in him. A buzzard.

Gila rubbed his corded neck. Then he slid from his seat and drew his long-barreled Spencer rifle from the wagon. "I'll be right back," he said.

Dan jumped from the wagon. "Wait," he said. He stripped the case from his new Winchester.

Gila whistled as he saw the fine weapon. "What is it? Rimfire?"

"Model 73. Brand-new. Caliber .44. Centerfire. More wallop than the old Model 66 rimfire."

Gila padded off through the brush with Dan close behind. "What is it, Gila?"

"We'll see in a minute. Didn't yuh see them hoss tracks in the soft sand near the road?"

"No."

"Get the crust offn them eyeballs! You're back in Apacheria, Danny."

Gila stopped in a clearing and eyed some horse droppings. He smashed them with his rifle butt. "Cavalry hoss. Oats in the droppin's. Dropped last night, I'd say." His eyes studied the harsh earth like a page in a book. "Hoss walkin' slow."

They went on. Gila held up a hand. A crumpled figure lay half-concealed beneath a mesquite clump. The half-inch yellow stripe showed on the blue trousers. "Come on," said Gila.

Dan levered a round into the chamber.

Gila rolled the body over. Dan looked into the bloody face of Corporal Tanner. The scalp had been cut neatly from the elongated skull. The jowls had loosened like wet pie dough. Flies rose in a buzzing cloud from the clotted red abomination of the naked skull. The mouth gaped open revealing the stained teeth. Gila spat deliberately. He pointed at the side of the skull, smashed like an egg. "They made damned sure his spirit wouldn't follow them for vengeance."

"Why a scalping? That usually isn't Apache practice."

Gila shook his head. The faded eyes held Dan's. "Not unless they plan a scalp dance."

Gila walked about. "Welcome back to Arizona, Dan," he said. "There's a blanket in the wagon. We'd better wrap him up so's Harriet don't see him."

The sun glinted on glass. Dan picked up an empty rye bottle. "When did it happen, Gila?"

Gila squatted by the corpse. "'Bout dawn, I'd say."

"Tontos?"

"*Quien sabe?* Tontos. Pinalenos. Mimbrenos. White Mountain, Chiricahuas."

"Much of this going on?"

Gila shook his head. "Once in a while we find a dead man in the hills. Ain't no way of tellin' who did the job."

Dan eyed the brooding hills. "You think we're safe?"

"The pass is wide. Not much cover. We got three good rifles and know how to use 'em. Harriet can shoot for record if she has to."

"Why in God's name didn't you bring an escort?"

"There hasn't been that much trouble. Besides, Cap'n Morgan said he couldn't spare the men."

"I don't like it."

Gila stood up. "Take it easy, Dan. This loco bastard musta been drunk when he reached here. Mebbe passed out in the saddle. Hoss walks offn the road. *Somebody* sees a chance to get a good rifle, pistol and hoss. Temptin' it was. They watches Tanner. Drops him. *Yah-ik-te*. He is not present; he is wantin'."

"Why would they scalp him? It's a dead giveaway."

It was a strange face that turned toward Dan. "I've done

a little myself, Dan. Wore Navajo hair on my leggins while scoutin' for Kit Carson's First New Mexico. I wasn't the only one. Somebody's brewin' medicine, Dan. *Big* medicine."

Dan went back to the wagon and had Booth unhitch a mule while he got a blanket. He did not look at Harriet. He rode the mule back to Gila, who was coming out of the brush. "They was three of them. One ridin' a mare. Three hosses was in the brush. Four hosses rides off. One of them without a rider."

The mule shied and blew as they placed the blanketed form across his back. Gila opened his hand and showed Dan a brass cartridge case.

"So?"

"Forty-four Henry rimfire. One shot. Not many repeaters in 'Pache hands around here."

"That doesn't mean much."

"Mebbe. Mebbe not." Gila dropped the hull into his pocket. "Looks like I got to get off my dead rump at Fort Costain and take a look-see into them hills when we get back."

They led the mule back through the brush. Now and then, Dan looked back over his shoulder. The desert was as silent as Corporal Tanner's grave would be.

The Dougherty bounced and swayed across the rough ground, sinking now into a deep sun-baked rut, and then bouncing out of it. Now and then, Dan glanced back at the still, blanketed form in the rear of the vehicle, but most of the time he scanned the low hills on either side of the quiet pass. As Gila had said, the pass was wide, without too much cover. Gila rode with his long Spencer butted on the floorboards, leaning on the weapon, eying the hills from beneath the sloppy brim of his Kossuth hat.

Harriet held Dan's forty-five in her lap. Her face was pale, but she had not gone into hysterics at the sight of the body. She was steady. Afraid, of course, but steady. There was a difference.

They rounded a sharp turn and Gila looked at Dan.

"We can turn off soon onto the fort road. Or do you want to take Harriet to her father first?"

"The ranch, Gila."

"Keno."

Dan slanted back his hat and looked toward the hills. A gaunt pinnacle of rock thrust itself up from the barren soil like a warning finger. Then Dan saw the strange figure seated in a hollow of the pinnacle, almost as though sitting in a comfortable armchair. Thin arms hung across the bony knees which protruded from beneath a greasy buckskin kilt. Loose moccasins hung about the skinny calves. The button-toed, thigh-length, hard-soled desert footwear of the Apache. The *n'deh b'keh*.

Booth reined in swiftly and scrabbled for his issue trap-door Springfield carbine.

Gila raised his head. "Looks like a damned mummy."

The four whites looked up the slope at the motionless seated figure. The Apache was old. His hair was dirty gray, bound by a calico headband. His ragged huck shirt hung open exposing his gaunt chest, the ribs protruding like ridges of granite through brown sand. He did not move.

"Is he dead?" asked Harriet softly.

"No," said Dan. The Apache was no more than fifty feet from the motionless wagon, as though graven from the very rock on which he sat. There was an uncanny stillness in the hot air. Even the mules stopped their small movements.

The Apache moved, raising a skinny arm. He spoke slowly in good Spanish. The voice was firm and clear as though a young man spoke. "Do not be afraid. None of the young men are here. Only I, who am old beyond belief, and harmless to you."

"What is it you want?" asked Dan in his rusty Spanish.

"I know you, Nantan Eclatten!"

An icy finger seemed to trace the length of Dan's spine. "No."

"We have fought against each other in years past. In the old days, before the great war of the White-eyes. You have been gone a long time."

"I do not remember, old man."

The Apache lowered his skinny arm. "Then, Nantan Eclatten, there is no respect in you for an old enemy? Was I not a good warrior? Did I not strike terror into you as you did to me when we fought?"

Dan shifted in his seat, moving his rifle. He had fought most of them before the war. Tontos, Pinalenos, Aravaipas and Chiricahuas.

"You do not remember Intchi-dijin?"

"Jesus!" said Gila. "Black Wind! I thought the old raider was long dead!"

Black Wind moved, and the sun glinted on a brass plate which hung from a thong about his withered neck. "Nantan Eclatten, in the old days you were but a boy, fit only to herd horses, and wear the head-scratching stick of the untried brave."

"Thanks," said Dan dryly.

"It is said that now you are a tried warrior. A chief wise in the ways of the white man's war. Why is it you come? Do the White-eyes plan vengeance on The People? Will there be war in this country again?"

"We are at peace with The People. But we have just found the body of one of our men. Scalped. Not five miles from here. Is this the doing of The People? If so, then it is *you* who plans war?"

Black Wind raised his head a little. "You are sure it was done by my people?"

"Yes. There has been smoke in the skies. Do you not have a treaty for peace with us?"

"Lies! Scraps of paper are covered with marks which have no meaning to The People. We are forced to make our marks on them. It says one thing. The White-eyed chiefs do another."

"*I* have signed no paper, Black Wind."

"It does not matter. Your people are not like mine. Each warrior has his say before he goes to war. Amongst your people a warrior does as he is told. You will go to war. There will be bloodshed."

"These are the words of a bitter old man."

"Listen, Nantan Eclatten! My people are angry. The young men sharpen their arrows and grease their guns. They buy fine rifles with the yellow iron which the White-eyes love more than anything else. They have asked my council and I have spoken. I advised peace, but if they do not heed my words your lodges will go up in smoke. Your wagons will be captured. Those of you who wear the blue suits will die in the mountains and deserts. The signal smokes will rise from here to Sonora."

"What is it they want, Old One?"

"Peace! But more than that! *Justice!* There is to be a meeting between your people and mine at San Ignacio Creek. It will end the same way!" Black Wind jerked the brass plate from the thong and held it out in a dirty claw. "This is the badge of betrayal! The reservation number given to a great chief as though he was one of your cows, sheep or goats! Am *I* to be only a number? I fled your reservation years ago, but I kept this badge of shame! Take it! Keep it! Remember it! For you shall not rest by day or night!" He hurled the plate into the roadway. It tinkled into a baked rut.

Dan felt cold sweat run down his sides.

Black Wind pointed a finger at the wagon. "There will come a time when you shall want to speak with me. Use that plate to pass through my warriors, before you choose the way of your dying! Farewell, Nantan Eclatten!"

The four whites looked down at the brass plate. When they raised their eyes again the ancient was gone, as though he had disappeared into the living rock itself.

Gila slid from the wagon and picked up the plate. He read it: "Black Wind. Number One. San Ignacio Reservation." Gila tossed the plate up and down in his hand. "I thought the old coot was long dead. He hasn't been seen around for years. He was the greatest of them all. A chosen son of Stenatliha. Knew every waterhole and rim-rock trail from the Mogollons down to Durango. No living man, white or red, knows this country like he does. It's a damned good thing he's as old as he is."

"I'm not so sure about that."

Their eyes met. "Somehow, I'm glad you're back, Dan," said Gila, "providin' you remember how to mix with 'Paches, and don't let your years in the war make you think you know everythin' about fightin'."

"I won't."

There had been an eeriness about the whole episode. The pass brooded in the hot sun. Harriet's face was tense as she looked at the pinnacle of rock. "He knew you."

"It's possible. I remember now fighting against a chief called Black Wind. He was an old man even then."

"Yes." Her face was strange. "But what you don't know is that Black Wind *has been blind for over five years!*"

Gila handed the greasy plate to Dan. "Yes. I remember now."

Booth nervously rubbed his jaw. "Let's get out of here!"

The Dougherty rolled forward. Dan fingered the brass plate. A feeling of foreboding surged over him. The rock was empty of life. Black Wind's Rock.

CHAPTER FOUR

Moore's Ranch was situated on a rocky hill overlooking the Mesquite Wells road. The walls were immensely thick, buttressed, pierced with narrow windows fitted with heavy metal shutters. The low roof was surrounded by a crenelated parapet. Beyond the house were high-walled corrals from which issued the bawling of mules. Heavy freight wagons stood near a field-rock warehouse. Outbuildings formed a quadrangle from which loopholes covered every foot of approach to the ranch.

Dan eyed the solid buildings. "Looks like a fort," he observed.

"It is," said Gila. "Jim built here right after the war. That was before Fort Costain's time. There was many a bloody wrangle around here before the 'Paches figgered the ranch was too tough a nut to crack."

Booth reined in the team near the main building. Dan helped Harriet down. She handed him his Colt. "Thanks. I'm glad I didn't have to use it."

"You might yet," said Booth gloomily.

Gila opened the thick door, and they entered a huge, pillared room. The floor was sand-strewn. Battered tables covered the floor. A long bar stretched along one wall. Shafts of sunlight peered through the narrow windows. A solidly built man hurried from behind the bar. "Harriet!" he said. "It's been a long time."

Harriet ran to him, and he drew her close with his left arm. The right sleeve was knotted just below the elbow. Jim Moore's face was seamed and furrowed; the face of a man who had spent most of his life outdoors in hard country. Harriet turned. "This is Major Fayes, Dad."

Moore held out his left hand. "The new C.O. of Fort Costain? Welcome, sir. The bar is open. I'd like to buy you a drink."

Dan shook his head. Booth wet his lips. Moore looked at the driver. "Is it all right if I buy Sam and Gila one?"

"Why not?"

Moore walked behind the bar. "Any trouble?"

Gila nodded. "Bob Tanner's tack is drove."

Moore turned quickly. "How so?"

"We found his body five miles the far side of the pass. Sculped."

Moore looked at Harriet and turned pale beneath the tan. "My God," he said, "I thought it was quiet."

"It ain't. We seen old Black Wind. He's hot under his stinkin' shirt. Claims his people are ready for war. Fact is, they ain't nothin' but a few rimrock *broncos* on the loose. Leastways, that's all that's been seen the last few months."

Moore nodded. "A commissioner is coming here one of these days for a conference at San Ignacio Creek." He downed a drink and eyed Dan. "I heard this morning that Hair Rope was seen near there with some of his *broncos*. He's pure quill, Major."

Gila refilled his glass. "Any of them carryin' Henry repeaters?"

Moore's eyes narrowed. "Damned if I know. Why?"

"Tanner was killed by one."

"That doesn't mean anything."

"Mebbe. Mebbe not. I've heard tell they'll pay up to two hundred in raw gold for one."

"You've been eating peyote."

"No. Last month three troopers went over the hill. One

of them stole Capn' Morgan's Henry rifle. I met him in Tucson. The drunken bum told me Hair Rope bought all three Colts and Springfields from him and his mates for one hundred and fifty apiece in gold dust. Two hundred for the Henry."

Moore refilled the glasses. "Can you blame the troopers? Even white men will pay good money for those weapons rather than try to collect twenty dollars for turning in a deserter."

Dan eyed the ranch owner. "Seems as though some of the whites out here are as much against the army as the Apaches, Moore."

Moore placed his one hand flat on the bar. "Not *all* of them, Major Fayes. Sure, we've got renegades, grafters and profiteers raising hell, but many of us are loyal citizens."

"Those people can raise hell out here."

"I'll agree to that. But as long as you have law officers, corrupt Indian Agents, yes, and even territorial and government politicians getting their cut, you're going to see a lot more of it." Moore turned to Gila. "You said Tanner was scalped."

"I did."

Moore rubbed his jaw. "Damned odd."

"That ain't all. Black Wind remembered Major Fayes here, and the old coot is stone-blind."

Booth nodded. "Puts the fear of God into a man sitting there and 'seeing that old bag of bones 'looking at you, 'knowing damned well he can't see you, and yet 'talking as though his eyes was as good as they ever was."

Moore waved his hand. "There's some explanation. He might have had someone with him."

"By God, he didn't, Jim!" said Booth.

"It still figures. How many times have you been shot at by Apaches without seeing them?"

Booth ran a finger inside his collar. "Too damned many!"

Jim nodded. "Black Wind got word that the command was changing at Fort Costain. He was wise that the major left Tres Cabezas. So the old goat sits in the sun like a Chinese idol and makes like a man that can see."

Dan took out a cigar. "It's possible."

Moore nodded. "Of course, it is. I've seen some of these Apache medicine men, the *diyis,* do some incredible stuff. Incredible until you analyzed it."

"We'd better get to the post," said Dan.

Moore reached for a bottle. "Compliments of the ranch, Major Fayes. Rye or bourbon? Perhaps you'd prefer *aguardiente* or good Baconora mezcal?"

Dan was about to refuse. "Mezcal," he said.

Moore placed the squat bottle on the bar.

"Thanks," said Dan. He turned to Harriet. "It was a great pleasure traveling with you, Miss Moore."

"Thank you," she said.

"I'm only sorry we found Corporal Tanner on the way."

"She's seen dead men before, Major Fayes," said Moore quietly.

Dan walked to the door and got into the Dougherty. Booth poured a quick drink and slopped it down, wiping his loose mouth. Gila grinned. They went out to the wagon.

Moore and Harriet stood at the door and watched the Dougherty roll down to the road. He looked at his daughter. "You've gotten over Jim Dunphy?" he asked softly.

"I think so."

Jim Moore leaned against the doorway. "When?"

She looked at him. "Why do you ask?"

Moore looked at the wagon. "Him."

She shrugged. "Another officer. They seem to come from the same mold."

"Not this one, Harriet."

"How do you know, Dad?"

He placed his arm about her slim waist. "Men have always been my business. Soldiers. Teamsters. Gamblers. Drunks. All the types and variations that make up the men of the frontier. Jim Dunphy was weak. Oh, he was a nice fellow. Many of the weak ones are."

She looked at the wagon. "And you think he's weak too?"

He laughed bitterly. "We all are. In this country a man's weaknesses show up better than most places. I wonder what his are? Women? Gambling? Liquor?"

"The unholy trio."

He nodded. "Yet there is something about him that *is* different."

"Why are you telling me this?"

He drew her close. "There was a way you looked at him. You've a great deal of your mother in you, Harriet."

"Is that bad?"

He shook his head. "You've much more understanding."

"Perhaps you weren't easy to understand, Dad."

Moore's face saddened. "Perhaps. But you try." He turned back into the big room. "Melva Cornish is still at the post, Harriet."

Her face tightened. "I thought she was going east."

He shook his head. "This time it's Ellis Morgan."

"And you're thinking that it will be Dan Fayes next?"

"Why not? It's always been the same. It was Jim Dunphy while he was C.O. Morgan took command and Melva is commanding *him*. Now Ellis will go back to Company A. Give Melva a week and she'll be after Fayes."

She laughed bitterly. "Why wait a week?"

Moore watched her go to her room. He shook his head and mopped the bar.

———

FORT COSTAIN SPRAWLED across a mesa top like a raw-boned trooper sleeping off a tequila drunk. The sun reflected from the whitish caliche of the parade ground and glinted from the brass barrel of the stubby mountain howitzer which sat near the warped flagpole. The parade ground was lined on two sides by adobe barracks and quarters. The third side was composed of the stables and corrals with a row of sun-faded Sibley tents flapping and bellying in the hot wind. Shaggy ramadas shaded the fronts of the buildings while on the low roofs of the adobes, vegetation had sprouted. Flash rains had cut deep gullies into the end of the parade ground where it dropped off in a steep escarpment to the creek bottoms to the east of the post proper. The post cemetery, on a low knoll, was perilously close to the deep gullies.

Dan eyed his command with some distaste. This was the post of duty which might save his shaky career. It was damned poor material from which to mold a model fort. Sherman had said Fort Costain had once been a key post in checking Apache ravages. There was little other reason for it to stand in stark nakedness on the sterile mesa top. In the distance, distorted by shimmering heat waves, rose the spectral mountains, the traditional stronghold of the rimrock Apaches.

Booth reined in the mules at the guardhouse. A trooper strolled out from beneath the shade of a ramada. His shirt showed white crescents of dried sweat beneath the armpits. He sported a day-old beard. The stock of his carbine had not felt the caress of a warm hand rubbing linseed oil into the walnut for many a day.

"Major Fayes, the new commanding officer, Krasner," said Booth.

Krasner eyed Dan and then gave him a sloppy salute. He pointed with his carbine toward a large adobe. "Headquarters. Captain Morgan has been expecting you, sir." He watched Dan through slitted eyes as the Dougherty rolled off.

Dan got down and slapped the dust from his clothing with his hat. "Find my quarters, Booth and put my gear in them."

Booth saluted and drove off. Dan touched the orders in his inner coat pocket and walked into the dim orderly room. In an inner office a bulky officer sat at a desk, looking through a window toward the mountains. He turned as Dan entered. "Yes?"

"Major Fayes," said Dan. There was a half-empty bottle on Morgan's desk.

The man stood up and saluted. "Morgan," he said. Dan

sat down in a chair and felt for a cigar. Morgan had a full face with small eyes. His black mustache was trimmed dragoon style. It was obvious that the big man was suffering from the heat. Not enough time spent in the saddle, thought Dan.

"How was the trip?" asked Morgan.

"Hot and dry."

"It's always hot and dry," said Morgan sourly.

From his speech he was a Border State man, thought Dan. His eyes were red-rimmed. There was a weariness in his almost handsome face. Weariness from boredom rather than hard work. The appearance of the post proved that. Dan offered Morgan a cigar. They lit up.

"Would you like to meet the officers now, sir?" asked Morgan.

"Not just yet. Keep them at their duties. I'd like a talk with you before I take over."

Morgan nodded. He leaned back in his chair, sizing Dan up, as though he expected a rawhiding. Like a schoolboy caught in some mischief.

"You know why I was assigned here, Morgan?"

"Reform. Tighten up the squadron and all that."

"You don't think it can be done?"

"I did my best." There was an edge in his tone.

"Obviously it wasn't enough."

Morgan eyed the end of his cigar with great interest.

"Shall I tell you what Cump Sherman told me about this post and the command?"

"What *did* they tell you, Major Fayes?"

"That it was rotten with insubordination. That the officers spent a great deal of time drinking and writing letters to their congressmen asking for transfers while they let the command go to hell." Dan puffed at his cigar. "But the worst part of the report was that the troopers acted like a bunch of rotten conscripts."

Morgan straightened up. "Did they tell you *all* of it, Major?" His face flushed. "Did they tell you that we've never been part of a regiment? That we've been in existence since

'67, as a so-called provisional organization? Did they tell you we were sent out here to fight Apaches with the roster loaded with green recruits and only a small leavening of veterans to ease the strain? They probably didn't tell you about the fight at Negra Pass last year when most of the officers, with one or two exceptions, were fresh from the Point? Captain Reichert didn't come back from the slaughter. He preferred to die there rather than return to face the Benzine Board. And he was one of the best officers that ever forked a McClellan!"

Dan eyed the blustering officer. "I read the official report. I don't know the personal facts. But I do know this! This squadron will be built into an efficient organization and incorporated into a newly planned regiment, or the men will be scattered to more efficient commands! I hardly need tell you what will happen to the officers!"

"Does that include you?'"

"It does!"

Morgan hesitated. "I wish I could speak freely."

"Shoot."

The small eyes narrowed. "I expected a rawhiding from you. General Crook came through here after the Negra Pass fight. There was an unholy rawhiding then. But did he attempt to build up the morale? Did he order us to a more decent post where we could feel like we were part of the military picture?"

"Obviously not."

"No. Damn him! George Crook worries more about what the newspapers say about him than he does about how *we* feel about him. He surrounds himself with a bunch of border riffraff he calls mule-packers! He treats Apaches like humans! By God, Fayes, in six months he hasn't once mentioned this command."

"Probably with good reason," said Dan dryly.

Morgan gripped big fists together. "Well, the command is yours. I'm through. Do I take over A Company?"

"Your old command?"

"Yes."

"Take command again."

Morgan had a choleric temper beneath his outward look of steadiness. "Anything else, sir?"

"Corporal Tanner has been killed and scalped. We found him beyond the pass."

Morgan paled. "The Apaches have been quiet."

"I've been told there have been smoke signals for some days."

"We see them now and then."

"Have you investigated them?"

Morgan flushed. "No."

"No scouting? No patrols?"

"No."

Dan stood up. He threw his orders on the desk. "We also met Black Wind. He had quite a lot to say about his people. It seems as though something is arousing them."

"The old man is blind. He hasn't been seen around here for years."

"He's around now."

Morgan bit his lip.

Dan left the building and crossed the sun-beaten parade ground to his quarters. He knew Morgan was watching him from a window. Booth was leaning against the wall of Dan's quarters. "Anything else, sir?"

"Not for the present. Take care of your team."

"You'll need an orderly, sir. I'd like the job."

"We'll see."

Dan walked through the hallway and into the left-hand room. Dust motes swirled in a shaft of sunlight streaming through a window. The beehive fireplace was littered with ashes and pieces of partially burned wood. The yellowed whitewash on the walls was streaked where water had leaked through the roof. Dust gritted beneath Dan's feet as he walked about. He sat down on the cot. Dust rose in a fine cloud around him.

Dan lit a fresh cigar. He knew now he should have told old Cump Sheridan to go to hell. Fourteen years of service and here he was, starting all over again. The army was like that. Work like hell on an assignment; get yanked from it when it's going well; start another dirty job.

Dan felt in his bag for the mezcal bottle. Someone had swilled out of it. Booth. Dan shook his head. He uncorked the bottle and took a long drink. He needed it.

CHAPTER FIVE

D an spent the afternoon unpacking his luggage, setting Booth to work cleaning his weapons and brass. Across the narrow hallway was another room which Booth had told him had belonged to Major Dunphy. It had not been used since Dunphy had shot himself in it. Booth looked in at the dusty quarters. There was a dark stain on the packed-earth floor near the bare cot. Hanging on the wall was a tattered guidon which Booth told Dan had been the flag of Dunphy's company in the Shenandoah during the war.

Retreat was long past when Dan gathered his toilet articles and walked through the hallway to the rear door on his way to the washhouse. The first stars blinked in the dark blue blanket of the sky. The odor of cooking drifted across the post

Dan bathed and shaved, taking his time, enjoying the sensation of the first real bath he had had since leaving St. Louis. Mess Call blew across the post. He threw his towel over his shoulder and blew out the candle lantern. The dry desert wind ruffled his hair as he stepped out into the darkness. The shadows in one place looked thicker. He slowed his pace. The shadow was a lot blacker and more solid than it should be. He reached out to touch it.

The shadow rose like an uncoiling spring. Dan caught the dull sheen of metal as he threw himself sideways. Something struck at the huck towel and stung his shoulder. The strong odor of sweat-soaked greasy leather clogged his nostrils. He brought up a knee, sinking it deep into his assailant's groin. The man grunted and went down.

Dan kicked out. His heel connected solidly. The man leaped to his feet and darted about the corner of the wash-house on silent feet.

Dan shook his head. It had been almost like a hallucination. Then his right foot struck something on the ground. He picked it up and held it close to his eyes. It was a thin-bladed knife, the haft bound tightly with rawhide. Dan walked into his quarters and turned up the lantern. His shoulder twinged. He threw aside the towel and pulled his undershirt free from his left shoulder. A shallow gash showed in the flesh in the hollow below the collarbone.

Dan wiped the cold sweat from his face. He poured mezcal on the cut and bandaged it. "The sonofabitch," he said. "Right on the post!"

He dressed carefully, slipping his derringer into his trousers pocket. He slanted his forage cap on his close-cropped head and blew out the lantern. He walked outside and breathed deep of the fresh air. It had been too damned close for peace of mind.

Lights from windows and doors threw their squares and rectangles on the hard earth. The flag halyards rattled violently against their warped pole. Dan crossed the parade ground to the officers' mess. It was well lit. A man laughed loudly as he pushed open the door.

Twelve officers came to their feet as someone called Attention. Dan walked to the head of the table. "Major Dan Fayes," he said quietly. "Please give your name, in order of rank, and present assignment."

Morgan did not speak. A broad-shouldered officer, with graying hair spoke up. "Captain Charles Norman, commanding Company B."

A smooth-faced man beside Charles was next. "Captain

Andrew Horace, commanding Company C."

"Captain Myron Cornish, surgeon."

The junior officers, four first and four second lieutenants, called off their names, rank and assignments.

Morgan turned to Dan. "First Lieutenant Dennis Halloran is in the hospital at Fort Grant with a case of varioloid fever, sir. He commanded Company A while I was acting post commander."

"Sit down, gentlemen," said Dan. He handed his cap to the mess orderly.

Morgan stood up. "Gentlemen, I'd like to propose a toast to our new post commander."

The orderly filled the wine glasses, and the officers drank the toast. Dan picked up his glass and returned the honor. The wine was rather good. It seemed to hit him right where it did the most benefit.

The meal progressed swiftly. Second Lieutenant Forrest Kroft toyed with his food and kept draining his wineglass. By the time the meal was finished his face was flushed and a silly grin passed over it now and then. Dan accepted a cigar from the box and lit up. The officers finished and eyed him expectantly. Dan spoke up. "Gentlemen, it is a pleasure to be here with you at Fort Costain. I realize it is not good manners to talk shop at mess, but tonight will be an exception." Kroft bowed his head slightly.

Dan leaned forward. "Is it customary to be ambushed by Apaches within the confines of the post?"

"What the hell!" blurted Horace.

Kroft raised his glass. "Welcome to our select circle, Major Fayes. You've joined the ranks of the initiated."

"Shut up, Kroft," said Norman angrily. Dan drew the knife from inside his blouse and threw it on the table. "As I left the washhouse an Apache nearly tried to see to it that I left this world. Where are the guards? Do they let *broncos* have the run of the post after dark?"

Morgan flushed. "They're devils for that type of work, Major. Although it has been some time since anything like that has happened."

"We usually carry sidearms after dark," said Adjutant Nat Woodridge.

"Thanks for letting me know about that matter of routine," said Dan dryly. "Who is the officer of the guard?"

All eyes turned to Sid Sykes of Company A. Sykes stood up. He wore Colt and sword.

Dan jerked a thumb toward the door. "Get out there! Make the rounds! Double the guards if necessary. Tell Gila Barnes I want to see him."

Sykes saluted and hurried from the mess hall. Dan placed his hands flat on the table. "I have a neat incision in my left shoulder, a souvenir of my first night on this J company post! I have been sent here to make a squadron out of this unit and I intend to do so. The alternative is the Benzine Board for every one of you seated here tonight!'"

Horace wiped a fat hand over his full mouth. "May I say a word, sir?"

"Speak up."

Horace glanced along the table as though for support. "This is a hell of a place, sir. Out on the devil's hind leg. We've been given dregs for recruits. Jailbirds. Snowbirds. Runaway husbands. We haven't even got a regimental number to call our own. Why, sir, believe it or not, but twenty per cent of my company is either over the hill or in the brig!"

"No reflection on you, I hope," said Dan sarcastically.

Horace compressed his soft mouth. "Sir!"

Dan looked along the table. Kroft was leaning back in his chair swilling the wine around in his glass. There was a vacant look on his handsome face. "One of your own junior officers, Captain Horace, hasn't got the sense to drink like a gentleman at mess. Yet you sit there and speak about your percentage of deserters and brig-birds' as though it was their fault."

Horace stood up. "I do not like to be called down in front of junior officers!"

"Sit down!"

Morgan coughed. "Sir, it's true we have been a bit sloppy.

Have we the promise of better men? Can we get new equipment?"

Dan shook his head. "You'll make or break the men you have. Congress hasn't seen fit to up the military appropriations bill. We'll get by on what we have." He stood up. "Corporal Tanner was ambushed and scalped five miles beyond the pass. We found his body this morning. There have been smoke signals for several days. Trouble is brewing in these hills and it's our job to stop it. I want a full field inspection tomorrow morning after stables."

Horace blinked. "The men won't be ready for it."

Dan eyed the flustered company commander. "See to it. Now, gentlemen, I have work to do, and I know you have. Good night."

The officers filed out. Dan drained his glass. Surgeon Cornish got his cap. He stopped beside Dan. "I'd better take a look at that shoulder," he said with a smile.

Dan nodded. Cornish wore the perpetual smile of a man who is always satisfied with himself. His dark eyes studied Dan through a cloud of tobacco smoke. He glanced down at the empty wineglass and then left the room.

Outside, Dan stood for a moment letting the dry wind sweep about him. A stooped figure rounded the corner of the mess building. Gila Barnes stopped and shoved back his battered hat. The strong odor of tobacco and sweaty clothing vied with the fresh desert wind. "Yuh want to see me, Dan?"

They crossed the parade ground together. Dan told him of the Apache. Gila nodded. "I'll leave right away. God knows I won't catch up with him, but I been wantin' to poke about the hills."

"How often has something like this happened?"

Gila spat. "Not for some time. Halloran was jumped once. Drilled the bushy-headed bastard with a slug. Denny is a cool man."

Dan nodded. "Take off then."

Gila saluted and vanished toward the stables. Dan went into his quarters and lit the lamp. He had been rough on his officers, but four years of war, and the years of duty as an inspector hadn't taught him any other system. The wine worked in him. He picked up the bottle of mezcal and drank deeply. He stripped off his shirt and undershirt and sat down on his bunk. He drew his revolving pistol from its holster and twirled the cylinder. The click of steel sounded loud in the stillness. He placed the Colt on the small table near the head of his bed.

The outer door opened. "Major Fayes!" called Cornish. "Come in, Doc!"

Cornish was carrying his medical bag. A woman followed him in. Dan reached for his shirt. Cornish smiled. "It's all right, Major. This is my sister, Melva. She's used to things like this. Helps me a lot. A good steady hand with the wounded or the sick." Cornish busied himself with his case.

Melva Cornish was a tall woman in her middle twenties. Her dark eyes held Dan's as she extended a hand. "Welcome to Fort Costain, Major."

"Thank you, Miss Cornish."

The faint odor of heliotrope had entered the room. Melva Cornish was full-bosomed, her breasts thrusting themselves out tightly against her dark dress. Her black hair was swept up and carefully arranged. Her mouth was full and ripe. She exerted a slight pressure on Dan's hand before she released it. Her eyes took in his muscular upper body and then the hastily bandaged shoulder. Dan suddenly had a feeling he had known someone like her before, in a place where a lady would have felt ill at ease.

"Take off the bandage, Melva," said Myron Cornish over his shoulder.

She came close to Dan and unfastened the bandage. Her cool fingers felt good on his warm flesh. "I heard you picked up Corporal Tanner on the way here."

"Yes." Dan looked away. He didn't want to talk about it.

Cornish looked up. "Neat job, Tanner's mutilation. Takes an expert to do it right. They never tear or peel it off. A quick incision to the bone and then a straight upward pull."

He thrust his left thumb into his mouth and popped his cheek. "Like that!"

Dan eyed the surgeon distastefully. Melva patted Dan's shoulder. "There," she said easily. She looked at her brother. "I agree with you, Myron. It was a nice job."

"You saw it?" asked Dan.

She raised her thick eyebrows. "Of course! They brought the body into the dispensary."

Dan felt the need for a drink.

Cornish worked deftly. The strong odor of carbolic filled the room. Melva bandaged swiftly. As she moved, Dan could feel the swell of her full thigh against his left leg. He looked at her. She flushed a little and stepped back. "Thanks," said Dan.

She smiled. "I like to help," she said. "Heaven knows there isn't much else to do here at Fort Costain."

"A rough place for a woman," said Dan.

Cornish grinned. "Melva likes it," he said.

Dan drew his shirt about his shoulders. "Drink?"

Cornish nodded. Dan filled two glasses. They downed the potent mezcal. Dan found his eyes wandering toward the full-bodied Melva. By God, she *was* a woman, double-breasted and firm.

Cornish eyed his empty glass. "Good stuff," he said. "I noticed the odor of it when I came in here."

"I cleansed the wound with it."

Cornish nodded. "Good stuff, inside or out. In moderation, of course." The dark eyes studied Dan for a moment. "Well, I have work to do. Coming, Melva?"

She nodded. As she walked to the door her hips swung easily. Dan put down his glass. A few more drinks and he would have followed her.

Dan dropped on his bunk. They were a queer pair. Then he remembered who Melva reminded him of. Kitty St. Clair in Washington. Kitty had fitted well in Dolly Aldon's establishment in the capital city. Kitty had spurned a wealthy congressman to give all her attentions to Dan. He closed his eyes. He wished that Kitty was with him now.

CHAPTER SIX

By noon of the day after Dan's arrival at Fort Costain he knew the squadron was almost as rotten as the post buildings. The inspection had been a farce. Carbine barrels were pitted, although none of the weapons were more than three years old, issue of 1869. In all three company barracks he had seen but half a dozen pairs of boots that looked like they had been shined. Cots were sloppily made. Uniforms had been superficially spruced. Dan learned that the company commanders made a practice of keeping the company Colts locked in boxes in their quarters, for on the frontier, Colts were better than currency, and most of the men could not be trusted with them.

Dan walked into headquarters. Adjutant Woodridge was still busy with the inspection records in C Company barracks. At Dan's request, Amos Linke, the squadron clerk, silently placed a bundle of service records before him. Dan scanned through them. The list of deserters was scandalously high. Drunkenness and insubordination topped the list of crimes for which men were confined in the guardhouse. Dan sat down and lit a cigar. He looked at Linke, a slight unsoldierly-looking man with thin graying hair. "Where's the sergeant major?"

Linke looked up. "Over the hill. Sergeant Major Haley."

"Hell," said Dan involuntarily, "him too?"

Linke nodded.

Dan flipped over the papers until he found Haley's record. He whistled softly. Twenty-seven years with the colors. Battles and campaigns: Mexican War, Civil War, and half a dozen Indian campaigns. Wounded four times. Cited three times for gallantry in action.

Linke coughed. "Sergeant Haley is a hard violent man but a splendid soldier. There is none better. For a time, he tried to keep up the efficiency of the squadron, but it could not be done by *one* man. Haley turned to steady drinking. One night at Moore's Hog Ranch, he went raving mad from the liquor. When the fight was over three civilians were badly beaten and Mike Haley went over the hill."

"Quite the bucko boy."

Linke smiled proudly as though Haley's sins were a thing he took pride in. "That he is. But a finer soldier, with drill, paperwork, fighting or any other part of the soldier's trade, there never was."

Dan puffed at his cigar. "You speak as though you've had an education, Linke. How do you account for Haley?"

Linke smiled. "Each of us is cast in a mold at birth, sir. Lawyer, doctor, beggarman or thief. Haley was *born* a soldier. But in him there is a flaw...for a soldier, that is. There is a sensitivity in him. Put him in a good unit and he'll make it better. Put him in a bad one and he'll make it good. But in him there is the same feeling we all of us have. Pride in our unit, and to hell with all the others, begging your pardon, sir." Linke shook his head. "His patience ran out here. Why else would he, a born soldier, do the one thing you'd expect from a nonmilitary man?"

Dan winced inwardly at the quiet words of the scholarly clerk. "It seems unanswerable. Where is he?"

Linke looked away.

"Come on! He must have been your good friend for you to know him so well and praise him so highly. *Where is he?*"

Linke looked squarely at Dan. "And if I tell the major, what will he do? Break his spirit in the guardhouse with the scum that inhabits it now? Shave half his head and drum him off the post to the tune of the Rogue's March?"

Dan shook his head. "I give you my word."

Linke smiled. "He is at Union, on the upper San Ignacio, twenty miles from here."

Dan did some quick calculating. "I'll leave here on a three-day pass. Reason: post business. Write that down." Dan stood up. "Captain Morgan will assume command in my absence." He looked at Linke. "I'm curious about you. You do not talk like the average yellow-leg."

Linke flushed. "I had a fine education, sir. But it taught me nothing of liquor and gambling." The little man smiled ruefully. "If there were no drunkards amongst educated men, sir, the army would have no fourteen-dollar-a-month clerks."

Dan left headquarters and met Morgan crossing the parade ground.

"I'm leaving the post for a few days. Take over in my absence."

Morgan was startled. "For what reason, may I ask?"

"Official business. Jack up this squadron, Captain Morgan. I want no repetition of this morning's inspection."

Morgan bit his lip. "A peace commissioner from the Indian Bureau is due soon."

"Let him wait."

Morgan eyed Dan.

Dan flipped away his cigar. "I want you to start officer and N.C.O. schools three nights a week. I want every man to fire for record starting tomorrow. Ninety rounds. Wingate's *Manual of Rifle Practice*. There will be full-dress parade at retreat until further orders."

Dan walked away leaving Morgan staring after him. He entered his quarters. Booth was whitewashing the walls. The ripe full odor of mezcal floated in the air even above the odor of the whitewash. Dan picked up his mezcal bottle. It was empty. "Booth," he said.

Booth turned. "Oh *that*, sir. I kicked it over by mistake."

Dan threw the bottle into the fireplace. "You misbegotten drunken bastard! Get me a horse. A good one. Fill a canteen. Bring him here."

"I'll get you Hardtack. One of A Company's bays."

Dan changed into an old pair of issue trousers and shirt. He pulled on his field boots and picked up his Winchester. Booth stuck his head in through the window. "All set, sir."

Dan walked outside and placed his blanket roll over the cantle. Booth tied it fast. Dan swung up on Hardtack and touched the big bay with his spurs. It was damned good to be in a McClellan again. A good ride would blow the stink of Fort Costain from his nostrils. He acknowledged the salute of the gate sentry and rode slowly down the winding road to the Mesquite Wells road.

Moore's Ranch seemed to be dreaming in the hot afternoon sun. Dan kneed Hardtack onto the short road that led up to the buildings. He slid from the saddle and walked in. The big room was empty. He walked to the bar and called out.

Harriet Moore, dressed in a simple gingham dress, came from a back room. "Hello, Major," she said.

"The name is Dan."

"Dan then."

He eyed her. She had changed her hair style, drawing it back from her oval face, and piling it on top of her shapely head. Her slim, full-bosomed figure fitted into the simple dress as though she had been poured into it. She flushed a little. "You're not leaving so soon?"

He shook his head. "How do I get to Union?"

She looked at him queerly. "Follow the road through Mesquite Wells. Beyond the town there is a fork, one leading northwest toward Beasley. The right-hand fork follows the San Ignacio. Union is about twenty miles up the valley."

"Thanks, Miss Moore."

She smiled. "The name is Harriet."

They eyed each other, and Dan suddenly knew what he had been missing while at the fort. "Is everything all right?" he asked.

"Yes. With me. Dad's feelings aren't so good right now."

"How so?"

"One of his teamsters was fired at in the hills. He got away from the wagon and hid. When he came back, he found that the wagon was looted."

"Who did it?"

"We don't really know. Apaches probably."

"What was in the wagon?"

"Flour. Bacon. Dried fish. Some reloading tools. Blasting powder. Three cases of Henry rifle ammunition."

Dan rubbed his jaw. "I'd like a report from your father when he gets back."

"I'll tell him."

Dan turned toward the door. "I'll only be gone a few days, Harriet."

"Be careful." She followed him to the door and winced a little when she saw the horse. "Hardtack," she said.

Dan eyed her. "So?"

"That was Jim Dunphy's favorite mount."

"I see." Dan mentally cursed Trooper Booth. "I didn't know."

She leaned against the side of the door. "It doesn't matter."

Dan swung up on the bay. He raised his campaign hat.

"I hope Mike Haley is still there," she said.

Dan lowered his hat and rested an elbow on his pommel. "Why did you say that?"

She tilted her head to one side. "Mike Haley is the best soldier Fort Costain ever saw. You need him. But be careful with him, Dan."

"Why?"

She straightened up. "He's a strong man with strong opinions."

"I have some strong opinions myself."

"Yes," she said quietly.

Dan touched the bay with his spurs and rode down toward the road. He looked back. The wind whipped her skirts about her long slim legs. There was a strange disquieting feeling within him. He looked back twice more before he reached a curve in the road. She was still standing there looking after him.

Union sprawled like an ugly excrescence on a pitted slope beneath shabby mine structures. Warped false-fronted buildings lined a dusty main street. Ore wagons groaned down the hill from the mines heading for the stamp mills Dan had seen three miles down the creek road.

Leaving the bay in the town's one livery stable, he walked up the street and entered the first saloon he saw, the Big Barrel. He ordered a beer and eyed the few other customers. Most of them looked like miners. None of them had the Regular Army stamp on them.

The batwings swung open, and a thick-bodied man came in with his head lowered as though he were primed for violent action. His slab of a face had the imprint of Erin on it. His blue eyes were red-rimmed and his mahogany face was covered with russet bristles. A filthy flannel shirt, open to the belly, showed a thick mat of reddish hair on the deep chest. His sleeves were rolled up on his powerful arms, exposing a Maltese cross tattooed on the left forearm. The insignia of the old Fifth Corps. There had been ten regiments of Regulars in the Fifth, commanded by George Sykes. Sykes's Regulars.

The bartender eyed him warily. "You've got no more jawbone here, Haley."

Haley lowered his bullethead. "So me credit is no good, you scut? I've thrown one hundred eagles across this mahogany in the past few days and ye'll give me no jawbone?"

The bartender shook his head.

"Throw the bum out!" a big miner roared from a poker table.

Haley turned slowly. His powerful hands gripped the bar behind him. "Now who said that?" he asked quietly.

The miner dropped his hands below the table. Dan could see a derringer in one of them. Dan slid his Colt free from the leather. "You there," he said clearly, "put away that stingy gun!"

All eyes turned toward Dan. Haley stared at him. The bartender leaned across the bar. "If he's a friend of yours, stranger, get him outa here. There's been a fight every night he's been in here and that hairy Irishman didn't lose one of them. There'll be a killin' if he ain't stopped."

Dan nodded. "Come on, Irish," he said, "let's go get a drink elsewhere."

There was suspicion on the homely face but Haley, surprisingly enough, preceded him out into the darkening street. "Thanks," he said over his shoulder, "I did not see the gun."

"It would have been the last reveille for you, Haley."

Haley rubbed his bristly jaw. "Where to?"

"I've got a bottle at the livery stable."

Haley threw a heavy arm about Dan's shoulders. His breath was like a rusty blade. "There's something familiar about ye. Something I do not rightly place."

The street was dark, lit only by the yellow light shining through dirty windows. Dan jerked his head. "The livery is down there."

Haley seemed satisfied. "There is a girl in Molly's who can give a man a fine go-around. Ye're interested?"

"Later perhaps."

They stopped in front of the livery stable. The big bay was in a rear stall. The liveryman was nowhere in sight. Haley swayed a little as he walked toward the back. He eyed the bay. "This horse is familiar," he said thickly.

Dan eased his Colt free and raised it.

Haley stared at the horse. "By God! 'Tis Hardtack!"

The heavy gun barrel struck just above Haley's left ear. The big man crumpled at the knees and went down like a falling pine. "Timber!" said Dan. He dragged the noncom into the darkness and went to look for the liveryman.

He met the man walking toward the stable, picking at his teeth with a straw.

Dan took out his wallet. "I want a horse," he said. "I'm taking a friend back to Fort Costain."

"I've a old gelding with one eye. Give him to you for thirty dollars."

"It's a deal."

They walked back to the stable. Dan saddled the raw-boned gelding. The liveryman helped him place Haley over the saddle.

Two miles from Union Dan stopped and dismounted. He stripped off his clothing and replaced it with worn cavalry trousers and a shell jacket. He remounted Hardtack.

The moon was up when Haley moved and groaned. Dan led the gelding down to the shallow creek and untied Haley. He lowered the big man to the ground and splashed water on his face. Haley opened one eye. "Hell-fire!" he said. "That last drink was a howitzer shell!" He looked up at Dan. "For the love av Saint Patrick! Who the hell are you?"

"Major Dan Fayes, the new commanding officer of Fort Costain."

Haley jumped to his feet. "I have no C.O., Mister. What's goin' on?"

Dan grinned. "You've been kidnapped, Haley. You're coming back to the blue where you belong."

Haley shook his head and worked his mouth, trying to free it from the fur. "Ah, to hell with that! They are not soldiers there. It is a reform school, and the officers are but lazy men who do not care about the squadron. I'm well out of it."

"You're coming back."

"To be thrown in a cell? No!"

"You owe me a favor. If you come back, I'll see to it that you don't go in a cell."

Haley squinted at Dan. "Ye're a strange one. Ye do have the look of a man and a soldier. But it is too late."

"Then I'll take you back at gunpoint."

"You?" Haley laughed. "I could crush ye wid one fist."

Dan grinned. "I'll strip off this coat and we'll settle it

right here. If I win, you come back. If you win, you take the gelding, fifty eagles, and my blessing."

Haley grinned craftily. "Ye're a man right enough. Come. I'll go easy on ye. I'll not mark ye up. I'll put ye to sleep easy-like."

Dan stripped off his gun belt, cap and shell jacket The moon was bright and clear. He had never been licked in his weight class at the Point, but Haley had thirty pounds on him. Dan had youth on his side. Haley had John Barleycorn riding his back, slowing him down.

Haley shuffled his big feet and spat on his hands. He moved in ponderously, his pale blue eyes alight with battle. Dan moved about studying the man. He was powerful, but there was a layer of fat about his middle. He was at least forty-five years old. Suddenly the Irishman closed in, throwing short hard punches, making no attempt to hit Dan.

Dan moved back. Haley grinned and moved in. Dan speared out a left and jolted home a smashing right to the gut. Haley's whisky breath came out in a gush. Haley bobbed about trying to clear his head. The liquor was still strong in him, although he wasn't really drunk. Haley feinted. A granite fist grazed Dan's jaw and another whizzed past his chin.

Dan moved about.

"Stand still, damn ye...*sir!*"

Dan threw a left. He threw a right which Haley easily blocked. He countered with a left to Dan's lean belly and skidded a right across Dan's jaw. The blow was enough to start dancing lights in front of Dan. The man was as rough as a cob. The blow which grounded him seemed to come from nowhere. Dan went down hard and looked up at the grinning NCO.

"Time," said Haley.

Dan got to his feet. He tapped Haley three more times and then went staggering back with a vicious right over the heart. He went down on one knee.

"Had enough?" asked Haley.

Dan shook his head. He sparred easily, keeping away from the sledgehammer blows. Haley was puffing. Haley lost his temper, triggered by a stinging left to the eye. He charged. Dan's forearms ached from the piston-like blows.

Dan sank home a left to the gut and followed through with a jolting uppercut which snapped the bullethead back. He followed through with a left to the jaw and a short right. Dan knew he had broken a knuckle as he looked down at Haley. "Time," he said.

Haley shook his head. There was a pale sickness on his face. He got to his feet and swung a hard right. Dan went under it, clipped Haley on the jaw with a left and sent him down again with a right jab.

Haley wiped the blood from his mouth. Doggedly he got up. Dan was after him like a wolverine. Haley covered up and retreated. His heel caught on a root just as Dan timed a smashing right to the jaw.

Haley went flat. His eyes closed and opened. "It's the liquor," he said.

"No alibis, Haley."

Haley sat up and felt his jaw. "I could lick ye if I was in shape."

"You're right there."

Haley grinned. "Few men have ever downed me, drunk *or* sober. Ye're a good man wid yer dukes, Mister Fayes."

Dan leaned against his bay. "You're coming back then?"

Haley stood up. "Yes. We made a bargain. 'Twill be hell not wearin' me stripes."

"We'll see about that"

Haley squatted by the creek and slopped water on his face. "Ye're a quare one, sir. I'm thinkin' we'll have some soldierin' at Costain from now on."

"We'll try."

The big mick stood up. "Aye, that we will."

Dan swung up on Hardtack. "Boots and saddles, Haley."

They rode back to the road and headed south.

CHAPTER SEVEN

It was almost noon when Dan drew rein in front of Moore's Ranch. Haley slid from his saddle and eyed the main building. He wiped his mouth on a hairy forearm. Dan shook his head. "There will be no drinking."

"Ah, sir!"

Dan slapped the dust from his uniform. "We made a deal," he said.

"When does it end, Major?"

Dan grinned. "When you get your stripes back."

"That may be a long time, sir."

"It may be."

The light blue eyes studied Dan. "You're not a drinkin' man yourself, sir?"

"At times."

Dan walked into the big saloon room. Jim Moore looked up from the bar. "I'm glad to see you back, Fayes," he said.

"How so?"

Moore came around the end of the bar. "I'm worried. Bertram Morris, a peace commissioner, arrived yesterday at Fort Costain. He went on to the reservation to meet with the Apaches. Captain Morgan sent Captain Horace and his company along."

"So?"

Moore shook his head. "I've known Morris for some time. He believes implicitly that the Apaches are well enough off at San Ignacio Reservation. He'll give them nothing. Morris is a small man, in stature and in mind. The Apaches hate him. He was the wrong man to send. Besides, Horace has an ungodly fear of the Apaches. If trouble starts he'll handle it wrongly. I'm sure of that."

Haley nodded his head. "He's right there, sir."

Dan lit a cigar. "When did they leave?"

"Shortly after noon. They'll be there by now."

Dan walked toward the door. "Come on, Haley. Do you know the way to the reservation?"

"Yes, sir!"

They mounted and rode on to the fort. The steady thump of carbine fire came from the range along the shallow creek. Haley cocked his head. "That's a sound I haven't heard for some time," he said. "Ye've done well for yer short time here, sir."

Dan dismounted at headquarters. "Stay here," he said. He walked in. Adjutant Woodridge was at his desk. "Glad to see you back, sir. Is that Mike Haley out there?"

"It is."

Woodridge shook his head. "I never thought anyone could bring *him* back."

"Tell Captain Morgan to come to my quarters."

Woodridge nodded.

"I'm leaving for the reservation right after I see Morgan." He left the building. "Haley," he said, "get into uniform. Get two fresh horses and bring them to my quarters."

"Yes, sir!"

Dan was shaving when Morgan appeared. The big officer's eyes were clouded with sleep. Having a siesta, thought Dan. "I brought Sergeant Haley back," he said over his shoulder.

"So? I'll have him put in the guardhouse."

Dan shook his head. "I'm taking him with me to the reservation."

"Why? Horace can handle it."

"Maybe. I want to hear what Morris has to say."

Morgan leaned against the wall. "He'll say plenty because you weren't here to meet him." Morgan's dark eyes studied Dan. "Bertram Morris has a lot of influence in Arizona, Major."

"Let's hope he has some with the Apaches."

Morgan laughed shortly. "They'll get nothing from him but big words and promises."

"Why did you send Horace in charge of the escort?"

"B Company is on guard. A is firing on the range."

Dan wiped his face and pulled on a fresh shirt.

Morgan lit a cigar. "You sound as though you don't like my choice of C Company for the escort."

"I didn't say that."

Morgan eyed Dan through a cloud of tobacco smoke. "Your tone did."

"All right then!" said Dan hotly, "I *didn't* like your choice. This may be a ticklish business. Horace didn't impress me as an officer who would keep his head under difficulties."

"It didn't take you long to form opinions of your officers."

Dan buckled on his gun belt and picked up his Winchester. "I've no time to talk about it," he said.

Morgan threw his cigar into the fireplace. "You don't seem to like anything on this post. Officers or men."

Dan walked to the door. "What's on your mind, Morgan? Get on with it."

The secretive eyes shifted. "You're in a hurry. This can wait."

Dan walked outside. Haley was leading up two fresh horses. A woman walked beside him. It was Melva Cornish, the strong wind pressing her dress to her full figure, outlining the deep breasts and the full thighs. She stopped beside Dan. "You're not leaving so soon, Dan?" she asked.

"Yes, Melva."

She bit her full lip. "I had planned a party for you tonight. Will you be back in time?"

He fastened his Winchester to the saddle. "I don't know."

"Well, perhaps we can plan it when you return."

He nodded. "That will be fine, Melva." His mind was far from parties and the ripe body of Melva Cornish. Then he saw the smoldering eyes of Ellis Morgan fixed on the young woman and he knew what was nettling the big officer.

The carbines thumped on the range and a cloud of smoke drifted up from the creek bottoms. Dan swung up on his bay and lifted his hat to Melva. Haley followed him as he rode toward the gate. Dan glanced at the noncom. Haley's left knuckles were skinned. They hadn't been that way the last time Dan had seen him. "You've cut your hand, Haley," he said.

Haley grinned. "The major doesn't miss much," he said. "I fell up against a tree."

"Yes," said Dan quietly. "There are a hell of a lot of trees on Fort Costain."

They passed the gate and Dan handed the ex-noncom a cigar. They both lit up. Haley drew the smoke deep into his lungs. "'Twas Trooper Skillings," he said. "Now Skillings always had the idea he could best me in a Donnybrook if I was not sergeant major. He didn't."

Dan nodded. "It's not easy to go back with the other men once you've been a sergeant major," he said.

"How the mighty have fallen, Skillings said. Trooper Skillings did a little fallin' himself." Haley touched the dark area on his faded shirt where his stripes had been. "All the same, sir, I feel a bit indacint ridin' about without me stripes."

"You'll get them back."

Haley shrugged. "I do not want them unless they are earned."

"Whatever gave you the thought that you'd get them any other way?"

The sun was low down in the west when Dan drew rein on the ridge that overlooked the winding, shallow waters of San Ignacio Creek. Smoke drifted up and then hung in a low cloud over the shadowy bottoms. The cavalry horses were picketed to the north on a grassy area. A row of cook fires glowed along the creek where the troopers of C Company were cooking their issue bacon in the spiders. The rich odor of bacon and coffee came up the ridge to the two men. Haley shifted in his saddle and eased his crotch. "The reservation proper is beyond that far ridge. This is the place where the bucks have their dances and soirees."

Almost directly below them were a number of wickiups, formed of thick whips of ocotillo, covered with skins and government blankets. A fire glowed in front of the biggest of them. Half a dozen men sat about the fire. Three of them were white men. Bertram Morris, Captain Horace and a third man he did not recognize. Dan touched the bay with his spurs and guided it down the brushy slope. "This place smells of trouble," said Haley quietly behind him.

"You're thinking too much, Haley." But Dan felt a cold sensation travel down his back. He eased his Colt in its holster.

"Ye feel it too, sir?"

"Yes," said Dan quietly.

The men about the fire turned toward Dan as he rode out of the shadows. He dismounted silently and let Haley take the horses to the picket lines. Horace flushed as he recognized the CO. He stood up. "This is Mister Morris, Major Fayes," he said nervously, indicating the little man who sat beside him.

Morris did not get up. He turned a petulant face toward Dan. "I expected to find you at Fort Costain," he said in an irritated voice.

Dan eyed the smooth, round face. The eyes were small. Dan suddenly had the impression he was looking at an angry porker. Morris' hands scrabbled at his plump thighs.

A lean civilian squatted beside Morris. "Ducey," he introduced himself, "interpreter." He was a man without an ounce of fat on his gaunt frame. Neatly dressed in sober black. A Sharps rifle leaned against a rock behind him.

Dan nodded. The three Apaches that faced the government commissioner were old men, wrinkled and skinny. Ducey looked at them. "These men are Cut Lip, Yellow Bear and Long Hat. Cut Lip is the chief." Ducey turned to the three impassive Tontos and spoke in swift slurring Apache. They eyed Dan and then looked at Morris.

Morris loosened his high collar. "The fools are angry," he said over his shoulder to Dan. "They present impossible demands."

"Be careful," said Ducey. "They understand English much better than they let on."

Dan squatted beside Ducey. Beyond the big wickiup were four warriors, squatting on the ground, idly watching the conference. There were no others in sight. Dan looked beyond them. The far ridge was thick with brush. There was no sign of life on it. A cool wind swept down the valley, chilling him.

Horace shifted a little and lit a cigar. "I don't like the smell of this, Major," he said.

Dan shook his head as Cut Lip spoke. At some time in his life the Tonto had been hideously maimed by a slash across his upper lip. The flesh had drawn back in a thick scar revealing the even white teeth. Ducey listened and then turned to Morris. "Cut Lip says that his people do not want trouble, but that they were promised blankets for the winter cold. They never came. They were promised fat beef cattle and received instead skinny beasts hardly fit for the teeth of a coyote. Do they get more promises, or do they get thick blankets and fat cattle?"

Morris wet his lips. "Tell him that the government has spent much money at San Ignacio. Building houses. Barns. Supplying clothing."

Ducey translated. Cut Lip's eyes flashed. He spoke again. "Cut Lip says his people do not live in the white men's lodges. That the coughing and spitting sickness comes upon the children. That the clothing was old and dirty, hardly fit for The People to wear. That the Tontos want permission to hunt in the mountains as they always have. Digging in the earth is not for the Tontos. They are hunters."

Morris cleared his throat. "There has been trouble in the hills. Men have been killed. Wagons have been robbed. Ask him if he knows who has done this thing?"

Ducey paled a little beneath his tan. "It isn't Cut Lip who is responsible, Mister Morris," he said.

"Ask him!" Morris' voice cracked a little.

Ducey looked at Dan. "I don't like to, sir."

"Then you'd better not."

Morris turned with all the outraged dignity of the little man who thinks a bigger man is overbearing him. "Sir! This is my duty. To track down these troubles."

"You'll get more than you bargained for."

The bluish lips drew back from the discolored teeth. "And what has the army done about these troubles in the hills?"

Dan relit his cigar. "We're working on it, Mister Morris."

"Pah!" Morris turned away in disgust. He looked at Ducey. "Ask him."

Ducey looked at Dan. Dan shrugged. Ducey translated in a low voice. Cut Lip fingered his hideous scar. Then he spoke slowly.

"Cut Lip says his people had nothing to do with the trouble in the hills. They want peace. Hair Rope is behind the troubles."

"Then Hair Rope must be turned over to the authorities!"

Cut Lip digested this. He spoke to Yellow Bear and Long Hat. There was feral hate in the liquid eyes of the old men as they spoke to each other. Cut Lip stood up. "There is nothing we can do," he said. "Hair Rope left us many grasses ago. Can we be responsible for what he has done?"

Morris smashed a pudgy fist into a damp palm. "Hair Rope must be brought to justice! Tell that old man that there will be no more cattle! No blankets! No food unless we get Hair Rope!"

Dan stood up. Tension settled over the little group. Suddenly Dan noticed that the four warriors who had been seated behind the wickiup had vanished into the lengthening shadows. He looked down toward the bivouac. Two troopers were wrestling in a cleared area, spurred on by the jibes of their mates. There wasn't a sentry in the area. There was no sign of the junior officers of the company, Cliff Rosin and Forrest Kroft. Dan stepped back from the fire. The shadows along the ridge seemed alive with impending danger and he had a naked feeling as though many eyes were on the group about the fire.

Cut Lip listened to Ducey. Then he stood up. "The little White-eye wants Hair Rope," he said coldly. "Then he shall have him." He turned to Yellow Bear and spoke tensely. "Get him."

Yellow Bear trotted off into the darkness. Horace grinned. "I knew damned well they wouldn't start any trouble," he said.

"My God!" said Ducey.

A silence fell over the valley, broken only by the distant cries of the wrestling troopers. Dan stepped back into the shadows. Morris dabbled at his round face with a bandanna. "A firm hand, Major," he said, "a firm hand."

"Yes," said Dan absently. There was a smell of trouble in the evening air.

The rifle cracked flatly from the western ridge, a spurt of orange-red in the shadows. Morris grunted. He turned, pawing at his back. "I," he said, "I..." Then he pitched forward across the dying fire as the echo of the shot slammed back and forth across the valley.

Dan jumped behind a rock. Ducey cursed as he sprinted for cover. The smell of burning cloth rose from Morris' clothing. Then all hell broke loose in the shadows. A ripple of rifle fire raced along both ridges. The wrestling troopers had stopped, looking toward the treaty fire. One of them sagged in the arms of the man who held him. Then his late opponent went down, dragging the wounded man with him.

Dan suddenly noticed that Cut Lip and Long Hat had vanished. He drew his Colt. "Get to your command, Horace!" he yelled. He darted to the fire and dragged Morris from the flames. Slugs whipped over his head. The cavalry horses whinnied and screamed in sudden panic. Some of them broke free, whipping their picket pins from the soft earth. A group of them thundered down the valley. The troopers scattered for cover as leaden sleet poured into them. Half a dozen of them were down, lying still or thrashing in agony.

Dan knelt beside Morris. The little man's eyes were open, but they did not see. Dan jumped into the brush. Something moved near him, and he cocked his Colt. It was Andy Horace. Then the officer was gone.

Sporadic carbine fire broke out from the troopers. Dan heard Haley's bull voice lashing at them. He plunged through the scrub trees and brush. A lean figure rose from the darkness and whirled, raising a rifle. Dan fired twice from the hip, leaped the fallen figure and snatched up his rifle. It was a new Henry rifle. Dan holstered his Colt and darted into thick brush, levering home a round. He fired at a shadowy figure and was rewarded with a muffled shriek.

Rifle fire poured down from the ridges. Dan dropped to his knees and crawled behind a rock ledge. A trooper turned and saw him. "God, sir," he said with gaping mouth, "we're sitting ducks."

"Shut up and shoot," said Dan.

Haley was driving the panicky troopers into cover. Then the rifle fire died away. Dan looked over the ledge. With the exception of the two Apaches he had fired at, there was not another buck in sight. He crawled to Haley. The big trooper spat. "Dammit," he said, "there ain't an officer with the men."

"Where are Kroft and Rosin?"

Haley gripped his carbine. "Corporal Denton said they rode over to the reservation to see the squaws."

Dan stared at the bitter man. "The fat's in the fire for sure. Morris is dead."

"Aye, and seven troopers are down." Haley threw a shot up the ridge. He flipped open the breech. The hot hull tinkled against a rock. "What now, sir?"

"Dig in. Below those rocks. Tell those damned noncoms to get control of their men."

Haley nodded and crawled off.

The valley was silent now. The fires glowed against the darkness. A horse whinnied up the valley. Dan crawled to the scattered company. Haley was lashing the noncoms into action. Gradually the company drew together. They piled rocks into a rude breastwork. Dan looked down the valley. Morris' feet protruded from behind a rock. There was no sign of life.

Haley squatted beside Dan. "What now, Mister Fayes?"

"They'll not fight at night."

"Aye, sir, but there's still the dawn to come. Shall I go back to the post for more men?"

"I'll go," a quiet voice said. Ducey appeared from the shadows.

"Look!" said Haley.

A squat Apache appeared on a rock, outlined against the western sky. "White-eyes!" he called. "You wanted Hair Rope! I am here!" Then he was gone as a cupful of slugs smashed about the rocks.

Dan felt a sickness within him. "Can you make it to the post, Ducey?"

"I think so."

"Go then. Bring a company if the post is safe. But for God's sake, tell them to watch for an ambush."

Ducey nodded and snaked off into the darkness.

Haley watched the interpreter until he was out of sight. "I've set a guard on the remainin' horses, sir."

Metal clinked against gravel as the shattered company dug in. The troopers worked with the few spades they had as well as mess knives, plates and their bare hands. In an hour they were partially below ground. A pale moon began to rise in the east. There was no movement on the overlooking ridges.

Dan placed his back against a rock and looked at the Henry rifle he had picked up. It was new. There had been other repeaters churning out death from the ridges.

"What about Lieutenants Kroft and Rosin, sir?" asked Haley.

Dan shrugged. He had no hope for them. But he had seen Captain Horace skulking in the shadows. There had been plenty of time for him to get back to his company. "Tell the men to get some sleep. Double guards. No shooting unless they're sure of a target, Haley."

"Yes, sir!"

Dan wanted a smoke but he satisfied himself by breaking up a cigar and chewing it. He had a full-sized outbreak on his hands now.

CHAPTER EIGHT

"Wake up, sir. 'Tis the false dawn."

Dan opened his eyes and shivered in the cold wind. Faint gray light was creeping into the valley of the San Ignacio. All about him he could see the sprawled troopers. Four of them lay near the stream that chuckled over its smooth stones. Haley had crawled out during the night with Corporal Denton to bring in the wounded.

"Trooper Wanska died durin' the night," said Haley. "Trooper Seligman has a slug in his chest. He's in a bad way. Troopers Lowell and Felton are hit hard but they will live."

Dan rubbed the sleep from his eyes and accepted a canteen from Haley. He drank sparingly. Haley brought out a twist of tobacco. "Chew, sir? It holds off the hunger for a smoke."

Dan nodded.

Haley handed him the cable twist. "'Tis Weddin' Cake. Strong, but the sauce ain't too bad."

Dan cut off a chew and stowed it in his mouth. "Anything stirring?"

"'Tis quiet as the grave, sir."

Dan looked across the creek and then sat up straight. A man was there, propped against a tree. He had been stripped. The head was drawn back tight against the tree trunk with a length of rope. The eyes stared across the creek. There was a curious lopsided look about the battered head. It had been crushed by a terrific blow. The naked body had been ripped open, letting the greasy entrails hang out over the mutilated crotch.

"Jesus," breathed a trooper, "it's Mister Rosin!"

A rookie suddenly retched and spewed a sour flood over his shirt.

Dan felt cold sweat work down his sides. The wind fluttered a scrap of paper pinned to the naked chest by a sharp stick.

"The 'Paches are gone," said Haley. "I scouted up the ridges. Nothin' but empty hulls up there." He poured a handful of them on the ground beside Dan. "Forty-four rimfire. Henry rifle ammunition."

Dan nodded. "It figures."

Somewhere over the hills they heard the brassy notes of a C trumpet.

Pale faces rose from behind rocks. A rookie laughed aloud. "Be quiet!" roared Haley.

Dan stood up and leaned on the Henry rifle. "Get a detail ready to cover and load those bodies," he said. "Cut Rosin down."

The trumpet sounded again, closer this time. Dan beckoned to the trumpeter of C Company, a skinny kid not more than eighteen. "Lip onto that trumpet," he said. "Let them know we're alive."

C Company's trumpet rang out brassily, if somewhat shakily.

Three men appeared atop the western ridge. Ducey, Captain Charles Norman and First Lieutenant Miles Danforth of Company B. Dan stood up and waved at them. Norman led his company down the slope in column of fours. Dan walked toward them. Norman reined in. "Hell to pay," he said. His face was serious. "I knew damned well Morris would create trouble. I had no idea how much."

Dan looked back over his shoulder. "Assign Danforth to C temporarily."

"Where are their officers?"

"Rosin is dead. Horace and Kroft are missing."

"For God's sake!"

The troopers of C had wrapped the bodies in blankets, and now lashed them across skittish horses. Haley led a detail to recover the body of little Bertram Morris. It had not been disturbed.

"What are your orders, sir?" asked Norman.

"Send C back to the post. Danforth can look for Horace on the way. We're riding to the reservation."

"Now? With Hair Rope on the warpath?"

Dan eyed the serious officer. "We've got to find Kroft."

A trooper led up Dan's bay. He swung up on the horse. "Haley!" he called, "accompany me as orderly!"

"Yes, sir!"

Danforth formed C Company. He mounted and led them toward Dan. "Your orders, sir?"

"Back to Costain. Keep your eyes peeled. The road is fairly open. You'll only run into an ambush if you get careless. Tell Captain Morgan to send word to headquarters about Morris' death. I'll send a detailed report when I return."

Battered C Company rode up the ridge, many of the troopers riding double. Behind them were the horses carrying the blanketed forms of the dead.

B Company rode up the valley with a point and flankers out. The sun tipped the eastern ranges as they debouched onto a level plain stretching along a branch of San Ignacio Creek. Several miles to the northeast a pall of smoke hung against the fresh-morning sky.

Ducey scouted ahead as they neared the reservation. He waved the company on from a low swale overlooking the creek bottoms. The smoke was thick along the edge of the swale.

Dan drew rein on the lip of the swale. Fires smoldered in the ruins of about half a hundred wickiups. There was no sign of life other than a skulking dog which ran off into the brush. On the far side of the creek, fires flickered about the foundations of half a dozen buildings. Scattered about the ground were iron bedsteads, pots and pans, smoldering mattresses, shattered boxes and barrels.

"The new buildings Morris was so damned proud of," said Ducey as he cut a chew. "A house each for Cut Lip, Yellow Bear and Long Hat. They didn't use them much. One of Cut Lip's young sons died in his house last year of the coughing sickness. Cut Lip left it and went back to his wickiup."

Dan looked up at the brooding hills. Somewhere in there was Cut Lip's band, now *broncos* as well as those of Hair Rope; warriors, squaws and children. "Mister Kelly," he said to the junior officer of the company, "take a platoon along the bottoms and see what you can find."

"Meaning Mister Kroft, sir?"

"If he's there."

Kelly jingled off with his men. Haley thrust a hand inside his shirt and drew out a scrap of paper, smeared and bloody. "This was stuck on Mister Rosin," he said.

Dan read it aloud. "To the White-eyes," it said in misspelt English, "We have closed the door on you. We have gone into the mountains as men and hunters. Do not follow. I have spoken. Hair Rope."

Norman spat. "I didn't know the bloody bastard could write," he said.

Ducey looked up. "His squaw can. She went to the reservation school."

Kelly brought back his platoon. "No sign of Kroft, sir."

"What now?" asked Norman. "Do we go into the hills after them?"

Dan shook his head. "That's what he'd want. Back to Fort Costain."

The column jingled off across the plain. The words of old Black Wind sifted back into Dan's mind. *Listen, Nantan Eclatten! My people are angry. The young men sharpen their arrows and grease their guns. They buy fine rifles with the yellow iron which the White-eyes love more than anything else. They have asked my council and I have spoken. I advised peace, but if they do not heed my words your lodges will go up in smoke. Your wagons will be captured. Those of you who wear the blue suits will die in the mountains and deserts. The signal fires will rise from here to Sonora.*

B Company received a smoky welcome when it reached Fort Costain. The smoke drifted up thinly from the stables, now nothing but great blackened rectangles on the barren earth. Ellis Morgan was stamping back and forth in headquarters, rawhiding the sergeant of the guard, when Dan came in. He stopped as he saw Dan. "God almighty," he said. "They fired the stables with naming arrows just before dawn. The wood was dry as old bones. Luckily we got the horses out."

"Who was officer of the guard?"

"Mister Baird. It wasn't his fault. Sergeant Bennett was asleep in the guardhouse instead of making his rounds."

"Confine Mister Baird to quarters. Break Bennett."

Morgan nodded sourly. "What happened at San Ignacio Creek?"

Dan sketched in the details. "Horace and Kroft are missing. Rosin is dead."

"Horace is here."

"Get him!"

An orderly was sent for Horace.

Morgan waved a thick hand. "One word of warning. Horace has friends amongst the high muckymucks. Go easy."

Horace bustled into headquarters. "Thank God you're safe, Major Fayes," he said.

Dan's cold eyes held those of the plump officer. "I see you're safe enough," he said quietly.

Horace flushed. "I was cut off."

"No more than I was."

Horace fiddled with his gun belt. "The brush was thick with them, sir."

Dan waved a hand. "I'll excuse you for getting cut off. There's no excuse for laxness at San Ignacio, however. Both of your junior officers were gone from your company. You had no sentries out. Rosin was killed and mutilated. Kroft is still missing."

Andrew Horace paled. "It was a complete surprise, sir."

"Damn it, Horace! You've been in this country for some time. You knew the Apaches were restless. Your company was cut to pieces through damned carelessness on your part!"

Horace raised his head angrily. "So? Where were you when the peace commissioner came? It was your duty to take him there. Not *mine!*"

Dan stood up. "You're confined to quarters until further orders."

"General Crook will hear of this!"

Dan smiled grimly. "Certainly, he will. Through my report."

Horace stamped out of the office. Dan turned to Morgan. "I'm promoting Haley to sergeant major."

"A deserter? You'll destroy the morale of the squadron!"

"*What* morale? Haley stepped in and held that John company together to keep them from being cut to pieces. Their own noncoms were panic-stricken. Their officers were all gone. Kroft and Rosin looking at squaws. Horace hiding in the brush. Haley is sergeant major. Post it."

Morgan's face went dark with the rush of blood.

"I want a patrol to go into those hills. I want one good officer to lead them. Picked men. Meanwhile clean up the post. You've got materials for new stables. Get the quartermaster busy on them."

Dan walked to his quarters.

Mister Sykes led out a ten-man patrol at noon, guided by Ben Ducey. At three o'clock smoke signals drifted up from the hills. They had been seen.

Gila Barnes came into Dan's quarters in the late afternoon. He squatted near the door and accepted a cigar.

"What did you learn?"

Gila lit up. "The hills are thick with *broncos.* I got as far as Skull Butte before I had to turn back. They've got a camp somewhere in the country behind Skull Butte. Found a prospector dead in the hills. Apache work."

"Beats me how Hair Rope cut C Company up at San Ignacio, got Cut Lip's band to pull out, and still had time to double back here to fire the stables."

Gila puffed at his long nine. "Hair Rope didn't fire the stables."

"The three top bucks of the band were at San Ignacio. Cut Lip. Yellow Bear, Long Hat."

Gila waved his cigar. "I was comin' out of the hills this mornin'. Saw dust. Ten bucks rode past. You'd never believe who was leadin' them."

"Keep talking."

Gila looked up. "Black Wind."

"Blind?"

"His cayuse was bein' led. There was no other buck of real warrior status with them. I overheard them laughin' about burnin' the stables."

"I wondered where the old coot was."

"Hair Rope is a killer. A real sure enough quill, but he hasn't got the brains to strike like Black Wind can. I'll be willin' to bet the shootin' at San Ignacio was Black Wind's idea."

Dan paced back and forth. "This is a mad business. A blind war chief."

"Not so mad. Black Wind is held in great respect by every Apache between here and Durango. Why, 'hell's fire, Dan! He fought with Cochise and Mangus Colorado! He was a great warrior when they were kids! If he stays on the warpath, you'll never know what hit yuh!"

Dan smashed a fist into his other palm. "Sykes is leading a patrol into the hills."

Gila nodded. "I met him. Told him to camp high at night. No fires. Ducey is a good man. He'll take care of Sid and his detail."

"This thing has turned into a stinking mess. With a record like this I won't be here long."

"They haven't relieved you yet, have they?"

"No."

"Then forget it."

"Those bucks had Henry rifles, Gila. New ones."

Gila nodded. "So did Black Wind's men."

"Where are they getting them?"

Gila stood up. "I'll mosey down to Moore's and then into Mesquite Wells. Might learn somethin'."

Dan walked to the small hospital and found Myron Cornish wearing his rubber apron. At the rear of the room was the line of dead from San Ignacio. Trooper Felton lay on the operating table in the deep sleep of chloroform. Cornish held out a mutilated slug at the tip of his Blasius pincers. "Forty-four caliber," he said, "Henry cartridge. Half-ounce ball. Felton will live. So will Lowell. Seligman is dead. The slug went into his chest and lodged near the heart. I probed with a Nelaton. Impossible to extract."

The mingled odors of blood, carbolic and chloroform were thick in the stuffy room. Cornish rinsed his hands in the pinkish water of a basin. "Rather interesting mutilations," he said.

Dan looked up. "What do you mean?"

Cornish jerked a thumb at one of the shrouded figures. "Mister Rosin. A good part of it was done while he was still alive. Rosin had a lot of resistance to live so long."

Dan felt a little sick.

Cornish dried his smooth hands. "They say an expert can keep them alive for hours, almost beyond belief."

Dan eyed the cold man with a little disgust.

Cornish removed his apron and shrugged into his fine uniform blouse. "Still, they say the Moors passed their skill on to the Spaniards. The Spaniards, in turn, taught them to the Indians. Rather interesting, isn't it?"

"Yes," said Dan dryly.

Cornish looked at him with mild amusement. "By the way. Melva would like you for dinner tonight."

"Some other time, Cornish."

The surgeon shrugged. "As you wish. She's all woman, and she likes you, Dan."

"Thanks." Dan left the reeking room and drew deep lungfuls of fresh air into his lungs. Over at the cemetery the burial detail had already started the row of fresh graves.

The sun had gone, staining the western sky with streamers of rose and gold. Dan went to his quarters. Melva Cornish was sitting on his bunk. She stood up as he entered. "Are you all right, Dan?"

"Yes."

She placed a hand at her throat. "I was worried about you."

He looked at her. A faint hunger crept over him. She seemed to be ripe for the taking. "I told your brother I couldn't make it for dinner tonight, Melva."

"That's quite all right. There will be other times."

She came close. "I'm so glad you're all right," she said. Suddenly she held his face in both cool hands and kissed him gently. Then she was gone leaving the imprint of her soft full mouth on his dry lips and the faint intriguing odor of heliotrope.

Dan saw a bottle of mezcal on the table. He uncorked it and drank deeply. There was a weariness in him, not so much of the body, as of the soul.

He lit his candle lantern and drew a chair to his desk. He started his report. His mind mechanically composed the details, as it had so often done before, keeping to the facts, eliminating unnecessary information. When he reached the part where he must write of the raid on the post, he put down his pen and took another drink. Who would believe that a *blind* chief, an old man, fit only for long hours of sleep and soft food, could strike as though he were young again? Yet Dan believed Barnes. He compromised by stating that the raid had been led by Black Wind, mentioning nothing of his blindness.

Someone tapped at the outer door.

"Come in!" called Dan.

Surgeon Cornish looked into the room. "I have a list of needed medical supplies, sir."

"Can't the quartermaster take care of them?" There was a faint note of irritation in Dan's voice.

Cornish eyed the bottle on the desk and then shook his head. "Department requires the approval of the post commander."

"Help yourself," said Dan, shoving the bottle and a glass toward Cornish.

Cornish poured three fingers and poised the bottle over another glass. He looked at Dan. Dan shook his head. Cornish shrugged and sipped at the liquor. "Ah," he said, "a man needs this after time in the dispensary."

The faint odor of carbolic seemed always to hover about Cornish, as heliotrope clung about his sister.

"You've done well here, Major Fayes," said Cornish.

Dan rested an elbow on the desk. "I'm glad *someone* thinks so."

Cornish waved a well-scrubbed hand. "You can't be blamed for that trouble at San Ignacio. Horace is a bumbling fool. Morris was so wrapped up in his own importance he never realized the Apaches are humans too. Morgan was always lax with Kroft and Rosin."

"You seem to have formed definite opinions about all the officers here at Costain, Cornish," said Dan dryly.

Cornish smiled. "I'm a scientific man, sir. The field of physical medicine will someday be well supplemented by that of the mind. In Europe there are men who probe the mind as we do bullet wounds. Man is a fascinating study. His foibles and weaknesses; his fears and ambitions. We all have our weaknesses." He looked pointedly at the bottle.

Dan poured a drink.

"You're West Point of course?" asked Cornish.

"Class of 1858."

Cornish refilled his glass. "It seems unusual for a man of your experience and record to be shunted aside to Fort Costain."

"I usually don't question my orders."

Cornish smiled. "Of course not. Yet, you were a colonel at twenty-three. Quite young."

"Volunteers."

"Even so. Still, they kept you on as cavalry inspector, with the rank of major. Very unusual."

Dan sipped his liquor. The man's probing questions and insinuations irritated him.

Cornish lit a cigar. "Let us hope your record continues. The Apaches are certainly riled up. New rifles. Plenty of ammunition. Good leadership. It will test your mettle...and ours, sir."

Dan fingered the requisition Cornish had placed on the desk. "I'll look this over."

Cornish nodded. "The way things look I'll have quite a drain on my supplies."

"I hope not."

Cornish stood up. He paused at the door. "If you have any problems don't hesitate to consult me. Most of us like to talk about our problems. A sort of mental catharsis."

Dan placed his hand over the papers on his desk. "These are my problems at the moment."

"A word of advice, Major Fayes. You're starting to drive yourself too hard. Perhaps you're also lacking the fuel that kept you going during the war."

Dan looked up quickly. "Just what do you mean by that, sir?"

Cornish glanced toward the bottle. "Nothing, sir, nothing at all." He left the quarters.

Dan got up and walked to the outer door to watch Cornish cross the dark parade ground. The man rubbed him the wrong way, yet he seemed to have Dan's interest at heart. Dan looked into Dunphy's old room. He lit a lucifer and looked at the dark stain on the floor. What had happened to him? *His* record had been good also. He had had the love of a fine woman like Harriet Moore. Yet the strain had been too much.

Dan went back to his room, looked at the bottle, then stoppered it and put it away. He could feel the little alcohol he had consumed already working within him. The old strain was getting hold of *him* again.

Mess Call sounded across the dark parade ground. Dan went back to his desk. Food had no interest for him, but the liquor did. He drew his report toward him and set to work, but every now and then he looked at the cabinet in which he had placed the bottle. It was almost as though he could look through the warped wood of the door and see the squat bottle sitting on the shelf.

CHAPTER NINE

S yke's patrol came back the second day after the fight at San Ignacio Creek. Men and officers gathered about the dusty, weary troopers. Three of the troopers were afoot, leading two horses apiece. Three others were in the saddle, bloodstained bandages showing against the dusty blue of their uniforms. Across three horses were limp bundles, troopers swathed in their blankets.

Sykes swung down from his horse and saluted Dan. "We were ambushed near Sand Springs, sir. Three men wounded. Three killed. One missing."

"Where's Ducey?"

Sykes wiped the dust from his haggard face. "He was separated from us."

"Come to my quarters." Dan walked across the sun-beaten parade ground.

Sykes dropped into a chair and accepted a drink. "I'm sorry about the whole thing, sir. Ducey led us into the hills. We watered the horses at the Springs and then climbed up onto a small mesa. I put out double guards and had the horses on one picket line. The night was quiet. Ducey left before dawn to do some scouting. Just as the first light came, we heard the howling of a coyote. It was repeated several times from different places." Sykes lowered his head.

"Go on!"

"They hit us right after that. Kepke and Riordan went down at the first fire. The horses almost stampeded. Corporal Clothier and Private Wascher went to quiet them down. That's the last we saw of Clothier. Later we found Wascher gutted at the bottom of the mesa. We holed up. We were in a bad way. Two men wounded. We hardly saw them, yet they covered every inch of ground with rifle fire."

"Repeaters?"

"Yes. Henrys, I think." Sykes drained his glass. "We stayed holed up until the sun rose. The Apaches were gone. I waited for Ducey and Clothier, but they never appeared. I came back as quickly as I could."

"Who was leading the Apaches?"

Sykes looked up. His dark eyes held a strange light in them. "I saw an old warrior high on a hill. He looked like a mummy up there, staring at us. Then he was gone."

"Black Wind?"

"I've never seen him, sir. The worst part of it was the laughing when we left the hills."

"The laughing?"

Sykes nodded. "Apaches. Somewhere. We never saw them. It was damned weird, hearing them laugh from the hills, the echoes carrying it along."

Dan eyed the young officer. He seemed to be of good material, yet his nerves were at the straining point. "Get some sleep," he said. "Make out your report when you feel better."

Sykes stood up. "Thank you, sir." He hesitated.

"What is it?"

"When do we get a crack at them, sir?"

"When we're ready. They'd like to have us come into the hills, bent on revenge, then shoot us up."

"This whittling process hasn't helped the morale any, sir."

Dan looked up. "We'll stop it."

After Sykes left, Dan called for his horse. He rode down to the road and headed for Moore's Ranch. The rancher was in the big barroom. He silently listened as Dan told him the story. "What is it you want from me?" he asked.

"How in God's name are the Apaches getting new Henry rifles?"

Moore leaned on the bar. "It's nothing new. I've known about it for some time. Hair Rope had new repeaters as early as the first of the year, six months ago."

"Perhaps he gets them in Mexico?"

"I doubt it. There are stocks of repeaters in Tucson, and other towns. A merchant can order as many as he likes and doesn't have to account for his sales. I myself have bought them there. I had twenty of them in stock as early as last March."

"How many do you have left?"

Moore looked quickly at Dan. "Ten. Why?"

"Just curious."

"I sold four of them to miners. Three to people in Mesquite Wells. One to Captain Morgan. One to Captain Norman. I can't remember where I sold the last of the ten." Moore's voice was cold.

Dan lit a cigar. "I didn't mean to imply that you had been selling them to Apaches."

"The only guns I ever sold them were some old Burnside single-shot carbines. That was last summer. Eight of them. I requested authority from the army to make the sale and received it."

Hoofs clattered on the hard earth in front of the big building. A familiar voice carried to them. It was that of Forrest Kroft. "We'll have a couple of drinks before we return to the post, Gila."

"You're carryin' a load now. You want Major Fayes to rawhide you?"

Kroft came into the barroom, followed by Gila. The officer paled as he saw Dan. He swayed a little. "Major Fayes. I'm reporting back to duty, sir."

Dan held back the acid in his voice. "Here? Where have you been?"

Kroft glanced at Gila. "Mister Rosin and I were at the

reservation. They shot at us from the brush. Rosin was killed. I managed to get away. I got lost in the hills."

Dan gripped the edge of the bar. "Rosin wasn't killed. He lived long enough to be tortured to death. Who did it, Mister Kroft?"

_ Kroft looked sullen. His handsome face was flushed with liquor and anger. "I don't know, sir. All I saw were rifle flashes and shadowy figures."

"How long were you in Mesquite Wells?"

Kroft bit his lip. He glanced at Gila. "A few hours."

Gila shifted his chew and looked at Dan.

Dan thrust out a hand toward Kroft. "Sober yourself up before you return to the post. When you do, write out a full report, then stay confined in your quarters."

Kroft saluted.

Jim Moore jerked his head. "There's coffee in the kitchen. The water bucket is just outside the door." He watched Kroft as he walked stiffly into the kitchen.

Dan turned to Gila. "What's the truth?" he asked.

"He was mixed up in a big poker game last night, started a fight and got damned drunk. I found him this mornin'. He asked me not to say anythin'. Hell, Dan, he's rotten clear through."

"Gambling on a shavetail's pay in Mesquite Wells?" asked Moore. "He couldn't have played very long with those sharpers."

Gila shrugged. "He's damned lucky Ace Deming didn't kill him."

Dan poured a drink and handed it to Gila. "Maybe his family has money?"

Gila shook his head. "His father went broke in the panic. He hasn't got a peso comin', outside of his army pay."

A pan clattered on the kitchen floor. There was a scuffle of feet and the sharp outcry of an angry woman. Moore ran to the door followed by Gila and Dan. Harriet Moore stood near the rear door holding a poker in her hand. Her face was flushed, and her breasts heaved. Kroft was holding his left shoulder. He turned as Moore closed in on him. "The bitch hit me with that," he said.

Moore's left fist shot out, connecting with Kroft's jaw. He staggered and swung wildly at Moore. The older man thrust out his right arm. The stub smashed against Kroft's mouth, driving him back over a chair. He tried to get up and then lay still. Blood poured from his slack mouth.

"The bastard," said Gila quietly.

Moore turned to Dan. Thin lines etched themselves from the corners of his mouth almost down to his chin. "Get him out of here," he said coldly, "or I'll kill him."

Dan strode to the unconscious officer. He picked up the water bucket and doused Kroft with it. Kroft opened his bloodshot eyes. Dan gripped him by the collar of his shell jacket and pulled him to his feet. He frog-marched him to the front door and shoved him toward his horse. "Damn you," he said thickly, "I'll break you for this."

Kroft dabbled at his smashed mouth. "She's nothing but a saloon bitch," he said drunkenly.

Dan hit him across the face with open hands. "Get back to the post, you drunken scum," he said.

Kroft swung up on his horse. "You'll pay for this. You and that woman in there. No one hits me and gets away with it." He spurred his sorrel hastily as Dan dropped his hand to his Colt. Dan watched him ride down the slope to the road. He turned in the saddle as he reached the road and shot a look of pure venom at Dan. Then he was gone.

Dan walked into the common room. Moore was filling whisky glasses. "I've had trouble with him before," he said.

Harriet stood in the kitchen doorway. "He's paid for it," she said. "You won't prefer charges against him, will you, Dan?"

"I'll give him a chance to resign."

Gila leaned against the bar. "They won't accept a resignation now, with the 'Paches on the war trail."

Moore tossed down his drink. "He's bothered her before," he said. "Kroft is the type that thinks brass buttons and a commission allow him free rein with any woman. No woman is a lady to him. They're all fair game."

Harriet smoothed her hair. "He's young," she said.

Moore turned angrily. "Not *that* young! He knows better! Keep him out of here, Fayes, or I'll kill him the next time he bothers Harriet."

Dan nodded. "Come on, Gila," he said quietly.

They rode toward the post. "What did you learn?" asked Dan.

Gila shrugged. "Not a hell of a lot. About the rifles, that is. It ain't hard to run in rifles. Any wagon can bring 'em in. The boxes can be marked anythin'."

"The whole thing is full of holes. Still, my job is to calm down this uprising, not to worry about gunrunners. God knows the *broncos* seem to have enough rifles."

"Yeh. But the more rifles they get the more warriors they can recruit. Bucks just waitin' to get their greasy hands on new repeaters." Gila bit off a chew. "Funny thing. Kroft had plenty of gamblin' funds from what I heard."

Dan looked quickly at him. "So?"

The faded eyes held Dan's. "He was usin' gold dust until he went broke."

"What are you driving at?"

"Nothin'."

They followed the fort road and passed the gate. "Where is Kroft quartered?" asked Dan.

"In Bedlam."

"Bedlam?"

"Yeh. The junior officers' quarters. At the end of Officers' Row."

"Dormitory?"

Gila shook his head. "They each have separate rooms." He looked at Dan. "You thinkin' the same thing I am?"

Dan nodded. "Can you get in and out of there without being seen?"

"At night mess the place is empty as last night's whisky bottle."

"Go ahead then."

Gila spat a stream of brown juice. "Dunphy had a hell of a time with Kroft. Kroft seemed to have some hold on him. Dunphy wasn't himself for a long time before he blew out his brains."

"Mister Kroft is quite a man for his age."

Gila nodded. "He likes money, liquor and women. He doesn't get them as a second looie of horse soldiers." Gila rode toward the corrals.

Woodridge, the adjutant, looked up as Dan came into headquarters. "Do you wish to reassign the officers, sir?" he asked.

"Why?"

Woodridge leaned back in his chair. "G Company hasn't an officer left, what with Rosin dead and Horace and Kroft confined to quarters."

Dan dropped into a chair and lit a cigar. "I see what you mean."

"Dennis Halloran reported in. He brought the dispatches from Fort Grant." Woodridge handed them to Dan.

Dan scanned the first two papers. They dealt with supply and transportation subjects. The third dealt with the messy affair at San Ignacio Creek. Dan read it slowly.

From: B. N. Curtiss, *Col.*

Dept. Adjutant, Department of Arizona Fort Grant, Arizona Terr.

To: Daniel R. Fayes, *Major*

Provisional Squadron, Cavalry Fort Costain, Ariz. Terr.

Subject: Apache Uprisings June 1873

As of this date there are no re-enforcements available for your command. One squadron of cavalry, regularly assigned to this Department, supplemented by three companies of infantry, has been temporarily transferred to the Department of California, for duty against the Modocs in northern California and southern Oregon, thus seriously weakening this command. These are your orders:

The murderers of Bertram Morris, peace commissioner, must be arrested and confined at Fort Costain.

In an effort to quell the uprising, you will take the field with your entire command, less one full company for garrison duty, which will remain at Fort Costain.

Details of troops will be assigned to duty in Mesquite Wells as per the request of a committee of citizens of that town, as well as any outlying habitations which may require them.

All reservation Apaches will be returned under guard to the San Ignacio Reservation. The band of the chief known as Cut Lip will be disarmed and kept under guard until further orders.

Upon completion of the above orders, you will hold yourself in readiness for travel to Fort Grant for a court of inquiry into the San Ignacio affair. This order includes the presence of A. N. Horace, Captain, U.S. Cavalry.

The subject matter contained herein will be strictly complied with as expeditiously as possible and will be held in confidence.

B. N. CURTISS, *Department Adjutant*

Dan placed the order on the desk and looked at Woodridge. "You read it?"

"Yes, sir."

Dan rubbed his jaw. "What is the present garrison strength?"

Woodridge took out his Morning Report. "Thirteen officers. One hundred and twenty-eight other ranks. One civilian scout. One civilian interpreter."

Dan shook his head. "With a handful of men, I have to garrison Costain—run down Hair Rope and Cut Lip—provide guards for Mesquite Wells and anyone else who feels the need of army protection. No matter which way you figure, we'll be stretched almighty thin, Nat."

Woodridge nodded. "You're damned if you do and damned if you don't."

Dan nodded. "Send word to Horace and Kroft that they are relieved from confinement to quarters. Assign Halloran to C Company. How many men in the guardhouse?"

"Seven."

"Have them released and return them to their companies."

Dan stood up and paced back and forth. He didn't trust G Company in the field. They'd have to stay at Costain as garrison. They had been whittled down to thirty-five men. Horace was of no use in the field, yet Black Wind's raid on the stables, had shown the contempt he had for the garrison of Fort Costain. The Skull Butte country was unknown to Dan. Gila Barnes knew it and so did Ducey, but it was one thing for a few good men led by capable scouts to penetrate hostile country; it was quite another matter to take a column of morale-rotten troops in there.

"Write out an acknowledgment of that order and send it to Curtiss," said Dan. "Captain Morgan can take his A Company to Mesquite Wells in the morning. He can arrange the details about guarding outlying houses. I'll speak with him about it tonight."

"Yes, sir." Woodridge stood up. "I must say, sir, that I feel a lot better with you in command here."

Dan walked to the door. "Thanks, Woodridge. We've got a tough job of work to do. There will be plenty of empty McClellans before we're through." He walked out of head-quarters.

CHAPTER TEN

D an dressed slowly for mess. He had no wish to look at the sullen faces of the officers he had released from confinement to quarters. Someone tapped at the outer door as he finished dressing. He started toward the room door and then stopped, glancing at his Colt. The wound on his left shoulder had healed but he had no wish to have a skulking warrior work on him again with a knife.

"It's Cornish, sir!"

"Come in."

Myron Cornish walked smiling into Dan's room. "Melva insists that you come over tonight. How about it? You've turned us down a few times already, sir."

Dan hesitated. It was a sure out from going to the regular mess. "All right, Cornish," he said.

"Fine! Say about eight?"

"That will be fine."

Cornish leaned against the wall. "Rumors are thick about the post," he said. "The sanitary sinks are buzzing with them."

"We have orders to pursue and arrest the Apaches who killed Morris and Rosin."

"The whole squadron?"

"No. C will garrison. A will ride to Mesquite Wells in the morning to guard civilians. I'll have to take B."

Cornish studied his neat nails. "What happens to me?"

"Have you a capable man or two to use as medical orderlies?"

Cornish nodded. "Sergeant French is a good man. Orderly Andersen has a great deal of experience."

"Andersen can go with A Company to Mesquite Wells. You can stay here with C or go along with the field column, whichever you prefer."

"I have some supplies coming in which I'd like to check."

"Then French can go with the field column."

"Fine. I'll help him prepare his panniers."

"How are Orskin, Mehaffey and Rinke?"

"Orskin and Mehaffey are all right. Rinke has a trace of blood poisoning. That's another reason I'd like to stay at the post. Rinke may lose his arm. Arrow wound."

Dan eyed the surgeon. "They used *arrows?*"

"Yes. I extracted a sagittate flint head from the wound. Poisoned, I think. You know how they make their poison?"

"No."

Cornish smiled. "Very interesting. They place a fresh deer liver on an anthill and let the ants fill it with their venom. The big Sonoran ants. When the liver is filled with it, they let it rot and then dry, making a powder of it which they mix with a little grease. This is daubed onto the arrowhead. Gangrene is usually the result if the wound isn't taken care of in time."

"Very interesting. But why would they use arrows when they have Henry rifles?"

The dark eyes studied Dan. "Fear, I suppose."

"What do you mean?"

Cornish waved a hand. "The whole post knows Rinke was wounded with an arrow. If gangrene *does* set in and he loses his arm, the thought of what happened to him will remain in the minds of the troopers who chase the Apaches. Psychology, Major."

Dan nodded. "Very efficient."

"They are. A remarkable people, the Apaches. I've heard it said that they know of hidden lodes of gold. Wealth that would turn any white man's head. Yet they rarely use it."

"You'd think they'd use it instead of waiting for government handouts."

Cornish eyed the glasses on Dan's desk.

"Drink?" asked Dan.

"If you'll join me."

Dan poured two drinks and handed a glass to the surgeon. Cornish eyed the liquid and then downed it. "Speaking of handouts. Actually, the reason they are so bitter against the government isn't that they really need handouts, as you call them, but rather because they feel that the government made them promises, and to an Apache, you must keep your word. It's as simple as that."

"I wish it was as simple to get them back on the reservation."

Cornish nodded. "By the way, Forrest Kroft is very bitter toward you. A very angry young man. Watch yourself, sir."

"What do you mean?"

Cornish smiled. "Kroft is unstable. He feels as though you destroyed his dignity. A bad place to hit a man."

When Cornish had gone Dan refilled his glass. Cornish was as smooth as silk, with his perpetual smile and insinuating talk. There was no real reason for Dan to dislike him, yet he was glad to see the surgeon leave.

It was eight o'clock by Dan's repeater watch when he walked down to Cornish's quarters midway down Officers' Row. The adobe was set farther back from the row line, overlooking the creek bottoms, placed on an outthrust point of ground with deep gullies on either side of it. Dan made a mental note that the gullies should be either filled or banked, for a heavy rain would eat away the earth dangerously close to the walls of the adobe.

Yellow lamplight showed between the trim curtains of the windows. Dan tapped on the door. It was opened by Melva Cornish. She wore a low-cut gown exposing the deep cleft between her full breasts which seemed to strain against the dress fabric. She held out a slim hand and gripped Dan's. "Just in time," she said. "Would you like a drink before dinner?"

"Yes."

Dan felt a fullness in him as she brushed past to lead the way into the snug living room. She spoke over her shoulder. "Wine? Brandy? Whisky?"

"Wine will be all right" The mezcal Dan had taken aboard had filled him with a comfortable warmness. He sat down in a big chair. Melva had done wonders with the poor quarters. Navajo rugs covered the packed-earth floor. A trim Argand lamp shed soft light from a marble-topped table. On the walls hung several oils of local scenery. Melva saw Dan look at them. "Some of my work," she said.

"You have talent, Melva."

She flushed a little. "Myron says so. It keeps me occupied in this lonely place."

She placed the glass on the table beside his chair. "I'm so glad you could come, Dan." She sat down and leaned back in her chair. "We'll dine in a few minutes."

Dan glanced at the table, covered with a heavy damask cloth. It was set for two. A smaller lamp brought out the highlights of the heavy polished silver. "Where is Myron?" he asked.

She leaned forward. The lamplight brought out the color of her firm breasts. "Didn't he tell you? Oh, that absent-minded man! He went into Mesquite Wells to consult with Doctor Walsh about poor Trooper Rinke's wound."

Dan nodded, as he sipped the wine. It was very cozy being alone with Melva Cornish. A commander who dealt with men all day needed a woman to come home to, even at a place like Fort Costain.

She eyed him. "I hope you're not disappointed."

"No."

"I know how you men like to talk business."

"I'm a little tired of business now, Melva."

He drained his glass and she rose to fill it. The fragrance

of her body and heavy perfume worked on him as the liquor did. Suddenly he felt completely weary of his profession.

They dined quietly. Melva was a skillful cook and a polished hostess. Dan found himself growing more interested in her. She still reminded him strongly of Kitty St. Clair in Washington, but there was a difference. Kitty had been easy to understand. In most ways, she was almost as simple as a man, while Melva had all the intrigue and challenge of her sex.

When they left the table, Dan sat in the big armchair and looked about the room. It would be fine to have quarters like this. Quite different from the monk's cell he lived in. On the mantelpiece sat some rock samples. Melva followed his glance. "Myron collects them while in the field."

"A man of many interests."

She laughed. "Yes. *He's* never lonely, Dan." She smoothed her thick hair. "What with his medicine and rock collecting he's quite contented."

"I often wonder why a doctor would enter the service. Low pay. Rough assignments. Little chance to get ahead in the profession."

The dark eyes flicked at him and then away. "There are times when I wonder about Myron myself. Before he went to medical school, he talked of nothing else. At school he astounded his professors with his quick grasp of any subject. After his internship in New York, in the tenement areas, he had a chance to go to Europe to study at Edinburgh, but he turned it down." Dan sipped his wine. "I wonder why?"

She clasped her fine hands together. "I'm not sure. Sometimes, I think it was because he worked so hard to go to medical school, depriving himself of everything but the bare necessities..."

"So he became an army surgeon for a pittance when he could be well paid for bis services anywhere else."

She leaned her head back against her chair. "Why did you become a soldier?" she asked. He grinned. *"Touché!"*

"I mean it Why?"

"My father was a soldier. Both of my grandfathers were soldiers."

"So it was the thing to do."

He shook his head and refilled his wineglass. "No. I would never have gone to West Point unless I had believed implicitly that I wanted to be a soldier."

"Then you might try to understand Myron."

"There's a difference. A soldier doesn't serve for pay. There are other things."

"Glory? Prestige?"

"In a way. There's more than that. It is a way of life to which one is committed."

She arose and paced back and forth, the odor of her perfume reaching tempting fingers out to Dan as she passed near him. Something about the comfortable room was also bothering his mind. The furnishings were expensive. The silverware on the table had cost a pretty penny. Yet she had said Cornish had deprived himself of everything but the bare necessities to gain his education. Money spoke in a metallic voice in that room, so different from other contract surgeons' quarters he had visited throughout the West.

She stopped beside his chair and looked down at him. Dan stood up and reached out a hand. She placed her warm one in it and Dan drew her close. He met no resistance. She raised her full lips to his. He crushed her soft body close and felt her smooth arms slip about his neck and draw him toward her, straining her body against his. His eager hands explored her upper body, the liquor he had consumed fueling the hot fire within him. They swayed a little as they experienced each other's lips and bodies.

She broke away and touched her hair. There was a strange look in her dark eyes. "I should never have let you come here to be alone with me," she said huskily.

He reached for her. "Why?"

"You know how talk gets around on a small post."

"I'm worried!"

She backed away from him. "It's getting late, Dan. Please! Some other time."

He closed in on her and drew her close. She struggled a little and then sought his lips eagerly. He drew her toward the couch and pulled her down beside him. It had been a long time since he had held such a woman in his arms.

Boots grated on the hard earth outside the quarters. She jerked upright. "Get away from me," she said.

"It's just some trooper."

She shook her head. "We're too far back from the other adobes for anyone to be walking around here."

"It's the guard," he said desperately.

She stood up and walked to the table. She picked up the decanter and filled his glass. Dan shrugged and walked to his chair. She stood looking down at him. "There is plenty of time in the future," she said.

He drank half of his wine. "Perhaps. I'll be leaving for the field very soon."

"You'll be back, Dan."

"Possibly. It's a dirty business, Melva."

Something brushed against the outer wall. She tilted her head. "You hear?"

Dan stood up. Every fiber in him cried out to take her now, completely. He picked up his forage cap. She was right. There would be plenty of time. "Good night, Melva."

"Good night, Dan."

She came to him as he reached the door and kissed him softly and then she was gone.

Dan shrugged. He opened the outer door and felt the cool night air rush about him. The moon hung in a cloudless sky. There was no one in sight. He walked slowly toward his quarters, feeling for a cigar. He stopped in front of the building and lit up. He drew the smoke deep into his lungs. Suddenly he had to fight down the desire to get his horse and ride into Mesquite Wells.

Dan opened the outer door of his quarters. Something moved at the far end of the hall. Instinctively he dropped to the floor. A spurt of flame reached out from the darkness. The roar of the gun was deafening in the low hallway. Then the rear door opened. He saw a shadowy figure against the light for a moment and then the door banged shut. He jumped to his feet and dashed out the front door. Feet grated on the hard earth behind the quarters. He ripped his derringer free from his pocket and ran around the adobe.

Something moved beyond the washhouse. He snapped out a shot and heard a muffled exclamation. A pistol flared again, and the slug slapped into the adobe inches from Dan's head. Shards of hard clay splattered against his face. Tears flooded his eyes. He ran toward the washhouse. His assailant would have to slide down the eroded escarpment behind it.

A man yelled from the guardhouse, followed by the steady pound of feet as the guard raced from the building.

Dan stopped beside the washhouse and looked down toward the creek bottoms. The area was bathed in silver moonlight, the shadows of the mesquite and cactus sharp on the pale earth. Nothing moved.

Dan turned as the corporal of the guard pounded up followed by four men. "Get down into the bottoms," he said. "It's only one man."

"Apache, sir?"

"Damned if I know! Get moving!"

The corporal plunged down the slope followed by his men. They spread out into a line and worked toward the silvered loops of the shallow creek. Dan walked back toward the parade ground. Ellis Morgan trotted toward him, breathing heavily. "What the hell is going on?"

"Someone waited in the hall for me. Shot at me. I got one shot in."

"Apache?"

Dan waved a hand. "I don't know. He was wearing boots."

"Some Apaches do."

Dan became irritated. "All right, all right. So they do. I *said* I didn't know who it was."

Morgan flushed. "I'll turn out my company to scour the bottoms."

"No. You're leaving for Mesquite Wells in the morning. Let the men get their rest."

Morgan wiped the sweat from his face. "I'd like to speak with you about that."

"Go ahead."

"I'm senior company commander. It seems to me that my company is getting the wrong assignment."

"It does? Why?"

"Hell, Major! I think I should stay here and command the post in your absence. Certainly, Horace hasn't got the ability to do it."

Dan raised his head. "It seems to me I was sent here to command this post, Captain Morgan. Are you questioning my authority?"

Morgan cut a thick hand sideways. "No."

"Then do as you're ordered. By God, I never saw a command like this. Every damned officer seems to think I'm riding him."

Morgan closed a big fist. He lowered his head. Almost as though planning to charge Dan. Then he looked down and saw the moonlight glinting on the silver-chased derringer. Slowly he raised his head and opened his fist. "Woodridge told me to report to you earlier this evening. I couldn't find you."

"I was dining at the Cornishes."

The dark eyes half-closed. "Myron is in town," he said.

"So?"

"You were alone with Melva?"

Dan slipped the derringer into his pocket. "Yes."

Morgan stared at Dan. "I hope you enjoyed yourself."

Dan came closer to Morgan. "Get the hell back to your quarters, Morgan! Another thing: Don't ever question my orders again!"

Morgan turned and strode off across the moonlit parade ground, slamming his heels hard against the earth. Dan watched him until he disappeared into the shadows at the far side of the post. He felt for a cigar and lit it. The big man was jealous. Damned jealous...and dangerous.

The corporal of the guard panted up the steep slope. "No sign of anyone down there, sir."

Dan nodded. "Take your men back to the guardhouse."

He walked into his quarters and lit the candle lantern.

He drank deeply and stripped off his clothing. As he closed his eyes to sleep, he thought of the warm voluptuous body of Melva Cornish. She was ripe for the taking but it would take time. A *little* time.

CHAPTER ELEVEN

The squadron officers were assembled in headquarters the morning after Dan's narrow escape. Dan leaned against the wall. "Read Curtiss' order," he said to Woodridge. Woodridge read in a clear strong voice.

Dan studied each man as Woodridge plowed through the order. Baird and Sykes of Company A seemed to be fairly reliable. Captain Norman of B was solid and unimaginative. Danforth and Kelly, his junior officers, were run-of-the-mill, although Kelly seemed to show some promise if he was handled right. They would be all right with Norman. Horace was a damned weak link in the chain and Dan had his doubts about his remaining in command at Costain, but Dan didn't trust him in the field. Kroft leaned against the wall, slowly turning his forage cap in his hands. He looked away sullenly as Dan glanced at him. His face was still bruised. Dennis Halloran, the first lieutenant who had returned from the hospital at Fort Grant, was a lean man with the Antrim look about him. He seemed to enjoy the admiration and respect of all the post personnel. He would fortify the weaknesses of Horace's command. Collier Crispin, the Q.M., was a scholarly officer, small and efficient with serious blue eyes behind his glasses.

Myron Cornish straddled a chair in a corner of the big

room. He smiled as Dan looked at him. Thoughts of what he had learned from Melva about her brother ran through Dan's mind. He wondered what Melva had told *him* about Dan.

Woodridge finished the order and looked expectantly at Dan. Dan stood up. "You may smoke, gentlemen." He lit a cigar as some of them got out their smokes. Cornish slowly tamped tobacco into a fine English briar.

Dan took his cigar from his mouth. "In that order we have the bare essentials of what we must do. Any questions?"

Morgan looked up. "Paragraph Two clearly states that you are to take your entire command, less one company for garrison duty, into the field, sir. Yet your orders are for my company to go to Mesquite Wells for guard duty, leaving you but one company."

Dan nodded. "Paragraph Three states that details of troops will also guard Mesquite Wells and vicinity. I don't see how it can be done with less than a company."

Morgan shrugged.

Dan puffed at his cigar. "I'm making one change. Mister Kroft will accompany B Company as junior officer."

Horace jerked his head. "I'll need him, sir!"

"You have Mister Halloran. There will be two other officers available should you need them. Mister Collier and Mister Woodridge. Surgeon Cornish will remain here as well."

Kroft glanced angrily at Cornish.

"There's no need to tell you gentlemen that we're stretching things pretty fine," said Dan. "Horace, I want double guards every night."

"The men will be tired."

Dan waved a hand. "You can eliminate all unnecessary details. The men can get plenty of bunk fatigue, Horace." He paced back and forth. "Morgan, I don't want you to spread your men too thinly. Keep two squads in Mesquite Wells. The citizens there have guns. If any attack is imminent, you can declare martial law and draft the citizens to help you. Detail a few men at each outlying house or ranch that requests them. Keep patrols, under competent non-coms, in the hills about the town."

"Yes, sir."

"That is all for Companies A and C. Morgan, you will move out as quickly as possible. Take enough escort wagons for your extra equipment and food. How many will you need?"

"At least four, sir."

Collier stood up. "We've only six on the post, sir. Six others were destroyed in the fire. That will leave only two for you, sir."

"We're not taking any where we're going. We'll use pack mules."

The officers of A and C saluted and left. Dan sat down and puffed at his cigar. "There's no need to tell you officers what we face out in the hills. Gila Barnes will scout for us.

Sergeant Andersen will go along as medic. His panniers are prepared, Cornish?"

"They're always ready, sir. I checked them this morning."

"Good. The head of B Company will pass through the gates at dusk."

"Why so late, sir?" asked Norman.

"There are probably Apache eyes watching this fort at this very minute. I don't want them to know we're leaving."

"Fine, sir."

"Full field equipment. Three hundred rounds of carbine ammunition per man. Fifty rounds per revolving pistol. Rations and forage for seven days. Officers' Call will be at 5:30 P.M. Co-ordinate your watches." Dan took out his watch and snapped open the case lid. "It is now 10:45 A.M. Officers may take repeating rifles if they have them. Any questions, gentlemen?"

Kroft raised his head. "I don't feel too well, sir."

Dan held the red-rimmed eyes with his. "Did you report for Sick Call, Mister Kroft?"

"No, sir."

Dan looked at Cornish. "Examine him after dismissal."

Second Lieutenant George Kelly, who stood beside Kroft, moved a little way from him. Tall Miles Danforth could hardly hide the disgust on his lean face.

"Dismissed, gentlemen!" said Dan. He watched them file from the room.

Woodridge spoke up. "Will you take Sergeant Major Haley, sir?"

"Can you spare him?"

"Yes. Linke is a good man. He can take over."

"Then Haley will go."

Woodridge grinned. "It would have broken his black Irish heart if he couldn't have gone. I feel rather badly myself about not going. Any chance, sir?"

Dan shook his head.

"I could take Kraft's place, sir."

"That young man is going to sweat. I'll dry the alcohol from his system. We'll make a sharp command out of this John squadron, Woodridge."

"I have no doubt about that, sir."

Dan was in his quarters when Gila Barnes came into the room.

"Did you check Kroft's quarters?"

Gila nodded. He thrust two fingers into the right-hand pocket of his worn coat. He brought out a small packet of paper and placed it unfolded on the desk. Gold dust glittered in the light that came through a side window.

"Where did you find it?"

Gila helped himself to a drink. "In the pocket of a pair of his trousers. There was a little more in a shirt pocket."

Their eyes met above the desk. "I think I'll take a ride into Mesquite Wells this afternoon," said Dan quietly.

Before Dan left the post after noon mess, Cornish had sent his orderly to tell him that Kroft was fit for field duty.

Mesquite Wells dozed in the afternoon sun. Here and there, amongst the false-fronted wooden buildings of the American period, were thick-walled adobes of the earlier Mexican period. The hills hung over the town. Smoke drifted up from the mine buildings on the rugged slopes.

Here and there the tailings from the mines erupted like great swollen scars, covering brush and earth.

Dan passed a peeled-pole corral at the edge of town and saw the bays of A Company there, under guard of two men. He dismounted in front of the marshal's office and went in. A thick-bodied man, wearing a star, stood up as he entered. "Can I help you, Major?" he asked. "I'm Ben Forepaugh, city marshal."

Dan nodded. "Major Dan Fayes, commanding officer of Fort Costain. I'd like to ask you a few questions in strictest confidence."

Forepaugh accepted a cigar from Dan. "Glad to be of help, sir. Damned glad you sent some of your men here to help out in case the Apaches attack. What can I do for you?"

Dan lit up. "I've a young shavetail on the post. A Mister Kroft."

Forepaugh's head snapped up. "Forrest Kroft. What do you want to know?"

"Something about his gambling."

"He's done a lot of it in the last six months or so."

"So I understand. Seems odd. A second lieutenant's pay won't stake a man very much."

Forepaugh's gray eyes held Dan's. "I've often wondered about it myself. Unless Kroft has been out prospecting, which I doubt, it does seem odd he should have gold dust to gamble with."

"I understand he was in here a couple of days ago."

Forepaugh nodded. "He was in a game with Ace Deming. Kroft claims Deming cheated. Deming almost drew on him."

"So?"

"Ace Deming is an honest gambler. Slick as goose-grease but no one has ever questioned his honesty. Kroft is damned lucky he didn't get killed." Forepaugh eyed Dan. "Just what are you driving at, Major Fayes?"

"The Apaches have been getting Henry rifles regularly

since the first of the year. I've heard they pay gold dust for them."

Forepaugh took his cigar from his mouth. "I can't believe it. An army officer! If you can't trust army officers out here, who *can* you trust?"

"*One* army officer, Ben."

Forepaugh nodded. "I'm sorry. Still, I don't think Kroft has the brains to work a gunrunning deal."

"Neither do I. But he may be fooling us. I'd like to talk with Deming if he'll keep his mouth shut."

"He will. He's my half-brother, Fayes. I'll get him right away."

Forepaugh came back with a slim man, dressed in sober black, his face freshly shaven but still showing the dark shadows of a thick beard on the smooth cheeks. He nodded as Dan was introduced. "How can I help you, sir?" he asked.

Dan spoke about Kroft.

Deming lit a cigarillo. "Up until three months ago Kroft always gambled with hard cash. Plenty of it and no dust. One night he got liquored up and ran out of cash. His credit stinks here in town. He was so damned mad he brought out a poke of dust. I didn't question it. Why should I? Gambling is my business; not Pinkerton work."

"How much would you say Kroft has shown in the last three months?"

Deming relit his cigarillo and eyed Dan over the flare of the block match. "Close to two thousand dollars, I'd say roughly."

"Damned near two years' pay."

Deming nodded.

Dan paced back and forth. "Keep your mouths shut about this."

Deming waved a slim hand.

Dan leaned on Forepaugh's desk. "What's your opinion on this gunrunning, Ben?"

"It would be easy enough to get away with. Buy guns in Tucson. Freight 'em up here. Run a wagonload out into the hills and bargain with the Apaches. They pay two or three hundred in dust for them."

"Anyone else use gold dust in town?"

"A few prospectors. The miners are paid in cash. As far as I know none of the men that pay their way with dust can be suspected. I may be wrong."

"Keep a record of them, if you will."

The gray eyes studied Dan. "And the officers?"

Dan nodded. "*And* the officers."

Deming looked up. "I'll help too, Major. I learn a lot across the green cloth."

"I'd appreciate it." Dan walked to the door.

Forepaugh stood up. "Jim Moore does most of the freighting around here, Fayes," he said.

Dan turned. "So?"

"It'd be damned easy for him to run in guns."

A cold feeling came over Dan.

"Just a thought, Fayes," said Forepaugh.

———

DAN PUSHED OPEN the thick front door of Moore's Ranch. The common room was empty. Someone moved in the kitchen. He walked to the door and looked in. Harriet Moore was taking some freshly baked pies from the oven. The heat had flushed her oval face. She carried a pie to the table and brushed back a wisp of hair.

"You seem to fit in a kitchen," said Dan softly.

She whirled. "You gave me a start," she said.

He leaned against the side of the door. "I'd like a piece of that pie, Harriet."

She pulled out a chair. "Sit down. There's fresh coffee. When do you leave?"

"After dusk." Dan eyed her as he sat down. She seemed very cool toward him.

She cut the pie and poured coffee for him. "I wish you luck," she said. "Surgeon Cornish told us last night that we'd be safe enough here."

"Behind these walls? I have no doubt about it."

She nodded. "We can take care of ourselves." He started on the pie. "You're quite a cook, Harriet."

"Dad thinks so."

"Where is he?"

"In the barn checking out a new shipment." He finished the pie. She offered no conversation as she worked. Dan lit a cigar and refilled his coffee cup. "You're still angry about Forrest Kroft?" he ventured.

She shrugged slim shoulders. "Why should I be? He learned a lesson. I've forgotten him."

"You seem put out with me then."

She looked at his plate. "Would you like more pie?"

He smiled. "I'd like one to take along. Seven or eight days' of field rations are rough on a man."

"I'll give you three. One for Sergeant Haley. You can give the other to your officers."

"That will include Mister Kroft."

"I don't begrudge any man on patrol a piece of pie, Dan."

He rested an arm on the back of his chair. "This is rather silly, isn't it?"

"I don't understand."

"Talking about pie...and Mister Kroft."

Her eyes held his. "What would you like to talk about?"

"I'd like to visit you when we return from patrol."

"The bar is always open, Dan."

"I'm not interested in the bar, Harriet."

"So?"

"I want to see you."

"I'll be here," she said coolly.

He got up and walked to her. "What's wrong, Harriet? He took one of her hands but she drew it away. "The least you could do is tell me what is wrong."

She looked up into his face. "It would be better if you stayed on the post and visited Melva Cornish," she said quickly.

"Well, I'll be damned! Begging your pardon, Miss Moore."

She walked to the rear door. "I must help Father now." She left the kitchen.

Dan walked out behind her. Jim Moore was standing at the tailgate of a freight wagon in front of the big barn. Harriet took the freight bill from his hand. "I'll finish this, Dad," she said. "There's pie and coffee in the kitchen."

Dan walked with Moore into the kitchen. "Harriet seems put out with me, Jim."

"So?" Moore cut a piece of pie and poured coffee.

"What's wrong?"

Moore sat down. "Myron Cornish was here last night. He mentioned the fact that you were dining alone with Melva."

"He was supposed to be there. I didn't know he was gone until I got there."

"I believe you."

There was something in his tone that caused Dan to look closely at him. "By God, Jim! I'm getting tired of this runaround. What's bothering Harriet?"

"Harriet likes you, Dan. A great deal. More than I had realized. She liked Jim Dunphy. I won't say she loved him. Jim was a good man but damned weak. I suppose it's the maternal instinct in women that makes them that way. My wife was like that. Harriet has a lot of Agnes in her."

Dan relit his cigar. "Keep talking, Jim."

Moore loosened his collar. "Melva Cornish set her cap for Jim Dunphy. Jim wanted nothing to do with her, but Melva is a strong-minded woman. She practically threw herself at him. She gave Harriet a hard time one night at a squadron dance at the post. Made remarks about a saloon-keeper's daughter. Harriet is too much of a lady to fight back. Things went from bad to worse. Dunphy drank a hell of a lot more. Then one night he went over the deep end and was found the next morning dead, with his service pistol in his hand. Harriet took it very hard. It didn't seem to bother Melva Cornish. She started after Ellis Morgan. It seems as though she must hold the affections of the post commander at Fort Costain. She can do it too."

Dan nodded. "She's all woman."

Moore looked up. "Myron Cornish laid it on damned thick last night, Dan. He seemed to gloat over the fact that Melva had an in with you."

"Melva Cornish has no hold on me."

Moore stood up. "Remember one thing. If she does interest you, I want you to stay away from Harriet. I don't want her hurt again." There was a quiet warning in Moore's tone.

"I won't hurt her, Jim."

"See that you don't!"

Moore followed Dan to the outer door. "Be careful," he said. "You've got a John squadron under you. I think you can whip them into shape. But no cavalry company carrying cookstoves can track down Hair Rope and Black Wind."

Dan mounted Hardtack and looked down at the one-armed veteran. "Say goodbye for me to Harriet, Jim."

Moore nodded. He watched Dan ride down the slope. His eyes were cold as ice. Then he smashed a big fist against the door and went inside.

CHAPTER TWELVE

B Company was butt-sprung and crotch-weary after four days on the trail. Dust coated the blue uniforms a neutral color and thickened the speech of the tired troopers. The hills about them were dim in haze. There was no sign of life. There hadn't been in the four days of the patrol. No smoke against the sky. No skulking *broncos*. Yet fear rode knee to knee with most of the men of Company B. There was nothing but the empty miles behind them and the unknown miles ahead. There was an aura about the slowly moving company with its tail of dusty mules. Sour sweat, the nitrogen odor of horses, dust and damp leather.

Dan looked from beneath the brim of his hat at a lone speck far ahead on a long slope. It was Gila Barnes, riding his ewe-necked roan in tight little circles. *Something* was up ahead at last. Dan thrust up an arm and heard the column come to a jingling, stamping halt. The dust swirled up about him. A mule bawled from the rear of the column where Mister Kroft cursed luridly as his long-eared charges milled about, trying to rub their packs off against each other.

"What is it, Dan?" asked Captain Norman.

Dan shrugged. He eased a dirty finger beneath his sweat-soaked collar and lifted the soggy cloth away from his sun-scored neck. "Sergeant Haley!" he called out.

Haley spurred his big bay forward and saluted.

"Come with me," said Dan. "Charlie! Ten minutes rest for the company. Loosen girths. Check those goddamned mules. Kroft is off in one of his tantrums again."

Haley took a chew from his pocket. "Ready for some Wedding Cake, sir?"

Dan grinned. "Strong, but the sauce is good. Is that it, Haley?"

Up ahead Gila had stopped circling his roan. He hunched in his battered Mexican saddle, like a gnome.

When they drew rein beside him, the scout jerked a thumb toward the steep slope behind him. "Look," he said laconically.

Wheel tracks showed in the loose sand at the bottom of a shallow wash. "So?" asked Dan.

Gila shifted in his worn saddle. "I was up the wash. There's been a camp there. Recently. A white man. Wagon. Four mules drew the wagon. Yuh'd better take a look-see, Dan."

"What the hell for?" demanded Haley. "What's wrong with a waggin bein' out here?"

Gila looked at Haley with ill-concealed disgust. "With no roads? Thirty miles from nowhere?"

"Gila, you stink."

"You're no Rose of Tralee, you ugly bastard."

They grinned at each other as Dan rode down the slope to follow the wagon tracks. The wash curved and a grove of smoke trees showed huddled against a rough wall of rock. Dan slid from his saddle at the sight of a circle of ashes on the earth.

Gila led up his roan. "Look," he said. He picked some partially burned pieces of wood from the fire. They were packing cases. He crossed to a hollow and picked up an object. It looked like a small mat of hair. He handed it to Dan. "Sculp," he said. "White man's." He felt about beneath a bush and brought up a small pot. It had been covered with cloth which had been tightly stretched and bound about the pot with strips of rawhide. There was a small, hooped stick at his feet. "'Pache water drum," said Gila. He picked up the hooped stick. "Beatin' stick."

Dan squatted in the shade of a smoke tree and looked at Gila. "Keep talking, Gila."

Gila shifted his chew. "There was a dance here. The ground has been tromped plenty. Apaches don't treasure sculps like other tribes. Use 'em for one dance and then throw them away. The medicine is gone outa them after the dance."

"What about the wagon?"

Gila nodded. "There was a white man here. Boot marks in with the moccasin tracks. Broken whisky bottles all over. Quite a baile they had." He walked to the fire and held out a piece of partially burned wood. "Take a look at this."

Dan examined the wood. It had been stenciled 'Dried Fish'. The other side was greasy to the touch.

Gila jerked a thumb toward the smoke trees. "Over there are a bunch of broken cases. All marked 'Dried Fish'. You note the grease on the wood?"

Dan nodded.

"That there is gun grease."

Dan rubbed it between his fingers and held it to his nose. He nodded.

"Damned queer," said Gila. "Dried fish cases with gun grease in 'em."

Haley eyed the gaunt scout. "So they had dried fish," he said.

"Yuh ain't got the brains yuh was born with, Haley. Dan knows what I'm drivin' at."

Dan threw the wood down. "Apaches won't touch fish, Haley. It's taboo. No one knows why. The reason is buried somewhere in their mythology."

"It's nice to have an education," said Gila dryly.

Dan spat out his chew and reached for a long nine. He lit it and eyed Gila through the bluish smoke. "Anything else, Gila?"

Gila thrust a dirty claw into a pocket and brought out

half a dozen Henry rimfire hulls. "Found these scattered up the wash, Dan."

Haley rubbed the reddish bristles on his jaw and looked at Dan. Dan tossed the hulls up and down in his hands. "Some white man brought guns in here, thirty miles from nowhere, packed in cases labeled 'Dried Fish'. He met the *broncos* here. There was a scalp dance. Some of the bucks tried out their new guns and left the hulls."

"Keno," said Gila.

"The question is: Who was the white man? We know too damned well who the *broncos* were."

Gila stood up. He pointed north. "Look."

A thin raveling of smoke etched itself against the clear sky, miles away.

"Haley," said Dan, "bring up the company. Where's the nearest water, Gila?"

"There's some *tinajas* two miles up the wash. Usually got water this time of year. Yuh kin bivouac up on a rock slope from there. Fairly safe position."

Haley swung up into his saddle and spurred his bay back down the wash.

Gila leaned on his long Spencer rifle. "How'd yuh like to take a walk with me tonight, Dan?"

"Toward the smoke?"

"Yes."

Dan relit his cigar. "You've read my mind, Gila."

"That ain't easy."

The company was bivouacked for the night on a rocky slope, the horses picketed against a wall of rock. The troopers lit no fires after dusk. A soft velvety darkness covered the low mesa which loomed behind them. Beyond the bivouac area a circle of troopers lay behind their saddles, fingering their carbines, listening, hardly daring to breathe for fear of not hearing.

Dan followed Gila through the darkness. The scout moved like a ghost, trailing an aura of tobacco smoke, sweat and greasy leather. Dan moved silently but clumsily in his spurless, cloth-wrapped boots. The wind whispered through the darkness, rustling the ocotillo and mesquite, mumbling strange thoughts to Dan. They had covered at least three miles since leaving the horses several miles from the bivouac area.

Beyond them the dim shape of the mountains showed blackly in the darkness. A coyote howled plaintively from the mesa.

Gila stopped. Dan halted just behind him. The scout seemed to be testing the night with all his senses. He spoke over his shoulder. "Smell it?"

Dan was about to say no when he caught the odor of bitter smoke, faint and tantalizing. "Apaches?" he asked.

Gila shook his head. "Not this low. The bastards camp high. The one thing they fear is surprise."

"White man then."

"Probably. *Quien sabe?*"

Gila leaned his long Spencer against a rock. "Stay here." He vanished into the darkness like an ill-smelling phantom.

Dan squatted beside a rock, fingering his Winchester. He hungered for a smoke and then remembered that Haley had given him a cut of Wedding Cake. He placed the chew in his mouth and worked it into pliability. He grinned as he thought of his last year in Washington. He wondered what some of his society drinking companions would think of him now, squatting in an Arizona gully, stinking enough to enrage his own sense of smell, chewing a wad of spit-or-drown. He needed a shave. He itched. His feet, socks and boots were larded together. *I'm crummy,* he thought, *lice-bitten and stinking, but I'm doing the job for which I was trained, and to hell with Washington society.*

The whipsaw scream of an eagle floated down to Dan from the dark mass of the mountain ahead of him. Far off to the right was the macabre bulk of Skull Butte, crannied and eroded, shrouded with brush, the top of a great granite dome. Like a decayed skull with some of the dry hair still clinging to it, two shallow caves marking the hollow eyes, a gully marking the nose hole and a rock ledge forming the slitted mouth. All the days of the patrol they had seen it, aloof and lonely, seemingly watching their snail-like progress across the desert and into the barren hills.

Dan scratched a dank armpit. The company had shaken down quite a bit. The recruits had learned to handle themselves in the field while the veterans had lost their garrison softness. He shifted his chew and spat into the darkness. In the final analysis it would be the showdown with the Apaches that would prove whether or not B Company was fit to call themselves U.S. Cavalrymen. It was one of the worries that gnawed at Dan's mind like a hungry rat.

The soft hoot of an owl came to Dan. He stiffened and then relaxed. An Apache wouldn't use the hoot of an owl for a signal, for Bu, the owl, was a harbinger of ill luck.

Gila seemed to swim up out of the darkness. He knelt beside Dan. "Camp up ahead. At a *tinaja*. One man. Four mules and a mountain waggin. He's asleep in the waggin."

Dan stood up. "Any sign of Apaches?"

Gila shook his head. "Shall we take him?"

"I want to question him."

"Go easy then. A man's liable to be jumpy out here at night."

Dan spat. "Why? He can't be worried. Camping here with a fire in hostile country."

They padded off into the darkness. The smell of smoke came strongly to them as the wind shifted.

Gila stopped in a thicket and held up a hand. Dan looked down into a wide hollow, thick with scrub trees and brush, dim and indistinct. Now and then the fire flared up from the bed of embers encircled by blackened rocks. Beyond the fire was the dim outline of the wagon. A mule stamped its hoof.

Gila eased down the slope. Dan squatted beside him. They scanned the area for long minutes, listening and sniffing. Gila nodded. Dan placed his ear close to Gila's ear. "Circle around. When you're ready, hoot like an owl. I'll close in. No shooting."

"Keno." Gila slipped into the enveloping night.

The owl hoot drifted across the hollow. Dan eased his

Colt out of its holster and padded down the slope. He circled the fire. The wagon was covered with a ragged tilt. The side toward the fire was rolled part way up, but the interior was too dark for him to distinguish anything. Dan approached the wagon. One of the mules bawled. One of his mates picked up the tune. Something moved in the wagon.

Dan stopped by the seat. The man in the wagon cursed softly. He bumped the sideboard as he thrust a long leg over the side toward Dan. Gila appeared near the tailgate. The man dropped to the ground and reached inside the wagon for something. Gila moved like a cat. The man turned. He was taller than Dan by a head. Gila closed in, striking out with his pistol. The man evaded the blow. Dan jumped forward. Gila was smashed against the wagon.

The man turned as Dan came in. He fended off the blow of the Colt and drove in a jolting blow to the jaw. Dan bounced off the wheel, his senses reeling. Gila drove a shoulder against the man. He went down. As Gila closed in, he was met by a long pair of legs. The socked feet drove into Gila's gut. The scout's breath went out of him in a gush.

Dan ran in again, smashing with the Colt. It was knocked out of his hand. He evaded a lashing blow, sank a left into the lean gut and followed through with a right hook. His opponent grunted in pain. He snatched up a stub of wood and threw it at Dan. It glanced from his shoulder as he charged in. Long arms reached out, gripped Dan by the shirt front and pulled him forward to meet a downthrust head. The skull crashed against Dan's chin. He brought a knee up hard into the groin, clasped both hands together and smashed them down on the back of the neck.

The man went down to meet an upthrust knee. He grunted in agony and rolled over toward the fire.

Blood dripped from Dan's chin as he pulled the tall man away from the hot embers. His clothing had already started to smolder. Dan squatted and scratched a lucifer on his belt buckle. He stared at the battered face. "Jesus," he said softly.

Gila spat. The juice slapped into the dust with the sound of a dropped pack of playing cards. "Ben Ducey."

Ducey moaned a little as he opened his eyes. "Who is it?" he asked.

"Major Fayes. Gila Barnes," said Dan quietly.

Ducey sat up. "What the hell kind of game is this?"

"That's what we'd like to know," said Dan.

Ducey tenderly touched his battered face. "You're a good man for the rough-and-tumble, Fayes," he said.

"Thanks. You're good yourself. Now start talking."

"What do you want to know?"

"Plenty. What happened to you after Sykes's patrol was ambushed?"

"I was cut off in the hills."

"Where'd you get the wagon?"

Ducey spat out some blood. "I always had it."

"What are you doing out here?"

"Looking around."

Gila looked at Dan. "Right out in the middle of nowhere with a waggin and four mules. How come yuh didn't ride a hoss or a mule, Ben?"

"A man can travel any way he wants."

Gila nodded. "Carryin' what?"

Ducey stood up. "You can look in the waggin."

"We won't find what we want in there, Ben."

Ducey eyed Gila. "What *are* you looking for?"

"Henry rifles," said Dan quietly.

"I got a Sharps."

"I said *rifles.*"

Ducey threw back his head and laughed. "You don't imagine I'd be gunrunning, do you?"

Gila leaned against the wagon. "Funny man," he said.

"Take a look in the wagon, Gila," said Dan. He cocked his Colt. "Now, Ducey. You've been missing quite some time. We find you out here with a wagon. There's no town or ranch within miles. The Apaches are raising hell. This has a damned queer look."

Ducey yawned. "I got tired of interpreting and scouting. Got too rough. Damned if I mind going out with experienced troops, but these John companies you have will only get cut up like Sykes was. A man has to look out for his future."

Gila poked his head beneath the tilt. "I'll bet you are," he said. "Not much in here, Dan. Blankets. Some food. Sharps rifle and a Remington pistol. No freight."

Gila slid from the wagon. "Seems as though someone had a waggin farther south, along a wash. Seems as though somebody was carryin' dried fish."

"What's wrong with that?"

Gila spat. "Dried fish packed in *gun grease?*"

"You've been eating peyote."

Gila shook his head. "Tastes like dirt. Never could stand the stuff. I'll stick to forty-rod."

The wind fanned the fire. Dan studied the lean face of the interpreter. Ducey's eyes shifted. "There was a scalp dance down the wash," said Dan. "Somebody was firing Henry rifles. We found the empty hulls. There were boot tracks mixed up in the moccasin tracks. Come clean, Ducey."

"I don't know what you're talking about."

Dan looked at Gila. "Search him."

Gila worked swiftly through Ducey's clothing. "Pipe. Tobacco canteen. Matches. Coupla pistol cartridges. Wallet. Loose change."

"Look around that wagon."

"He's been in there," said Ben Ducey.

"*In* there," said Dan. "I'm thinking of the rest of the wagon."

Ducey fingered his lower lip, watching Gila from beneath drawn brows.

Gila crawled beneath the wagon. "Water bucket," he said, "Tar bucket." He opened the toolbox ironed to the side of the wagon. He lit a match and poked about in it. "Jack. Hatchet. Nails. Auger. Rope. Linchpin. Kingbolt. Some strap iron." Suddenly he stopped and lit another match. He lifted out a can. "Grease," he said.

The fire flared up. Something glittered on the side of the greasy can. Dan took it from Gila's hands. He held it close to the fire. Flecks of gold dust showed just beneath the rim of the lid. He took the lid off and poked through the grease. Some of the grease came out in a thick ball. The bottom of the grease was caked with gold dust. The can was filled at least half an inch deep with the precious ore. "What's this?" asked Dan quietly.

"You can see! Gold dust."

"Yes, I know. But where did you get it?"

Ducey grinned. "Prospecting. I carry it in there for safe-keeping."

Gila scratched his scrawny neck. "Get your boots on," he said.

"You've got no right to arrest me!"

"We'll worry about that later," said Dan. "What happened to Corporal Clothier?"

"How should I know?"

"He went missing at Sand Springs."

"Too bad!"

Ducey pulled on his boots. He lit a cigar and watched his two arresters. "You'll get yourself in trouble," he said. "I've got friends in this country."

"Yeh," said Gila, *"Apache* friends."

"You've got nothing on me."

Gila grinned. "No? Mebbe you was carryin' dried fish to sell to them."

"It's possible. God knows they don't get enough food from the Bureau."

"You've been an interpreter for quite some time," said Dan. "Too bad you didn't spend a little more time studying Apache customs as well as their language. Or you'd know they won't touch fish or animals associated with water."

Ducey glanced nervously at Gila.

Gila shifted his chew and spat leisurely. "Yeh. Anyways they wouldn't touch food packed in gun grease. They ain't *that* hungry!"

Gila hitched up the team. Dan put out the fire. They led the mules up the draw back toward where the horses had been picketed. Ducey walked easily, sucking at his cigar. Dan knew they didn't have a hell of a lot on the interpreter, unless they tied in some other evidence. Ducey wouldn't break easily. The evidence was all circumstantial. The source of the gold dust was unknown. The fact that Ducey had cached it in the grease can meant nothing.

Dan looked back over his shoulder. The moon was pale in the sky, hardly showing enough light to see anything. Somewhere behind them the *broncos* were gloating over their fine weapons. They had magazines that held fifteen rounds, enough to blast hell out of a cavalry unit armed with single-shot carbines. The one advantage the cavalry had was their marksmanship. Few Indians had the patience to practice shooting. Yet Dan knew that his squadron was woefully inefficient in shooting for record. The scales were swinging down for the *broncos*.

CHAPTER THIRTEEN

B Company cooked their bacon and brewed their issue coffee. The thin smoke of the fires hung low in the early morning sky. Dan squatted beside a rock with Captain Charlie Norman. "We've really nothing on Ducey as yet," he said.

Norman swallowed his food and sipped his coffee. "You think he's alone in this deal?"

"No." Dan put down his plate. "I've reason to believe we might blow the top from this thing before long. I've had my eye on someone for a little while."

"So? Who?"

"I'll tell you when I learn more."

Norman stood up. "What are your orders?"

Dan looked at the mountains. "I'd like to probe farther into those mountains but I'm getting worried. We'll swing back around Skull Butte and head for the upper San Ignacio. If Hair Rope has any idea of hitting Mesquite Wells, we may cut him off."

"Supposing he's already been there?"

"I doubt it. No Apache in his right mind would buck up against a cavalry company behind 'dobe walls. Besides, the civilians in Mesquite Wells are not exactly soft touches. The combined fire power of a cavalry company and a score of straight-shooting civilians."

"I'll agree to that." Norman strode down the slope to where his noncoms were eating.

Dan felt for a cigar. Suddenly he raised his head. Corporal Ferris had been assigned to guard Ben Ducey. The noncom was filling his plate at a cook fire. Dan dropped his own plate and hurried over. "Who's guarding Ducey?" he asked.

Ferris smiled. "He's all right, sir. The officer of the guard told me to come and eat."

"Who's officer of the guard?"

"Mister Kroft, sir."

Dan threw away his cigar and walked swiftly through the brush to where Ducey's wagon sat beneath an overhanging rock wall. There was a quick movement in the brush. Forrest Kroft moved across an open space. He whirled as Dan appeared. Then he plunged into the brush. Dan ran after him. Boots grated on the hard earth. Ben Ducey emerged running from the brush, looking back over his shoulder. Dan freed his Colt from its holster. "Kroft!" he yelled.

Ducey slammed his feet down hard. Kroft whipped out his Colt. He raised it as though on the pistol range.

"Kroft!" yelled Dan. "Don't shoot!"

The revolver shot punctuated Dan's order. Smoke drifted back over Kroft. Dan cursed as he plunged down into a hollow. Ben Ducey lay on his face. His long fingers dug into the ground. He jerked spasmodically and then stiffened. Blood soaked through the back of his huck shirt.

Dan knelt by the side of the interpreter and turned him over. His eyes were open.

Troopers yelled in the camp. Captain Norman plunged through the brush followed by half a dozen troopers. Forrest Kroft slipped a cartridge into his Colt and holstered the weapon.

Dan looked up at Norman. "Dead," he said.

Kroft walked to them. "He made a break for it," he said

easily. "I yelled at him to stop. I didn't mean to kill him. I wanted to wing him."

Dan stood up. "Bury him," he said to Norman.

Kroft looked down at the man he had killed. "I feel terrible about this," he said.

Dan held out his hand. "Give me that pistol. You're under arrest."

Kroft shrugged. He handed Dan the Colt.

Dan and Charles Norman walked behind Kroft as he returned to the bivouac area.

"There goes our lead, Charlie."

"Funny thing. Kroft could have winged him."

"How so?"

"Kroft has won many a squadron pistol-shooting match. I've seen few men as good as he is with a handgun."

Dan eyed the young officer. If there was any connection between him and Ducey there was no way of proving it now. "Boots and saddles as soon as Ducey is buried," he said.

The company pulled out at eight o'clock. Ducey's grave was left to its lonely place. One of the troopers had fashioned a crude cross which stood out above the rocks piled over the grave.

It was late in the afternoon when the company reached the San Ignacio. The point dipped down into a hollow heading for a draw which led down into the bottoms. Something cracked in the brush atop a rock formation. A trooper of the point threw up his arms and slid from the saddle. The point scattered for cover. Then rifle fire broke out behind the company. Slugs whipped into the small column of mules. Norman roared out his orders. The troopers slid to the ground. The horse-holders led their charges into a hollow. Carbine fire ripped out, but there was nothing to shoot at but thin wisps of smoke in the thick brush overhead.

Dan squatted behind a rock. The sun beat down on the rocky earth. Now and then a shot broke the quiet, swiftly answered by the crackle of carbine fire. Three troopers were down. One dead and two wounded. Yet they had seen nothing of the *broncos* beyond the rifle smoke. Charlie Norman crawled to Dan. "What now?"

Dan took his cigar from his mouth. "There can't be more than a dozen or so of them."

"Yes. But we can't get across the open ground to root them out."

"I don't want you to."

Norman wiped the sweat from his broad face. "I figure this way, Dan. They were watching us. They had orders to slow us or stop us near the San Ignacio. Why? Because there's something going on up ahead they don't want us to find out about."

"This trail leads to Mesquite Wells."

Norman raised his head. "You don't suppose?"

"What else?"

"It's loco. They can't take Mesquite Wells."

Dan rubbed his jaw. So far, his command hadn't done much to compete with Hair Rope.

Gila squirmed through the brush. "They pulled foot," he said. "'Bout ten of them ridin' north through a draw. Long Hat was leadin' 'em."

"You're sure they pulled out?"

Gila nodded. "Just saw 'em. See? The dust?"

Dust rose beyond a low ridge.

Dan stood up. "Send a squad up there, Norman. Gila will go with them. I want that ridge combed."

The company waited in the solid heat. Now and then the sun flashed on metal as the squad moved through the thick brush. Then Gila stood up on a rock and waved his arms in the All Clear.

B Company moved out, taking with them the two wounded troopers. Trooper Archer lay beneath the earth to one side of the lonely ridge. The sun was low now, barely clearing the western ranges. Dan looked back at the lone grave. Suddenly he felt like a damned fool or a green shavetail on his first patrol. The *broncos* had all the cards. The days of the patrol had not netted Dan one arrest, nor one dead Apache.

The stench of burnt flesh hung thickly in the valley of the San Ignacio, mingled with the odor of burning wood and hot metal. Norman had halted the head of his company on a rise looking down on the Mesquite Wells road. Spaced equally apart were five glowing beds of coals, fanned into flaring life by the night wind which crept down from the ridges. Here and there were huddled figures. Something hung against a wagon wheel which had fallen back against the burned wood and iron of a freight wagon.

Dan jerked his head at Norman. "Stay here. Gila!"

The scout kneed his roan next to Hardtack.

"Come with me," said Dan. "I want a squad, Charlie."

The squad followed Dan and Gila down toward the burned wagons. They rode slowly into the heavy hot air. Wisps of smoke rose up from the wagon ruins. "Seven men," said Gila.

"Never had much of a chance," said Sergeant Bostwick.

"It stinks," said a trooper.

"What did you expect?" asked Trooper Lane, hatchet-faced and lean. "Oh dee cologne?"

"I'm sick."

"Dismount and puke," said Bostwick. He looked at Dan. "It hits 'em hard the first time, sir."

They dismounted. The green trooper hurried into the shadows. They could hear his retching as they walked about the area. Gila eyed a stripped body. The right shoulder was reddened by the recoil of the rifle. "Put up a fight," he said. "Guess it didn't last long."

The ground was littered with yards of cloth from bolts. Glass crunched underfoot as they walked about. "Whisky," said Bostwick, "cases of the stuff."

"Some drunk," a trooper said. "No wonder they cut up them bodies."

An Apache uses a knife like an extension of his arm, swiftly and without mercy. The honed blades of the *besh* had had their fill of hot blood. Empty cartridge cases littered the torn earth.

Gila stopped beside Dan. "Take a look at this," he said.

He walked to the burned and maimed carcass lying on top of the metal of the wagon wheel. Dan eyed the big corpse. The right arm was missing from the elbow down. "Jim Moore," said Gila.

There was a sour taste in the back of Dan's throat. He fought it off and turned away. "Maybe this was why we were held up back at the creek, Gila."

Gila nodded. "Probably had an ambush ready and knew we were in the area. Gave them just enough time to finish the job." He toed a smashed bottle. "By God, they must be plannin' a time tonight up in them hills."

"I feel like a John recruit," said Dan. "They hit and vanish."

Gila cut a chew and stowed it in his mouth. "They sure ain't doin' anythin' to increase your military reputation, Dan. You're losin' face. Fast."

Dan looked south. Somewhere down there Harriet Moore was in her kitchen, preparing a hot meal for Jim Moore and his teamsters. He'd have to tell her. It was his job. A terrible hunger for liquor swept over him. He needed his glass crutch again.

"Bostwick!" said Dan. "Get the company down here."

The company filed down into the massacre area. Norman dismounted and came to Dan. "Now we know," he said.

"Bury them," said 'Dan, "This was Jim Moore's outfit, Charlie. That's him on the wheel."

"Good God!"

Dan walked away. He left the burned area and took off his hat. His foot struck something on the ground. A bottle. He picked it up. It was untouched. He worked the cork out and raised the bottle. Suddenly he threw it with all his strength into the brush. A trooper looked curiously at him as he walked past carrying a shovel.

Spades and shovels thudded against the earth. The bodies were rolled in blankets and placed in a neat row. Dan smashed a dirty fist into his other palm. He paced back and forth alongside the shallow creek. There was a coldness in him now. A dark anger against the men who had supplied the *broncos* with repeaters.

Dan felt for his cigar case. His fingers touched the brass reservation plate Black Wind had cast so contemptuously into the road at Dan's feet. He fingered the smooth metal. *Take it! Keep it! Remember it! For you shall not rest by day or night!*

The bitter voice seemed to live again in the night wind. *There will come a time when you shall want to speak with me. Use that plate to pass through my warriors, before you choose the way of your dying.*

Dan looked up at the dark sky. "Maybe you'll die, Black Wind," he said aloud, "and there will be no way for *you* to choose *your* way of dying!"

———

HARRIET MOORE'S eyes were dry as she listened to Dan's story of her father's death. She sat at the kitchen table with her slim hands clasped together. When he had finished, she bowed her head.

The clock ticked steadily. Dan turned his dusty hat around in his hands, wishing he were anywhere else, yet wanting to be with her.

She looked up. "Thank you, Dan," she said quietly.

"Is there anything I can do?"

She shook her head.

He hesitated. "Have you enough money, Harriet?"

"My father was a wealthy man, Dan. I don't need anything." She stood up and paced back and forth. "I wanted him to retire but it wasn't in his heart."

"What will you do?"

She shrugged. "Stay here, I suppose."

"It will be a rough job for a woman."

"Yes. But it will keep me busy. I have no other place to go, Dan." She bent her head. "Why did it have to happen?"

"What was he hauling?"

"Liquor. General supplies. Two wagonloads for Pastor's General Store in Mesquite Wells."

"Any rifles or ammunition?"

She glanced quickly at him and then went to a desk. She took some papers from a drawer and ruffled through them. "Two cases of Henry rifle ammunition. One case of .44's. One case of .45's. One case of .50's." She scanned another sheet. "Ten Henry rifles."

Dan nodded. "Who knew what he was carrying? Beyond your father and yourself?"

"The teamsters, I suppose. The distributor who orders for us." She looked at the last sheet. "There were also some medical supplies for your post. Quite a lot in fact."

Dan walked to her and looked at the sheet. They were items listed which he remembered from Cornish's requisition. Medical alcohol. He knew where *that* had gone. Various medicines. Lint. Retractors. Glassware. "Funny thing," he said, almost to himself, "I saw none of these items in the area."

She shrugged. "Apaches are like children. They'll take anything which strikes their fancy."

Dan nodded. "Will you be all right?"

"Yes. There are four employees here."

"I'll detail a guard."

"Is it necessary?"

"Yes. I feel as though I'm responsible for your safety."

"Do as you think best." She looked up at him. "Will you take me to the grave when you have time?"

"Certainly." He touched her face. "I'll have him brought here for burial if you like."

She shook her head. "Let him stay with his men."

Dan left the building. The dust from the passage of his command hung low on the road farther south. He mounted Hardtack and rode slowly toward the fort. Captain Morgan was damned flustered when Dan asked him why he had allowed Moore on the road without a proper escort. Morgan claimed he had not known Moore was with his wagons. Mesquite Wells had not been bothered. Dan ordered out a strong patrol to search the San Ignacio Valley for possible raiders. It was all he could do.

Dan sat up late in his quarters the night of his return. A pile of orders, requisitions and other military work lay on his desk. He lit a cigar and read again the report which had come in from Department Headquarters. All hell had broken loose in Dan's absence. Three teamsters had been killed on the Union road. A prospector had been tortured to death near Little Wash. A cavalry patrol from Camp Hayes had been ambushed and cut to pieces. Two ranches in the Green Mesa area had been gutted and their occupants massacred. A mining camp near Bitter Water had been besieged, all the horses and mules driven off, and some of the outbuildings burned to the ground. Dan stood up and looked at the map which hung on his wall. He circled each of the points mentioned in the report. He drew a pencil line from the fight which had involved the Camp Hayes patrol, through each of the circled area. It covered a great arc from thirty miles west of Fort Costain, up through the hills close to Union, then down past the San Ignacio, through the Skull Butte area to Bitter Water, far to the southeast of Fort Costain. All of this had happened in the days of Dan's search for Hair Rope and his *broncos*.

Dan sat down and lit a cigar. He would need at least a brigade to patrol all those square miles. Gila had told him that Hair Rope had never had more than twenty bucks in his band. Add forty more from the San Ignacio band. That would give Hair Rope a total of about sixty braves. Figuring each war party would number at least twenty to thirty men, it seemed an impossibility for Hair Rope to do what he had done.

Dan eyed the map. The center of the wide radius was north of Skull Butte. That area was malpais. Cut-up land, a jumble of rugged mesas, peaks and hills, in which a cavalry unit could easily get lost, surrounded and smashed. There was no chance for reinforcements. He had to handle his job with the troops he already had.

Dan took the brass reservation plate from his pocket and looked at it. Cooke's *Cavalry Tactics* didn't cover the situation. The *broncos* had the advantage of knowing the country like the palms of their greasy hands. When they needed horses, they stole them. They could live off a country, where even a veteran frontier trooper would have starved to death. Water was a problem for anyone in that country, but the Apaches had the long hard training of doing with as little water as possible. They'd never face a cavalry unit in a knock-down-drag-'em-out fight. It wasn't their way. Strike when the odds were with you. Avoid a head-on clash. Hit hard and then vanish. Guerrilla fighting at its best. That was the Apache way of war.

Dan leaned back in his chair. Gila knew the area where the *broncos* were hidden better than most men and even he admitted that it was a matter of less ignorance of the country, than a real knowledge of it.

"No trooper, carrying a cookstove, can ever catch an Apache in his own country," Dan said aloud. Some of the hard-earned lessons of '59 and '60 came slowly back to him. It wasn't really cavalry country. It was brutally rough on horses. The enemy used horses to get from place to place with incredible speed, made their ambush, fought on foot, then used their horses to get the hell out of the reprisal area. If a horse was run to death a warrior wouldn't be charged one hundred and thirty-two dollars and fifty cents for it. A warrior could get more mileage out of a horse than any trooper. They had ways. If the horse died, they cut off the best meat and left him for the buzzards.

The whole damned setup in Arizona was wrong. No Apache chief would have a chance against Jeb Stuart or Phil Sheridan in a *civilized* cavalry encounter. Dan half-closed his eyes. He thought back on the great cavalry commanders of all time. Genghis Khan. Prince Rupert. Murat. Light-Horse Harry Lee. Tarleton. None of their lessons applied here. They might work against Kiowa, Comanche or Sioux with some success, but never against The People. Hair Rope had the advantage that he had made the White-eyes lose face. He would press that advantage to the limit. Every psychological factor was working with him.

Dan got up and paced back and forth. His one advantage

was in the white man's ability to outthink the savage. But how? *Break loose from the past* he thought. Think of *something* where your one advantage will even up the odds.

There was a light tap on the door. Dan picked up his Colt. "Who is it?"

"Gila."

"Come in."

Gila dropped into a chair, shoving back his sloppy Kossuth hat. He eyed the map. "Courier just came in from Fort Grant. Good news. In a way."

Dan poured two drinks. "Good news?"

Gila accepted his drink. "Hair Rope was killed two days ago in the Galiuros. Him and five warriors. They raided the corrals and was driven off. They headed west and run plumb into a strong patrol. Never had a chance. Cut Lip was captured."

They looked at each other over their glasses. "You're thinking the same thing I am, Gila?" asked Dan.

The scout nodded. "Who in hell's name has been raisin' the devil in this area?"

Dan downed his drink. "Hair Rope a good eighty miles from here. Cut Lip with him. Long Hat held us back at the San Ignacio while Moore was cut down. That leaves Yellow Bear."

Gila spat into the fireplace. "He's got the mind of an idiot. More interested in squaws than fightin'. He's a *diyi*, anyways, a medicine-man, and ain't supposed to fight."

"So who's leading the *broncos?*"

Gila eyed Dan. "One man. Black Wind!"

"Impossible! He's old! He's blind!"

"Yeh. *But who else is there?*"

Dan refilled the glasses. "My God! A pack of *broncos* ripping the country apart, led by a blind chief."

"It's loco. But it's true."

Dan placed a hand on the map covering the area behind Skull Butte. "What do you think the odds are of us getting in there?"

"Jeeesus! Fiddle-footed troopers crashin' through the brush in boots. Blind as bats. We'd be wiped out."

"Exactly. That's what Black Wind expects."

"So?"

Dan straddled a chair, resting his arms on the back. "Our trouble is just as you say. Mounted men trying to track down guerrillas that can outmaneuver us easily. We're limited too much. Now supposing we hand-picked our men. Veterans. The best shots. Got into the hills without being seen by traveling at night. Left our horses and went in on foot."

"You'd have to get rid of those damned stovepipe cavalry boots."

"Make rawhide moccasins."

"The light is dawnin'."

Dan spoke swiftly. "I'll get repeaters. Enough to go around. If I have to buy them myself. Take the best men from each company. Travel lightly. Do you get it?"

"You're wreckin' history, Dan. It just ain't in regulations!"

Dan grinned. "Listen, you hairy-eared bastard! It isn't really new. The British formed light infantry companies in the 1750's, while fighting against the French and Indians. They were trained in scouting and skirmishing. Moved about quickly and quietly. Hand-picked men who could use their own initiative. It was a high honor to be picked for this type of duty."

"What did it prove?"

"That white man *can* use Indian tactics."

Gila pulled at his lower lip. "Waal, it's worth a try, Danny. What do you want me to do?"

"Make a sketch map of the area north of Skull Butte. As well as you know it."

"Keno."

"Meanwhile I'll pick out the men and get the repeaters."

Gila helped himself to a drink. "You'll either make a damned hero out of yourself or end up getting court-martialed...providin' yuh don't get killed."

CHAPTER FOURTEEN

D an stood at the edge of the parade ground looking down at the firing range. Sergeant Major Haley was at work with the picked men of Dan's new organization. It hadn't been too well received by Captains Ellis Morgan and Andrew Horace. It was usual army practice to get rid of the misfits and curdle-heads on a new organization. Horace had blustered and Morgan had grown sullen when they saw their best men drawn from their companies to get quartered with the picked men of B Company.

The shining new Henry rifles flashed on the range. A relay was firing. The crackling reports echoed from the low hills and the bluish smoke drifted upward. The shiny brass hulls were ejected from the magazine rifles to clatter on the hard earth. Dan had secured some from Harriet Moore, others in Mesquite Wells, while the remainder had been found at the fort.

Dan lit a long nine. Gila was at work with Corporal Kemper, who had been a shoemaker in civilian life. The two of them were making up knee-length rawhide moccasins, soled with tough leather. Two pairs for each of the forty men of Dan's organization. Farrier-Corporal Brogan was fitting rawhide boots to the picked horses of the command. There was another detail to be taken care of. Dan wanted a medic. Medical-Sergeant French was a good man, skilled in his line, with ten years' frontier service behind him.

Dan opened the dispensary door. French jumped to his feet from behind his desk. "Sit down, French," said Dan. "Is Surgeon Cornish here?"

"No, sir. He went down to Moore's Ranch."

Dan sat down. "How'd you like to join my scouts. French?"

French grinned. "Can I, sir?"

"I'd like to have you if Surgeon Cornish can spare you."

"My medical orderly is a good man, sir. Used to be a medical student before he took to liquor. He can fill in for me any time."

"Good. Then if Cornish agrees we'll assign you to the scouts."

French nodded.

"By the way, Sergeant. Tell Surgeon Cornish his medical supplies were lost in the attack on Moore's wagon train. He'll have to make out another requisition."

French looked at Dan. "Medical supplies, sir? We didn't requisition any."

"There were medical supplies in Moore's wagons. Alcohol. Various drugs and medical supplies. Lint. Retractors. Glassware."

French tilted his head to one side. "We've got five gallons of alcohol in stores, sir. All the lint we'll need for months. We order retractors about once a year. I know that we don't need any glassware."

"Look up the copy of that requisition."

French looked through his files. He turned to Dan. "The last requisition we made was two months ago. One hospital bed. Two bedpans. Two scalpels. That was all."

"You must be mistaken."

French shook his head. "No, sir. There's no copy here, nor did Captain Cornish mention it to me."

Dan puffed at his cigar. "I see. Tell Captain Cornish I'd like to see him when he comes back." Dan stood up and walked to the door.

French spoke up. "I don't like to get Captain Cornish in trouble, sir, but this happened twice before. Once when Major Dunphy was in command. Later when Captain Morgan took over."

Dan turned. "Speak up!"

"Is that an order, Major Fayes?"

"It is!"

French rubbed his jaw. "I got hell from Major Dunphy at the time. Captain Morgan didn't bother about it when he was in command."

"Well?"

"Both times the supplies came in. In large boxes. Captain Cornish took charge of them. The first time I was out with a patrol and heard about it from the orderly. The second time I received the shipment and Captain Cornish took charge of them too. I never did see what was in the boxes."

"Keep talking."

"Well, sir. I never saw any new stores in the storage room. Whatever was in those boxes was never put in there."

The rattle of firearms came from the range. Dan looked across the parade ground toward Cornish's quarters. Melva was seated beneath the ramada. "Did you make a report on it to Lieutenant Collier?"

"No. Captain Cornish told me not to bother anyone about it."

"Seems like a hell of a lot of medical supplies for a post that hasn't done much field duty until lately."

"Yes, sir."

Dan turned. "Keep your mouth shut about this, French."

"I will, sir."

Dan walked across the parade ground. There had been a contract surgeon in his brigade of volunteers who had always ordered excessive amounts of alcohol for his own use. There had been a quartermaster officer in a camp along the Rapidan who had done a thriving business in selling issue supplies until he had been caught. Cornish lived well. Far too well for the pay of a surgeon.

Dan sent Booth for Hardtack. When the orderly returned, Dan ordered him to clean up Dunphy's old quarters. Dan rode down from the mesa. It was a beautiful day, but the sun was hot as the hinges of hell's own door. It would be worse in the hills when he led his scouts after Black Wind.

Cornish's mare was standing hipshot in front of Moore's big building. Dan walked into the common room. Cornish was at the bar idly swilling liquor around in a glass. He turned as Dan entered. "Just in time for a drink, Major Fayes," he said.

"I'm on duty, Cornish."

Cornish smiled. "Here?"

Dan nodded and leaned against the bar. "I want to talk with you about those medical supplies you recently ordered."

"That's why I came down here. Moore was freighting them in. I thought some of the items might be salvaged."

Dan felt for a cigar. Cornish knew there had been nothing salvageable from the burned wagons. The secretive eyes held Dan's for a moment and then looked away.

Dan puffed at his cigar. "It seems as though there is no record of that requisition in your files, Cornish."

"French is careless. I'll speak to him about it."

"It also seems as though some of the items you ordered were not needed."

"For instance?"

"Alcohol. Five gallons are already in your stores. Lint. You've all you'll need for months. Retractors. It seems as though you're well supplied on those. Glassware. You have plenty. I ordered Sergeant French to tell me about it."

"Have you taken over the surgeon's duties, Fayes?"

There was an impulse in Dan to smash the smooth face before him.

Cornish sipped his liquor. "Another thing: Department Headquarters requires the signature of post commanders on all requisitions. It seems as though you neglected that little detail, sir."

Dan flushed. The surgeon was right. He had told Woodridge to O.K. it.

"I suggest that you find those duplicates, Captain Cornish."

"I'll try."

"There is such a thing as the Inspector General Department, Cornish. I wouldn't like to inform them of this carelessness."

"Whose? Yours or mine?"

"Dammit! Watch how you address me, sir!"

Cornish flushed. A tiny muscle worked in his jaw. "Listen, Fayes! You're a career man. I am not. I'm fed up with duty out here. My contract ends in a few weeks. I don't have to renew it. Congress is contemplating the reduction of the Medical Corps, as badly as it needs expansion. I can leave the service easily. Such is not your case. Your record was shaky before you came here. It hasn't gained any luster since. A mess in the requisitioning of supplies wouldn't help you any."

"I see," said Dan quietly. "How did *you* know about my record since the war?"

Cornish smiled. "I have friends in Washington. Some information was passed on to me."

Dan almost lashed out at the smooth smiling face. He controlled himself. "Get back to the post," he said. "You and I will settle this later."

"Any time, Fayes. I always did like a good battle."

The surgeon walked out of the common room. Dan heard the steady beat of his horse's hoofs on the hard road. He took the cigar from his mouth and dropped it on the sanded floor. He ground it savagely beneath a boot.

Harriet came into the room. "I didn't know you were here, Dan."

He took off his hat. "I wanted to see Cornish."

"A strange man."

"I understand he was asking about his medical supplies."

She raised her brows. "No. He wanted to buy the place. He knows it's a gold mine."

"Are you planning to sell it?"

"I don't want to. For a time at least."

"Why?"

She looked steadily at him. "Do I have to tell you, Dan?"

He took one of her hands in his. "I had hoped a little," he said quietly.

She raised her face to his. "Now you know."

He drew her close and kissed her. She placed her head against his chest. "Do you think me bold?" she asked.

He held her close and pressed his lips against her hair. "I'm a fool," he said.

She shook her head. "I didn't know about it until Captain Cornish told me you had been with Melva. Then I was jealous. I fought it off, but it was no use."

"Why did you fight it, Harriet?"

She looked up at him. "I lost Jim Dunphy," she said. "Now I know I never really loved him."

He kissed her, feeling the softness of her slim body. It was something wonderful; something he had never hoped for.

"You will be careful, Dan?" she asked. "I couldn't bear to lose you too."

"I'll be all right."

"I hope so. Cornish hates you. Morgan and Horace would ruin you if they had a chance."

"How do you know this?"

"They were all against Jim. They fought him from every angle. He told me about it. Drinking was his outlet. It eventually caused his death."

"It's hard to think of a man having your love and then committing suicide."

She drew away from him. "Jim Dunphy was weak, but he wasn't the type to commit suicide, Dan."

"What do you mean?"

She shrugged. "I just never believed he would do it. I still don't."

He eyed her closely. "Just what do you mean, Harriet? I

want to know. There are a lot of things I don't know about Fort Costain."

"I'll tell you then. Cornish worked on Jim. Melva worked on him. There were times when Jim was too drunk to attend to his duties and the other officers had things their own way."

"Morgan and Horace?"

"Yes. And Kroft. Kroft hated field duty. Horace protected him. Morgan wanted Jim's command. Oh, it was terrible. I don't want to see it happen to you."

He drew her to him. "It won't."

"Cornish told my father about you. How you were sent out here to salvage your career." She looked up at him. "It was liquor, wasn't it, Dan?"

He flushed. "In a way."

"I remember the night we were at Tres Cabezas. Your screaming woke me up. I couldn't believe it was you. It was terrible."

He dropped his hands. "A man hates to see his inner soul stripped for inspection," he said quietly. "Perhaps we'd better forget about the two of us, Harriet."

She shook her head. "I can help you. My father had those nightmares after the war. His arm would bother him, and he took to heavy drinking. It caused his separation from my mother. He fought it off out here." She looked up at him. "You will let me help you, Dan?"

"Yes," he promised. He kissed her. "We'll work it out together." He walked to the door and looked back at her. "You seem doomed to help men like me, Harriet."

She shook her head. "Not *doomed*, Dan. *Blessed*."

Dan mounted Hardtack and turned him toward the road. He looked up at the mesa and at the smoke wreathing up from the unseen fort. Suddenly he smashed a fist down on his pommel. They might get him in the end, but they'd have one hell of a battle before they did. A battle they'd never forget.

CHAPTER FIFTEEN

Gila Barnes was waiting in Dan's quarters with another man when Dan returned to the post. Gila jerked a thumb at his weather-beaten companion. "Sage Winters," he said. "Lives near Union. Come here to tell you somethin' of interest."

Dan gripped the old man's hand. "Drink?" he asked.

Sage wet his lips. "Don't mind if I do."

Dan poured two drinks and handed them to his two guests. "What do you have to tell me, Sage?" he asked.

Sage drank half his liquor and wiped his mouth. "Like Gila says, I live near Union. I do some prospectin' in the hills when I want to get away from my old lady. I was up in the hills the last month or so. Didn't know the 'Paches was on the loose from San Ignacio. Anyways I never take chances with the bushy-headed bastards. I seen Old Cut Lip's band in the hills near Skull Butte. Hair Rope, the misbegotten bastard, was with 'em. They headed into the malpais country."

Dan refilled the old man's glass.

Sage nodded and raised his glass in salute. "Coupla weeks later I'm far north in the malpais. Suddenly the goddamned country is thick with 'Paches. Tontos. Coyoteros. Even some of the Girls!"

"Girls?" asked Dan.

"He means Aravaipas," said Gila.

"Yeh," said Sage, "Parties of half a dozen or so, all ridin' into the Skull Butte country. I skites outa there and finds myself trapped in a damned box canyon. I'm backtrailin' when I sees a mess of 'Paches camped in the canyon where the box canyon ends. Christ! It was enough to give a man the chills! I had to kill Bessie to keep her mouth shut."

"Bessie?" asked Dan.

Sage nodded soberly. "My old mule. She was a good one but had too big a mouth. I hides out on the canyon wall with a little water and. grub, hopin' the red bastards would pull out. They don't. They have a big feast. It was a dandy, Gila. They cooked an unborn foal in its mother's juices. Golden brown it was."

"Delicious," said Gila.

Sage grunted. "Gila is half heathen, Major Fayes."

"I've always thought so."

"Go to hell," said Gila with a sly grin.

Sage glanced wistfully at his glass. Dan filled it up. Sage brightened. "Waal, they had quite a *baile.* Plenty likker and food. Scalp dance. Hell, it was enough to make your hair stand on end. Screamin'. Whoopin'. Hollerin'. There musta been at least a hundred and fifty bucks down there, with enough Henry rifles to equip a squadron. Brand-new they was! That old devil Black Wind squats in the middle of the uproar passin' out cartridges. He had boxes and boxes of 'em. The warriors whoop and holler, wavin' them damned rifles. Then they tortures a white man. By God, I got sick. Lost what little food I et. The poor bastard stays alive for hours, though you couldn't tell he was a man when they was done. I was tempted to blast him between the eyes with my big Sharps but I knowed they'd get me less'n I kilt myself."

Recall blew across the post. Horses trotted past the quarters. Sage swilled his liquor in his glass. "Can I have a cigar, Major?" he asked.

Dan gave him one and lit it. Sage puffed steadily. "Then old Black Wind makes a speech. It was a dandy. He tells them they got the White-eyes scairt to death. He says they cut 'em up at Sand Springs. That they raided Fort Costain and burned the stables. He goes on and on talkin' about what he done. How he can get all the rifles he wants from White-eyed friends for *pesh-klitso*."

"He means gold," said Gila.

Dan felt cold all over. He poured a drink. "Go on," he said quietly.

Sage sucked at his cigar. "He says the Long Knives are ascairt to come in after old Black Wind, the greatest of all chiefs. Funny thing though, he talks like *he* led the raids. Blind and old as he is."

Dan nodded. "We've suspected it."

"Waal, you can *bet* on it. That greasy old mummy knows this country bettern' God who made it."

"You're sure you understood what he was saying?" asked Dan.

Gila grinned. "Sage talks 'Pache like a real quill. Seems as though Sage had a 'Pache squaw once."

Sage licked his thin lips. "Yeh. Plump as a grouse. Soft as down. Kept her mouth shut when a man wanted to think."

Dan paced back and forth. "Seems like we're sitting on top of a powder magazine with the fuse lit."

He handed the old man a box of cigars and a bottle of mezcal. "Thanks, Sage."

Sage waved a dirty claw. "Fergit it. Glad to be of help."

"Did they mention who was running the guns in?"

"I caught somethin' about Ben Ducey. Didn't believe it. I've known Ben for years. We was livin' with sisters before the war. Apaches they was." The old man stood up and walked to the door. "Got to get back to my old woman," he said. *"Adios, amigos."* Suddenly he turned. "Gila, you keep that double-hinged jaw of yours shut about that squaw if you see my old lady. Hear?"

Gila nodded. Sage left. Gila looked at Dan. "I thought you might be interested in what Sage had to say."

"I was. The prospect scares me."

Gila nodded. "Yeh. But if we don't root Black Wind out it'll be a hell of a lot worse, Danny."

"One hundred and fifty blood-hungry bucks led by one of the greatest war chiefs of them all. It isn't a pleasant prospect, Gila."

"For this you're a soldier, Dan."

Dan nodded. "Yes."

Gila jerked a thumb at Dan's desk. "Sam Booth cleaned up Dunphy's room. He burned the trash. He said he thought you might want to look over that stuff." Gila left the quarters.

Dan poured a drink and lit a cigar. He looked at the things on his desk. An old leather corps badge from the cavalry outfit Dunphy had probably served with. A hunting case watch. A japanned pen case with several pens and steel points. A traveler's ink vial a quarter full of dried ink. Several tarnished sets of major's leaves. A dusty black velvet cap patch with the crossed sabers of the cavalry embroidered on it. Spare coat and overcoat buttons. An officer's belt plate.

Dan downed his drink. He wondered if Harriet would want these pitiful relics of the weak man she had thought she loved. He shrugged, opened a drawer and swept them into it. He shut it and then saw the folded papers lying on top of some of his own. They had been stained by water. He unfolded the top one. It consisted of notations on grading and reinforcing the end of the parade ground to prevent further erosion. The second sheet was a list of post officers and their duties. The third was a note from Jim Moore containing a list of enlisted men who owed him money for drinks.

Dan lit his candle lantern and opened the last paper. It was a double list of figures. Each line of figures was dated. The left-hand column consisted of figures labeled "Pay". The right-hand column was of a greater sum with notations to the right of them. The notations were about liquor, furniture, silverware and other household and personal items. There were four dates, all of them the end of the month. The paper was hardly legible because of water stains.

Dan studied the faded writing. Possibly Dunphy's pay and his expenses. Yet a major's pay was more than the pay figures listed. They were a captain's pay. He walked outside. A trooper was passing. "Get Private Booth," said Dan. "Tell him to report to me here at once."

Dan was looking over the sheet again when he heard a tap on the door. The door opened and Trooper Sam Booth came in. "You wanted to see me, sir?"

Dan nodded. "Where did you find the things you left on my desk?"

"The stuff from Major Dunphy's room?"

"Yes."

"There was a niche in the closet That stuff was in a cardboard box. Looked like water leaked through the roof. I guess it was overlooked when Major Dunphy's things was sent away to his folks at home."

Dan rubbed his jaw. Booth looked at the bottle. "Have a drink," said Dan.

"Yes, sir!"

Booth filled a glass and downed it. He looked at the paper on Dan's desk. "I can tell you about that, sir."

Dan looked up. "So?"

Booth nodded. "I was Major Dunphy's orderly too. Got kicked out of the job when Captain Morgan took over. Major Dunphy was a real officer. Like you, sir. Always had a drink or a smoke for an enlisted man."

"Keep talking."

"I was cleaning out the washhouse one afternoon. I sneaked in here to see if Major Dunphy might have a dollop left in one of his bottles. I was coming up the hallway when I hears him arguing with somebody."

"So, being a good soldier, you went right out to the washhouse again."

Booth looked pained. "I stuck around figuring he might need me."

"Listening."

"Well...yes, sir. Anyways it was something about money.

Seems as though this other officer was spending a hell of a lot more than he was drawing."

"No crime in that."

"I guess not. Well, the argument got hot. Dunphy says something about the Inspector General. Captain Cornish don't seem worried."

Dan looked up quickly. "Captain Cornish?"

"Yes, sir. I always wondered where he got his money. The whole damned post knows he ain't got a cent beyond what he draws as surgeon."

"How long ago was the argument?"

"About three days before Major Dunphy shot himself."

"I see." Dan fingered the paper on his desk.

"I remember that paper because I put it away in with his other papers. One day he comes in and asks me where I put it. I told him and he took it out. Today was the first time I saw it since then."

Dan stood up. "All right, Booth. One thing. Keep your mouth shut about this."

The trooper saluted and left.

Dan sat staring at the papers on his desk. Dunphy had had trouble with Cornish. Something about Cornish's high expenses. Then Dunphy had committed suicide. Yet Harriet had said Jim Dunphy wouldn't have done it. Then Dan remembered the night someone had lain in wait for him in his quarters and had shot at him. Cold sweat worked down his sides, soaking his shirt.

Dan lit a cigar and dropped on his cot. Kroft had had gold dust. Kroft had shot and killed Ben Ducey out in the hills. An attempted escape. More likely the *ley del fuego*. Let the prisoner run and *then* execute him.

Dan put on his cap and crossed to headquarters. "Linke," he said to the little orderly clerk, "go and get Mister Kroft."

"He's under arrest in quarters, sir."

"Dammit! Go get him!"

Linke scurried from the room. He was back in five minutes. "He isn't there, sir."

"Did you look for him?"

"Yes, sir."

"Get the officer of the guard."

Linke brought back Halloran of G Company. He wore his sash across his chest signifying his duty as officer of the guard. "Halloran, find Mister Kroft. Bring him here under arrest."

Halloran looked strangely at Dan, saluted and left.

Dan waited impatiently. He'd wring the truth out of that goddamned shavetail if he had to beat him to a pulp.

The sun was long gone when Halloran returned. "We found him, sir," he said quietly, "out at the range. I left a man to watch him."

"Dammit! I told you to bring him here!"

"Yes, sir. But I had to leave him where he was. You see, sir...he's dead."

Dan hit the floor. "The hell you say? Apaches?"

Halloran shook his head. "His service pistol is in his hand. He shot himself, sir."

"Come on!" Dan ran across the parade ground and down the wooden stairs that led to the bottoms. He ran through the darkness to the firing butts.

"He's over there, sir," called Halloran. "In the trees beside the creek."

Dan pushed his way through the brush. A corporal leaned on his carbine beside the sprawled body. Kroft lay on his back with his eyes open. A bluish hole showed at his left temple. A little blood and matter had oozed from the purplish hole.

Dan knelt beside the body. He touched it. It was still a little warm. Dan stood up. He looked at Halloran. "Get a detail to take the body up to the post."

"I wonder why he did it?" asked Halloran.

Dan shrugged and walked off through the darkness. His foot struck something. He bent to pick it up. It was a short-handled spade. He eyed it and then looked back at Kroft. He placed the spade against a tree and walked up to the post. Dunphy a suicide. Ben Ducey shot down by Kroft. Kroft dead by his own hand. Dan suddenly felt as though he were in the coils of some twisted problem, impossible to decipher. The smiling smooth face of Myron Cornish seemed to show up in the shadows.

CHAPTER SIXTEEN

F orrest Kroft was laid out in the hospital covered by a
sheet. The thin material outlined his face. A strong
draft blew in from the open door and swayed the lamps on
their chains. The shadows covered the still form or swept
away from it as the lamps moved. Dan stood beside the
body and drew the sheet back from the bluish face. The lips
had drawn back slightly from the white teeth.

Feet grated on the gritty floor. Dan turned. Sergeant
French approached him. "Seems like the ones you least
expect to kill themselves are the ones that do it. Now I
never thought of a man like Mister Kroft going this way."

Dan lit a cigar and studied the handsome face, now cold
in death. "Kroft was right-handed, French."

"Yes."

Dan pointed at the hole in the temple. "Then how could
he have shot himself in the left temple. It's possible, but
damned awkward."

"By God, sir! I never thought of that. What does it
mean?"

"I'm not sure. Was the slug extracted?"

"Yes, sir. Forty-five caliber. One cartridge had been fired
in his Colt."

Dan drew the sheet over Kroft's face. "You were here when Major Dunphy committed suicide?"

"Yes."

"That was also a forty-five?"

French rubbed his jaw. "I'm not sure."

"What do you mean?"

"His Colt had been fired once. Captain Cornish extracted the slug."

"So?"

"I'm not sure it was .45 caliber, sir. It seemed smaller to me. More like a .41, but I was never sure. I had forgotten about it until tonight."

"But you aren't sure?"

"No, sir."

Dan relit his cigar, eying the noncom over the flare of the match. "Keep your mouth shut about this, French."

"I will, sir. What is it...murder?"

Dan threw down the match. "I don't know. Good night, French."

Dan went to headquarters. Woodridge was still at work. He looked up as Dan entered. "I have the roster of your scouts, sir," he said.

Dan held out his hand. He scanned the list. His junior officers were Halloran and Sykes, both men of promise. Sergeant Major Haley. Medical Sergeant French. Sergeants Bostwick and Cutter. Corporals Denton, Ferris, Moylan and Crispin. He scanned the list of troopers. "We've made quite a drain on B Company, Woodridge," he said.

Woodridge nodded. "B has always been the best company in the squadron, sir." He grinned. "Captain Horace has been raising hell about losing his men. He and Captain Morgan have been sympathizing with each other." Woodridge leaned back in his chair. "Can I speak plainly, sir?"

"Certainly."

"You've done a good job so far, sir. In *some* ways. You have been rather ruthless in not sparing the feelings of

Morgan and Horace. I don't think they'll take much more of it."

Dan waved a hand. "Have you started to prepare a report on Kroft's death?"

"Not yet, sir."

"Hold off on it for a while."

"It isn't regulation, sir."

Dan looked steadily at the adjutant. "It isn't regulation if the report you submit is erroneous, is it?"

Woodridge stared at Dan. "No, sir."

Dan turned to the door. "I may have more information for you before long on the subject."

Dan tapped on the door of the surgeon's quarters. Melva opened it. She smiled as she saw Dan. "I haven't seen much of you, Dan."

"I've been busy, Melva."

"Do come in."

He followed her through the hallway to the snug living room. A fire burned in the fireplace. It was then that Dan realized Melva was not wearing a dress. Only a thin wrapper clung to her full figure. As she walked ahead of him, he could see the full length of her legs silhouetted against the firelight. She turned. "You must excuse me," she said. "I thought it was Myron when you knocked. I was getting ready to dress."

"I'm sorry I interrupted you. I wanted to see your brother."

"He's at Captain Morgan's quarters. He should be back shortly."

She made no move to leave the room. "Would you like a drink, Dan?"

He nodded. She filled the glass and brought it to him, looking up into his face. The fragrance of her perfume and body drifted about him. She was expecting something. Dan took the glass and turned away.

Melva sat down in the big armchair and looked curiously at him. "What's wrong, Dan?"

"Nothing."

"I don't believe you. You're under a strain."

"Yes," he admitted.

"Because of Forrest Kroft?"

He looked at her. "Partly. It just added to the trouble."

"Myron said he always suspected Forrest would crack someday."

Dan sipped his wine. "Sometimes I think your brother is more interested in the mind than he is in the body."

"I agree. He seemed to know Jim Dunphy would kill himself."

"A prophet."

She looked at him queerly. "Why do you want to talk with Myron tonight?" she asked.

"We had a little trouble about some requisitions of his."

She paled a little and touched her smooth throat with a slim hand. "Myron gets angry when line officers question him about his duties."

"He's a soldier, no matter what his duty is. As his commanding officer it is *my* duty to question him."

She leaned her head back against the chair. "I see. He has been talking about leaving the service."

"To go into private practice?"

"I don't think so. He wants to make a great deal of money."

Dan looked about the expensively furnished room. "It seems as though he has already done well for himself."

She lowered her lids and studied him. Then she stood up and got the decanter. "Let me fill your glass, Dan."

As she came close to him her leg pressed against his. He stood up and drew her close. She did not resist. Her body was soft and warm, hardly protected by the thin material of the wrapper. She placed the decanter on the table and slid her smooth arms about his neck, drawing his face down to hers. Her lips parted as she kissed him.

Minutes drifted past as they stood there. There was a roaring in Dan's ears. She was no amateur at lovemaking and once again he thought of Kitty St. Clair in Washington. She turned away from him and walked to the couch, looking back over her shoulder. Dan followed her and placed his hands on her full hips. She turned and sat down, drawing him down to her. "You're tired," she whispered.

The fire was burning low. There was no other light in the big room. Her breath came quickly as he kissed her and passed his hands over her full body. "Come back later," she said softly. "Myron is going off the post tonight."

"I must see him."

"Not tonight. You're angry. It will only end in a quarrel."

He straightened up and looked at her. "What makes you say that?"

She kissed him. "I know. Please go now, Dan."

He stood up and looked down at her. She was like a lazy cat crouching there, soft and warm.

"Come back about nine," she said.

Dan picked up his forage cap and left. It wasn't until he was in his own quarters that he realized she had staved off the meeting between him and her brother.

Dan peeled off his shell jacket and scaled his hat at a chair. He dropped on his bunk and reached for the bottle of mezcal in the cabinet. He drank deeply, again and again, thinking fleetingly of Harriet Moore but more often of Melva Cornish.

Tattoo rang out across the post. Dan opened his eyes. The room was dark, the candle lantern having guttered out. The darkness seemed to swim around him, and Dan knew he was as close to being drunk as he could be. He dropped his legs to the floor and ran his tongue over his dry lips. He reached for the half-empty bottle and then shook his head. He picked up a towel, thrust his Colt beneath his waistband and headed for the washhouse. He doused his face in the water and slowly dried himself. It was close to ten o'clock.

He went back to his room, lit the lantern and dressed quickly. His head still swam a little as he blew out the lantern and walked outside. The post area was dark. He crossed quickly toward the surgeon's quarters. A horse whinnied from the darkness. Cornish's fine mare was tethered at the back of the quarters. Cantle and pommel packs were on the mare and the saddlebags bulged. The rear door was part way open. Dan could hear voices inside.

"You've got money, Melva," said Cornish. "They won't bother you."

"But why are you leaving, Myron? What has happened?"

Dan looked through the doorway. Cornish had his back to Dan. He was dressed in field uniform, booted and spurred.

Cornish waved a hand. "I haven't time to tell you about it now. Fayes suspects something. I can't take a chance on him having me arrested for investigation."

Melva stared at him. "What have you done?"

"I told you I don't have time. His orderly told me he's asleep. When he wakes up, he'll be here, if you've played your cards right."

"I did. I'm sick of this business, Myron! First it was Jim Dunphy. Then Ellis Morgan. Now Dan Fayes. What am I to you? A lure to keep your superiors from watching you too closely?"

Cornish slipped a Colt into his holster. "All you need to know is that you've done a damned good job."

"I hate it!"

"Yes. But you like the money that goes with it. It's all over now."

"He'll suspect something. How long can I hold him?"

Cornish laughed. "You'll hold him all right. I can trust you for that."

She turned her face away from him. "There's something you've been hiding from me. I worked with you believing you'd make enough money and stop your illicit dealings. Why can't you stop now? Dan doesn't know enough to arrest you."

Cornish picked his hat from the table. "Listen," he said quietly, "Fayes was questioning Sergeant French. He suspects something about Kroft's death."

Her eyes widened. "What? It was suicide, wasn't it?"

"No! Kroft killed Ben Ducey to make him keep his

mouth shut. Fayes would have wormed the truth out of him. I couldn't take a chance on that!"

"What are you driving at, Myron?"

"Kroft knew I had a cache down near the creek. He went down there to find it when I wouldn't give him any more dust. I followed him. We had words. I killed him."

Her hand went to her throat. "Why didn't you tell me? They'll think *I* had something to do with it."

"Dammit! I told you they had nothing on you. Keep Fayes here tonight. I've got to have time to get away!"

Dan eased through the doorway. Melva's eyes widened in terror. Cornish whirled. He jerked his Colt free and swept the Argand lamp from the table, crashing it to the floor. Melva screamed as Dan closed in. Cornish lashed at Dan with his Colt. Dan blocked the blow and hit the surgeon in the belly. Cornish grunted and dropped the pistol. His strong hands closed about Dan's throat. They went back against the wall. Cornish tightened his grip. Dan brought up a knee into the surgeon's groin.

Cornish grunted. He kicked Dan in the belly. He snatched up a glass pitcher and struck hard at Dan. The pitcher shattered on Dan's head. He went down on his knees with the shock. Blood veiled his face. Cornish laughed wildly as he battered at Dan's head with the remains of the pitcher. Dan gripped Cornish by the knees and dumped him back over the table. He hammered blindly at the smooth face, feeling his knuckles rip against the teeth.

Melva slammed the door shut. Cornish rolled sideways as Dan felt his fists smash teeth. The surgeon wrapped his long legs about Dan's waist and raised his upper body. Dan fell backward with Cornish on top of him. Cornish broke free and scrabbled for his pistol in the darkness. He gripped it and swung hard. The barrel clipped Dan across the side of the head. Dan fell behind the table.

"Don't shoot!" screamed Melva. "You'll rouse the post!"

Dan came up from behind the table to meet a savage slashing blow of the pistol. He hit the floor hard, dimly hearing the smash of boots against the floor. The door opened and slammed and then Dan went down into a pit of swirling darkness.

Dimly he heard the grating of feet on the floor and the low talking. He opened his eyes. Ellis Morgan was standing with his arm about Melva Cornish's shoulders. Captain Andrew Horace leaned against the wall looking down at Dan.

Dan touched his slashed skull. It throbbed like a drum. There was a lump over his left ear.

"Get up," said Morgan thinly, "you drunken scum!"

The strong odor of whisky clung about Dan. An empty bottle lay at his side. He got to his feet and stood there swaying, holding his battered head. Then he looked at Melva. "Where is he?"

She drew her ripped dress closer together. "Who?"

"Your brother."

"It's a good thing he isn't here," said Horace. "He'd have killed you for what you tried to do."

Melva turned her face away. "It was terrible. He knew Myron was gone. I was just getting ready for bed. He tried to attack me. I struck him with the pitcher. Thank God he went down."

A cold feeling came over Dan. "She's lying," he said.

Morgan walked toward Dan. "Are you armed?" he asked.

Dan shook his head.

Morgan drew his Colt. "I'm placing you under arrest, Major Fayes," he said.

"On what charge?"

"Drunkenness. Attempted rape. You'd better come with me."

Dan looked at Melva. "Tell him the truth!"

She looked away.

Dan gripped Horace by the arm. "Cornish was here. He admitted he murdered Kroft. We fought. He's riding away from here right now while we stand here like idiots!"

Horace drew away from Dan. "You've ruined yourself," he said. "I knew it was only a matter of time. Riding the officers and destroying the squadron with your insane ideas. Proving what Captain Cornish said about you."

"What was that?" asked Dan quietly.

Horace smirked. "He prepared a report saying you were an alcoholic and unfit for command. He gave it to Captain Morgan and myself. We're forwarding it to Department Headquarters. You're through, Fayes. And I'm damned glad of it."

Morgan jerked his head. "Come on," he said.

Dan walked to the door. Unless Cornish was caught there was no way he could clear himself. He wiped the blood from his face. A dry wind swept about him as he rounded the corner of the building. The gully was just to his left. He lurched against Morgan, and the heavy man stumbled. Dan ducked and darted to one side. He plunged down the eroded slope as Morgan cursed. The Colt flamed in the darkness. Dan hit the ground hard and raced through the darkness toward the creek.

Horace and Morgan were yelling for the guard. Dan reached the trees. He ran to the creek bank and jumped into the shallow waters. He splashed across and gained the far shore. The yelling grew fainter behind him as he trotted through the trees toward the north. The fat was in the fire now, but he had to get Myron Cornish. He needed a horse and a gun. Moore's Ranch was his best bet. He looked back over his shoulder. A lantern bobbed about on the edge of the parade ground. He increased his pace although has battered head pounded fiercely.

There was a faint moon rising in the eastern sky. The wind swept across the hills, moaning softly. Dan crossed the creek again and worked his way up a slope. Two miles further on he saw the dim outline of Moore's Ranch. Only one light showed in the big house.

Dan stopped and listened. There were no sounds of pursuit. He stood there with the faint moonlight shining on his bloody face, and there was cold hate in his eyes. Then he pushed his way through the brush toward the ranch.

CHAPTER SEVENTEEN

The wind soughed about the ranch buildings and flapped the wagon covers. The bunkhouse was off to one side, dark and silent. Dan padded across the yard behind the main building, where one window showed yellow light. The house seemed closed for the night. The heavy shutters were closed. He tried the front door. It was bolted.

Dan walked around and tried the back door. It swung open easily at his touch. He eased himself inside the dark kitchen. The building was as quiet as the grave except for the steady ticking of the waggle-tailed clock on the kitchen wall. Dan crossed the dark barroom to the large room which served as the general store. He lit a match and looked about the well-stocked chamber. Light showed in a thin line beneath a door at the rear.

He eased the doorknob and opened the door a crack. It was a bedroom. Harriet's. The bed was still made. The lamp flared a little in the draft. The room was empty of life. A closet door gaped open. Some clothing lay on the floor. Dan shoved back his cap and looked about with a puzzled expression on his battered face.

An icy feeling formed within him. Harriet was gone, and he suddenly knew she had not left of her own free will. He put out the lamp and returned to the store. He helped himself to a Colt .45 and cartridges. A Henry rifle. Canteens, food and blankets. He buckled a gun belt about his waist and slid the Colt into it. The rest of the things he placed in a sack. He blew out the lamp and walked out of the building.

In the big stable he picked a stocky dun and saddled it. He formed cantle and pommel packs and lashed them in place. Then he led the dun out into the wide yard. On a sudden thought he walked to the bunkhouse and tried the door. It opened. He lit a match. A man lay face downward on the packed-earth floor. The back of his gray head was stained with blood. It was Sim Eames, one of the employees.

Dan rolled the little man over. He was still alive. Dan wiped the face with cold water. Eames opened his eyes. "Jesus," he said, "my head's explodin'."

"You'll live. What happened?"

Eames sat up and gingerly touched the back of his head. "I helped Miss Harriet close up for the night. Then I comes over here. Joe Steiner and Casey Duncan had gone into Mesquite Wells. Whilst I was thinking of goin' to bed, I hears this horse outside. I goes to the door and sees Captain Cornish out there. He asks me if he can get some supplies. He says he's leavin' Fort Costain. I tells him Miss Harriet has closed for the night. When I turns away from him it seems like the floor comes up to hit me in the face. That's all I know."

Dan stood up. "Harriet's gone," he said. "Cornish has taken her with him."

"She wouldn't go anywheres with that cold-eyed bastard."

"She probably had nothing to say about it. Listen, Sim, you didn't see me here."

"I get it."

"When the other men get back, I want you to go up to the post and get hold of Gila Barnes. Tell *him,* and him only, that I've gone after Cornish."

"Keno!"

Dan left the bunkhouse and swung up on the dun. He spurred it toward the road. The wind shifted. He heard the thud of hoofs on the road in the direction of the fort. He looked back. A dark group of horsemen topped a rise. Troopers. He kneed the dun off the road into the brush and headed for the creek. Odds were that Cornish had gone north. If he had gone south toward Tres Cabezas he would run the risk of being picked up.

Dan crossed the creek and rode swiftly toward the north.

It was close to dawn when he noticed the bitter odor of wood smoke. A banner of gray smoke hung low along the creek bottoms. He drew rein on a rise and looked down toward a burned-out ranch-house. The wind fanned the huge beds of ashes, revealing bright eyes of fire. He rode slowly toward it. In the graying light he saw a dog sprawled across a flat rock. His skull had been cleft by a terrific blow.

Dan slid from his saddle, slipping his Henry rifle from its sheath. The wind moaned through the trees, fanning the beds of ashes into fiery life. Scattered about the trampled ground were battered pieces of furniture. Two men lay beneath the trees, with the curious lopsided look a smashed skull gives the faces of the dead. Dan picked up a war club. The tip was clotted with blood and hair.

Dan wet his lips. The air was oppressive with the heat from the embers. Unshod pony tracks pocked the earth, with a great litter of empty cartridge cases scattered about them.

The Apaches were getting bolder. The small ranch was no more than three miles from Mesquite Wells. Then the ghastly thought struck him that Cornish might have run into them.

Dan walked about the area in the graying light. The pony tracks led north through a draw. He followed them and then stopped. Mingled with the unshod tracks were those of two shod horses, a big one and a smaller one. Dan squatted by the trail looking north toward the hills. A worm of bitter thought crept slowly into his mind. Cornish was the mastermind behind the gunrunning. The Apaches had allowed Ben Ducey free passage through their land. *Why not Cornish?*

Dan lit a cigar and passed a dirty hand across his sore jaw. Where else could Cornish go? Harriet wouldn't have gone with him without resistance. In Mesquite Wells, Union or Beasley someone would have noticed she was a prisoner. The pieces of thought moved about, adjusted themselves and then formed an unholy pattern. He was sure Cornish was with the only friends he had...the Apaches he had so well supplied with rifles.

Dan went back to the dun. He mounted it and passed from the ruined ranch, never looking back.

The trail was well marked, revealing the contempt the raiders felt toward any pursuers. Here a pair of gaudy galluses hung over a mesquite bush. There a battered clock lay in the dust.

By noon Dan was high above the valley of the San Ignacio, looking northeast to where a plume of smoke drifted upward. Burning ranch or Apache signal fire?

Dan kneed the dun to one side, following a faintly defined trail. He couldn't go back. Morgan might have a patrol looking for him. Going ahead didn't make much sense. What could he do against a war party of blood-hungry Apaches? He wasn't even sure Harriet was with them.

The lone man to the rear led his horse across the flats, kneeling now and then to examine the ground. Then he would look up at the ragged hills and plod on.

Dan touched his cracked lips with the tip of his tongue. He had had no water since the day before. The sun beat down on the hollow, making the rocks almost too hot to touch. Dan slid his Henry rifle forward and sighted the lone man. The sights seemed to swim in the hazy heat. The dun nickered from the bottom of the hollow.

Dan studied the approaching man and then stood up. There was no mistaking the battered Kossuth hat and the ewe-necked roan. Gila looked up and jumped to one side, raising his long-barreled Spencer. Then he stared and ran to the roan. He mounted and spurred it up the slope. He slid from the saddle and eyed Dan. "Jesus," he said, "you leave a trail like a travois."

Dan grinned. "I thought I was pretty careful."

Gila spat. "It's a damned good thing I found yuh before yuh got any farther into these goddamned hills."

"How's the water?"

"Just enough for a swallow or two." Gila unhooked a huge canteen and handed it to Dan. Dan sipped a little and then wet his scarf. He wiped the dun's mouth with it.

Gila squatted on the hot rocks, oblivious to the heat, and studied Dan through half-closed eyes. "There was hell to pay when you escaped. Morgan took command and ordered Charlie Norman to go after you. Norman refused. Morgan put him under arrest Then we get a message that Black Wind struck the mines at Union. Killed seven miners and set fire to one of the buildin's. Got away with thirty horses and mules. Morgan gets scared. He orders out the scouts."

"So?"

Gila waved a dusty arm. "They're back there five miles. Denny Halloran is leadin' 'em. Morgan ordered me to track you down. I leaves the post and waits for Halloran. I didn't want to see him get into this country and get cut up."

"Will Halloran attempt to arrest me?"

Gila shook his head. "Morgan had enough sense to keep his mouth shut about that hassle in Cornish's quarters. Ain't no one knows about it but Morgan, Horace and Norman, exceptin' me of course, and I won't talk."

"So?"

"This is your chance. The chance you was so all-fired eager to get. Yuh got your scouts. Yuh got me. All we have to do is surround one hundred and fifty 'Paches in their own country and make 'em say Mama."

"They're up there ahead of me. In the hills. And I think Cornish is with them." Dan puffed at his cigar. "Let's get the scouts."

Gila walked to his roan and drew Dan's new Winchester

from its slings. "I thought yuh might want this. Brought along some mocs for yuh too."

"Thoughtful of you, son."

Gila shrugged. "By the way," he said with a sly grin, "how was it?"

Dan looked up. "What?"

"Melva Cornish, yuh idjit."

Dan spat. "I didn't get that far. It was a rigged job, Gila. Melva was just giving Cornish time to make his break."

Gila shook his head. "Just when yuh was makin' time too. Oh, well."

They mounted and rode down the slope with the late afternoon sun shining against their dusty faces.

It was dusk when Gila and Dan rode into the bivouac. Halloran had picked a good place for it, on a slope with a clear view of the surrounding terrain. The horses and four pack mules were in a hollow on individual picket lines. The cooking fires were already out.

Halloran showed a look of relief on his lean face when he saw Dan. "I wasn't too keen on this jaunt, sir."

Dan looked quickly at him. "Why?"

"The scouts were the major's idea. The men seemed to think you'd lead them. It makes a difference when someone else takes over the command."

Dan nodded.

Halloran swept an arm to indicate the command. "Each scout carries one hundred rounds of Henry rifle ammunition. Twenty-five for the Colts. In reserve we have another two hundred for each carbine and twenty-five more for each Colt. Water for one more day. Cooking rations for two more days and enough embalmed beef to carry us along for three more days."

"You brought the rawhide boots for the horses and mules?"

"Yes, sir. Two sets for each animal. The men are wearing one pair with an extra pair tied to their saddles."

"There is water for the animals in a *tinaja* behind those rocks. A little green but palatable."

A trooper took the two tired horses to water them. Dan squatted beside a rock and accepted a cigar from Halloran. "Get Sid Sykes," he said.

The junior officer came through the darkness and squatted beside Denny Halloran. Sergeant Major Haley loomed behind him. He grinned as he saw Dan.

Dan lit his cigar. "The Apaches struck near Mesquite Wells, evidently after hitting Union. I trailed them into some malpais and lost them. But they're up ahead of us somewhere."

He took his cigar from his mouth. "We'll stay here until midnight and then move out. Gila, you take a corporal and four men and leave an hour ahead of us. Keep us posted by courier. We'll cross the flats and take that shallow canyon northeast of here. If we don't run into them, we'll bivouac near the place we found Ben Ducey."

"Keno," said Gila.

Dan turned to Halloran. "I want a quiet march. Send Mister Sykes to check each man before we leave. I want no jingling, squeaking or knocking. We'll travel like ghosts."

"Yes, sir."

Dan yawned. "I want some sleep. Keep a moving guard below these rocks. If anything looks suspicious wake me up!"

Dan made his bed beneath an overhang. He lay there a long time listening to the muted voices of the men. More than one of them had eyed his battered face but had said nothing. There was a feeling of hopelessness in him. He doubted if Cornish had any interest in Harriet beyond using her as a hostage. It wouldn't be past the surgeon to leave her with the Apaches when he pulled foot. The rest of it wasn't fit to think about.

The command moved out at an easy walk. The saddles were cold and there had been no coffee. The men were sour. The moon shed enough light for them to see their way. It was as though they were moving on another planet or as the last survivors of humanity on a deserted earth.

The first courier met them a mile from the canyon mouth.

Gila was far up the canyon. No signs of life. But they had found tracks. Mingled with the tracks of the Apache horses were those of two shod horses. A big stallion and a small mare.

The second courier met them at the designated bivouac area. Gila and Corporal Moylan had gone deeper into the hills and would return during the day. The command went into a fireless bivouac, eating stringy embalmed beef.

Dan allowed fires of dry wood just after dawn for heating coffee. The men slept heavily after their slim meal. Dan sat for a long time scanning the hazy hills with Halloran's field-glasses, but he might as well have saved his eyes. Not even a wisp of dust moved in those barren heights. Water was the big problem for Dan's command. The water at the bivouac served to refill the canteens and the horses and then was gone. The small water casks on the mules were kept filled as a reserve.

Corporal Moylan reported back at noon. "Gila has gone deeper into the hills," he said. "He doesn't like the looks of the canyon up ahead. The walls are sheer. A perfect place for an ambush. However, sir, there is a sort of rough pass which cuts to the west. Beyond that pass is a way to circle far behind the area where Gila thinks the Apaches have holed up."

"So?"

Moylan shrugged. "Gila is not sure of how we can get into the Apaches' canyon. It's a long shot, sir."

Dan eyed the rough map Moylan had sketched in the sand. "What about water?"

"He says there is water at Roca Roja. Big natural tanks there. They run dry about this time."

Dan nodded. "Halloran," he said quietly, "we'll pull out at dusk. Moylan will guide us."

THE BOOK HAS explicit rules on the march of cavalry. Space out to fifty-five paces, stagger the files to keep the dust down and give the mounts a chance to breathe. Unfit to graze, even on the shortest halts. Halt ten minutes on the hour and allow forty minutes every sixth hour for watering. Trot twenty minutes every second hour and lead for the full hour preceding water call. Treat a horse like the best friend you've got and talk to him like a brother.

But how can a command be spread out to fifty-five paces and staggered twenty yards to the right when you're traveling in a narrow slot of a canyon no more than fifty feet wide at the bottom? Forty minutes every sixth hour is fine for watering when you have an unlimited supply of water, and you have six hours to travel in. You can't trot big cavalry mounts in rocky country when a hoof striking a stone can be heard by Apache ears for an eighth of a mile.

Dan tugged at his dun's reins. "Come on, *amigo*," he said to himself, "we've thrown away the book."

The day's heat hung in the narrow canyon like an issue blanket, forcing rivulets of sweat to break out on bodies and soak dusty uniforms. The command traveled silently in a heavy cloak of sweat-soaked wool, the acid smell of horses, the sweetish odor of damp leather. Even the moon did not penetrate the narrow slot. Thirty-seven men plunging through the darkness following an unknown trail to face four times their number of Apaches in the hostiles' back yard.

The pass was worse than the canyon. Great shattered heaps of rock obstructed the way, forcing the scouts to wind through a bewildering trail. Catclaw, cholla and prickly pear reached out thorny hands to tear at the soldiers' dusty clothing. Here fragments of the moonlight speckled their dirty faces. Each man worried only about himself and his horse, now and then looking up to see the sweat-soaked man ahead of him, leading his dusty horse.

Dan looked back along the struggling column. Doubts gathered in his mind like buzzards settling on the dead. The one thing that kept him going was the fact that he had one sure weapon. The white man's ability to outthink the savage. Even of this he wasn't too sure, for old Black Wind had proved quite a few times that he could think himself.

The gray light of false dawn filtered down on the little command. Dan turned to Denny Halloran. "Bivouac up that slope."

The area was a jumble of craggy rock, well-armed with thorny vegetation. To the right rose a great knife-blade of a ridge, seemingly impossible to climb. Ahead of them was more of the country through which they had just traveled. Dan looked at his men, held in yellow-legged discipline. He beckoned to Haley. "Pass the word around that a white woman is in the hands of the Apaches."

Haley looked at Dan. "It will help, sir."

The whites of the men's eyes showed up against their tanned faces, coated with dust They didn't say much, but there was a perceptible tightening in the command. Hands closed on pistol butts. They looked at each other and then went to take care of their horses. Tracking down hostile Apaches was one thing; saving a white woman from greasy exploring hands was another.

CHAPTER EIGHTEEN

The scouts were far below Dan as he stopped for a breather. Gila looked down from a rock slab. "Winded?" he asked with a sly grin.

Dan's breath was harsh in his throat. He looked up at the gaunt scout, perched like a crow on the lip of the rock. "Hell, yes," he gasped.

Gila cut a chew. "I got fifteen years on yuh, Dan."

"Yes, you bastard, but you're part mountain goat."

Gila chuckled as he slipped the chew into his mouth. "Never knew who my pa was, Dan."

"*I* know."

Dan leaned back against a rock. The heat seemed to shift about in heavy veils. They had been on the move all morning since Gila had found the Apaches. There were none on this side of the ridge according to the scout.

Dan slanted his hat brim over his reddened eyes and looked west. The terrain was fantastic. Frosty blues and cavalry-scarf yellows; broiled lobster-claw reds and hazy purples; grassy greens and dull golds. All of it blended together in a phantasmagoria of color.

"You're sure Harriet is still alive?" he asked quietly.

"Yeh. I think I seen her. Ridin' with the squaws. Cornish was with Black Wind."

Dan forced himself to his feet. His left moccasin had split along one side. His Winchester butt was scarred from his using it as an alpenstock to aid the hazardous ascent.

Gila went on tirelessly and then dropped to his knees. He waved a hand to Dan. Dan went to his knees and snaked along behind the scout, brushing against rock you could fry bacon on.

Gila was crouched in a cleft like a lizard. He shoved back his battered hat and wiped the collected sweat from his lined face. "Look," he said.

Below them a wide canyon cut like a trough through the harsh earth. The far wall was hung with great masses of rock waiting for the next frost to loosen them enough for their downward plunge to the great talus slope far below. Here the canyon had a great indentation in it, caused by a naked shoulder of rock that thrust like a ship's prow into the trough. At the end of the shoulder was the mouth of another canyon, narrow and shadowy. A wisp of smoke drifted up from it. Along the base of the far wall was an indistinct line leading to a place where a humped ridge of rock followed the direction of the canyon wall.

Gila shifted his chew. "Yuh see that low ridge?"

"Yes."

"Behind that is a deep gully. Like a natural trench. That ridge is like a fort wall with loopholes in it."

"So?"

Gila eyed Dan. "This is the place. Holy ground it is for the Tontos. They've never been rooted outa here. In '63 the California Volunteer Cavalry tried to root 'em out. Lost twelve killed and seventeen wounded. In '68 a squadron tried to get in here. They was badly cut up."

"I thought no troops had ever been in here."

"They ain't. The Californians got it ten miles from here in the canyon I come up. Full of twists and turns it is. A dozen warriors could hold it against a regiment. Believe me, Dan, there ain't been a yellowleg in here yet."

"We're here."

Gila spat. "Yeh. Where? Behind this ridge. All Black Wind has to do is hole up behind that low ridge. Yuh can't get at 'em from the south. They got a fine field of fire there. Yuh can't get at 'em from the north. That rock shoulder cuts into the canyon. Look, the canyon ain't wide enough for a wagon to get through. Yuh figger on slidin' down from here? In daylight you'd be cut to pieces. At night you'd lose half your men on the way and the rest would chew Apaches' slugs once they hit the bottom. Now why in hell's name did yuh want to come in here?"

Dan uncased his glasses. Gila shaded them with his stinking Kossuth hat. Dan studied the far wall. Gila was right.

"They got a cinch here," said Gila, "Ain't no one gonna pry 'em out. The women and kids is up that narrow canyon. It's a box with a damned dangerous trail outn it. Sage told me that. So the women puts up the wickiups. They roasts mezcal and broils horsemeat. They got water in there. Natural tanks, always in shade. Holds water most of the year. The bucks take it easy with a few warriors on guard."

Dan looked down toward the low ridge. There was a movement in the brush. A warrior walked past an open area. The sun glinted dully on the brass trim of his Henry rifle.

Dan put down the glasses. It was a tactical problem hard enough to analyze when a man was at his best. Lack of sleep and short rations hadn't helped Dan's weariness. He flogged his tired brain. *Always attempt to make the enemy think you are in force. Frighten them if possible. Trust in your luck.*

Using forty men to delude the Apaches into thinking he was in force would stretch things wire-thin. How in God's name could he frighten them? They were secure in their ancient natural fortress. Trusting in luck wasn't much of a sheet anchor to windward.

Dan looked north. "What's up there?"

"The bitchiest jumble of rocks yuh ever saw."

"Can we get up there from where we are?"

"Yeh. But what then?"

Dan rubbed his bristly jaw. The skin was taut from wind and sunburn. He remembered then he had cursed Trumpeter Criswell for letting the sun flash on his instrument just that very day. A trumpet had a brassy, far-carrying voice. He mentally placed that piece of the puzzle to one side for future use.

"Let's go," said Dan.

They worked their way down the steep side of the ridge. The men were scattered among the boulders, breathing hard in the heavy heat. Halloran, Sykes and Haley squatted in front of Dan. He wiped the sweat from his face and then sketched a map on the sand at his feet. "Mister Sykes will take a corporal and seven men back down this canyon to a point where they can climb the ridge and look down into the next canyon."

"I saw a place about a mile and half back," said Sykes.

"You will take Trumpeter Criswell as one of your men."

Sykes looked puzzled.

"Halloran," continued Dan, "you will take the bulk of the scouts up to where Gila and I just were. Take all the ammunition you can carry. I want absolute silence in the climb and while you are up there." Halloran nodded.

Dan looked at Sergeant Major Haley. "You will accompany me and Gila. I want eight men. The best shots and the toughest men in the unit."

Shadows were beginning to form in the canyon. The men eyed Dan. "At the first light of dawn, Mister Sykes, I want Criswell to lip onto that trumpet and put some spit into it!"

Sykes wet dry lips. "Yes, sir."

"Halloran," said Dan, "you will have that ridge top lined with your men. When the Apaches hear Sykes's trumpeter, they should boil out of that box canyon like bees and take up position behind the rock barricade below the overhanging canyon wall. You will open fire."

Halloran tilted his head to one side. "But the major said they had perfect cover behind the rocks. What do we shoot at, sir?"

Dan waved an arm. "At the rock wall behind them. You've played billiards, Mister Halloran?" "Yes, sir."

"Then you know how to bank your shots." A great light dawned in Halloran's blue eyes. "The angle of rebound is the same as the angle of incidence."

Dan took off his stinking hat and bowed his head. "You're a man of quick perception, Mister Halloran."

Dan looked at Gila and Haley. "We will pull out now and go north, coming down into the canyon. When Halloran plays the opening waltz, we will come down the main canyon and attempt to get into the Apache camp. Our goal is to save Miss Moore and find Surgeon Cornish." Gila whistled softly. Haley let out his breath in a soft rush.

Dan stood up. "Any questions?"

"Supposing it doesn't work?" asked Sykes.

Dan looked down at the young officer. "Why," he said, "they will close the book on Fayes' Scouts."

In the silence that followed they looked at each other. Then Sykes spoke up. "The odds are long, but I don't know where I'd rather be than here."

The canyon was already deep in shadow when Dan and his detail moved out. Riding behind him and Gila were Haley and Troopers MacDonald, Abruzzi, Schaefer, Hanson, Garrity, Delano, Black and Willis. Top shots. Rough-and-tumble boys.

None of them spoke as they picked their way through the darkness. For there are times when words make no sense, and when a man is better alone with his own secret thoughts.

Dan awoke with a start as a hard dirty hand clamped down on his working mouth. He looked up into Gila's shadowy face. The scout leaned close. "Yuh was talkin' loud, *amigo*."

Dan nodded. Gila withdrew his hand. The canyon was dark. A cool wind crept through the chaotic jungle of rock. Dan shivered. He looked at Gila. "What was I saying?"

Gila stowed a chew into his mouth. "Somethin' about the war. The woods. The rain."

Dan sat up and leaned back against a rock.

"One of these days you'll forget all that," said Gila.

Dan looked up at the sky. There was the faintest trace of gray light. "It's about time," he said.

"Yes."

"Awaken the men."

"Keno."

They rose from among the rocks like a crew of dirty tramps. A rifle butt clicked, and Haley cursed in fluent style. "Dammit, Delano! You're clumsy as a cub bear!"

They sipped their stale water and chewed without appetite on their embalmed beef.

Dan stood up and tightened his gun belt. "All right, Gila," he said.

Gila walked off through the wilderness of rocks. Dan and the men followed him. The sky was lighter now. The shoulder of rock which jutted out into the canyon loomed high above them. An eagle screamed like a file scratched across hard metal.

Fear descended upon them like a soft flying ghoul. It eased its skinny arms about Dan's neck and settled its body comfortably on his back. Each man has his own picture of fear. Dan's had somehow taken the shape of a skinny Apache, with tight parchment for skin, drawn over protruding bones, staring at him with sightless eyes. Intchidijin. The Black Wind.

Gila stopped at the base of the huge rock shoulder. He held up a dirty hand. They stopped silently on rawhide moccasins.

Then far away down the canyon, carried on the cold wind, came the brassy tone of the trumpet. Mister Sykes was in position.

Dan looked up at the knife-edged ridge. There was no sign of life, but Halloran would be up there. His men gripping Henry rifles greasy with cold sweat, staring with strained eyes at the far wall of the big canyon.

Gila dropped to his hands and knees and crawled on,

followed by Dan and the troopers. Gila stopped. "Look," he whispered.

Dan stared into the dimness. There was movement at the mouth of the box canyon. A long line of trotting Apaches, carrying their repeaters. They vanished behind the rock barricade. Minutes drifted past. Dan pictured the Apaches secure in their natural fortress, laughing at the foolish White-eyes.

It grew lighter. Now and then an Apache head popped up, to stare down the canyon and then sink down again, as though worked by a string.

Dan looked up at the ridge. "Jesus," he husked, "what's wrong?"

As though in answer he heard a faint roar of command. Then rifles sparkled along the ridge. Smoke drifted with the wind. The slugs smashed against the rock wall behind the barricade. An Apache whooped derisively. The Henry rifles on the ridge churned steadily. The echoes slammed back and forth. The whoops changed to screams. Lead pattered down behind the barricade. The two hundred and sixteen-grain slugs, driven by twenty-five grains of powder, slammed into the wall and ricocheted downward. The mutilated bullets whined through the air.

Dan stood up. "Now," he said, and took the lead, running at a crouch between the rocks.

Dan's breath came hard in his throat as he went up the rough slope. There was a feathery feeling in his lungs. This was the job for which they had been trained. The apex of the years of training and parade-ground soldiering. To shoot and be shot at.'

Dan stopped behind a slab of rock. Halloran's men were emptying their fifteen-round magazines. Then the fire died away. The screams and groans of the warriors rose in a bitter crescendo. Dan went on again, glancing to his right. In the dimness behind the barricade, he could see thrashing bodies and others that were still. Then he passed the mouth of the box canyon.

A young buck stood up behind a rock and looked toward the barricade. He never saw the steel-shod butt of Dan's rifle drive in to smash his skull. Dan hurdled the body. Another young warrior stared at him with gaping mouth. Haley fired from the hip. The slug whirled the Tonto around. He dropped.

The canyon opened up. Wickiups showed in the dimness, like great beehives. Shadowy figures scuttled about them. The squaws hurrying their kids to safety. "Don't shoot at them unless they attack us!" yelled Dan.

"Nits breed lice!" yelled MacDonald.

"You heard the major!" shouted Haley.

Five young bucks charged Dan's party. Young men who still wore the head-scratching stick and drinking cane of the untried brave. It took guts. But guts was no defense against Henry rifle slugs fired at fifty feet. The charge was ripped apart like tissue paper and the rushing white men were through into the canyon proper.

A squaw dropped to one knee and fired a double-barreled shotgun. Both barrels flamed. Willis staggered sideways as the shot caught him in the left thigh. Then he was down, gripping the shattered limb, with gouts of blood streaming through his dirty fingers. Garrity fired twice, driving the squaw back into a hollow.

The driving crashes of Halloran's fire ripped out again. The main canyon was a hell of rifle fire and agonized screaming.

A mixed group of squaws and young warriors closed in on Dan's men. The command came automatically from Dan. "At twenty yards! Fire by squad! Aim is left oblique! *Fire!*"

Henry slugs smashed home, drove brown bodies back and down like so many bundles of clothing.

Delano went down with a thrown knife in his left shoulder. Schaefer grunted as a pistol flamed at his feet and smashed him back against a rock with half his face a bloody mask.

"There's the girl!" screamed Abruzzi.

Harriet was running up a slope pursued by a screaming squaw, whose knife-fanged claw was reaching out for the white girl's back. Gila raised his long Spencer, steadied and fired. The squaw staggered forward. The knife tip sliced through the back of Harriet's dress. She darted sideways and came on toward them.

Dan hurdled a boulder. Here and there in the rocks were half-naked boys, fighting like warriors with old Burnside carbines, shotguns and bows. Dan's men dived for cover and began to pick them off one by one. A buck leaped on Garrity. Garrity came up from the ground like an uncoiling spring. His rifle barrel smashed the Tonto's skull.

Dan dropped a warrior and drew his Colt. He placed it on the rocks in front of him and began to reload his Winchester. Harriet was safe behind him. His fingers fumbled with the cartridges as he fed the magazine.

"Look!" said Gila.

The squaws had retreated with their young ones up a narrow trail that clung like a string to the almost sheer walls. "Don't fire!" yelled Dan.

Suddenly, behind them, from the main canyon there came a roaring noise and then the smash of tons of rock. Dust billowed into the box canyon. A dozen warriors rounded the turn, full into the fire of the freshly charged Henry rifles of Dan's little command. The slugs ripped them apart, scattering them across the rocky ground.

Above the crashing of rifles came hoarse cheering from Halloran's men.

Dan crawled to Harriet. She did not speak as he slid his arm about her.

Gila ran to Dan. "Look," he said.

At the rear of the canyon a man dressed in blue was running for cover.

"Cornish," said Dan quietly.

"There's the old man," said Gila.

Black Wind was crawling up the rocks, feeling his way with clawed hands. Black raised his rifle. Dan struck it down. "Let him go," he said. "He's trapped. They both are."

Now and then a shot ripped out from the rocks as a

Tonto made a last stand. The squaws were high up on the trail now.

Haley trotted up from the canyon mouth. "Halloran's fire loosened the rocks from the canyon wall. The whole goddamned mess came down on the bucks. There ain't but thirty or forty of them still alive."

Dan picked up his rifle. He looked at Harriet. "Stay here."

"Where are you going?"

Dan jerked his head. "Captain Cornish and I have a debt to settle."

"Don't go, Dan! He's mad!"

Dan picked up his Colt and slid it into his holster. He climbed over the rocks, crouched, and ran for the back of the canyon.

Dan crawled up the slope. Two hundred yards from the towering canyon wall he heard the dry voice. "Nantan Eclatten," the voice called out, "are you there?"

It was like a voice from the grave. Dan looked up. Black Wind was perched on a rock shelf above him. Behind the skinny Tonto was the mouth of a cave.

"Nantan Eclatten!"

Dan crawled closer. "I am here, Black Wind," he called out in Spanish.

The old chief nodded. "I knew it."

"Come down, old man. You are safe."

A rifle shot split the quiet.

Black Wind shook his aged head. "No. This is my last place to stay. Here I stayed for the last five years, thinking of the white man's perfidy. When the time was ripe, I went back to my people."

"You have lost, Black Wind. Your warriors are all dead or captured. Your women and children have fled."

Black Wind wet his thin lips. "Yes, Nantan Eclatten. Your medicine was good. Mine was not."

Dan looked at the strange figure seated on the rocks. The wind flapped his dirty buckskin kilt. "You are safe," he said again.

Black Wind shook his head. "I will not see many grasses. I will not go to the reservation to be looked at and spoken about. I am not a child to be so treated."

"You are a great warrior, Black Wind."

"You are a greater one."

Dan looked down the slope. He could see the tall form of Denny Halloran beside Mike Haley. Halloran's men were rounding up the survivors of the *bronco* band. Sergeant French was busy with his medical panniers.

Dan looked up the slope. Myron Cornish was climbing the canyon wall. Above him there was no trail.

Dan slipped a hand into his pocket and touched the brass plate Black Wind had cast with scorn into the road at Dan's feet. "Come down," he called. "You will be treated with the honors of war."

Black Wind shook his grizzled head. "Am I only to be a number?"

"You will be treated as a great warrior."

"I once said that you should choose the way of your dying. I was wrong. It is I who will choose the way of my dying. I will die here. Alone with the gods who did not smile on me in my last fight."

Dan shrugged. "As you wish." He crawled through the rocks. The canyon was light now. Cornish was high on the slope, looking down now and then with white face at the canyon below him.

Dan worked forward. Cornish opened fire at too great a range. The spent bullets spattered on the rocks.

Dan worked closer and closer until he was just below the rock wall. He left his Winchester and began to climb. His skin was ripped and abraded by the keen-edged rocks. Sweat broke out and soaked his filthy uniform.

He rested on a ledge fifty yards from Cornish.

"Fayes!" called out the surgeon, "can you hear me?"

"Yes."

"Then listen! I have thousands in gold. I'll split with you if you let me go."

"Go to hell!"

"I'll kill you if you come up here!"

"We'll see."

Far down the canyon Dan could see the white faces of the troopers as they watched the two men high on the rock wall.

Cornish raised his voice. "I'll give you *all* the gold!"

"You bastard! You think you can buy your way out of this?"

Cornish began to shoot. Slugs smashed against the rocks and keened off into space.

Dan worked upward. His left leg was numbing from the strain.

Rocks fell from the ledge above him. He eased himself up on the ledge. Cornish was trying to batter a foothold in the canyon wall with his rifle butt. Dan stood up and edged behind a rock shoulder. "Cornish," he called out, "drop that gun!"

Cornish turned. He threw it down and jerked a pistol from his belt. His thin lips worked as he looked at Dan. "You spoiled the sweetest plan a man ever made up," he said.

Dan cocked the Colt. "Throw down that gun, Cornish!"

Cornish fired. The slug whipped past Dan. Dan snatched his hat free from his head with his left hand and scaled it at Cornish's face. Cornish automatically threw up his left hand to guard his face. Dan fired. The big Colt kicked back hard into his hand. Dust puffed from the dusty blouse.

Cornish took two steps forward and then swayed toward the lip of the ledge. His eyes were glazing even as he fired. The slug picked at Dan's left shoulder like a burning iron and then Cornish went over the ledge. He screamed once as he turned head over heels and struck with a sickening smash far below.

Dan walked to the edge of the ledge and looked down. The dead man's head was twisted hard to one side. Blood flowed from the slack mouth.

Dan holstered his Colt and started down.

Harriet came to meet him. The sun had tipped the

canyon rim, shining down on sprawled bodies and empty wickiups; on empty cartridge cases and bloody knives.

Halloran grinned as he saw Dan. "You've written a new page in the book," he said.

Harriet rested her head on Dan's shoulder.

Gila looked up at Black Wind. "What about him?" he asked.

"Let him be."

As though in answer Black Wind raised his cracked voice. "Nantan Eclatten!" he called.

Dan turned.

The old chief raised his skinny arms. *"Dih asd-za hig-e balgon-ya-hi dont-e shilg-nli-dah!"* he intoned.

Gila shifted his chew. "This I have done and what has come about is all the same to me!" he translated.

The command was silent as they looked at the old man.

"The last of the rimrock *broncos,"* said Dan.

Gila nodded. "One of the greatest. Yuh know somethin', Dan? I got a lot of respect for that old bastard."

The scouts moved out at noon, leaving a plume of smoke rising from the burning wickiups. The blue-faced dead were buried in a rock cleft, troopers and Tontos alike. Dan looked back as they reached the canyon mouth. The old man had toppled sideways against the side of the shallow cave. High above him a buzzard floated on the still hot air, drifting through the veil of smoke, patiently awaiting his time for the feast.

"He won't get much," said Gila dryly.

Down the canyon Trumpeter Criswell lipped into Assembly, bouncing the brazen notes of the C trumpet from the ancient walls. The troopers rode loose and easy in their saddles.

Dan looked at Harriet. She smiled through the dust. He held out a hand and gripped hers.

The Tontos were broken but the Chiricahuas still held their mountain fastnesses to the south. There was a long trail ahead of any soldier in Arizona Territory. But soldiering was a way of life to which he was dedicated. A hard life without monetary award. But his command had been blooded properly now. The long years of his near disgrace had been burned out in the hell of canyons and chattering rifle fire. He had squared his account.

Dan looked back at the wreathing smoke drifting high above the canyon. *"Yadalanh,* Intchi-dijn," he said quietly. "Farewell, Black Wind!"

SHADOW VALLEY

CHAPTER ONE

The distant whistle of the departing locomotive moaned through the Wyoming night, echoing from the bald hills which ringed the town. One of the three loneliest sounds in the world, Holt Cooper thought as he stepped from the station platform and walked toward the central part of Rockyhill. The other two were the melancholy howl of a coyote and the crunching of a stranger's boots on the streets of a new town.

He swung along easily despite the weight of the rim-fire saddle on his left shoulder and the war bag and Winchester gripped in his right hand. Rockyhill should have been just another town to him, like dozens of towns in Texas, New Mexico and Arizona, but he found himself looking with interest at the same old false-fronted buildings. For Rockyhill *was* different. It was the closest town to the ranch he had never seen. *His* ranch.

A tall man stepped out of the shadows and stopped in the yellow light of a store window to fashion a smoke. A queer feeling roiled in Holt as he saw the lean planes of the tanned face, and the big brown Stetson shoved back on the graying black hair. The man reminded him of his half-brother Niles. He knew damned well it wasn't Niles, but for some strange reason Holt had expected his brother to meet him at Rockyhill. Niles wouldn't be there. He'd never be there. He was buried out at the ranch with a bullet hole in the back of his head.

The man lit his smoke, saw Holt and nodded. "Howdy," he said politely.

"Howdy," Holt said.

"Nice evenin'." The man glanced curiously at the saddle and then down at the Winchester. "Just get in, I take it?"

"Yes. Can you tell me where Minner's Emporium is?"

"Corner of Front and Willow. You can't miss it. Biggest store in Rockyhill."

"*Gracias.*"

"You're welcome."

Holt walked on. The tall man leaned against the wall and watched Holt. Then he crossed the street and walked under the wooden awnings, keeping a hundred yards behind Holt, never taking his eyes from him.

The man had been right. It was hard for a man to miss Minner's. Buckboards and spring wagons lined the street in front of it. Poke-bonneted women stood talking on the boardwalk. Holt suddenly realized that it was Saturday evening.

The women eyed him as he stepped up on the walk and passed them. He pushed open the glassed door and entered the big general store. Half a dozen women lined the cluttered counter. Two clerks passed swiftly back and forth filling orders. Holt looked at the gangling man who stood behind the counter. It must be Sloan Minner.

The man behind the counter looked over the head of a woman. "Help you?" he asked.

"I'm Holt Cooper."

The faded blue eyes squinted a little as they studied Holt. "Sloan Minner. Kinda busy right now, Cooper."

"I'll wait."

"Put your things on the back counter. Cheese and crackers there. Help yourself. Be with you soon as I can."

Holt worked his way past the women and placed his saddle on the floor in front of the rear counter and then put his war bag and rifle on the end of it. He contemplated the cheese and crackers, hunger gnawing in his lean belly. He had promised himself a steak and trimmings after six hours on the train. He comforted himself by lighting a long nine.

Sloan Minner was at his best, as he always was on Saturday evening, passing the time of day with the ranch women, keeping a cold eye on his perspiring clerks, and mentally tabulating the day's profits. But this was a different Saturday night. The big man in the rear of the store had changed things. Sloan had been expecting Holt Cooper for over a week, thinking that he would know Niles Williston's half-brother the instant he saw him. Sloan Minner was usually damned sure of himself in everything but this time he was wrong.

Minner tried not to let the big man know he was studying him. The flat-crowned hat with the *barbiquejo* strap. The dusty gray suit coat a little too tight for the wide shoulders. Black pants over the uppers of high-heeled boots. Minner couldn't see the six-gun because of the coat but he knew it was there, for the big buckle of the cartridge belt shone dully in the lamp light. Cooper resembled half a hundred cowmen Sloan Minner knew, but somehow, he was different.

Holt Cooper was one inch under six feet tall, and built in splendid proportion, from the wide shoulders down to the lean horseman's waist. The hands were big and capable, equally able in making a horsehair bridle, dogging down a steer—or handling a six-shooter. The hair which showed under the dusty brim of the hat was fair. The nose, big in the lean face, reminded Sloan Minner of an Arapahoe he had once known. Big Hawk had been his name. The name would fit the big stranger equally as well, unless Sloan Minner's judgement had faded with the years. But the eyes clinched Sloan's mental argument. They had a level directness and a hint of coldness in them that boded no good for anyone who crossed him.

Holt leaned back against the counter trying to relax after the grueling train ride. But it wasn't easy. Not with his thoughts and the stares of the shopping women. Worst of all was the steady secretive scrutiny of Sloan Minner. He had been one of Niles' best friends but that didn't give a man call to study another man like a horse he was thinking of trading for.

Holt glanced at the fly-specked crackers and the dusty cheese. He shook his head and walked to the longer counter. "You're busy, Minner," he said. "I'll take a walk and get some fixings."

For a moment Minner looked as though he might stop Holt, but then he nodded. "Try the beanery across the street, next to the Stockmen's Bar. It isn't half bad."

Holt walked to the door, feeling every pair of eyes in the place boring a hole into his back. He stopped on the board-walk and slid a hand into his inner coat pocket to touch the letter he had received from Minner. He knew the contents by heart. Niles had been drygulched by an unknown person, one of a series of killings in the Rockyhill area. He had left his spread in Shadow Valley to Holt, his only living relative, but Minner had cryptically mentioned that Holt must not mention being willed the ranch when he came to Rockyhill. It would be better to keep his mouth shut until Minner could talk with him in private. After that Holt could do as he judged best. Keep the ranch or sell it.

Holt crossed the rutted street. A cool fall wind swept along, driving dust and scattered refuse ahead of it. He looked through the window of the beanery. The place was filled, tables and counter. He shrugged. There was a saloon on the corner, and although he didn't feel like drinking, he sure didn't want to wander up and down the dusty street alone.

He pushed through the batwings and walked to the end of the bar. The place was filled. Rockyhill seemed to be a popular place on a Saturday night. "Rye," Holt said to the perspiring barkeep.

The first drink cut the dust in his throat. The second he took as a matter of course. The third one was the charm. It seemed to take some of the stiffness out of his soul. A pang of remorse shot through him. It had been three years since he had seen Niles in Pueblo. Niles had been on the way to Shadow Valley then and tried to talk Holt into throwing in with him. They differed in many ways. One trait they had in common was the lone wolf streak. Sure, they got along. Niles had taken Holt as a kid and taught him everything from throwing a Blocker loop to a poker chip draw. Their ten years' difference had made Niles seem like a father rather than a half-brother. But they hadn't been bred to work together as partners.

The tall man who had followed Niles along the street suddenly saw him standing at the end of the bar. "That's him, Lew," he said to a squat man bucking the tiger.

Lew nodded. "Find out what you can, Walt." He looked up. "No trouble, mind!"

Walt grinned. "Lay off, Lew. I know my business."

"I hope to God you do." Lew eyed Holt. "This hombre is no saddle tramp."

Walt waved a hand and sauntered from the smoky room. He crossed the street and checked Minner's. The stranger looked as if he meant to stay with the bottle for a time. Time enough for Walt to get a few facts. He walked into the general store.

Holt shoved the bottle back after the fourth drink. He had learned long ago not to fill up on an empty belly. A few more drinks and his temper would hone down to a razor edge.

He walked outside and stood there letting the fresh wind dry the sweat on his face. It soothed him. Maybe his wandering was over. This was good cattle country. Niles' last letter had been full of enthusiasm, and he had been doing well. Holt was thirty years old and most of the sharp edges of his character were being rounded off in the mill of time and experience. Maybe Niles had been right in the first place. Maybe Holt should have thrown in with him. "Too late," he said aloud.

Two women passed. One of them looked back at him.

"Did you hear what he said, Martha? Too late! It's only half after seven."

Holt grinned. Speaking aloud was a habit he had never learned to break, the habit of a man who had spent too much time riding alone. He crossed the street and opened the door of Minner's General Emporium. His face tightened as he saw the tall man standing at the rear counter. The man had slid Holt's Winchester out of its saddle scabbard. Sloan Minner paled as he saw Holt. He opened his mouth to call out a warning and then he shut it, because Holt Cooper had passed him like a great lean cat.

Holt stopped behind the tall man. "That's my Winchester," he said quietly.

Walt turned quickly. He grinned. "Sorry. I thought it was for sale. I'm looking for a new saddle gun."

"It's not for sale," Holt said.

Walt avoided the hard gray eyes. "I been looking for a fairly big caliber Winchester."

The long gun rack behind the counter held at least a dozen new and used Winchesters, as well as Spencers, Sharps-Borchardts, trapdoor Springfields and other makes. "Look up there," Holt said coldly.

Sloan Minner came to the end of the counter and shook his head at Holt. "Can I help you, Walt?" he asked.

Walt stepped away from Holt. "I just wanted some chewing," he said.

"He wants a Winchester," Holt said. "Fairly large caliber."

Sloan Minner stared at them. "Why, hell, Walt," he said, "I just sold you a .45/90 not more than two weeks ago."

Walt reddened under his tan.

Holt looked at his war bag. It had been untied. He said, "What's your game, Walt?"

"Get out of my way, stranger." Walt shouldered past Holt.

Holt spun the tall man around. "I asked you a question," he said.

"Here's your answer!"

Walt swung from the hip. Holt blocked the blow with his left forearm. His right fist drove like a piston into the lean belly just above the big belt buckle. His left dropped in time to meet the descending chin with a snapping uppercut. Walt went over backwards, driving against the cracker barrel which toppled and spilled its contents. His outflung left arm knocked the cheese tray from the counter. He hit with a hard thump which raised the dust from the floorboards.

"Jesus Christ!" yelled Sloan Minner. "Sorry, ladies!"

Holt stepped back, resting his hands on his hips. "Have some cheese and crackers, Walt," he said.

The tall man wiped the blood from his mouth, then looked at his reddened hand. He came up like an uncoiling spring, dropping his right hand down for a draw.

Sloan Minner saw it, and yet he didn't see it. One second Holt Cooper was standing there grinning down at Walt Short, with his hands on his hips. The next second he was standing there ramming the muzzle of a six-gun into Walt's gut.

During that fleeting interval Sloan Minner figured he was going to have a killing in his place of business. Then he began to breathe again as Holt Cooper lowered the gun, sweeping back his coat to slide the Colt into the forward tilted Missouri holster.

Walt stepped back gingerly, crunching through soda crackers and yellow cheese, waiting for that swift movement —the movement he had never seen—to come again. Then he realized that the big stranger had merely warned him. He wanted to do something to prove himself in front of the women who stood pale-faced at the front of the store, but he didn't want to be a dead hero. And that's what he might be if he matched draws with this vinegarroon. Walt Short turned and walked from the store, and killing hate clouded his vision every step of the way.

Sloan Minner came down behind the counter. He surveyed the wreckage of his cheese and crackers.

"I'll pay for it," Holt said.

"You sure as hell will," the storekeeper said, "and I don't mean the cheese and crackers. You know who that was?"

Holt smiled. "Name of Walt."

"Walt Short!"

Holt raised his eyebrows. "So?"

"Fast as greased lightning and eleven claps of thunder. One of Lew Manning's top guns."

"You should have told me."

Sloan wiped the sweat from his thin face. "Yeah. I should have told you. How the hell did I know what I let myself in for?"

Holt leaned back against the counter and retied his war bag. "You saw him fooling around with my gear, didn't you?"

"Yes—no! Hell, I don't know what I mean!"

Holt took out the letter. "You sent this to me," he said. "You mention a lot of secret hokey-pokey. It's about time you began talking, isn't it?"

Minner nodded. "Hollister!" he called to a clerk. "Get this mess cleaned up. Close at eight tonight." Minner jerked his head at Holt. "Follow me, Cooper." He led the way into a back office and seated himself before a battered rolltop desk. His hands shook a little as he took a bottle from a drawer and filled two glasses. "Before God," he said, "I never seen such a draw. Reminds me of someone."

"Who?"

The faded blue eyes held Holt's gray ones. "Niles Williston. That's who!"

"He taught me, Minner."

"I might have figured." Minner downed his drink. "I wish to God I never got mixed up in this mess."

CHAPTER TWO

Holt could hear the clerks sweeping out the store as he sat in Minner's cluttered office. By this time the news of his ruckus with Walt Short would be all over Rockyhill. Maybe he should have pretended that he hadn't seen Short messing with his gear, but that wasn't his way. The liquor had worked quickly on his empty stomach, and his temper had never been of the best when someone crossed him.

Minner kicked the door shut. "We can go out the back way," he said.

"Why?"

Minner filled his glass. "My first thought is that you might be stupid to ask such a question. Giving you the benefit of the doubt, I'll have to say you're just ignorant of this country."

"I'm getting damned tired of this country, Minner."

"Then you'd better get to hell out of it!"

Holt leaned forward. "You talk too much nonsense," he said. "Start talking sense."

Minner flushed. "What do you want to know?"

"Who killed Niles?"

"No one knows."

"Why did you want me to keep my mouth shut about being willed the ranch?"

"Two reasons. First, Niles told me long ago to do it that way. And even if he hadn't, I would have done it anyway." Minner lit a cigar and eyed Holt over the flame of the match. "You don't know this country. I'll go back and give you a little of the history. Times are rough around here. The big ranchers are against the little ones; the farmer is against the cowman; the cowman is against the sheepman; the cowman is being bled white by the rustler. Bullets are against ballots in this country. Rustlers and small ranchers have been ambushed and killed. Some of them have just vanished. People say they've either been run out of the country—or their bodies haven't been found yet."

They heard the front door bang shut and the key turn in the lock. Minner got up and pulled down the faded window shade.

"Where's the law around here?" Holt asked.

Minner turned. "We've got law all right. The sheriff and his deputies. Association men. Pinkertons. Stock detectives. Crawling all over the county suspecting each other. Getting in each other's way. It'd be comic if it wasn't for the fact that a good many men have been murdered."

"There will always be a certain amount of killings in any county, Minner."

Minner sat down heavily. "Yeah. We know that. But that isn't what bothers everyone. It looks like most of the killings, including Niles', have been done by one man."

"One man! How do they know?"

Minner leaned forward. "The last seven killings seem to prove it. Bullet hole in the back of the head. .38/56 caliber. Every time."

"That doesn't prove anything."

Minner raised his eyebrows. "No? Well, by God, Cooper, you can look all over this town and you won't find a rifle in that caliber. There may have been some before the killings got started but there aren't now."

"You're wrong there," Holt said slowly.

Minner paled. "What do you mean?"

"My Model 1886 is .38/56."

"Did Short know that?"

"I don't see how he could miss."

Minner filled Holt's glass. "Look," he said, "give me power of attorney to sell that damned ranch. Leave a forwarding address. I'll get rid of the spread and settle with you by mail, keeping myself a fair commission. Agreed?"

Holt grinned. "I'm not selling the place until I see it and make sure whether I want it or not."

Minner tapped Holt's knee with a long forefinger. "You *don't* want it. No use in your wasting your time going out there."

"You heard what I said. What's your angle, Minner?"

Sloan Minner flushed. "Niles Williston was my good friend. I don't make friends easily. *Close* friends, that is. Folks around here think I'm somewhat of a stingy curmudgeon. Well, I'm not. Niles knew that. I was always welcome out there until the trouble started, and then Niles warned me to keep out of it."

"Keep out of what?"

"There was trouble. A lot of trouble. You know Niles wasn't the kind of a man to take bull from anyone. Seems to me you're like him in that respect anyway."

"Always have been."

"Niles didn't look for trouble but he sure as hell didn't run away from it neither. Shadow Valley is good land, but it always did have a curse on it."

"I don't get it."

"You will if you stick around long enough. The Indians wouldn't go near it. There was a real nasty killing there in the early days. Niles bought it from the widow of a man who was supposed to have committed suicide. It was hard to get vaqueros to work there. But, like I said, it was good grazing land. Plenty of timber and water. Niles was prospering. Then all hell broke loose around here. The Mannings accused Niles of rustling. They sent men onto his land to check his cattle. Niles ran them off. They were afraid of him."

Holt smiled reminiscently. "Niles would give the devil a run for his money."

"He was all horns, hoofs and rattles. But times got rough. Some of his cattle was run off. He kicked about it to the sheriff. He was told he had probably rustled them in the first place and had gotten rid of them before someone knew he had. He hired three hands from out of the county. Two of them were scared off. The other was shot through the shoulder and eventually lost an arm from gangrene."

"Nice country," said Holt dryly.

Minner nodded. "I wish to God I didn't have every cent I own invested in this place or I'd be somewhere else right now. Anyway, Shadow Valley has a bad name. Niles was working alone with a two-bit herd. He wouldn't even leave the ranch. I used to send Ab Chisum out there with supplies. One day Ab goes out there. House empty. Barn burned to the ground. Horses gone. Ab finds Niles near the west waterhole with a slug through the back of his skull. No tracks. Nothing."

"Except that the slug was a .38/56?"

"Yeah. There was that."

Holt reached for the box of long nines on Minner's desk. He lit up and watched the smoke drift about in the draft.

"Well?" Minner asked.

"I'm staying."

Minner groaned. "Listen," he said. "Niles seemed to know he might get it. That's why he entrusted his will to me. I'm a notary public. Niles told me that if anything happened, I was to contact you. Explain the circumstances and talk you out of taking over the ranch. I can make it look like I sold the estate and sent the money to a distant relative back east. Niles figured it smart. You have different names. You don't look alike. That's why I sent for you. I can clean up this business and wash my hands of it, though God knows I'd like to see Niles avenged."

Holt inspected his cigar. "I've been a drifter ever since

we sold the old man's ranch in the Panhandle. Maybe I should have thrown in with Niles. I was too damned anxious to see the elephant. Together we might have whipped this thing."

"Then you'll leave?"

Holt stood up. "No," he said.

"You're a damn fool!"

"*Gracias*. But this damn fool is going to find the man who killed Niles. That's final, Minner."

CHAPTER THREE

S loan Minner unlocked the rear door of the store and poked his head out like a Christmas turkey awaiting decapitation. "Looks clear," he said softly over his shoulder.

Holt turned sideways to get his saddle through the doorway. "They drygulching here in town too?"

"No. But you got Walt Short's tail in a crack and Walt won't forget it. He always was proud of his fast draw and you sure boogered him tonight."

Holt peered up and down the dark alley. "I'll have to get a room, which means I'll have to walk Front Street."

"You will like hell!"

Holt grinned in the darkness. The older man was sure building up a case. "Maybe you've got a room at your place."

"I have. I've got a horse too. You'll be up and out of here before dawn too, or I'll know the reason why." Minner locked the rear door. "Let me carry that saddle," he suggested.

"I can handle it."

Minner took the hull. "Now carry that war bag in your left hand."

"You figure he might come shooting?"

"Dammit! I don't figure anything around here anymore."

They walked two blocks up the alley, then Minner cut

through to the next street north of Front and stepped up on the porch of a small frame house. "I can fix you grub," he said. "Nothing fancy. Side meat and beans. I don't eat much in the house."

Holt shook his head. "Look, Minner," he said quietly. "I may have caused you trouble in the store. I don't aim to cause you any more by having you take sides with me. I'll go on tonight."

"It's twelve miles out there, Cooper."

"I can stand it if the horse can."

The older man seemed relieved. "All right then. I'll fix you some riding chuck."

"No. I'll eat out at the ranch."

"As you say. Ab Chisum is out there as caretaker."

"Isn't he afraid too?"

Minner shook his head. "Ab knows everybody. Hasn't got an enemy in the county."

Holt walked back to the small barn behind the house. He lit a lantern and saddled the mild roan. He put out the lantern and led the roan back to the street. Minner was still on the porch. "Pokey won't give you any trouble. Don't get much chance to straddle him anymore. He's as gentle as a hound dog."

"I'll send him back with Ab."

Minner nodded. "Follow the road west. Second creek you cross is the Cottonwood. Half a mile beyond the bridge a road cuts south. You're on your own land there. Follow that road about two miles into the valley. The ranch house is below a low bald butte. You can't miss it."

Holt fastened his rifle scabbard and war bag to the saddle. "Thanks for everything," he said.

"I'm not doing you any favors, son."

Holt mounted and thrust out a big hand. "I'd be proud to consider you a friend, Sloan."

The older man shook with him. "You can. Like I said, I don't make friends easy, but you'll sure as hell's fire need one in Rockyhill."

Holt touched the roan with his heels and rode west

along the dark street. The tinny tinkle of a piano drifted to him from the main stem of the town. It was good to feel a horse under him again.

Sloan Minner stood on the porch until Holt was out of sight. Then he shook his head and went into the house. He turned the big Bible on the marble-topped table and opened it at random. Placing a finger on the page, he read aloud in a dry voice: *"The people of the land have used oppression, and exercised robbery, and they have vexed the poor and needy; yea, they have oppressed the stranger wrongfully."*

CHAPTER FOUR

There was a sickly moon in the cloud-dotted sky when Holt Cooper drew rein on a rise and looked for the first time across Shadow Valley. The place was quiet except for the rush of the night wind which moaned softly around the bald butte to the west. Ranch buildings stood out in sharp relief on a grassy slope and a rectangle of yellow light showed starkly in the black bulk of the house.

"Ab must be a nighthawk, Pokey."

The roan slung his hammerhead back and forth as though to agree.

Holt shivered a little in the searching wind. It would soon be time for the fall gather. He built a fresh smoke and touched Pokey with his heels. The valley floor was nearly level except at the far sides. The west side slope was steeper, leveling off into a benchland where the ranch buildings stood almost under the shadow of the butte. The butte itself was rough and stippled with scrub timber and brush. To the south of the valley, he could see dim, humped mountains brooding in the night.

He caught a dull pewter trace beyond the motte of trees which stood to the east side of the valley. The creek wound along the eastern wall of Shadow Valley. The grass was deep everywhere. No wonder Niles Williston had settled down there after several years of wandering. It was just such a place as he had often mentioned to Holt in the old days when they let their imaginations run riot on the ideal spread. Good water, grass and timber. Sheltered from winter winds. From all that Holt could see in the silvery light, it was a lovely place.

A mule bawled from the corral as Pokey passed through the gate at the bottom of the slope. He blew out his brains again as Holt neared the house. The yellow light winked out. Holt drew rein a hundred yards from the house and waited.

There was no sign of life.

"Hello, the house!" he called.

Still no sign of life. Holt felt like a yahoo for coming up on the house like this at night. Then he heard the creak of an opening door. He eased his hand down to his Winchester. There was vague movement in the dark shadow of the porch roof.

"Who is it?" a man called.

"The name is Cooper. Holt Cooper. You Ab Chisum?"

"I know who *I* am. I sure as hell don't know who *you* are."

"Sloan Minner knows me. Name of Holt Cooper."

"Niles Williston's brother?"

It was a surprise to Holt until he realized that Minner must have confided in Chisum and that Chisum had hauled supplies for Niles. "Yes," he said.

"I see yore ridin' Pokey. Guess yore all right. Git down off that hoss and lead him up here."

Holt did as he was told. A short, bench-legged man stepped off the porch and leaned a Winchester against a post. He thrust out a hard little hand to grip Holt's. "It's you all right," he said. "I'da knowed yuh anywhere."

Holt grinned. "You're joshing," he said.

"No. I kin tell. Breed marks, Cooper. Yuh might not look like yore brother to most people. Me, I know people by breed marks. Ears, eyes, noses and suchlike."

"Well, I'll be damned."

Chisum swelled up a little. "I'll take Pokey to the corral.

Go in the house and set. Damned nice of me to ask yuh, ain't it?"

"How so?"

The little man chortled. "Yuh own it, don't yuh?"

Holt laughed. He took his war bag and Winchester into the house. He struck a match and lit an Argand lamp. The living room was like many another he had been in. Field-stone fireplace with antlers above it. Rough furniture, built for wear and not for beauty. A pinto pony hide hung on one wall. An old slant-breech Sharps rested on pegs driven into the long wall.

Holt blew up the fire and placed wood on it. Boots popped on the porch and the little man came in. Ab Chisum had squirrel-bright eyes and when he grinned, his wide mouth cut his brown face in half. "Sure pleased yuh come," he said. "I been feelin' porely. Ain't sleepin' well and I'm off my feed."

It suddenly registered on Holt that he had never eaten that thick steak he had promised himself. "I'm hungry as an Apache," he admitted.

"Fine. I got a beef quarter coolin' in the shed. Built myself some pies today. Set tight. Have a smoke. I'll rustle up the chuck."

The little man was as good as his word. In a remarkably short time, Holt sat down at a table spread with loin beef, beans, biscuits and lick. He ate like a famished coyote and ended up with two slabs of pie.

"Makes a man feel fine to see his chuck et like that," Ab said. "Yuh want to sleep or play the coffee pot awhile?"

Holt fashioned a smoke. "I can't sleep too well when I'm not working," he said. "But that reminds me. You mentioned not sleeping. You worried about being drygulched?"

Chisum shook his head. "Ain't no one after me. Sure, I was friendly with Niles, but I was friendly with everyone else. too. I'll admit this ain't an easy country to stay neutral, as they say, but I've managed so far, and I aim to keep on doin' so."

"Looks like Niles was pretty much on his own then."

The bright eyes held Holt's. "I ain't one of these waddies who'll get hisself kilt fightin' for his boss, if that's what yuh mean."

"I didn't mean it that way."

Chisum shrugged. "Even if I had been it wouldn't have done much good. He was a marked man. It was in the cards. Sometime, someplace they woulda got him."

"They?"

Chisum glanced at the open window and then lowered his voice. "Yuh heard about the killin's from Sloan Minner. Makin' it look like it was the work of one man. Mebbe it was but yuh kin bet your bottom dollar he was paid to do the job."

"Hired killer?"

The little man nodded. "The country is crawlin' with Association men and Pinkertons. Lotsa other sneakin' coyotes as calls themselves stock detectives. Stock detectives! Rustler killers is what they oughta call theirselves!"

"Niles was no sticky looper."

"Never said he was. But he didn't take no hurrahin' from the Mannings nor the Owenses nor anybody else that braced him."

"Owens?"

"Link and Perry Owens. Brothers. They own the spread west of here. Mannings own the spread east of here. Manning land curls around the bottom of this spread and borders on Owens land."

"Why did the Owens brace him?"

"Water trouble. Nothin' really serious but the Owens boys was cobby and so was Niles. Didn't take much for them to tangle horns."

"Nice country."

"Ain't nothin' the matter with the country. It's the dod-dummed people in it, sonny."

"Same thing everywhere."

Ab yawned. "'Bout time to turn in. I suppose yuh want to look over the place."

"Who said I was staying?"

Ab grinned crookedly. "It's writ on the wall in letters of fire. Mebbe gunfire."

Holt dumped his dishes into the roundup pan. "Where do I bunk?"

"Take the big room. I never used it. There's soogans in there." Ab went to a kitchen cupboard and opened it. The shelves were filled with bottles the same size and with the same flamboyant labels. Ab took one from the end and pried off the cap. He drained it and tossed the empty into a box. "Best stuff in the West," he said chokingly.

Holt took one of the bottles from the shelf. "Abyssinian Desert Companion," he read. "Recommended for flux, looseness of the bowels, bots, fevers, fits, the mad staggers, headaches, boils, galls, flatulence and many other troubles common to man. For bots it has no equal." He looked at the bright-eyed Ab. "You suffer from any of these?"

"No. But I ain't about to get any of 'em neither. Take a bottle a day." Chisum thumped his narrow chest. "Sound as a silver dollar."

Holt grinned as he put the bottle back on the shelf. "That why they call you Ab."

"Short for Abyssinia. My real handle is Hardin. Hardin Chisum."

"Well, good night, Ab. I'm dinked."

"Sleep easy, son. Try a bottle of the Companion."

Holt shook his head. "I'll stick to rye, Ab. Thanks just the same."

Tired as he was, Holt lay awake for a long time staring up at the dim ceiling. The wind whispered softly around the log house. From somewhere up on the bald butte a coyote welcomed Holt Cooper to Shadow Valley.

CHAPTER FIVE

Ab Chisum squatted at the edge of the trampled mud border of the waterhole. "That's the spot, Holt. Right there. I found him there at dusk one day. I been into Rocky-hill for supplies. Come back to find the new barn flamin'. All the hosses was gone includin' Niles' bay. I was some worried, I tell yuh. So I goes to find him. I did. Right here. Bullet in the back of his head. The coroner dug it out. .38/56."

Holt squatted beside the little man in the hoof-pocked mud. "Did you cut for sign?"

Ab wet his lips. "Yeah."

"Find anything?"

"No."

Holt turned his head to look at Chisum. "I'm not about to call you a liar, Ab."

Ab rubbed his bristly jaw. "What do yuh mean?"

Holt stood up. "I just have a feeling you haven't told the whole story."

Ab spat into the mud. He shifted his chew. "Waal. Yore his brother. I kin tell yuh. Come on up here a piece." Chisum walked along the rim of the pool and started up a brushy slope. Three hundred yards from the waterhole he stopped. Holt stopped beside him. They were about a hundred feet above the pool level. Behind them loomed the rough hills.

Ab pointed his toe at the ground. "I found somethin' right here the day after the killin'."

"So?"

"There was an empty .38/56 hull here. That's what made me come up here. The sun was shinin' on it. But there was somethin' else. Right here." Ab placed his foot on a rock. "It was a footprint. A nekkid footprint, Holt."

A jay chattered from a tree overlooking the slope. The sun warmed Holt's back. It was all so damned peaceful.

"There," Ab said. "I knew yuh wouldn't think it made sense."

"I didn't say that, Ab."

"But yuh kin see why I wouldn't tell anyone. Any man as would walk over this ground with nekkid feet would have to be loco."

Holt nodded. "Or he didn't want to leave boot tracks."

"So he left *feet* prints."

"The difference is that he was so damned anxious not to leave boot prints he went barefoot and figured he was safe enough."

Ab spat. "The print weren't easy to see. Yuh know how it is. If the sun is just right sometimes yuh kin see an outline. Yuh coulda come up here a dozen times in the same day and never seen it, lessn' yuh was part Injun."

"I'll buy that."

"Gives a man a queer turn to think of that dry-gulcher lying up here waiting for Niles. Mebbe he was here for hours. Days even."

"You figure it was not an impulse?"

Ab tossed a stone up and down in his right hand. "Let's put it thisaway: Niles didn't make no friends around here outside of Minner and me. He was rough as a cob on anybody that fooled around here. The Mannings hated his guts, and he wasn't exactly loved by the Owens boys. The thing as sticks in my craw is that the Owens boys are fighters from who laid the chunk. If they had it heavy against Niles, they woulda braced him one at a time. Six-shooters, Winchesters or fists."

"And the Mannings?"

Ab tossed the stone at the chattering jay. "Lew is a fighter right enough. Drake is a good man with a Colt, but he's got a yella streak or my name ain't Abyssinia Chisum." Ab scratched his jaw. "Still, Niles was kilt just like the others was—.38/56 in the back of the head. No tracks. No trace."

Holt looked down the long sunlit slope. It took a good shot to hit a man's head at that range with a saddle gun. He felt cold despite the warmth of the day. The .38/56 soft-point packed a tremendous wallop.

"Yuh wanta continue the Grand Tour?"

Holt nodded. They walked down to their horses and rode south toward the far limits of the range. Only a few cattle dotted the valley. Herefords, Durhams, and some crosses.

"Two years ago, Niles had over three hundred head," Ab said. "Last year he was down to one hundred an' fifty or so at the fall gather. Damned near mint him he said, bein' as he wasn't grass-bellied with *dinero*. This spring there weren't no more than a hundred of 'em. There may be some in the breaks but I dunno. Like as not they've strayed over on other ranges. I can't run the dod-dummed ranch all alone. Leastways on what Sloan Minner pays me. He's stingy enough to skin a flea for its hide and taller."

"I'd like you to stay on, Ab."

The little man looked sideways. "Yuh aim to ranch then?"

"I'm not selling."

"Then you'll get the squeeze the same as Niles did. I just hope to God yuh don't get paid off with a .38/56 bottleneck."

Nothing more was said until they stopped their horses to let them blow on the eastern rim of the valley. Ab thrust out an arm. "That's all Manning land down there. The MM Connected."

Holt fashioned a smoke. "I never paid much attention to Niles' brand."

"Diamond W."

"I like it."

Ab shrugged. "Niles useta have NW Connected. He changed the brand when he was sparkin' Vivian Leslie.

Seems he sent plumb to Cheyenne for a diamond ring, figurin' he'd brand Viv with it. Even changed his dod-dummed brand to Diamond W, he was so light in the head about that filly."

Holt's hand had stopped halfway to his cigarette with the match flaring in the wind. "Niles? Sparking a woman?"

"What the hell yuh expect him to spark?" Ab asked testily.

"Dammit!" Holt dropped his match as it seared his fingers.

Ab grinned. "Surprised yuh, eh? Waal, I'll allow Niles wasn't much of a ladies' man, but Viv Leslie was a fine lookin' female. Kinda tall for a woman, leastways the kind I like. Dark hair and eyes. I always thought she had some Injun blood in her. She liked Niles in a way. Never told him she was leavin' town."

"When did all this happen?"

"'Bout a year ago. Niles was off his feed for a week. Never seen a man take it so hard."

"Seems like there was a lot about Niles I didn't know," Holt said, and then noticed Ab squinting down at the Manning range. Three horsemen had broken from a motte of cottonwoods near a small creek. They rode steadily toward the ridge.

"Comp'ny," Ab said.

"Who are they?"

Ab stood up in his stirrups and studied the trio. "Lew and Drake Manning. That's Caleb Clarke with 'em." He sat down. "Yuh better think of a story."

"Why?"

"From what yuh told me happened in Rockyhill last evenin', I think Lew already knows yore takin' over the Diamond W."

"So?"

"He wants this range. Never got anywheres with Niles like I said. Mebbe he figgers he kin talk yuh out of it."

"He'll have some talking to do."

Ab spat. "He ain't exactly the kinda man who hides his light under no bushel. Still, Lew is pretty fair when it comes to business."

Holt kneed his horse close to Ab. "As far as you're concerned, Ab. I'm only interested in buying this spread. I'm not Niles' half-brother."

"I get it." Ab rolled another smoke. "Sloan Minner is goin' to have some explainin' to do to Lew though."

"How so?"

"Lew's been pesterin' him to sell the spread to him. He wants it so bad he can taste it. If'n Lew knew yuh was Niles' half-brother he wouldn't take it so hard. This way he's goin' to figger Sloan pulled a fast one on him. Lew don't like anyone to grease around him."

Holt shifted in his saddle. He could tell by the way the three men rode that they meant business.

CHAPTER SIX

They came up the slope and drew rein ten feet from Holt and Ab. Lew Manning was squat and burly with a beak of a nose that jutted out from his square face like the bill of a bald eagle. His Boss Stetson was set squarely across his brows, shading bold black eyes that could have belonged to an Indian brave.

"You Holt Cooper?" he asked.

"I am."

"I hear you're thinking of buying the Diamond W."

Holt took his sack of Ridgewood from his shirt pocket and began to build a smoke.

"Well?" Manning snapped.

"I didn't get the name," said Holt softly.

The second man of the trio was dressed to the nines in the height of town cowpoke fashion. He wore twin Colts on a buscadero belt. Thin lines formed at the corners of his full-lipped mouth. "He's Lew Manning," he said loudly. "Everybody around here knows my cousin Lew."

Holt lit up, eyeing the two cousins above the flare of his lucifer. "Who're you?" he asked casually.

The handsome face tightened. "Drake Manning!"

Holt lowered his hand. "Pleased to meet you," he said.

Lew jerked his head. "Shut up, Drake," he said. "I didn't come up here to pass the time of day."

"What did you come up here for?" Holt asked.

"I want this range. Sloan Minner knows it. The whole damn county knows it. Minner should have given me first choice."

"That so?"

Manning's big hands gripped his saddle pommel. "Don't play cosy with me, Cooper. What's your angle? Where you from?"

"I don't have any angle other than I want this place and aim to take it. I'm from Texas."

Drake Manning spat. "A Texan is considered just as good as a white man around here as long as he behaves."

Holt raised his head a little.

"Maybe you'd like to back up what you just said, Manning. Make your play if you've got the guts."

Lew Manning kneed his horse in between them. "Dammit! I come up here to talk business, not to get on the peck. You had no call to say that, Drake. You ain't got the sense God gave a rat."

"Go to hell!" Drake Manning said.

Caleb Clarke had dropped his right hand against his gun belt buckle. His blue eyes never shifted from Holt.

Lew Manning raised a thick hand as though to strike his cousin. Then he controlled himself. "I shoulda known better than to bring you along on a business deal," he said. "Git!"

Drake bit his lower lip. "All right, Lew," he said. "Do it *your* way. You always do anyway. Come on, Cal."

The two men rode down the slope looking back over their shoulders. Lew Manning felt for a cigar and lit it. "Pay no mind to him, Cooper," he said. "He's young and ringy. He don't like to take pills from no one but he takes them from me. I took him in when his folks passed on. Give him too much money and freedom, I guess. I'll apologize for him."

"The next time he shoots his mouth off," Holt said, "he'll either apologize himself or back his play."

Manning sucked at his cigar. "All right! All right!" he said angrily. "We know you're a fast man, Cooper. Everybody in Rockyhill knows how you took care of Walt Short last night. But don't throw your weight around too much. There are other good men around here."

"I imagine," Holt said dryly.

Manning hooked a leg about his saddle horn. "I'm not interested in gunplay. I'm interested in business. Now I want the Diamond W. Why don't you go somewheres else and look for a spread?"

"I like this one."

Lew Manning inspected his cigar. "It's got a bad name," he said quietly. "Killings and suchlike."

"Most ranges have had at least one killing."

"Not like these."

"What do you mean?"

"Nothing. Nothing at all. Tell you what I'll do. You forget about this place, and I'll pay you five hundred in cash."

"You can bid for it with Minner."

"*That* sonofabitch? He wouldn't give me the time of day. He's got the right to sell the place. Seems like Williston has some relatives back East. He left the place to them and they ain't interested in it. Well—*I am!*"

"So am I," Holt said. "I'm going to take it over, Manning."

Manning threw away his cigar. "All right! All right! Buck me! But before you buy, you think it over. Think it over for twenty-four hours, and then if you're damned fool enough to buy it, go ahead!"

"I aim to. I don't need twenty-four hours."

"So?" Manning said softly. "*I'm* saying you *do*." He circled his horse and touched it with his spurs. "Remember that, Cooper."

"I'll remember," Holt said.

Ab Chisum shoved back his hat and wiped the sweat from his forehead. "My God," he said. "I could smell the flowers and hear the organ playin' Abide with Me."

"I thought there might be gunplay," Holt admitted. "For

future, reference, how good is Drake Manning?"

"He practices all the time. Poker chip draw and such like. He's pretty good. So is Lew. Come to think of it, there ain't a man on the MM that ain't better than average."

Holt turned Pokey. "Let's go home," he said.

They crossed the sunlit valley toward the ranch house. The sun glinted from the windows and shone down on the blackened outline of the barn which had been burned.

"I'm riding into town this afternoon," said Holt.

"Why? The dod-dummed ranch is yours, ain't it?"

"I want it to look like I bought it."

"You got a loco streak, Holt."

"Maybe."

They reached the fence which surrounded the buildings. "Go get some chuck," Holt said.

"Where you goin' now?"

Holt indicated the two graves situated in a sunny glade. "Up there, Ab."

"Keno." The little man rode toward the house.

Holt ground-reined Pokey and walked up to the graves. The first one had a simple wooden headboard marked *Samuel Chase 1845-1886 Gone From This Earth To His Reward In Heaven.* The second had a marble stone marked *Niles E. Williston 1849-1889.* There was no inscription.

Holt took off his hat. It was hard to realize that big Niles lay quietly under that sod. Holt had always taken him for granted. He had always thought he knew Niles like a primer book. He had never known him to pay much attention to any women other than the occasion doxies he took up with when he went on a high lonesome. Holt wondered what Vivian Leslie was like. She must have had something above the ordinary.

Holt picked up a striated stone and placed it on the grave. Then he walked slowly down to his horse and led him down to the corral. The wind freshened as he turned the old roan into the corral. It brought with it the odor of drying grasses and fall flowers. The sun was warm, beating gently down on the wide valley. It all seemed so peaceful.

CHAPTER SEVEN

The sun glinted from the waters of the creek and flashed now and then from a shining leaf in the row of trees which bordered the creek. Holt drew rein and looked over the sagging rail of the old bridge. A fish darted for cover as Holt's shadow fell over the rippling surface of the water. Holt shoved back his hat and felt for the makings. He was in no hurry to get to Rockyhill. He rolled his smoke. Pokey jerked as a fly bit home.

Holt lit up and raised his head. Something glinted on a knoll beyond the east bank of the creek. Too bright for a leaf reflection. He eyed the knoll. Pokey eased away from the bridge rail. Then Holt slid sideways, throwing his right leg high to clear the saddle as he jerked his Winchester from its scabbard. The rifle flatted off on the knoll. Pokey jerked and reared as the slug whipped across his shaggy rump.

Holt hit the bridge flooring hard, squirting dust from between the planks. He rolled toward the far end of the bridge as the rifle cracked again. This time the slug gouged into the flooring. A splinter lanced into Holt's right cheek, bringing tears to his eyes. He shook his head as he cleared the bridge and rolled into the brush, levering a round into the chamber.

Pokey was off down the road, heading for Rockyhill and his quiet stall behind Sloan Minner's house.

Holt slid the rifle barrel through the brush and cuddled the stock against his cheek. He could feel the blood run down his jaw as he plucked out the jagged splinter.

His eyes still swam. Then he saw the movement. A thickness in the shadows. He fired, cursing because he knew he had missed. The rifle report died away in the hills.

Then it was quiet again with little sound other than the murmuring of the shallow creek and the soughing of the wind in the willows.

Holt waited fifteen minutes and then bellied through the brush. In twenty minutes, he reached a place where he could see the knoll. He Indianed up on it, cursing the stones which ripped the knees out of his best pair of pants. He eased up behind a thick cottonwood. The view was good. He saw no one, nor had he heard the distant thud of retreating hoofs.

He walked up on the knoll and squatted behind a bush. The sun shone on an empty brass hull. He picked it up. It was a bottle-necked .38/56 hull, the same type his Winchester used. He slipped it into his pocket and worked his way down the far side of the knoll. He walked carefully through the murmuring trees. Two hundred yards from the knoll he found a soft spot where the creek had overflowed. Three imprints showed on the ground. Imprints of the bare toes of a running man.

He circled the soft spot. Another two hundred yards brought him to the edge of the trees. He found a pile of fresh horse droppings.

He stood there for a long time looking out across the open country. The only sign of life was a ragged hawk circling high over a ridge. As he watched the hawk, he saw it suddenly dip and then shoot off down the wind as though disturbed.

Holt walked back to the road. Old Pokey was grazing quietly, jerking as the flies settled on the fresh blood on his dusty rump.

Holt mounted and touched the roan with his spurs. He looked to the south. The hawk was long gone, and so was the man who had killed Niles Williston.

Holt mounted and clattered the bridge at the eastern edge of Rockyhill. The moon had not yet risen, and...

CHAPTER EIGHT

T he moon had not yet risen when Holt clattered over the bridge at the western edge of Rockyhill. The mingled odors of smoke and cooking food hung over the town. Lamps glowed in the houses and stores. Holt rode easily down the center of Front Street. A woman hurried past carrying a paper sack of groceries. Two boys loitered near the blacksmith shop. A drunk lay in the bed of a ramshackle spring wagon. It seemed like a quiet evening in Rockyhill.

Holt swung down from Pokey in front of Minner's store. He walked in. One of the clerks looked up. "Evenin'," he said, then paled a little as he recognized Holt. "Mr. Minner is in his office," he said.

Holt walked back through the cluttered aisle and tapped on the office door. Minner's crabby voice told him to come in.

Minner was sitting at his desk. He had a welt on his left cheek. "You!" he said.

Holt grinned as he sat down. "What's riling you, old hoss?"

Minner spat angrily into the cuspidor. "I wish to God you'd stayed out of Wyoming," he said. "Nothing but trouble since you got off the train."

Holt helped himself to a super and lit it. "What's happened now?"

"Lew Manning came by my place night before last. Braced me about buying the Diamond W. By God his eyes looked like the open windows of hell when I told him you were going to take it over. Then this afternoon he came back with Drake and braced me again. What the hell did you do out there?"

"I talked to Lew."

"There must have been some trouble, then."

"There was a little," Holt admitted.

Minner touched his bruised cheek. "That sonofabitch Drake waled me one when I told him to mind his own damned business. I don't like this, Cooper. Why don't you tell people that you're Niles' brother?"

"I'm not ready yet."

"When *will* you be?"

Holt took the cigar from his mouth. "When the time suits me."

Minner grunted. "Puts me in a hell of a spot."

"It might be worse if they knew."

"They will! I have to take care of the legal matters. Then they'll know you were willed the Diamond W."

"When?"

"I can't stall too long."

"Once you file, they'll know who I really am."

"Yes."

"Then stall on it."

"Good God! You want me to get waled again?"

"I'll see that you don't."

"Yeah! All I have to do is send for you when the Mannings show up. By that time, I'll have a broken jaw."

Holt leaned back in his chair. "Who is Vivian Leslie?" he asked.

Minner flushed. "Ab tell you about her?"

Holt nodded.

"Always did talk too much. I think that rotgut he drinks has addled his brain."

"That may be. You didn't answer my question."

Minner lit a cigar and reached for a bottle. He filled two glasses. "Vivian showed up here a little over a year ago. Fine looking woman, although not the type I'd hanker after. Too much woman, if you know what I mean."

"Yes."

"Niles went for her in a big way."

"I know all that. But who was she?" Minner shrugged. "No one knows where she came from. She had some money when she came here. Lived high on the hog at the Stockmen's Hotel. Then she went broke. Quite a few of the boys got an itch for her. Drake Manning. Niles. Niles seemed to have the inner track. Drake insulted her one night. Niles like to beat Drake's head off one night in the Stockmen's Bar. Took two men to get Niles off of him. Drake drew on Niles, but Lew stopped him before any shooting started. It was a mess."

"Seems as though Niles was ready to marry her."

"Yes. I ordered the ring from Cheyenne. He even changed his brand to Diamond W in honor of the occasion."

"An occasion that never came off."

"Yeah," Minner said dryly. He downed his drink. "She left town on the quiet one night. I heard later she was in Denver and had gotten married. Later I heard she had died of pneumonia after a sickness. I never told Niles."

Holt leaned back. "I'm one of the initiated now."

"How so?"

"Someone shot at me twice near Cottonwood Creek while I was coming into town."

"Twice?"

Holt looked narrowly at Minner. "Yes. Why?"

Minner refilled his glass. "Nothing. Drink up."

"Here's the empty hull, Sloan."

".38/56."

"Keno."

Minner rubbed his lean jaw. "Now you see what I mean. Why don't you pull out? I can sell the place for a good price. A fair commission is all I ask."

"To Manning?"

Minner looked away. "Who else? He'd kill me if I let anyone else get it."

"You already did."

"No use asking you to go again. You'll end up like Niles."

"Maybe."

"Dammit I *know!*"

Holt stood up. "I'm staying. I'll need supplies. Flour. Sugar. Frijoles. Coffee and canned milk. Side meat. Couple cartons of Ridgewood and some supers. Plenty of dried fruit. 'Bout four boxes .38/56 cartridges and two of .44s for my Colt."

"You'd better get rid of that damned .38/56."

Holt shook his head. "I'll need a hoss."

"See Lem Condon down at the livery. Tell him I sent you. Lem will give you a good deal."

"*Gracias,* Sloan."

Minner stood up. "You might never live long enough to eat all that chuck," he said gloomily.

"I'll take that chance. Where's the newspaper office?"

Minner stared at him. "Corner of Front and Cottonwood. Why?"

"Nothing. Just want to know where it is."

Minner sighed. He walked to the door of the office and watched Holt walk through the long store.

At the *Clarion* office, Holt found a baldheaded little man working alone. "Evening," the little man said.

"I'm Holt Cooper. New owner of the Diamond W. I'd like to enter a subscription."

"Twenty-five cents a month, Mr. Cooper."

Holt placed three silver dollars on the counter. "Put me down for a year. Can I look through your morgue or are you getting ready to close?"

The little man laughed. "When does a newspaper close? We go to press tonight. I'll show you the morgue." As Holt followed him into a back room, he spoke over his shoulder. "I'm Judson Millar, owner of the *Clarion.*"

"Pleased," Holt said.

"Can I help you?"

"No. I just want to get acquainted with some recent history around Rockyhill."

Millar leaned against the wall. "I can help you. They call me the local history book around here."

"I might call on you some time. Don't let me keep you from your work."

"I'd rather talk."

Holt shook his head. "Some other time, Millar. Now, if you'll excuse me—"

Millar sighed and left him alone.

Holt worked through the issues of the last four months. There was no need to read about Niles' murder. Minner had sent him copies of the paper which dealt with Niles' story. But Holt was curious about the other mysterious killings. Somewhere there might be a peg on which to hang a clue.

The records were striking in their similarity. Small ranchers living in the vicinity of the Manning spread and the Owens' ranch. Suspicion of rustling. Trouble with the Mannings and Owenses. Shot down from behind. .38/56 caliber rifle had been used for the killings. No trace of the killer or killers.

Holt turned a page and paused to examine the picture of a dark-haired woman on the society section. Miss Vivian Leslie, the caption stated, a visitor in our fair town, now residing at the Stockmen's Hotel. Miss Leslie was from Denver and was in Rockyhill for an indefinite period of time.

Holt rolled a smoke and leaned back in his chair. She was a looker, all right. But there was something about her that might have warned a man with more experience about women than Niles had possessed.

Holt walked into the front office. "Thanks, Millar," he said.

"No trouble. Come any time. I'd like a news item about you, Mr. Cooper."

"Some other time, Millar."

"Well, good luck with the Diamond W."

"Thanks. Good night, Millar."

There was a feeling of rain in the night air as Holt rode across the bridge at the edge of town. The big dun paced easily. He ought to, Holt thought. He sure cost enough.

Holt reached down and eased his Winchester in its scabbard. The rain started when he was half a mile from the town. He took his slicker from the cantle and shrugged into it, leaving the front open for easy access to his Colt.

CHAPTER NINE

The rain-laden wind slapped steadily at the log walls of the house. In the little kitchen, a roof leak dripped monotonously into a pan set on the table. The steady banging of the barn door came to Holt as he dried the last dish from the roundup pan and placed it on the shelf. The place was damned lonely without gabby Ab Chisum. The little man had left at noon with the buckboard to get the supplies Holt had ordered from Sloan Minner. Holt grinned as he remembered Ab storing away two bottles of Abyssinian Desert Companion beneath his worn slicker to fortify himself for the long trip.

The rain had been beating down steadily all day after a night of intermittent showers. The creek was rising, and the cattle had drifted into shelter. The wind was cold and boisterous.

Holt lit a cigar and listened to the banging of the barn door. The house was so comfortable that he hated the thought of plowing across to the barn. He emptied his coffee cup and reached for the pot to refill the cup. "Dammit," he said. "I might just as well close that door or it'll keep me awake all night."

He reached for his slicker and hat and put them on. He opened the door and stepped out onto the streaming back porch. Then he reached inside and took his Colt from its holster and thrust it beneath his belt.

The wind drove past him, banging open the kitchen door. Glass tinkled as the Argand lamp was swept to the floor, crashing in ruin with a stink of hot oil. Holt went back in to make sure the flames were out. He didn't bother to light another lamp.

He walked across the windy yard to the barn and went inside. The big dun nickered. "How are you, Panhandle?" asked Holt.

Holt checked the west windows of the barn, making sure they were tight. The roof was dripping in a dozen places. He shifted Ab's mouse-colored horse into the stall next to Panhandle and then patiently rigged an old tarp to keep the leaks from bothering the two horses.

There was a rumble of thunder and a flash of lightning as he walked to the door and stepped outside. He closed the door and stood with his back against it, watching the wild electrical charges lancing into the bald butte. It was one hell of a night to be outside.

Holt hunched into his slicker and walked across to the front of the house. He ducked under the sluicing water pouring from the roof. He turned to look across the streaming valley, lit by occasional eerie flashes of lightning, and then went into the house. He took off his slicker and hat and hung them up. The fire was smoldering low in the fireplace. He crossed to it to stir it up and then stopped short. A sixth sense rang a warning in his mind.

Holt stopped by the door which opened into the hallway which in turn led to the kitchen. He waited, thinking that the loneliness of the place might be working on his nerves. The stories Minner had told him hadn't helped any. The Indians wouldn't go near the valley. A man had committed suicide there. The waddies didn't like to work there. Ab had made it worse with his tall tales of ghosts and mysterious noises out of the dark nights.

He gripped the butt of his Colt, reassuring himself with the solid feeling of the worn wood. Then he eased into the dark hallway and padded halfway to the kitchen. He stopped. Minutes ticked past and then he heard a scuffling noise. Some animal was in the kitchen rustling up some chuck. Still, he remembered he had closed the door tightly after the wind smashed the lamp.

His breathing seemed loud in the stillness. He went to the door and listened. There was no sound. He placed his hand softly on the doorknob. Something bumped against the table. It was a faint noise, barely audible above the lash of the wind.

Holt threw back the door and jumped into the kitchen, raising the Colt. Faint light issued from the ill-fitting door of the big stove. Something moved hurriedly toward the back door. Holt kicked a chair aside and closed in on a figure. Then he heard the doorknob turn.

The lightning flashed and he looked into the staring eyes of a woman, the eyes seemed like black marbles in the intensely white face. Then suddenly the kitchen was plunged into darkness again. Holt stood there as though transfixed. He had seen that face before. *Vivian Leslie.* But she was dead.

The woman, or ghost, moved swiftly. Holt instinctively threw up his right arm. Metal scraped on his gun barrel and there was a biting pain in his right wrist. He felt warm blood run down his forearm as he hit the woman with his left shoulder, dropped the Colt and gripped the slim wrist above the knife.

They struggled in the darkness, breathing hard. The knife pinked his right shoulder before he twisted it viciously from her grasp and threw her back against the door. She slumped at his feet and screamed wildly.

Holt stepped back, flicking blood from his hand. He felt for matches and lit the spare lamp. She lay on the floor with her face toward the door. Holt kicked the bloodstained knife under the table. He knelt beside her and turned her around. She looked up into his face and fainted dead away.

The thunder seemed to chuckle uproariously as he picked her up, feeling the softness of her beneath the soaked clothing. He carried her into the living room and placed her on the couch. The woman must have been out in the rain for hours. He wasted no time in fueling up the fire and going into his room for warm soogans.

She was still out when he came back. He set to work, stripping the soaked clothing from her. Her skin was smooth and like ivory. He dried her with a towel and then wrapped her in the soogans. Then he stepped back to look down into the oval face. No wonder Niles Williston had gone haywire over her. Holt knew damned well he hadn't been the only one.

She opened her eyes as he set the broth on the marble-topped table. Then she looked down at her pile of soaked clothing. "Who are you?" she asked shakily.

"Holt Cooper."

"I—I thought the house was empty."

"You could have seen the light in the barn."

"I didn't."

Holt shrugged. He squatted beside her. "Try some of this," he said.

"Thanks."

She ate greedily. Holt placed the bowl on the table. "Coffee?" he asked.

"No thanks." She looked up at the ceiling. The rain was lashing down as though determined to drive the house down into the mud. "My horse is near the creek. She broke her leg."

Holt reached for his slicker and hat.

"You didn't ask who I was," she said.

"I know. You're Vivian Leslie."

The big eyes were half veiled. She nodded. "You know me then?"

"I know of you."

Her eyes flickered, then. Holt smiled. "Stay tight," he said. "I'll take care of the mare."

The wind lashed at him all the way across to the roaring creek. The lightning showed him the mare. She was down on her side, lying still as the rain pelted her. She was far gone. Holt guessed she had been ridden into exhaustion before she had broken her leg. He shoved back his hat and drew out his Colt. She did not move as he placed the muzzle close to her head. The thunder almost drowned out the flat crack of the big six-shooter. The mare hardly moved as she died.

Holt always felt a little sick when he had to finish off an animal. He turned away and trudged across to the slope. He looked at the house. Where had she come from? Minner had said she was reported dead. He shook his head ruefully as he thought of the turn she had given him there in the kitchen when the lightning revealed her pale face and staring eyes. But then another thought took hold as he remembered her body as he had seen it stripped of the soaked clothing.

She was lying back against the arm of the couch when he came in. "Do you work for Niles?" she asked.

He hesitated. "Didn't you know about him?" he asked.

"I've been out of this area for a long time."

Holt hung up his slicker and sat down in a chair. "Niles is dead," he said. "Shot from the back."

She placed a hand at her white throat. "My God," she said. "Who did it?"

"No one knows."

"When did it happen?"

"Some weeks ago."

She looked away from him. "He was a good man."

"Why did you leave him then?"

She started. "You know about that? Of course, you do. Everybody around here does."

"Why did you come back?"

"To see him."

Holt rolled a smoke. "Cigarette?"

She nodded. He placed it between her full lips and lit it. She drew the smoke in gratefully. "I should say I'm sorry about him. I am. But my marrying him wouldn't have stopped a killing."

"You seem pretty sure of that."

"I'm not the only one who thought so. Niles was looking for it. He got it. It's as simple as that."

There seemed to be a coldness in her not engendered by the soaking she had undergone. She sat up and the comforter slid down, revealing the swelling of her breasts. She made no effort to pull it up. The faint odor of perfume drifted to Holt from her warming flesh. He stood up. "I'll dry out your clothes," he said.

He looked at the garments curiously as he hung them up behind the old wood-heater. They were of fine material. A traveling dress of serge, a chemise, embroidered drawers and long black hose. She travels in the latest styles for a ghost, Holt thought. He hung up the long black shawl beside the other clothing. Then he picked up the knife. It was a fine Mex *cuchillo* with engraved blade and silver-wire wrapped handle. He placed it atop a cabinet. He filled two cups with coffee and took them into the living room. She eyed him from under heavy lids as he placed the cups on a stool beside the couch. Her perfume enveloped her as if it were part of her.

Holt poked the fire. "You're a long way from anywhere," he said over his shoulder.

"I came from Lupine Gap," she said.

"That's south of here."

"Yes. I left Bedloe this morning."

"Alone?"

She smiled as he turned. "I'm used to it."

"Quite a ride through those brakes on a sidesaddle."

She shrugged shapely bare shoulders. "I learned to ride before I learned to walk," she said.

"Still, it's a long rough trip for a woman, particularly in a downpour like this."

She did not answer.

Holt sipped his coffee. "You can rest here tonight. Ab will be back in the morning with the buckboard. I'll have him drive you into Rockyhill."

"No!" she said sharply.

He looked quickly at her.

"I'm sorry," she said.

"I can have him take you back to Bedloe. But it will take three days by road."

She sipped her coffee. "Do you own this place now?"

"Yes."

"I'm surprised Lew Manning didn't grab it."

"You know about that then?"

"I lived in Rockyhill last year. I know all about the hell's delight which has been going on around here," she said bitterly.

He nodded. "It's late," he said. "You'd better get some rest. With that soaking you could catch your death."

She drew the soogan about her and finished her coffee. She stood up and then swayed. Holt gripped her and held her up. "I'm weaker than I thought I was," she said.

He picked her up. She was a real bundle of woman. He carried her into his room and placed her on the big double bed. Suddenly she placed an arm about his neck and drew him down to meet her full lips. She kissed him and held on tightly for one so tired. "Thanks again," she said sleepily.

Holt covered her with blankets. Queer fires raging through him, but he left the room. He lay for a long time on Ab's hard bed, listening to the rain drum on the old roof. He could see now why Niles had gone loco over her. It was a long time before he dropped off to sleep.

CHAPTER TEN

The rain had died out during the night, leaving bright pools in the grassy meadows along the rushing creek. Holt was up early, inspecting the damage done during the storm. He turned the horses into the corral, for the old barn was soaked and damp. That was one job he had to do—build a new barn or put a new roof on the old one.

A horseman was making heavy going up the muddy road. Holt walked down to the Texas gate and waited for him. The man drew rein fifty feet from Holt. "You're Holt Cooper, ain'tcha?" he asked.

"Yes."

"I'm Pete Disken from the Box RB. Ab Chisum give me a message for yuh."

"Shoot, Pete."

"Seems like Ab got mired down just outside of Rockyhill. Broke a wheel and a axle. He says to tell yuh he'll be along as soon as he can git the rig fixed."

"Thanks, Pete. How about some jamoka?"

Disken shook his head. "I'm late gettin' back," he said. He grinned. "I went on a high lonesome in Rockyhill last Friday. Just come around yesterday afternoon. Don't remember a thing but they tell me I had one hell of a good time. I'm wonderin' now whether old man Birney will fire me."

"I'll need hands," Holt said. "Come back here if you're fired."

"That's right nice of yuh, but if he fires me, I'll travel on. Got a hankerin' to see Utah anyways."

Something in his tone told Holt that he wouldn't work at the Diamond W for twice the wages. "I've heard it's hard to get waddies to work here," Holt said.

Disken felt for the makings. Holt tossed him a full sack of Ridgewood. "Thanks, Cooper," he said. "Yeah. The Diamond W ain't too popular. Lots of queer stories about this place."

"Old and new ones," Holt said.

Disken wet his cigarette paper and rolled the cylinder. He placed the smoke between his lips and looked keenly at Holt. "You've hit it," he said. "Killin's and suchlike. Started before that though. Seems as though the place always had a bad name." Disken lit up. "Things come in threes," he said darkly.

"What do you mean?"

Disken raised his head and flicked away the match. "Sam Chase hung hisself here—leastways they *said* he hung hisself. Missus Chase sells the place to Niles Williston. Williston loses the filly he figgers on hitchin' up to, then he gets it in the back of the head. Now you're here. Things come in threes."

"I'm not superstitious."

"No?" Disken spat. "Well, it don't make a damned bit of difference whether a man's superstitious or not. Shadow Valley ain't right, nor will it ever be. They's a curse on the place, pretty as it is."

Holt shrugged. Vivian was still asleep. If Disken saw her, there would be some juicy gossip in Rockyhill and the whole damned county. "I'm much obliged to you, *amigo*."

"No trouble a-tall."

Disken waved a hand and rode down toward the valley

road. Then he turned and rested a hand on his saddle cantle. "Whyn't yuh sell to Lew Manning?" he called back.

"I thought you said the place was jinxed."

"It is. That's why I'd like to see Lew and that Goddamned cousin of his here. See you, Cooper."

Holt watched the Box RB man disappear around a curve. He frowned as he walked up to the house. It was the first time anyone had hinted that Sam Chase had been other than a suicide.

Holt opened the kitchen door. The odor of cooking came to him. Vivian Leslie was at the big range. "Be ready in a minute," she said as she pushed back a lock of her hair.

Holt took off his hat and sat down. "I figured on cooking for you," he said. "How do you feel?"

"Wonderful. The air here is so good. This is a perfect place, Holt."

Holt snubbed out his smoke. "Yes. Why didn't you marry Niles Williston when you had the chance and take over here?"

She whirled. "Damn you!" she said.

Holt leaned back in his chair. "Sorry. I was just curious."

She bit her lip. "Look, Holt, as long as I'm here I'll try to get along with you. But don't talk about Niles Williston!"

He said nothing.

"What was Niles to you?" she asked.

"You said you didn't want to talk about him."

"Set the table," she said. "I'm hungry."

He eyed the simple gingham dress she wore. "I didn't see that last night," he said.

"I found it in a closet. I suppose Mrs. Chase left it here."

The dress looked as though she had been poured into it. Holt couldn't imagine her coming through those rough hills to the south on horseback through a downpour. "I'll get your saddle and saddlebags after breakfast," he said.

"I'll go with you."

"You'll stay here!"

She filled two plates. "Why?" she asked after a time.

"Niles Williston may be dead, but Drake Manning isn't."

"So?"

"You know of the trouble that's been going on around here. You know Williston had trouble with the Mannings and Owenses. Well, it seems as though I've inherited some of that trouble. I don't know how much Drake Manning was interested in you, but I know well enough that if he knows you're here it won't make things any easier on me."

She sat down across from him. "So you'll hide me here until you can get rid of me."

"I'm not running a boardinghouse for women, Vivian."

She did not speak until they were through eating. Then she stood up. "All right," she said. "I'll stay out of sight. When will your man be back?"

"Late today or early tomorrow, I'd say."

"I'll be ready to leave then."

Holt emptied his coffee cup and built a smoke. She busied herself with the dishes. After a time, he left and got his horse and rode to the creek.

He managed to get the sidesaddle off the dead mare by cutting the girth. He loaded saddle and saddlebags onto Panhandle and then rummaged through a saddlebag. It held a box of cosmetics, extra linen, mirror, hairbrushes and combs. He unstrapped the second bag, thrust in a hand and drew out a small pistol. A New Line Pocket Model Colt, caliber .41. The sun glinted from the nickel-plated barrel. Holt hefted the little handgun.

"Prostitute's Special, Panhandle," he said to the dun. He slid it back into the saddlebag. He felt around in the bottom of the bag. More odds and ends. A tin plate and cup with knife, fork and spoon. Then he came up with a picture frame in plush covered metal. It was of a blond young man whose light eyes seemed to stare coldly into Holt's. Holt turned it over. "Fisher's Photographs," he read from the dim lettering. "Denver, Colorado."

Holt strapped down the bag and then swung up on the big dun. There was a lot of unexplained history about Vivian Leslie. Maybe he'd find out why she had left Niles. For all her warm looks there was a diamond-hard core in her, or

Holt hadn't learned as much about the female of the species as he had prided himself in.

Still, as he rode across the soft meadow toward the ranch buildings, he was aware of an odd lift of spirits. A tendril of smoke drifted up from the fieldstone chimney of the house. The woman had walked out on Niles. He should hate her. He didn't.

CHAPTER ELEVEN

I t was heavy going across the soft land, but the big dun took it in stride. Holt dismounted at the bottom of a slope near the west waterhole and led the dun up the grade. He was all the way to the top within view of the waterhole when he belatedly saw the two mounted men sitting their mud-splattered horses. He stopped, instinctively reached for the Winchester, then thought better of it. He led the dun to within fifty yards of them. They were both big, blocky men, and they didn't seem in the least worried about him.

The older of the two strangers leaned forward in his saddle. "Who're you?" he asked.

"Holt Cooper."

"This is Diamond W land. You working for Sloan Minner?"

"No."

"I'm Link Owens. This is my brother Perry."

Holt nodded. "I've heard of you. What are you doing here?"

"None of your God-damned business," said Perry.

They looked a lot alike. Solid, as though carved in native rock with little regard for niceties. Big of bone and solid of muscle. Reddish hair showed beneath their hats. But it was the hard green eyes that held you.

Link shifted in his saddle. "Take it easy, Perry. We're checking the waterhole," he told Holt.

"Why?" Holt asked. "This is Diamond W land."

"I already said it ain't no concern of yours," Perry said.

"Happens it is," said Holt easily. "I own the Diamond W."

The two brothers glanced at each other. Link shifted his chew and spat to one side. "Then we'll tell you Sam Chase useta let us use this waterhole. We've got a good range except for water. Happens Sam and us made a deal some years ago. Williston was hard to get along with. He cut us off."

"After the rain you should have all the water you need."

Link nodded. "We will. For a time. Runs off too easy around our place. We was just checking things around here."

"I haven't given anyone permission to use water from my range."

"Do tell," Perry said politely.

Holt could see why Niles had had a run-in with them. He had plenty of water—more than he'd ever need—but their possessive attitudes galled him.

Link rubbed his blocky jaw. "We won't use any for quite a spell. We kin put a Texas gate in your west fence to run the cows through."

A horseman appeared on top of a low ridge and rode swiftly toward them. "Charley Benton," Link said. "Guess we're wanted. Perry."

Perry nodded. "I'll get the gate started today. I like to get things done right away."

The high-handed attitude of the two brothers almost got Holt on the prod. He glanced at the approaching vaquero. Three against one in a shooting country. The two brothers studied him, waiting for him to make his play.

"You won't start any Texas gate," Holt said slowly. "Nor any other kind."

Link glanced sideways at his brother. "Tough nut, ain't he, Perry?"

Perry grinned. "All alone, he is. A real tough hombre.

Texas man. Leastways he throws his weight around like a Texas man. I ain't worried, not so long as we're facing him."

Anger welled up in Holt, but he didn't show it on his face. "Texas man or no," he said, "keep off my land."

Benton slid his sorrel to a halt.

"Around dozen of 'em are missing, Link. Found tracks near the brakes. Hoss and cow. Rustlers I'd say."

"Sonofabitch," Link said.

Perry wet his thick lips. "We'll be right with you, Charley, soon's we straighten out this tough nut here."

Benton was a sad-faced man with ragged dragoon mustaches. "You want I should go back and round up some of the boys?"

"Set tight," Perry said.

"Well?" Link asked of Holt.

Holt placed his right hand on his hip just above the butt of his gun. "You heard me. Stay off my land."

The three men sat their horses looking down at him, "Real tough nut," Perry murmured.

Benton pivoted in his saddle, scouting the land for a hidden rifleman. It didn't figure *one* man would brace up the Owens brothers.

Perry kneed his horse closer to Holt. "Yuh heard what we said. We put up the gate. We use the water when we need it."

"Stay off of my land," Holt said between his teeth. "Stay off or get shot off."

Link laughed. "Come on, boys. We've got work to do."

Holt built a smoke as he watched the trio ride west toward the Owens range. He was beginning to wonder how Niles had stuck it out as long as he had. Hell, he would have allowed them the use of the water, but their damned overbearing attitude had forced him to buck them. He lit up and swung up on Panhandle. "Salt, pepper and gravel in the beans," he said. "I wonder what will happen next in this pleasant country."

He could see the buckboard as he neared the ranch house. Ab was carrying supplies into the house, and even from a distance Holt could tell that Ab was on the prod. Ab splashed through a shallow pool as he came toward Holt. He stopped and placed his hands on his hips. "Dod-dummed country," he said waspishly.

"What's riling you, Ab?"

"Two things. First, some sonofabitch took a shot at me near Cottonwood Crick. Gouged a three-inch splinter offn the back of the buckboard seat. Come within inches of killin' me, Holt."

"Who was it?"

"How in hell should I know? And I didn't go to find out. I come up the road like the devil was proddin' me in the rump with a pitchfork. I tell yuh, I could feel that damned bushwhacker's eyes a-borin' into me over his sights until I was a half-mile away."

Holt could see that the little man had reached his boiling point. "Well, do you have any *idea* who it was?"

"Hell yes! I seen Drake Manning on the road. He tells me to quit out here. I tells him I'll quit when I damned well feel like it. Drake slaps the butt of his carbine and tells me there's other ways of convincin' me. Dod-dum him anyways! Who in hell does he think he is?"

"God, I guess," Holt said dryly. "You think it might have been him?"

"I ain't accusin' him, if that's what yuh mean. But he was on that knoll near the crick about five minutes before I reached it. I could see him. Then he goes into the brush. There wasn't nobody else around. Besides, that bastard kin shoot the wings offn a fly with a saddle gun. If it *was* him, he was shootin' to scare me an' not to kill."

Holt rolled a smoke. "What else is bothering you?"

Ab jerked a thumb at the house. "That woman. Yuh got any sense at all you'll get her outa here right now. She's bad luck, man. Plumb bad luck!"

"She showed up here in the middle of the storm, Ab. Horse dead and her soaked to the hide. You couldn't expect me to boot her out into the rain again."

"By God, I woulda done it."

"We're different then, Ab."

"Yeah. Yeah. I'm clost to fifty years old. I wasn't never one to cotton to women anyways. Trouble-makers they are. But you—ain't yuh got sense enough to know her for what she is?"

"Take it easy, Ab."

Ab spat sideways. "Sure. Sure. She's got the Indian sign on yuh. Wigglin' around like a worm on a hook waitin' for a bite. Yuh dod-dummed fool."

"Shut up!" Holt snapped.

Ab thrust out his chin. "Go ahead! Belt me one! But yuh ain't goin' to change my mind even if yuh wale hell outa me!"

Holt controlled his temper. "I've had enough today," he said. *"Don't rile me, Ab."*

Ab stepped back. "All right. All right. I'll unload the supplies and put 'em away. I'll stay with yuh until yuh get another hand. Then yuh kin pay me off." The little man stamped off careless of the mud which flew away from his rundown boots.

Holt looked up at the sky. "Oh God," he said. "What next?"

Vivian Leslie was in the kitchen storing away food supplies as though she had been at home in the little kitchen for years. She smiled at Holt, and then her expression changed. "What's wrong?"

Holt filled a coffee cup and sat down at the table. "Nothing," he said.

She pulled up the barbiquejo strap of his hat and took the hat from his head to hang it on a peg. Her hand had been cool against his face. "Don't lie to me," she said.

"It doesn't concern you."

She sat down opposite him. "Is it about me?"

"Partly."

"What else is wrong?"

"I ran into the Owens boys at the west waterhole. They say Chase—he's the original owner of this ranch—said they could use the water when they needed it."

"Niles wouldn't let them."

"Neither will I."

"They're hardcases," she said, and frowned. "What else is bothering you?"

He waved a hand.

"It's me, isn't it? Ab's been talking?"

"Yes."

"He wants me to leave."

"I'll have him drive you to Bedloe," Holt said.

"And leave you alone?" She leaned forward. "Ab was fired at. You'll be next. I know these people around here. They know no law but bullet law—"

"I'll get along."

"Uh-huh. Niles thought the same thing. No one could tell *him*."

Holt drained his cup. "I've got enough trouble without having a woman here."

She smiled ruefully. "It isn't having a woman here. It's having *me* here, isn't it?"

He stood up. "You're dealing," he said shortly.

She stood up and came close to him. "I'll go then. Alone. Let me have a horse and some food."

Suddenly he swept her close. She raised her face to meet his searching lips. They clung together and all the banked fires of loneliness within Holt flared up into hot life.

Ab opened the door, and they broke apart. Holt's face felt hot. Ab stamped past them, took a bottle of the Companion from the cabinet and walked outside. A moment later, they heard a smash of glass.

She smiled. Holt couldn't help but grin. She ran a slim hand through his thick hair. "Maybe we ought to try the Abyssinian Desert Companion," she suggested. "It seems to be the answer to all Ab's problems."

"I wish I had an answer," he said. He kissed her. "Don't worry about staying, Vivian."

"You'll have to throw me out, Holt," she said softly.

Holt walked outside. Ab had emptied the buckboard and was carrying feed into the barn. Holt looked at the back of the buckboard seat. There was a gouge in the silvery wood.

Holt took out his case-knife and opened it. He cut out the embedded slug.

Ab came from the barn and looked at the mutilated soft lead slug. "Yuh see?" he snapped.

"I didn't doubt you, Ab."

The little man took the slug. ".38/56," he said, and paled beneath his tan. "Now I'm mixed up in this thing."

Holt sighed. "Seems as though all a man has to do in this country is to carry or shoot a .38/56 and everybody heads for the brush."

"Yuh think it's a joke? Do yuh? Well it ain't! Not by a dod-dummed sight it ain't. That's a callin' card with my name on it."

Holt tossed the slug up and down in his hand. "Figure out your time, Ab, and I'll pay you off."

"Go to hell," Ab snarled, and stalked off to the barn.

Holt walked to the corral and got his dun. He tightened the cinch and swung up on Panhandle. Ab appeared at the barn door. "Where yuh goin'?"

"Taking a little ride, Ab. I'll be back later this afternoon."

Ab watched Holt ride down toward the gate.

"Dod-dummed fool," he said.

CHAPTER TWELVE

The MM Connected was situated in a wide valley thick with timber. Beyond the ranch buildings the open range stretched far to the south toward the low rough hills. Cattle dotted the land as far as Holt could see. The place looked as though it had always prospered.

Holt rode up to the gate below the big ranch house. A limping waddie came around the side of the house. "Where's Lew?" asked Holt.

"He ain't here."

"Where is he?"

"In Rockyhill. Drake's here though."

"Tell him I want to see him."

"Keno." The man limped across to the big barn and went inside. Minutes later, he limped back to Holt. "Drake's busy with a sick hoss. He says if yuh want to see him yuh kin come to him."

Holt swung down from the dun and ground-reined him near a fence. Then he walked to the barn. Drake was standing in a stall, looking down at a blanketed colt. "What's on your mind?" he asked over his shoulder.

"I wanted to talk to Lew."

"He ain't here."

"That I know."

Drake turned. "Well, get on with it. I'm partners with Lew."

Holt began to build a smoke. "You and your cousin have been pressuring Sloan Minner about me taking over the Diamond W."

"That so? He's got a big mouth, that Minner."

"Seems as though you waled him, Drake. He's a little old for you to be pushing around, isn't he?"

"I don't like his lip. Furthermore, I don't like yours, Cooper. Let Minner fight his own battles."

Holt lit up. "Happens that Sloan and I made a legal transaction for the Diamond W. There wasn't any dirty work connected with it. I consider Sloan a friend of mine. I'd advise you to stop bothering him about the Diamond W. It's mine and I aim to keep it. He's out of the deal now."

Drake leaned against a post and glanced down at Holt's six-gun. "You're talking mighty big for a man who has only one hand working for him. We've got thirty-five men here, Cooper. Good men."

"I fight my own battles, Manning."

"That's what Niles Williston said. That's what Joe Stroud said. I can name a few others around here that talked big. They're all gone now."

"Shot in the back of the head with a .38/56."

Drake frowned a little. "Well then—maybe you get the idea."

"You're threatening me with the same treatment?"

"I don't know who bushwhacked them if that's what you mean."

Holt nodded. "That's what I mean."

Drake stood up straight. "Get to hell off of my place! Get off or I'll run you off!"

"With thirty-five men behind you?"

"I can do it alone, Cooper. And don't ever get the idea I can't."

Holt dropped his cigarette and carefully ground it out. "Seems as though you also stopped Ab Chisum on the road this morning and warned him to quit me."

"I like Ab. I don't want to see him get mixed up in a fracas."

"What makes you think there *will* be a fracas?"

Drake grinned coldly. "I got the second sight."

"Well, use it and figure out what's going to happen to you if you shoot at Ab again."

Manning stepped forward. "What the hell was that you said?"

"You heard me!"

There was a soft movement behind Holt. He turned and saw Walt Short. He dropped his hand to his Colt and knew he had made a mistake. He caught the soft whisk of leather and the double-click of a six-gun being cocked, and turned again, slowly. Drake was holding one of his fancy Colts on him.

"Thanks, boss," Short said. "I been wanting to work this smart bastard over for what he done to me in Rockyhill."

"Take his six-shooter," Drake said. "Close the door. Ain't no one around but Limpy, and he knows enough to keep his nose out of here."

Walt took Holt's pistol and tossed it atop a bale. He closed the big door and came back. A shaft of sunlight struck the side of his set face. Drake said, "Walt claims you got the edge on him in Rockyhill. Maybe you *can* beat him to the draw. But I know one thing. He'll take you in a fair fight."

Holt glanced down at Drake's pistol. "Fair?"

Manning slid the Colt into its ornate holster. "Shuck your gun belt, Walt." He looked at Holt. "I don't want any killings here, but I aim to see you marked. That's so you'll know enough to keep away from the MM boys."

"Why don't you try me yourself?" Holt asked, but Drake said, "He's all yours, Walt."

Holt eyed Walt. He saw lumps around the thin mouth. The nose had been broken and badly set, giving it a curious twist. There was some scar tissue above the eyebrows too.

Walt unbuckled his gun belt and placed it beside Holt's six-gun. He shrugged his shoulders back and forth loosening the long muscles. Then he danced about, shifting his weight from one foot to the other.

"I'm ready, Drake."

"Go get him then."

Walt moved in swiftly, thrusting out a long left. He held his right cocked beneath his narrow chin. Holt raised his guard and circled about, watching the cold eyes of his opponent. Then Walt tapped him twice with a left, feeling him out. The right came so quickly that Holt felt the wetness of the floor through his thin Levi's before he knew what had happened.

"Have some cheese and crackers, yuh sonofabitch," Walt said. He threw a few feinting punches. "Get up. I ain't broke sweat yet."

A thin trickle of blood seeped from Holt's mouth. He got up and raised his guard. Walt's attack varied this time. He threw lefts and rights from wide out, tapping Holt hard each time. Holt blocked with elbows and forearms, riding the battering blows. The uneasy thought came to him that here was a man who could hit equally well with either hand. And then he was down in the stinking muck again.

Drake grinned. He picked at his even white teeth with a straw. "My, my," he said. "And him from *Texas* too."

Holt got up. Walt moved in. Holt tied up his arms, rode him around a bit and then threw him back. Walt slipped in the muck, throwing himself off balance. He threw out his arms to balance himself. Holt moved in, driving a short left into the lean gut. As Walt bent forward, he met a cracking uppercut. He straightened up and went back against a post. Holt tapped him twice on the lean chin with a left. Walt slid down along the post and shook his head.

Holt moved back. He had been lucky. This time Walt would pull out all the stops. It might be rockabye for Holt if he didn't watch out.

Walt got up and shook his head. "You've had your turn," he said deep in his throat.

The tall waddie closed in throwing fists from all angles. One hit Holt's mouth, starting a fresh flow of blood while another half-closed his eye. Holt gave ground, taking the fierce attack until Walt tired a little. He managed to hit the MM man twice. Walt backed away, blowing and snorting.

"He ain't marked enough yet," Drake said.

"I ain't done either," Walt said.

Holt knew Walt could stand off and cut him to bloody ribbons. The man was too good for him in a stand-off fight. Holt had a few shots left in the locker, but he had to use them quickly or he wouldn't be able to see Walt Short. When that happened, he'd end up with more scar tissue on him than Walt carried.

Walt bobbed and weaved a little, coming in cautiously, with some respect for the big man he was facing. The big Texan hit hard in his style of cow camp fighting. He'd have easily taken any other MM waddie by now. Walt speared Holt with a left and drew back his right for a hard hook. Holt blocked the left and closed in, taking the smashing right on his ear. Bells rang loudly as he hammered at the lean gut, throwing his shoulders in behind the short blows. Walt gasped. He retreated, stabbing at Holt's battered eye.

Holt brought up a left uppercut and then slammed a right to the gut again. Walt slipped a little in the muck. His left spur tripped him. He staggered to the right. Holt back-handed him across the side of the head. Walt turned to meet the attack and Holt brought up one from waist level. Walt caught it flush. He banged off the wall and went down.

Holt closed in. He gripped Walt by the shirt and dragged him up. Holt's breath was thick and bubbly in his throat. He slashed at Walt's eyes with his free hand and then belted him in the gut. Then he smashed linked hands atop the man's head, driving him down to meet an up-thrust knee. Walt lost all interest in marking Holt.

"Jesus Christ!" yelled Drake.

The fires of hell were raging in Holt now. He scooped up a handful of mud and manure and cast it at Drake. The filth splattered his face. Before he could dash it away Holt was on him. He drove in fierce short punches to gut and face. A pounding right caught Drake three times over the heart. He went back against the side of the stall. Holt drove in a left that split a knuckle. He finished with a right that damned near broke his fist and Drake's jaw.

Holt staggered back. He picked up bis Colt and slid it into his holster. His lungs seemed to be on fire. He spat out blood. Then he swayed toward the door. He slid it back in time to look in the frightened face of Limpy. Before Limpy could move he felt the muzzle of a Colt in his belly. "Hey, mister," he said. "I got nothin' against yuh."

Holt came back to his senses. He walked away from the little man. He made it to the fence and managed to climb into the saddle. After passing through the gate, he turned the dun westward. He should have known better than to brace the MM men on their own ground, but by God, the next time he met Drake and Walt it would be a shooting matter.

CHAPTER THIRTEEN

Ab Chisum took his fourth biscuit and spread it with molasses. "I been off my feed lately," he said. "But maybe it's been my own cookin'. You handle the pots and pans right nice, Miss Vivian."

"That's a compliment coming from you," she said.

Ab grunted. He surveyed Holt's battered face, and he examined Holt's swollen fists, all with approval.

"Yuh must be a ring-tailed whizz with red striped wheels," he observed. "Walt was champeen two-three years ago when they had the Cowboy Show in Rockyhill. I heard once he licked Ben Holmes from Cheyenne. Ben was champeen of the old Sixth Cavalry."

"You're lucky you walked away from the MM as well as you did," Vivian told Holt.

Holt nodded. "I set the fat on fire there," he agreed, and sat back in his chair and sighed.

The west window of the kitchen smashed into shards. An instant later they heard the crack of a rifle. Ab hit the floor as the slug struck the far wall of the kitchen. Holt jumped to his feet and gripped Vivian by the arm, dragging her to the floor. He got between her and the window and turned off the lamp just as another slug whipped through the window and sang off the stove.

Holt felt her warm body soft against his. "Don't move," he said. "Ab! Hand me my rifle!"

Ab crawled across the kitchen and reached for the Winchester. A third slug sang through the window and smashed through the thin wood of a cabinet door. There was the muffled smash of glass. A pungent odor drifted into the room to mingle with the stink of the lamp fumes.

"Dod-dummit!" Ab roared. "They got my Abyssinian Desert Companion! Gawd dammit! It's enough to make a man kill!"

Holt took his Winchester from Ab's shaking hands. "Stay low," he said. "They can't shoot through the logs." He crawled into the hallway and to the front of the house. He eased through the doorway and rolled over to the end of the porch. He dropped to the damp ground and wormed his way to the end of the house. He crouched behind a pile of firewood and looked up the slope toward the bald butte. A rifle winked in the darkness. The slug thudded into the back door of the house.

Holt crawled across the muddy yard to the barn and into the dark building. He ran to the back of it. He eased through the far door and stopped at the rear of the barn. The rifle flashed again. Holt levered a round into the .38/56 and rested the rifle atop a barrel. He sighted approximately where he had seen the flashes and then waited.

The rifle spat flame two hundred yards from the house. Holt fired and then churned out three more shots. He dropped behind the barrel and rolled away from it. The unseen marksman fired twice. The slugs thudded into the barn. Holt went back into the barn and ran to the front. He raised his rifle and waited. Then the wind picked up the thud of hoofs. The sound gradually faded away near the face of the butte.

Walking back to the house, Holt tapped on the south window. "Don't show a light!" he called. "Get out of the kitchen. Stay on the floor."

Holt padded toward the west fence and crawled under it. He Indianed up the slope, stopping frequently to watch and listen. There was no sound except that of the night wind soughing through the scrub trees.

He stopped near a rock outcropping and listened. He shrugged and walked down to the house. The Owenses, the Mannings or the barefooted unknown had been at work.

He went into the living room. "All right," he said. "I think they're gone."

Vivian came to him in the darkness. He kissed her. "Let's get out of the valley," she pleaded.

"No, Vivian. I'm sticking."

"Next time they might shoot to kill."

"So will I. Go to bed. Ab and I will take turns staying awake tonight."

She obeyed him like a child. Holt went into the kitchen. Ab was holding a candle up, surveying the ruins of his stock of tonic. "Three bottles," he said sourly. The pungent odor of the Companion seemed to flood the room. Ab took a bottle and uncapped it. "Have a slug," he said.

Holt shook his head.

Ab drained the bottle. "Ah! That's the ticket."

Holt took out his knife and pried the slug from the back of the cabinet, cutting his finger on the broken glass. He eyed the slug. .38/56.

"I'll take the first watch," he told Ab. "Fill up the coffee pot. I'll call you at midnight."

Ab filled the pot and placed it on the stove. "Dod-dummed business," he growled. "Now a man can't even get his sleep around here."

"You can leave, Ab."

"Me? Not after some sonofabitch shoots up my stock of the Companion. I don't stand for that!"

The little man went to his room. Holt fastened the doors and leaned a chair against the kitchen wall. He dropped on it and placed his rifle across his lap. Tomorrow he'd go over the ground for tracks with a fine-tooth comb. The ground was soft. It shouldn't be too hard to find tracks.

CHAPTER FOURTEEN

The steers were scattered over an area of several hundred square yards. Fifteen of them had been slaughtered—shot at close range, for some of them had powder marks on their hides and intermingled with their hoof tracks were the deep indentations of horse's hoofs. The killer had ridden around and around the steers until he finished them off.

Holt sat on his dun eyeing the scene of death. Already there were buzzards in the clear sky, circling patiently, waiting for him to leave. They had plenty of time and no worries about the food supply running short.

At least a dozen .38/56 hulls lay scattered about the carcasses. The murdering sonofabitch had had a field day. Holt figured the steers had been killed just about dawn.

There was nothing he could do. The place would be an abomination for days until winged scavengers and their four-legged allies, the coyotes, cleaned up the stinking mess. He had seen only four steers on his ride. The rest of them had probably spooked off into the brakes. The fence would hold them there until he and Ab could round them up and drive them back north.

He drew his Winchester from its scabbard and levered a

round into the chamber, then placed it across his thighs and rode toward the brakes.

In an hour's ride he found only three strays. The reason was plain enough. Yards and yards of fence had been cut and the posts had been pulled from the soft earth. He looked to the south where the rugged hills, broken and ridged by naked outcroppings of sharp rock, held the remainder of his diminished herd. It would take days to round them up— unless they had drifted far south toward the Colorado line. He was out of business as a cattleman.

It went from bad to worse. The south waterhole held two dead steers and the decaying carcass of a long dead coyote. Marks showed plainly that it had been dragged there from some distance.

Ab was up on the barn roof when Holt returned. He came halfway down the ladder and listened as Holt told him of the havoc done. "I figured somethin' like this." He came all the way down the ladder. "We'll need a lot of shingles. That roof is shot."

"Is that all that's bothering you?"

"No. It's that woman."

"So?"

"She's a jinx, a hoodoo. She was to Niles. Now it's happenin' to you. What's she doin' here anyways? Where'd she come from?"

"She came from Bedloe."

"Yeah. That's all you know! Don't it strike yuh damned funny she shows up on a pourin' rainy night ridin' from Bedloe? Yuh know any woman would be loco enough to do that unless she had a reason?"

"She probably did."

"Yuh ain't got sense enough to boot her out. There's more too."

"I've heard enough."

"No, yuh haven't. Mebbe yuh didn't know she was bein' sparked by Drake Manning before Niles tried to put his brand on her. They had a hassle about her. I've heard it said she was scared off by Manning because she had taken up with Niles. Mebbe she was the cause of him gettin' killed and not because somebody wanted to get rid of him for the Diamond W."

Holt frowned. The little man was probably right. She'd have to go, but he'd be damned if he'd let Drake Manning scare him into making her go.

Ab shifted his chew and spat. "Yuh want I should go in and get the shingles? There'll be more rain afore long."

"All right, Ab."

"I'll push the team. I can make it back here right after dark if I make good time."

Holt watched him hitch up the team of mules. Ab placed his rifle in the buckboard. Then he looked at Holt. "Keep your eyes peeled. That sonofabitch who shot us up last night is a good man with the long gun. Wouldn't be no problem for <u>him</u> to Indian up and plant a slug in yuh. Mind now."

Holt grinned. "All right, Dad."

"Go to hell, boss."

Ab pulled out. Holt unsaddled the dun. He'd have to talk with her. She'd have to go. Maybe he could get her back some day, but he wasn't sure he really wanted her to come back. Good cook or not, she wasn't the type to make a rancher's wife.

CHAPTER FIFTEEN

S he was in her big room when he came into the house.
He could hear her moving softly around in there. He
knew he'd have to tell her she'd have to go. He had known
the usual quota of women, good and bad, in his years of
drifting. The realization suddenly came to him that maybe
Niles had gone through the same thing he was experiencing
now. Wanting a woman. But there was no place for her here
now. Still, he hesitated, for if he once let her go, he might
never see her again.

"'Damned fool," he said as he walked into the kitchen
and poured a cup of coffee. No word had passed between
them about any permanent affiliation. Yet she had accepted
his kisses and returned them. Maybe it was her way of
paying him off for what he had done. The sly thought came
to him that maybe he hadn't demanded enough.

"I'll take some too," she said behind him.

He jumped guiltily as he turned. She had piled her dark
hair atop her shapely head. Her face was flushed and there
was a new freshness about her. She must have been bathing
in her room, for her skin was still damp. The aura of
perfume clung about her. He remembered vaguely seeing a
bottle of it with her cosmetics when he had salvaged her
saddlebags.

He slipped an arm around her waist and drew her close. There was no resistance as she lifted her face for his expected kiss. This time he bent her backward as his free hand searched her upper body, feeling the fullness of it.

Her teeth sank into his lip. She turned her head away and forced her hands up under his chin. "Damn you," she said. "You're like all the rest of them after all."

He released her. She adjusted her dress and walked around the table.

"You'll have to leave," he said.

"Why? Because you didn't get enough from me? Is that it? I might have known this would happen."

"No one asked you here, Vivian. I haven't bothered you with questions anyone else might have been free to ask you."

She sat down and rested her arms on the table. "So that's it? What is it you want to know?"

He began to fashion a smoke. "A woman shows up at an isolated ranch in the night—the ranch of a man she was once engaged to. She claims she came through the hills from Bedloe which is a helluva long ride for a good man on a good horse. She doesn't want to leave the ranch. Yet she knows she can cause more trouble because Drake Manning took a fancy to her once and might do it again."

"I once told you I'd go. You didn't seem anxious for *that* to happen."

He lit his smoke. "You haven't answered my questions."

She stood up. "I don't intend to."

"You will."

She laughed. "You're a soft touch, Holt. You won't force me to."

"I might. No one knows where you came from the first time you showed up in Rockyhill. Then you vanish the same mysterious way. Why don't you tell the real story about yourself?"

She walked to the hall door. "I'll get my things together," she said. "There's one thing you have forgotten, Holt."

"So?"

"I've tried to be your friend. From the looks of things

around here you could have used one." She closed the door behind her.

About an hour after twilight, Ab Chisum stopped the buckboard beside the barn. Holt leaned his rifle in a corner and came out of the barn. The little man shook his head as he dropped to the ground. "Got the dod-dummed shingles, an' that ain't all. There's more hell to pay. Sim Pastor was found dead with a .38/56 plumb through his left ear. Sim had the Lazy S southeast of here."

Holt didn't quite know what to make of it. Ab gripped him by the arm.

"Two witnesses claim they saw you near the scene of the crime this mornin'. Ridin' like hell, they said."

"That's a damned lie. I was never off the Diamond W."

"That's it! That's it! Sim was found near the south water-hole on *this* range!"

Holt felt an icy finger trace the length of his spine.

"There was no body there this morning, Ab."

"Dammit! I know that or yuh woulda told me."

"Who are the witnesses?"

"Drake Manning and Walt Short."

"That figures," Holt said.

"Sheriff Tim Conlon is headin' this way. I got outa town as fast as I could and run hell outa these mules to get here. Pack some grub and take off into the hills. Tim Conlon got elected because the Mannings backed him."

"I might have figured that too."

Ab took a folded paper from his pocket. "Sloan Minner give me this for yuh. Said it was important."

Holt took the paper into the barn and held it close to the lantern. "Dear Holt," he read aloud. "The news around town is that you had something to do with the killing of Sim Pastor, which I know is a damned lie. But feelings are hot around here. People know you carry a .38/56 and I have already warned you about that. Times are rough in a country when a man can't carry a certain caliber of rifle without being suspected of dry-gulching, but that's the way it is. Take my advice and pull out now while you have time. I can sell the ranch for a damned good price and forward you the money. Less a fair commission of course. Lew Manning has upped his price ten percent. You'd be a fool not to take it and then get shut of all this trouble. Leave your forwarding address with Ab and make damned sure he don't let anybody but *me* know what it is. Good luck. Sloan Minner."

Holt folded the paper and lit it with a lucifer. "Minner sure as hell is in a big hurry to get me to sell. Him and his fair commission."

Ab grunted. "That old sonofabitch has pitch on his fingers so's he don't lose a penny. What are yuh goin' to do?"

"Stick."

"I knew yuh would. Actually, they haven't got much on yuh, but feelin's is high. Some of these people around here would string up anybody, even *me,* if they thought they had anythin' to do with all these killin's."

Holt nodded. "Get some food. I'll unload the shingles."

As he carried the last bundle into the barn, he heard the soft thud of hoofs on the road. He picked up his Winchester and went down to the gate. Three horsemen drew rein. He didn't have any trouble identifying two of them: Drake Manning and Walt Short. The third man was tall and gangling, wearing a huge Stetson. The faint moonlight shone dully on the star on his vest.

"What can I do for you?" asked Holt.

"That's him," Manning said to the tall man.

"I'm Tim Conlon," the tall man said. "Sheriff in these parts."

"Pleased to meet you," Holt said politely.

Conlon looked down at the rifle. "Put that down," he said.

"Not while you're in MM company, I won't."

Conlon tugged at his ragged dragoon mustache. "You ain't about to resist arrest I hope."

"Am I being arrested?"

Conlon tilted his head to one side. "A man was shot to death on your range. Sim Pastor from the Lazy S. Shot plumb through the head with a .38/56. Is that a .38/56?"

"It is."

"These two men said they seen you riding like hell away from there about the same time."

"What time was that?"

Manning looked at Short. "A little after ten this morning," Short said.

"Where were you at that time?" Conlon asked.

"Back here."

"He's lying," Short said.

Holt tilted the Winchester a little higher. "You're another, Short."

"Let's take him," Manning said.

"Wait!" Conlon said. "I'm the sheriff here."

"Jeeesus," Short murmured.

Conlon flushed. Holt leaned against a gate post.

"Before you go any further," he said. "I'd like to report that my house was shot up last night. This morning I found many of my cattle slaughtered. My fences were cut. One of my waterholes was polluted."

"Yeah? Who did it?"

"That's your job to find out, isn't it?"

"You file a report and I'll see to it. Then you *were* out on your south range this morning?"

Holt nodded. "I didn't kill Pastor. I didn't see his body. Nor did I see these two hombres anywhere around at the time."

"Two witnesses said you was there. I'll have to take you in."

"You have a warrant?"

Conlon straightened up. "Dammit! Of course, I do! I know my job, Cooper, and don't you ever forget it!"

Holt heard a soft footfall behind him. He turned. Vivian Leslie stood there in her serge traveling dress. "He was with me from nine until eleven this morning, Sheriff," she said quietly.

Drake stared at her. "Vivian!"

"Hello, Drake," she said.

Short whistled softly.

Conlon shoved back his hat. "You sure of that, ma'am?"

She linked her arm through Holt's. "Certainly. Wasn't I, Holt?"

He bobbed his head mechanically. One of these days he *might* figure her out.

Conlon glanced angrily at Drake Manning. Drake spat. "I don't know how the hell she got out here, Tim. There's something mighty peculiar about this. But I know *one* thing for sure. She's lying the same as he is."

Holt shoved back the hammer of his Winchester with his left hand. "Seeing as how she's a lady, Manning, you'll apologize for that."

Conlon kneed his horse to one side. "Wait, Cooper!" he said hastily.

Drake Manning's hands rested on his pommel. He wanted to draw on Holt. It showed all over him. But he remembered the clobbering he had taken in his own barn and only his tongue moved as he wet his lips. "I'm sorry, Vivian," he said.

Holt said, "Sheriff, you can stay here as long as you like. I'd admire to have you for supper. The rest of you, git!"

Manning sank the guthooks into his gray and rode a hundred yards down the road. Short followed him. Conlon lifted his hat. "Evenin', Miss Leslie. Evenin', Cooper."

"Evenin'," Holt said.

Conlon turned his sorrel and rode to join the two waiting MM men. Holt grinned as he heard them arguing. "What the hell did you want me to do?" Conlon rasped. "Her word's as good as yours. Besides, that bastard looked like he meant to use that Winchester. I ain't no Goddamn hero. And I didn't see *you* going for your gun."

"Oh, go to hell," Manning snarled.

Holt grinned. "Trouble in the enemy camp," he said, and looked at Vivian. "Thanks. I've been wondering if I would have made Rockyhill alive with those three riding herd on me."

She avoided his gaze. "I'll ride on tonight," she said.

"No."

"Why not? You've as much as told me I'm not wanted here."

He held her by the elbows. "That was before. I have a feeling you saved my life, Vivian."

She looked up at him then. "Perhaps. I know I've done one thing that will cause more trouble. I let Drake Manning see me. That's another thing he'll have against you, Holt."

"I'm worried."

"You're a fool. You don't really know him. When he wants something, he lets nothing stand in his way. I know from bitter experience. He gets insane with jealousy."

"You know him well then."

She started up the pathway toward the house. "Yes. I know him too well."

"Ab will get supper," he said.

She spoke over her shoulder. "Then I'm allowed to stay?"

"Do you want to?"

"Yes. Before God I know it's wrong, but I want to stay, Holt."

He kissed her before she went in. He stood for a long time on the dim porch, smoking one cigarette after another. The odds were piling up against him. First the Mannings, then the Ovenses and now the sheriff. All he had on his side was his own gun, a little peace-loving cowpoke who drank medicine that was mostly alcohol, and a woman he didn't understand.

CHAPTER SIXTEEN

An uneasy peace hovered about the Diamond W for three days. Holt stood it as long as he could, and then he saddled Panhandle and rode south. He spent a good part of the day exploring the rough brakes, familiarizing himself with them as much as he could, but the place was a mare's nest of jumbled rock, scrub trees and thick brush.

The sun was low over the western hills when he rode fence toward them. He stopped to build a smoke at the far southwest corner of his range. It was quiet and peaceful, and again he found himself thinking of Vivian Leslie. Something drew him to her, and something else kept urging him to drive her away. Yet he couldn't get himself to force her to leave. He grinned wryly as he lit up. It had been a comeuppance for Drake Manning when he saw them together. And when she...

The rifle shot flatted off to the west, carried to Holt on the wind. He raised his head and stood there listening. Two more shots cracked from somewhere over on the Owens spread. He swung up into the saddle.

"I should know better, Panhandle," he said. "But we'll take a look over there." He spurred up the slope and rode through the trees. The dying sun glinted from a shallow pool of water. Hoof marks showed on its margin. The tracks of two horses heading off to the northwest.

Holt ground-reined the big dun in a hollow and took his Winchester from its sheath. As he turned, he heard a fourth shot. He padded through the brush and came out on a bald knoll which overlooked the Owens spread. A man lay face down in a clearing. A horse grazed fifty yards away from him.

After easing through the brush and under the fence, Holt bellied through the trees. There was no sound other than the wind soughing through the branches. The odor of burnt gunpowder drifted to him. Holt crawled through the brush to where he could get a clear look at the man. "Uh-oh!" he said. The man was Link Owens.

Holt walked forward with ready Winchester, eyeing the shadowy trees. He stopped and knelt by Link. The man was dead, shot through the side of the head. Grayish matter oozed from the blackened hole above his left ear. Holt threw himself flat as he heard the thud of hoofs. A horseman left the shelter of the trees, raised a rifle, then dropped it. He sagged over his pommel and gripped the mane of his horse. It was Perry Owens. Blood stained the back of his shirt. But he had clearly seen Holt. "Cooper, yuh sonofabitch!" he yelled weakly. Then he spurred his horse over a rise, swaying from side to side as he rode.

Holt shoved back his hat. He turned to eye the encircling trees. The sun flashed on something on the ridge behind him. He jumped over Link and dropped flat, using the big men for a shield. A rifle spat flame and smoke and the slug hummed just over Holt's hat. He slid his Winchester forward. Another slug keened past his ear. He fired toward the smoke and then rolled over into a shallow hollow.

Minutes ticked past. There was no movement on the ridge. Holt bellied into the shelter of the trees and then stood up. He advanced at a crouch with his Winchester cocked. He worked his way up the slope as if he were stalking a wounded deer. He stopped at the edge of a grassy clearing. This was the place from where the shots had been fired at him. The light was failing as he looked about the clearing. Six empty cartridge cases lay on the grass. He knelt and picked one of them up. .38/56. There was a slight depression in the grass not far from him. He examined it. It was the faint impress of a bare foot. A cold feeling came over him as he left the clearing and started through the trees.

Two hundred yards from the clearing he found another footprint—and a bright droplet of blood on the grass.

Holt circled back for the dun. He led it to where he had found the footprint and blood. The sun was almost gone as he took up the faint trail.

He cast about for twenty minutes before he found the trail again. A bare footprint, with the shape of a gun butt pressed into the soft earth beside it as if the man were using the rifle as support. The ground was rougher now as he progressed into the brakes. Ledges of naked rock thrust themselves up from the earth like dislocated bones. Trees and brush stippled the slopes. There were narrow passage-ways between the big rock outcroppings. A hell of a place to be stalking a killer.

He left the dun and worked his way through the rock jungle, padding softly, stopping often to listen. He wanted to turn back out of that mare's nest of rocks, but something drove him on.

He was high on a slope when he heard metal click against rock. The rifle roared not fifty feet from him, but he had been warned by the metallic click. He dropped, thrusting his rifle forward. He fired directly into the smoke puff among the trees and heard the unmistakable belly grunt of a man hard hit. Something hit against rock. Holt rolled over, levering in another round as he came to rest behind a rock.

There was no other sound. He waited. Then he bellied into the trees to his right and worked his way through the trees.

A man lay face down. His muddy bare feet showed below

his rolled-up pants legs. His slim hands gripped a Winchester. Holt rolled him over and looked into the thin, pale face. The wide-open eyes did not see Holt. Blood had spread across the front of the dirty checked shirt. The slug had caught him through the heart. A lucky shot if Holt had ever seen one. Blood also stained the right ankle and foot, mingling with the mud.

Holt eyed the dead man. Fine blond hair showed beneath the black hat brim. A wisp of a mustache in Mexican dandy style traced the short upper lip. Holt felt through the clothing. There was no wallet or other means of identification. "I've seen you somewhere before," Holt said softly. He walked about the motte of trees. There should be a pair of boots and a horse somewhere around. A man didn't travel far in that country without a horse and boots.

The sun was gone by the time he found the cave buried among the jumbled rocks. He lit a lucifer and entered the cave. A bedding roll lay to one side. A fire-blackened circle of rocks showed at the rear of the cave. Holt lit a candle stub. The guttering light revealed extra clothing, saddlebags, a partially empty carton of .38/56 cartridges and other odds and ends. From the looks of the place and the depth of the ashes in the fireplace, the unknown resident had been there for quite some time.

Holt patiently went over the cave inch by inch. There were no clues as to who the man might be, but Holt felt sure he had killed the man who had terrorized the countryside. Also, he did not doubt that the unknown was a paid killer. "But who was paying him?" he said to himself. He sat down on a rock and built a smoke. There would be hell to pay now. Perry Owens had seen Holt near the body of Link. Perry had been wounded but he could still talk.

Holt went outside and dragged the dead man into a rock cleft. Maybe he should take the corpse into town, but it wouldn't prove anything. It might serve to incriminate Holt instead. The man had been shot with a .38/56, and that seemed to be enough evidence for a hanging.

He covered the corpse with brush and rocks and then

took the Winchester to the cave. He placed it in a deep cleft. Holt wondered how many men had died of slugs shot from the Winchester.

As he walked back to the dun, he tried to think of a way out of the mess he was in. Perry would shoot off his mouth.

The sheriff would ride to the Diamond W again and this time Vivian Leslie couldn't save him.

A rangy clay bank was grazing near Panhandle when Holt reached the dun. A pair of figured boots hung from the saddle horn. Holt let the clay bank nuzzle his hand. It wasn't too hard to hide a dead man but hiding a live horse was another matter. He took the boots from the saddle horn and unsaddled the clay bank. He hid the boots and saddle in the brush and slapped the clay bank on the rump. The horse wandered off in the darkness.

Holt angled back over the ridge toward the Diamond W. A cold wind swept through the trees and moaned through the hill gaps, increasing his deep uneasiness. He had seen the dead man somewhere. He was sure of that. But his memory took him no farther.

CHAPTER SEVENTEEN

Ab Chisum squatted on a hay bale in the barn, soberly listening to Holt's story. The little man kept shaking his head. "Salt, pepper and gravel in the beans," he said when Holt finished. "What do you aim to do?"

"Go into Rockyhill and tell Sheriff Conlon that I rode up after the shooting."

"Yuh said Perry had a good look at yuh. He knows yuh was there. Jesus, man! Yuh can't go into Rockyhill now. It'd be like stickin' your hands into a rattler den."

"If I stay here, they'll come for me again."

"Yore damned if yuh do and damned if yuh don't."

Holt relit his cigar. "Maybe if I tell the whole story they'll believe me."

"Don't be a dod-dummed fool!"

"You think I want to stay here and have a mob come after me?"

"Yuh kin pull out for the hills, Holt."

"And get hunted down like a mad dog?"

Ab slapped the side of his head. "I just can't think."

"You're not alone in that."

"Supposin' yuh let me go into Rockyhill and tell Conlon? Then we could come back here and yuh could show him that dead man. Mebbe Conlon will know who he is."

"It's too thin a story. All Conlon will know is that the stranger was plugged with a .38/56. And there I'd be, blaming him for bushwhacking the Owens brothers. A sure out."

"It might work."

"No," said Holt quietly. "Dead men can't talk."

Ab got up and walked back and forth. "Go ahead then. I'll stay here. What about her?"

"She can do as she likes."

"Yuh goin' to tell her about the stranger?"

Holt shook his head. "I'll tell her nothing. I don't trust her too much, Ab, even if she did save me from getting arrested by Conlon."

"Now you're talkin'," Ab crowed. "The light has dawned in that thick skull of yours."

Holt massaged his temples tiredly. "If I don't get back here by tomorrow afternoon, Ab, you'll know Conlon didn't believe me."

"If he puts you in the calabozo I wouldn't give a plugged centavo for your chances of livin', Holt."

"I'll take the chance. I know one thing. I'm not taking to the owlhoot trail for a murder I didn't commit."

"Mebbe you'll wish yuh *had,* son," Ab said gloomily.

Shortly after ten o'clock, Holt reached Rockyhill. He left Panhandle at the livery stable and walked up a side street toward the calabozo. Holt opened the door of the office and saw a plump man sitting at the desk with his feet propped up on it. A newspaper covered his face, rising and falling gently with his breathing. Holt rapped on the desk.

The plump man slowly took the newspaper from his face and looked sourly at Holt. "What you want?" he asked.

"Where's Conlon?"

"Having a few drinks."

"I want to see him."

"He's at the Stockmen's Bar."

"I want to see him here."

The plump man spat leisurely into a filthy cuspidor. "Then you'll have to wait until tomorrow, mister. He gets in around half past ten in the morning."

Holt placed his hands flat on the desk. "Go get him," he said. "This is business, mister. Damned important business."

The man dropped his feet to the floor, opened his mouth to argue, and then thought better of it. "All right. All right. Who shall I tell him is waiting?"

"Just a stranger."

The man grunted. He took his hat from a hook and jammed it on his head. He slammed the door behind him.

Holt rolled a smoke and sat down on the edge of the desk. Conlon, for all his obvious affiliation with the Mannings, seemed to be a right hombre.

Conlon opened the door. "What the hell you—" His voice trailed away as he saw Holt. "My God!" He slammed the door shut behind him. "What are you doing here? You plumb loco?"

"Sometimes I'm not sure."

Conlon glanced at a window. "I sure hope no one sees you here."

Holt took his cigarette from his lips. "I was riding fence late this afternoon. I heard shooting. Found Link Owens dead just over my line. Perry Owens had been winged. I heard shooting before I saw Link, as I said. Someone shot at me too."

Conlon squinted suspiciously. "Who?"

"I don't know. I wanted to tell you before Perry Owens filled you up with a lot of bull about me shooting at them."

Conlon stepped back. Suddenly he whipped out his Colt. "You're a little late, Cooper."

Holt eyed the six-shooter. "How so?"

"Perry Owens made it to the ranch. Said you killed Link."

"He's a liar. Ride out there with me and I'll prove it. I'll throw the lie in his teeth."

Conlon shook his head slowly. "You're too late, like I said. Perry Owens died after he got home. The last thing he said was that you had killed Link and him too."

Holt stared at the sheriff.

"It's your word against that of a dying man, Cooper. And

a dying man don't generally lie if he knows he's going to meet his Maker. Stand up! Turn around!"

Holt stood up and raised his arms. He turned around and felt Conlon remove his six-shooter from its sheath. "I'd like a chance to clear myself," he said.

"Fat chance of that. Charley Benton brought in the news about Link and Perry. He also said he'd been with the brothers when they hassled with you about using your waterhole. He said you'd told them to stay off your land or get shot off."

Holt walked down the row of cells with the Colt muzzle nuzzling between his shoulder blades. He went into the end cell. Conlon slammed the door shut "Where's your horse?"

"At the livery."

"Your rifle with it?"

"Yes."

"I'll need it for evidence. .38/56, ain't it?"

"Yes."

Conlon locked the cell door and sheathed his Colt. "You're a damned fool in more than one way, Cooper. Riding in here looking for trouble. Knocking down Walt Short. Riling the Mannings and the Owenses. Worst of all carrying a .38/56. A .38/56 in *this* country. My God!"

Holt opened his mouth to tell Conlon about the stranger he had killed and the hideout he had found, but something warned him, and he closed his mouth.

Conlon walked heavily to the front of the jail. "There'll be hell aplenty around here," he said over his shoulder. "The Owens boys was well liked by most."

Holt dropped onto the hard bunk and rolled another smoke. All he could do now was wait.

CHAPTER EIGHTEEN

The thud of boots against the street and the murmuring of voices awakened Holt. He sat upright and listened. There were many men in front of the calabozo. He could hear Tim Conlon walking around in the darkened office. "What is it, Conlon?"

Conlon came down the corridor. "That big-mouthed turnkey of mine has been at it," he said. "Jonas never could keep his mouth shut. Drake Manning's out there with a lot of MM men. Bunch of Owens' men are out there too, and a lot of drunken saloon crawlers. They're after you, Cooper."

Holt stood up. He had seen a mob take a man from a jail in New Mexico and what they had done to him had caused Holt a few nightmares in the following weeks.

Conlon cleared his throat. "I'm all alone," he said, and Holt felt sorry for the sheriff despite his own nervousness.

"Can you hold them off?"

"Alone? I don't think so."

"What are you going to do?"

Conlon tapped his Colt. "Lot of people around here say I'm a front for the Mannings and the other big cattlemen. Without their votes, they say, I'd never of got elected. Maybe they're right. But I took an oath for the office, and I aim to keep it until you go to trial. Guilty or innocent, you're under my protection."

"Thanks," Holt said.

"I've got no love for you, Cooper. I'm just doing my job."

"That's why I thanked you."

"Oh," Conlon said. He checked the back door. "There's a wooden shutter near that window," he said. "Hooks on the wall. Put it up."

Holt placed the shutter across the window. "Look, Conlon," he said over his shoulder. "Let me out of here. I can make it to my horse. I'll hole up near my ranch and tell Ab Chisum where I am. You can get me when you want me."

Conlon blew out an explosive breath. "You want *me* to get strung up? Fat chance, Cooper. You'll stay here. Maybe I can chase 'em off."

Holt listened to the men outside. "You've got a job cut out," he said.

Something thudded against the door. "Open up! Open up, Tim!" a man yelled. "We want that killer!"

Conlon looked at Holt. "Drake Manning."

"That figures."

"Funny thing. Drake hated Link and Perry like loco weed. Now all of a sudden, he's trying to get the man accused of killing them. It's a crazy world, Cooper."

Conlon walked to the front of the jail and lifted a shutter. "You men are breaking the law," he said. "Go on back to the saloons."

"We'll celebrate there after we get Cooper!" Drake Manning yelled.

Conlon cursed. "Get out of here! I warn you!"

"Taking your job seriously, Tim?" jeered Manning. "You're nothing but a front and you know it! Now open up!"

Stones pattered against the shutter. Conlon dropped it. He took a double-barreled shotgun from a rack and broke it to check the loads. Wood smashed against wood as the mob tried to ram in the door. Conlon took a six-shooter from a rack and brought it to Holt.

"Take it," he said. "If they get past me, you'll be on your own."

"Let me out to back your play."

For a long moment Conlon eyed Holt. Then he opened the door. "Come on," he said.

They stood in the dim office and listened to the insensate growling of the mob. A bottle smashed against the wall. Holt raised his head as he heard a metallic rapping at the rear door. Conlon turned. "A trick," he said. He walked to the rear door. "Who is it?"

The voice was muffled. Conlon unlocked the door and let a man in. The two of them came into the front office. Holt looked at Lew Manning. Manning rested his thumbs in his gun belt and eyed Holt. "It sure didn't take you long to get crotch deep in trouble," he said.

"What's he doing in here?" Holt asked Conlon.

"He's the only man around here they'll listen to," said Conlon.

The ram thudded against the door. A board split and plaster rattled on the floor.

"That's Drake out there," Lew Manning said softly. "I mighta known."

Holt leaned against the wall. "He's got no love for me."

"Neither have I," Manning snapped. "There ain't been nothing but trouble since you showed up."

"Trouble because I bucked against you. Who are you? God?"

"Dammit!" Conlon roared. "The man came here to help, Cooper! Keep a civil tongue in your head!"

"Shove it," Holt said.

Conlon groaned. "What do we do?" he asked Lew Manning.

Manning took a sawed-off Greener from a rack. He broke it and inspected the loads and then snapped it shut. "Open that God-damned door," he said.

Conlon unlocked it and took down the bar.

"Open it," Lew said.

Conlon opened the door and then jumped to one side. A rock thudded against it. It broke and a piece of it struck Lew on the face. He shoved the door with his shoulder and stepped out on the stoop, holding the scatter-gun across his left forearm.

"Go on back to the saloons," he said.

Drake Manning stared at his elder cousin. "What the hell are you doing mixed up in this?"

"I might ask you the same thing, Drake."

"Cooper bushwhacked the Owens boys!" yelled a drunk. "Probably killed Sim Pastor too! We aim to string him up!"

Tim Conlon picked up his shotgun. He looked at Holt. "Showdown," he said.

Lew Manning said, "Listen to me, you drunken fools! I got no love for Cooper! You all know that! Innocent or guilty a man is entitled to a fair trial. I think he's guilty as Judas, but I ain't about to see him lynched. Not in *my* country!"

"Talks big, don't he!" yelled a puncher.

Charley Benton was at the front of the mob. "He threatened my bosses, Lew! I heard him. Perry gets back to the ranch and dies. Link is killed outright. Ain't that enough proof?"

Lew shook his head. "Just what *did* Perry say, Charley? Come on! Speak up!"

"He said Link had been drygulched. Said the same man shot him. Then he was quiet for quite a spell. There was blood in his throat, I guess. He coughs hard, mentions Holt Cooper and dies."

"Did he say Cooper killed Lew and shot him?"

"Well—no. Not right out."

Lew looked from one to the other of the angry men. "You hear that?"

"For God's sake," Drake said. "What more proof you want, Lew?"

"The man will be tried. Now git!"

Drake edged toward the porch. He stopped as Lew

swept back both hammers with his right hand. "Tim keeps split wads in this scattergun. I can't miss at this range. Think it over. If you get me you've got to face Tim and Cooper. It isn't worth it, men."

The men at the rear of the mob drifted backward. The front rank shifted. Then slowly they too drifted back, leaving Drake Manning alone. Cold hate twisted his handsome face. "I won't forget this, Lew," he said, and turned on a heel and strode down the street.

Lew Manning's shoulders sagged as if he were suddenly very tired.

"They won't be back," he said. "I'll stay in town tonight at the Stockmen's Hotel, Tim."

Conlon wiped the cold sweat from his face. "God," he said. "I want no more of that."

"I'll straighten Drake out." Lew looked at Holt "Get back in your cell."

Holt handed Conlon the six-gun. "Thanks, Manning," he said.

"Go to hell. I'd have done it for any man." The big rancher leaned the scattergun in a corner and walked out into the night.

Holt rolled a smoke. "Queer duck," he said.

"Lew is always getting Drake out of scrapes. I know one thing—Drake Manning ain't got a tenth the love for Lew as Lew has for him. One of these days those two will tangle. It's in the cards."

"How so?"

"Lew took Drake in when he was just a kid. Gives him money. Made him a partner. Raised him from a pup. In my opinion Drake don't appreciate a damned thing Lew ever done for him. Drake wants to be the bigshot—the boss. Mark my words. One way or another he'll have a showdown with Lew one of these days."

"Nice hombre."

"Yeah," Conlon said dryly. "Like a sidewinder. Leastways a rattler is honest enough to warn you before he makes his play. That ain't Drake Manning's way. He won't never forget what Lew did tonight."

Conlon locked Holt in his cell. Holt lay for a long time on the hard pallet, staring at the dim ceiling. Finally, he slept.

CHAPTER NINETEEN

A long about noon, Tim Conlon came down the cell corridor and unlocked Holt's cell door. "Someone to see you," he said.

Holt followed the sheriff into the front office. Sloan Minner stood there. "You sure can get into a mess when you have a mind to," he said.

"I'll admit it looks bad," Holt said.

Minner was nervous. He kept glancing back over his shoulder. "I talked to Judge Ames this morning. He's willing to let you out on bail."

"Nice of him," Holt said.

"I'd almost rather you stayed here," Minner said. "I'll put up the bail but what happens once you go back to the ranch?"

"Let me worry about that, Sloan."

"He's right, Cooper," Conlon said. "One way or another you'll get into trouble."

"Pay the bail," Holt said shortly.

They walked out into the sunlit street. People stared curiously at them. "I'll buy," Holt said.

"You're loco."

"Why?"

"Most everyone believes you bushwhacked the Owens boys."

"Do you?"

"I don't know what to believe."

Holt walked up onto the porch of the Stockmen's Bar. "I'll be all right," he said, and Minner trudged after him.

The barkeep got nervous the moment he saw Holt. He mopped the bar, glanced at the other men in the big saloon, and finally produced a bottle of rye in response to Holt's second request.

Minner downed two drinks in rapid succession. "There's a train outa here in an hour," he said. "Take it. I'll sell the ranch. I'll tell Conlon where you can be found, but nobody else. What do you say?"

"I'm staying."

"You're as loco as Niles was. Threats didn't bother him either. You know where *he* ended up."

Holt downed his drink and slowly built a smoke. "Why are you so damned anxious to have me sell? You won't make a fortune on a commission, Minner."

Minner smashed his glass down on the bar. "You're a plumb fool! You rile the Mannings. Get accused of killing Sim Pastor, Link and Perry Owens. Damn near get lynched. Take my advice and get out of here or I'll let you walk right into another killing. And this time it'll be *you!*"

"Let me worry about that."

"I will!" Minner jammed his hat down on his head and stamped from the bar.

Holt grinned as he filled his glass. The old boy was really worried...

The barkeeper came along the bar. "How long you planning on staying?" he asked.

"Why?"

"I don't want no trouble, mister. Drake Manning's still in town."

Holt emptied his glass and paid for the drinks. "You don't have to take the mirror down," he said. "I'll go."

A man came up the porch stairs as Holt reached the

batwings. Holt looked into the eyes of Drake Manning. The rancher stopped short and looked quickly up and down the street.

"Nervous?" Holt asked.

"Get out of my way, Cooper."

"You can walk around, sonny. What's wrong? Walt Short missing? You can make your own play, or don't you have the guts?"

Manning's lips peeled back from his teeth.

"One of these days, Cooper, I'll get you. *One way or another.*"

Holt grinned. "I'll be around."

Manning edged past him. "You think you're a lot of man," he said.

"Texans have a habit of being just that."

Manning placed his back against the wall of the saloon. He glanced down at the Colt in Holt's Missouri holster and then up into the cold eyes.

Holt stepped down into the street and walked toward the livery stable. If he had gauged Drake right the man lacked the guts to draw on him. He glanced back. Manning was gone.

He got his dun and rode out on the sunlit road.

CHAPTER TWENTY

Shadow Valley seemed as peaceful as the Garden of Eden. Holt stopped now and then in his shingling and looked across the sunlit valley. Smoke drifted up from the house where Vivian Leslie busied herself preparing dinner. Ab Chisum had ridden to the brakes to see how many steers were still left on the ranch. Holt wasn't optimistic about Ab's success. If the little waddie found a dozen steers Holt would consider himself lucky.

Holt worked steadily, while his mind sought to unravel the mystery that seemed to get more tangled with the passage of time. Five men had died on or near the Diamond W range. Sam Chase, supposedly a suicide, might have been murdered. Niles had died because he bucked the Mannings and the Owenses. But then the Owenses had been killed by the mysterious sharpshooter Holt had found in the hills. Sim Pastor had been suspected of rustling and died because of it.

The slaughter of the Owens brothers had cast a different light on the whole matter. It narrowed the killings down to the Mannings. Yet Lew Manning didn't seem the kind of man who would hire a killer. If he wanted a fight to the death, he would sling his own lead. Holt stopped his hammering and looked east across the valley toward the MM.

"Drake Manning," he said softly.

Holt had run into night riders along the Pecos in New Mexico and in the Sulphur Springs Valley of Arizona. They had created a wave of terrorism which proved so damned effective that many small-time ranchers had been forced to sell out to bigger and more powerful interests. He also remembered the stories old Cass Apperson had told him about the Ku Klux Klan.

He could see Ab riding down a long swale toward the ranch houses. "Nary a steer," he said aloud. It was what he had expected all along.

Holt went down the ladder and placed his hammer atop a pile of shingles. The roof could wait. If his plan didn't work, it wouldn't matter to him how much the damned roof leaked.

Ab led his horse up to the corral. "Nothin'," he said soberly. "They either drifted clear into Colorado or someone picked them up. Yore out of business, Holt."

Holt nodded. He tossed the makings to Ab. "Stick around," he said. "I've got some riding to do."

"Best let me go with yuh."

"This is my fight, Ab."

"One man against how many? Yuh dod-dummed hard-headed jackass!"

Holt grinned. "I like the respect you have for your boss, Ab."

The little man was troubled. "I don't mean it that-away, Holt. Yuh been square with me. I'd rather never see yuh again than to have yuh buck such crazy odds."

"This is my ranch," Holt said. "No one is going to drive me from it." He got his saddle and swung it up on Panhandle.

"Yuh want me to keep on with the shinglin'?" Ab asked.

"No. Stick close to the house. They can't do much to my range now other than to cut fences, but they sure as hell can raid the ranch and burn down the buildings like they did Niles' new barn."

Ab took his Winchester from its sheath. "I'll be the best watchdog yuh ever seen."

Holt rode toward the hills where he had killed the barefooted man. Somewhere there must be a clue as to who had hired him.

The hills were quiet and peaceful. The wind breathed cold as he led the big dun through the jumbled rock passages and carried a stench of death as he passed the place where he had hidden the body of the unknown killer. He'd have to take care of that.

The cave was as he had left it, being well hidden from prying eyes, shielded by brush, trees and rocks. He wasn't sure if it was on Owens or Manning land. He went over the cave with a fine-tooth comb. Rocks had tumbled from the roof at the rear of the cave, and he pried some of them out. There was a large cavity behind the rocks. He crawled through a hole and lit his candle. He studied the back of the cave. Cigarette butts lay on the floor and in one place smoke had stained the low ceiling. He rubbed it with his fingers. It was from a lamp.

His boots grated on a broken whiskey bottle. Two other empties lay in a corner. He felt the walls and lifted loose rock although he wasn't at all sure what he was searching for. He scanned the walls. There was a loose rock wedged in a cleft. He took it out and felt about in the cavity. His fingers touched leather. Holt took out a limp leather notebook similar to the type used by tallymen. He opened it. The first pages had been ripped from the book, making it about two thirds its original size.

He took the book out of the cave and sat down on a rock to study it. The initials D.B. had been crudely burned on the leather cover. He studied the entries on the first page. Beneath the heading of July were the initials J.S. and the date July 7th; the initials R.B. and the date July 15th; the initials C.K. and the date July 21st. Under August he read the initials O.B. and the date August 10th; the initials D.C. and the date August 21st. Under September the initials N.H.

and the date September 1st; the initials N.W. and the date September 17th. October had but one set of initials, that of S.P. and the date October 8th. All the entries except the last ended with the word *Paid*.

After he studied the book, Holt slowly lowered his hands to his lap. N.W. was Niles Williston, because Niles had been found shot to death on the 17th of September. S.P. must be Sim Pastor, who had been killed on the 8th of October. The barefooted sharpshooter had been the killer. The book proved it. But who had paid him?

A jay chattered angrily and flew off from his tree perch. Holt reached for his rifle and faded into the brush. Something clattered on the rocks south of the cave. He waited. The noise came again. The brush rustled. Then he breathed a sigh of relief as the big clay bank he had turned loose poked his head through the brush and whinnied.

Holt eyed the big horse. Someone would know whose mount this was. There could be only one solution if Holt meant to carry out the plan he had been mulling around in his mind. He stood up and walked to the big clay bank. He led him through the winding passages to a place where he had seen a sheer drop of seventy or eighty feet of crumbling rock. He shook his head as he raised the rifle. He fired. The clay bank went down heavily, crashing down the slope in a welter of loose rock to strike at the bottom of the drop half buried by the fallen rock. The echo of the shot died away in the hills.

Holt pried rock loose and tumbled it down until the clay bank was completely covered. He felt half sick as he went back to the cave.

He found a battered spade in the cave and went to the place where he had hidden the body of the unknown. It was a sickening job to uncover the swollen body and rebury it in the soft ground not far from the cave. He replaced the neatly cut sod and tramped it down to conceal the lonely grave.

The initials in the book kept running through his head.

He thought back on the *Clarion* stories he had read about the killings which had taken place before Niles had been murdered. One man had been Dan Casner, which would fit the initials D.C. Another had been named Norris Hayes. He had been found on the MM spread several weeks before Niles had met his death. That might account for the initials N.H. and the date of September 1st

He sat by the cave for a long time thinking of what he had discovered. Drake Manning was ambitious and probably murderous. He had a cruel, sadistic streak. He resented Lew and was afraid of the man who had taken him in and made him a partner.

Holt swung up on Panhandle and looked at the cave. Whoever had marked the men to be killed also must know of the cave and the coldblooded killer who had lived there while he pursued his deadly line of work. The thing that kept bothering Holt was the impression that he had seen the killer somewhere before, or someone who was a close ringer for him. But where?

The sun was dying in a glorious welter of rose and gold when he reached his fence line. He rode toward the brakes, and in the late twilight he saw the Manning range ahead of him. There was movement in the trees on both sides of the line. Holt slid from the dun and took his Winchester from its scabbard. He worked his way through the brush until he could see Lew Manning and Caleb Clarke on his side of the fence. They were examining something on the ground.

Holt grinned as he loaded the rifle. He rested it on a boulder and sighted just above the two men. He squeezed off and then dropped to the ground as the echo of the shot slammed back and forth between the hills. He could still see the two men clearly. Lew jumped for his horse. Clarke reached for his rifle and then swung up on his gray. The two of them dug in the hooks and raced for their own land, bending low in the saddle. Holt raised the Winchester and sent a slug whining over them. They vanished beyond a low ridge. Holt picked up the two hulls and put them in his pocket.

Someone had wanted a reign of terror. Holt Cooper would see that it went on, with a slight change of emphasis, until the man footing the bill came out to learn what had gone wrong.

CHAPTER TWENTY-ONE

The moon was faint in the western sky when Holt drew rein in a motte of cottonwoods and once again looked down at the Manning spread. Lamplight showed in the big house, but the bunkhouse was dark. A mule bawled from a corral as Holt tethered Panhandle to a tree and took his rifle from its scabbard. He walked to the edge of the motte and worked his way across a rock-studded meadow until he was within two hundred yards of the house.

He loaded the rifle and rested it on a rock. He sighted on the uncurtained window at the front of the house and waited to make sure no one was directly behind it. There was no movement in the room. He fired. As he reloaded he heard the distant smash of glass. He walked fifty yards to his left and smashed another window as the lights went out in the big house. A door banged and a man yelled. Holt grinned. A bucket hung from a post at the rear of the house. His third shot missed but the fourth one smashed into the bucket. He heard it bang on the ground as he reloaded.

Holt waited a little while. He detected a movement near the bunkhouse. He fired high. Then he emptied the magazine, peppering the upper walls of the big barn where he had fought Walt Short and flattened Drake Manning.

After that he walked back to the dun and mounted up.

He rode north and then followed a rocky patch of ground toward the creek. He urged the dun into the water and rode toward the bridge. He came out at the east end of the bridge and crossed the road into low hills. He rode north for half an hour, picking the rocky patches of ground, then trended west until he came out on the road again. Finally, he rode into his own valley.

Ab Chisum was in the kitchen. The little man looked suspiciously at Holt. "Yuh been actin' right queer lately," he said.

"Yeah?" Holt filled a cup with strong black coffee. "Where is she?"

"In her room. She's nervous, Holt."

"Why?"

"She don't like this night ridin' business."

"Too bad."

Ab lit a cigar. "Where did yuh ride tonight?"

"Around."

"That's a big help."

"Anything happen around here?"

Ab shook his head. "It's too damned peaceful, Holt. I don't like it."

Holt built a smoke. "Can you remember the names of the men who have been drygulched around here in the last three months?"

"I reckon so."

"Shoot."

Ab half closed his eyes. "Last July it was Joe Stroud and Ray Bascomb. Charlie Krico just vanished. Some say he was killed; others say he got scairt and bought a trunk. Then there was Oscar Brink back in August. 'Bout a week later Danny Casner got it. Norris Hayes was either killed late in August or early September. I disremember which." Ab paused, then added, "An' there was Niles on the 17th of September."

Holt nodded. He had read the entries in the leather book so many times that he knew the initials by heart.

"What are yuh drivin' at anyways?"

"Just thinking. What kind of men were they?"

"I didn't know Stroud. He was a small-time rancher livin' southeast of the MM. Ray Bascomb and Charlie Krico was partners. Sticky loopers some folks say. But I never thought they was any different from some others around here. Oscar Brink was a nice fella. Dan Casner came up here from Colorado an' bought a small spread south of here. Kept pretty much to hisself. Norris Hayes was kinda mysterious like. Some say he was an Association man. Others say he was a Pinkerton. I don't know. Spent most of his time pokin' around in the hills. When they found him he'd been cleaned out. All identification missin'. The sheriff didn't know who to notify about his death."

"Seems as though everyone around here, with one exception, has been terrorized or killed."

"You mean—the Mannings?"

"I mean the Mannings."

Ab looked back over his shoulder as though he feared someone was listening. "Watch what yuh say," he whispered.

Holt grinned at the little man's discomfiture. "It's true, isn't it?"

"Yeah. Yeah. But don't say it. For God's sake don't say it!"

Holt rested his elbows on the table. "Still, I think Lew Manning is the kind of man who invites a knockdown, drag 'em out fight."

"I'll buy that, Holt."

"That leaves Drake."

Ab filled his cup. "Drake ain't about to go over Lew's head. Not if he knows which side his bread is buttered on."

"I'm not so sure about that."

"Drake don't like takin' pills from Lew, but Lew is the boss and don't yuh forget it. If Drake took over there'd be more hell to pay around here than we already got."

"There *will* be more hell around here, Ab. You can bet on that."

The squirrel-bright eyes studied Holt. "What yuh got up that dirty sleeve of yours?"

"Nothing but a dirty arm."

Ab grunted. "Yuh been mighty quiet about things. Just what *are* yuh up to?"

"Nothing. Nothing at all."

Ab watched Holt as he got up and left the kitchen. He drained his coffee cup and then walked over to the cabinet where he kept the Abyssinian Desert Companion. He uncapped a bottle and drank it down. Then he picked up Holt's Winchester. He opened the breech, placed his thumb in it so the nail would reflect lamplight, and peered into the muzzle. The rifle was fouled with powder. Ab closed the breech and put the rifle back where he had found it. He looked at the hallway door and scratched his bristly jaw. Dod-dum it, who did that Holt think he was foolin'? Shootin' a rifle on the sly an' then not cleanin' it till mornin'!

But what in tarnation was he goin' around shootin' at?

CHAPTER TWENTY-TWO

H olt was awakened by the noisy banging of the windmill in a high wind. He shivered as he got out of bed and dressed himself. The days were gradually getting colder. He walked out into the hallway and banged on Ab's door as he passed it. The kitchen was cold and empty. Usually, Vivian was up before both of the men, preparing breakfast. Holt started the fire and placed the coffee pot on the big range. He cleaned his rifle while he waited for the coffee to boil. Now and then he caught himself listening for sounds in Vivian's room.

Ab stamped into the kitchen. "Winter's a comin' on, Holt," he said. He looked at the stove. "Where's breakfast?"

"She isn't up yet."

"Dod-dum it! I got to finish that roof afore the wind rips the new shingles off. I ain't in the mood to work in that wind without some chuck in my belly."

"Make it yourself."

"Hell with that. She took over the job."

"Go get her then."

Ab stamped back through the house. The little man was usually in a foul mood until he had eaten. Holt grinned as he heard Ab call her name. Then he heard the door creak open. Ab came back into the kitchen.

"She ain't there."

"Look outside."

Ab peered through a window. "Don't see her." He went outside and returned in a few minutes. "Guess it's up to me to make the chuck. She just plain ain't here."

Holt stood up and leaned his rifle against the wall. A chill came over him. "Do you have any idea—"

"Dod-dummed if I know. Lately she's been borrowin' my hoss and ridin' around when yore gone. I don't know where she goes."

Holt grabbed his hat. "I'll see you later."

"Yuh think she's gone for good? Is that it?"

Holt didn't answer. He picked up his rifle and went out to the barn to get his horse. The wind battered at the old barn as he saddled the dun. He rode down to the road and looked both ways. On an impulse he rode south. There was no one in sight in the wide valley. The trees thrashed in the wild wind.

He was two miles from the house when he saw her guiding Ab's mouse-colored horse down a steep slope. He kneed the dun into the shelter of the trees and watched her. She vanished among a jumble of rock knolls. Holt spurred the dun and rode swiftly to where he had last seen her. She was gone.

Holt rode to the west waterhole. There were fresh tracks on the margin, leading southwest, almost in a general line with the hills where he had found the cave. He rode toward the cave area and drew rein half a mile from it. Then he dismounted and went in afoot. Twice he saw fresh tracks and then he reached a rocky area which showed no sign of passage.

He stood there for a long time. There was only one way through that chaos of rock and trees. It led to the vicinity of the cave. But he didn't want her to know he had been there. He went back to the dun and rode back toward the ranch house. Time and time again he looked back but there was no sign of her.

He unsaddled the dun and led him into his stall. Back in

the house, he found Ab picking his teeth over a recently emptied plate.

"I'll rustle some chuck for yuh," Ab said. "Yuh see her?"

"No."

"She'll be back."

"It doesn't make any difference. I'm glad she's gone."

"Yeah, and yore a dod-dummed liar too."

Holt sat down at the table. Ab filled his coffee cup.

"Whyn't yuh get the truth outa her, Holt?"

"What do you mean?"

"She don't say nothin'. Stays around here like a respectable woman. Yeah, almost like a wife." "Shut up and get me some grub!"

Ab stamped to the stove and began to cook. He served Holt silently. Holt was done eating when they heard the stamp of hoofs outside of the kitchen. Ab peered through the window. "It's her," he said, and Holt's heart bucked. As a countermeasure, he scowled.

"Keep your mouth shut about me riding out this morning."

"Why?"

"Goddammit! Because I *say* so! That's why!" Ab looked at Holt for a moment and then he said, "I guess yuh know what yore doin'. I'll get busy on that dod-dummed roof. She kin rustle her own chuck."

She came into the kitchen and smiled at Holt. "I'm sorry," she said. "I wanted some fresh air. I thought I'd be back before you got up."

"We don't sleep late, Vivian."

Her clear skin was flushed with the beating of the cold wind. She stripped off her gloves and coat and put on an apron. "You've eaten, I see."

"Yes," he said shortly.

She studied him. "You're angry."

"Where did you go?"

"South. Then over toward the east. Why?"

He stood up. "I want you to stay close to the house, Vivian."

"Who would bother me?"

"I didn't say anyone would bother you."

"Then why do I have to stay close to the house?"

"Because I *say* so."

"I don't take orders from you or any other man, Holt."

He jerked his head toward the door. "Then you can leave."

For a moment their eyes clashed, and then she looked away. "All right," she said quietly. "I'll do as you say."

Holt walked outside. Ab was busy on the barn roof hammering angrily away. A sudden feeling came over Holt that he'd like to pull out and forget the whole damned business. But there was one thing that had to be done or he'd never be able to live with himself. He had to find the man who was responsible for the death of Niles. He glanced back at the house. Vivian was another problem. She hadn't been riding for her health.

Holt took out his sack of Ridgewood and began to build a smoke. Suddenly the face of the man he had killed flashed before him. He knew now where he had seen him. He was the man whose picture he had found in Vivian Leslie's saddlebag.

CHAPTER TWENTY-THREE

Lew Manning tethered his blocky gray to the fence and walked up the path toward the house with the deliberate stride of a man who means business. Caleb Clarke stood by Lew's horse, holding the reins of his own sorrel. Vivian Leslie stirred in her chair. "I'd better go inside," she said.

Lew stopped at the foot of the steps. "You got time to auger?" he asked Holt. He touched his hat brim and nodded to Vivian.

Holt said, "What's on your mind, Manning?"

Manning looked at Vivian. She stood up. "I was going in, Lew," she said.

Manning waited until Vivian closed the door behind her. "Somebody shot up my place a couple of nights ago, Cooper. That evening, before the shooting, somebody took a couple of shots at me and Caleb there, while we were looking for missing cows along your fence line."

"So?"

Manning leaned against a post and lit a cigar. "I don't know who did it. Do you?"

Holt shrugged. "Somebody shot up my place. Shot at me and Ab Chisum."

Manning puffed at the cigar. The glow of it lit up his

broad hard face. "There's been shooting around here aplenty, but none of it's been done at houses."

"Just men," Holt said dryly.

Manning nodded. "Now I ain't saying that you shot up my place and potted at me and Caleb. But I am saying that I had nothing to do with your place being shot at."

"I'll take your word on it."

Manning looked out over the dark valley. "I want this place so bad I can taste it, but I ain't the kind of man who uses night riders to get his way. I fight clean and in the open, Cooper."

Holt yawned. "It's a damned curious thing that none of your men have been killed by the mysterious man with the .38/56."

Manning spat. "We dug .38/56 slugs out of my house walls."

"Any name on them?"

"Damn you!"

"Why have you come here?" Holt asked.

Manning straightened up. "You won't sell the Diamond W. All right. I'm a businessman. I've got work to do. The fall gather is due. I'll give you my word that I haven't been terrorizing you. I want your word that you won't bother me."

Holt couldn't help but like the man's straightforward manner. "I'm all alone here, Manning. You've got thirty-five men in your corrida. Do you think I'd buck up against a hand like that?"

Manning puffed at his cigar. "It wouldn't surprise me. You're a hardheaded jackass, always on the prod."

"I go on the prod when I'm choused by men like Walt Short and your cousin."

Manning waved a hand. "I fired Walt for that business of going after you in my barn."

"What about Drake?"

"I need him for the fall gather, but I told him I'd had enough of his carousing and troublemaking. He's taking the train for Cheyenne tomorrow. I want him to take care of some business there for me. It'll take quite some time. That satisfy you?"

"Fair enough."

Manning stuck out a big hand. "Let's shake on it then."

Holt gripped the rancher's hand. Manning walked toward his horse. Then he turned. "One thing. I don't like to give advice. But I'm going to do it now. Get rid of that woman, Cooper."

"You can keep your advice."

Manning untethered his gray and swung up on it with a smash of leather. "Some of my men will come over on your range to check the brakes for strays."

"You'll notify me first."

Manning scowled. "That ain't necessary."

"It is with me. I want to know who's on my range."

Manning kneed the horse away from the fence. "Like I said, you're a hardheaded jackass to do business with."

"Just keep your nose clean, Manning, and you won't have any shooting trouble."

Holt watched them ride toward the road. Somehow, he believed the big man. Maybe Holt was a damned fool, but Manning's talk had had the ring of sincerity.

Holt walked to the corral and got Panhandle. Ab came out of the house. "I was listenin' through the window," he said.

"You got a big nose, Ab."

"I ain't ashamed. You believe him?"

"What do you think?"

"He usually keeps bis word."

"I'll chance it then."

"Where you headin' now? More night ridin'?"

"I'll be back in about two hours."

Ab watched Holt ride off into the darkness. He shoved back his hat and scratched his head.

Holt rode south and then turned toward the hills where the cave was hidden. Somebody had paid the killer to do his bloody work. A contact had to be made. The man who showed up would be the man Holt wanted. It was as simple as that.

At midnight, Holt finally gave up his chilly vigil. He picked up his rifle and walked to where he had left the dun. Maybe the payoff man was too slick to come into the hills. Maybe the killer had received his blood money somewhere else.

Holt rode swiftly from the hills and headed for the ranch. The wind shifted when he was a mile from the house. He drew rein and listened. Then he heard it again. The distant crack of a rifle. He drove in the steel and raced the dun down the slope until he was a quarter of a mile from the house. He could see flashes on the steep slope behind the house and answering flashes from the house. The crackle of gunfire carried clearly to him.

He urged the dun up the slope and into a motte of cottonwoods. He ripped his Winchester from its scabbard and trotted up the slope, picking his way through the loose talus from the crumbling face of the butte. Half a dozen rifles were blasting away on the slope. As he stopped, he heard the smash of glass in the house. A rifle flared from a kitchen window and was answered by half a dozen slugs. The echoes rose and died away from the face of the butte.

Holt worked his way through the thick brush and came out two hundred yards behind the unseen marksmen. He dropped behind a rock ledge and slid his rifle forward, levering a round into the chamber.

A shadowy figure moved from behind a tree. Holt fired. The man jumped as though stung by a yellowjacket. Holt pumped out three more rounds. Men yelled. Two rifles flashed in his direction. The slugs slapped into the butte face. Holt dropped. He crawled fifty yards to his left and opened fire again. Then he crawled up the slope and ran swiftly to the south. He dropped behind a boulder and reloaded.

Scattered fire broke out. They were searching the dark slopes to the north of Holt's position. He fired at a flash and a hoarse yell rewarded him. Then there was a long silence, broken at last by the thud of hoofs. He churned three shots toward the sound and walked back to the dun.

Hoofs drummed on the valley road as he mounted. He touched the dun with his spurs and rode toward the house. Cautiously he dismounted behind the old barn and padded through it afoot. "Ab!" he yelled as he reached the door.

"That you, Holt?"

"Yes."

"Come on in. I think they're gone."

Holt sprinted across to the house and walked into the smoky kitchen. Ab lit a candle. Blood dripped from his cheek. "You hurt, Ab?" asked Holt.

"Glass cut. Vivian was hit."

"Where is she?"

"In her room."

Holt hurried to her. She lay on the bed. Her left dress sleeve had been ripped away and a bloody bandage was bound about her upper arm. Holt dropped beside her. She opened her eyes. "It's all right," she said faintly. "Just a flesh wound."

He kissed her. Ab came into the dimly lit room. "They showed up about an hour ago. It was Drake Manning and some of the MM boys. They wanted you."

Holt stood up. "Why?"

Ab wet his dry lips. "They yelled out that they come for you. That you laid in ambush for Lew Manning."

"That's a damned lie!"

Ab's eyes were steady and cold. "Mebbe. But Lew Manning is dead. Shot through the head. Caleb Clarke was with him when he got it. Caleb rode to the MM and said Lew had been killed on the Diamond W."

"Just talked to him tonight! We made a deal!"

Ab nodded. "I overheard it. If I was you, I'd pull out of here. Hide in the hills. Yuh skinned outa that Sim Pastor killin'. Yuh won't skin outa this one."

Holt stared at the little man. "You don't think I killed Sim, do you?"

"No. But a lot of people around here think you did. Yuh

ain't got time to stand there talkin' about it. Yuh gotta move!"

Vivian said, "He's right, Holt. Drake will hound you down. Get away from here while you have the chance."

Holt looked from one to the other of them. They were right. Drake would be back with the whole damned MM corrida, and this time they wouldn't let rifle fire scare them away. Lew Manning had been a popular boss.

CHAPTER TWENTY-FOUR

Holt carried his gear into the hideout he had picked high on a hill which overlooked the rugged brakes and part of his range. It was the time of the false dawn, and the eastern sky was gray with the promise of the rising sun. He rigged a tarp across a sapling and placed his hot-roll and war bag inside the shelter. The dun was picketed in a deep gully half a mile from camp.

From his place of vantage, Holt could see anyone approaching long before the visitor found the way to his hideout. When the valley grew lighter, he took the field-glasses Ab had given him from one of his saddlebags and began to search the terrain far below him. There was no sign of pursuit. They'd be back at the house before long. Maybe they were there now.

Holt pulled off his boots and unrolled his hot-roll. He lay there for a long time, smoking and wondering what in hell's name would happen now.

It was late morning when he awoke and began his survey of the sunlit valley. A steer grazed not far from the creek. A hawk hung high in the cloudless sky. That was all.

He sat there for an hour and then restlessness slipped the bit into his mouth and urged him to do something. He took off his spurs and picked up his Winchester. He slipped biscuits and a can of beans into his coat pocket and padded down the rocky slope to the south.

It was quiet in the rock passages which led to the cave. A lizard darted for cover in front of him. A jay chattered angrily and then flew off. He stopped in front of the lonely cave and looked about. Nothing had been changed. He went in, looked around, and came out again.

Something fluttered at his feet. He stooped and picked up a piece of linen. A handkerchief. He spread it out. The initial had been worked into one corner with fine thread. "V," he said aloud. "Vivian." A dark uneasiness stole over him. She *had* been here. The morning he'd followed her, she'd come here.

He placed the handkerchief in his shirt pocket. If he ever got out of this tight, he'd force the truth from her.

Holt went back to his hideout. Just as he arrived, he saw the distant movement in the valley. He focused his glasses and saw five men, riding with rifles across their thighs, heading toward the brakes.

An hour later, he saw four men ride out of a motte close to the MM line and then head north. The MM boys were on the prod all right.

"Damned convenient for Drake Manning," he said aloud. "Just as he's about to be exiled to Cheyenne his cousin gets killed, supposedly by me. Puts the MM in his hands and puts the blame on me. Once he gets me, he can pressure Minner into selling him the Diamond W."

Holt placed the glasses on his bedroll. Two men knew he was the owner of the Diamond W through Niles' will. Everyone else thought he had bought it. He took a pencil from his shirt pocket and opened the leather book he had found in the cave. He wrote slowly for twenty minutes and then signed what he had written. He placed the book back in his coat pocket.

Holt had never been on the run in his life. It bothered him, but there was nothing he could do about it. Just sweat it out, hoping for some kind of break, he thought.

Well after dark, Holt left the hideout and rode down

toward the house. He studied it at a distance, not daring to go any closer. There might be men waiting there for him to return. He rode toward the road that led into Rockyhill, turned the dun into the brush, and heard the steady beat of hoofs. Several men riding swiftly to the west.

He followed the creek to the south until he was even with the Manning buildings and then he dismounted. He left the dun in the motte of cottonwoods on the Manning side of the line. He took his Winchester and climbed to the top of a low ridge which overlooked the Manning spread. Now he could see men moving back and forth in the light from doorways and windows. Some of them rode north. Another party left soon after that, heading toward the brakes to the south.

Holt waited until the activities died down, then he worked his way through a deep ditch until he was a hundred yards from the big barn. He squatted there, patient as an Indian, chewing on an unlit cigar. The lights went out in the bunkhouse. A man carrying a lantern walked from the barn to the bunkhouse and extinguished the lantern. The only light on in the big house was in the kitchen. Now and then the vagrant wind picked up the rattling of pots and pans from the house. Then the kitchen light winked out and a moment later the rear door of the house opened and closed. A man stopped to light a smoke and then walked over to a small shack near the bunkhouse. The light went on and then a few minutes later it too went out.

Holt cached his rifle and pulled off his boots. He worked his way closer to the barn. The rear door gaped open. He padded into the big building. A horse whinnied from a stall but quieted when Holt spoke softly to it. He walked to the front of the barn and waited twenty minutes, listening to every night sound.

He crossed swiftly and silently to the house and eased through an open window. The odor of cooking hung heavily in the darkness. There was no sound in the house except the furious ticking of a waggletail clock on the living room wall. Holt moved down a hallway, listening for heavy breathing.

He looked into a big bedroom. The bed was empty. He checked another bedroom, but it was empty also. A door opened to his left and he slipped into a small room. A big rolltop desk stood against the south wall. He listened for a time and then eased up the cover of the desk.

The window shade had been drawn down, so he risked lighting a few matches. He found the usual things—account books, bank book, tally books, a wad of old letters and the miscellaneous objects a man will keep in a desk.

He went to the smaller of the two bedrooms. A picture on the bureau showed Drake Manning sitting a fine black. Holt rummaged through the small desk and then through the bureau drawers. If Manning had been paying his killer he must have a record of the payments somewhere, and quite likely he wouldn't carry it on his person. Holt felt under the mattress with no luck. He didn't dare stay in the house too long. He rubbed his jaw and looked about the room. A small shelf of books offered possibilities. He took each book out in turn and riffled through the pages. Still no luck.

A dog barked sharply just outside of the house. Holt stood still and waited. The dog barked again, then padded alongside the house and stopped below the bedroom window. A deep growling came from his throat. A door banged somewhere in the darkness.

Holt replaced the last book and walked into the hallway. The dog began to bark at the front of the house.

"Shut up, Bonehead!" a man yelled from the side of the house.

The dog growled, barked once more, then suddenly yelped and ran off. "That'll learn yuh!" said the man. Boots thudded alongside the house.

Holt walked into the big kitchen. The sound of footsteps died away. The dog was near the big barn now and he began to bark again. Holt eased through the back door and looked toward the barn. The dog barked louder. Holt moved swiftly toward the side of the house and crashed squarely into a man. "What the hell!" the man said.

Holt drove a left into the man's gut. As his head came

down Holt slid his arm around it and clamped a hard hand on the mouth. He grunted as the man brought up a knee that barely missed his groin. The man opened his mouth, and his teeth sank into Holt's hand. Holt winced in pain. He hammered away at the bristly jaw with bis right fist. The man was strong and big and he struggled like a wildcat. Holt's hand was bleeding, but he managed to pinch his opponent's nostrils together with his thumb and forefinger.

They went battling back against the house. Holt clamped his hand tighter on mouth and nostrils. A fist bounced from Holt's jaw. He began to drive hard upper-cuts and felt the man weaken. The man broke away and sucked in a noisy breath, enough to yell. Holt whipped out his six-shooter and laid it cleanly alongside his opponent's head. The man went down like a sack of wheat.

Holt sprinted for the west fence. The dog tore after him, barking. Holt reached the fence. He whirled, cocking the Colt. It crashed once. The slug struck the dog in the head. He thrashed about as Holt got through the fence.

Holt raced for his horse, hearing men yell back at the bunkhouse. A door banged open, and boots thudded on the hardpacked earth. Holt jumped into the ditch and grabbed his boots. As he pulled them on, he looked back. Shadowy figures milled around the dog. A rifle spat flame. Holt snatched up his Winchester and sprinted down the ditch, making heavy going in the soft earth. He heard the fence wire twang as the men came through. He whirled, levered in a round, and snapped a shot over their heads.

The dun was still in the cottonwoods. Holt swung up on him and gave him the steel. He rode south. He could see lights on at the Manning place, but no signs of pursuit. He had done nothing to further his purpose except buffalo a man and kill a dog.

CHAPTER TWENTY-FIVE

T hey swept over the Diamond W like a plague of locusts, and they were just as thorough. They used wire cutters, bullets and fire, and they did not stop until the Diamond W had been ravaged except for the house which sat on the benchland overlooking the only thing that was left. They could not hurt the valley itself unless they plowed it up and sowed it with salt, and that would have been against their purpose. But the fences were down, the few cattle lay bloating in the sun, and the outbuildings were rectangles of blackened ruin on the ground.

There was one thing left for them to do—to find Holt Cooper. In this they failed. They saw him and heard the eerie whine of his bullets, but it was like chasing a ghost When they cut his fences, he cut theirs. For every Diamond W steer that died, he collected the life of an MM critter. Three of the MM line shacks burned to the ground. A greenish, bloated carcass lay in each of their waterholes. One night fifty head of MM steers vanished through a wide gap in the wire and were lost in the brakes. When the MM waddies went in after them, whining .38/56 slugs turned the expedition into a panicky flight

It was time for the fall gather but the men of the MM dared not go into the broken country. Three of them pursued the big man who fired at them. Two horses were killed, and one rider went home with a bullet-smashed shoulder. That night an outbuilding of the MM, packed to the rafters with hay, went up like a torch. Bullets chased the would-be firefighters back to the protection of thick logs.

The time of the moon came again, bathing the country in silver light, softening the rocky hills. Shadow Valley had lived up to the curse which was supposed to have been laid upon it, but it was beautiful under the soft night light.

Holt Cooper had one magazine load of rifle cartridges left. His clothing was tattered and stinking. His boots were paper thin, and his dun needed shoeing. His ragged beard mantled his face and his belly needed other food than meat.

He came down out of the hills at night and looked at his house through his field glasses. The house was dark and cold. For a time, he had wondered why they spared the log house, and then the lobo instinct in him had warned of a trap. Vivian and Ab must be gone. He had seen no signs of life about the house for days. There were no mules nor horses in the peeled pole corral. The barn roof was still half shingled.

He left the bay hidden in an arroyo and went forward with rifle ready. The moonlight glinted now and then from the shards of glass which still remained in the window frames or littered the ground below them. Yard by yard he came down the slope until he could lie concealed in the brush one hundred yards from the deserted house.

He watched for a long time, then stood up. There might be some food left. And a few cartridges for his best friend—his Winchester.

He took one step forward and stopped. The vagrant wind had carried a faint sound to him. He waited. The sound came again. A cough.

The wind stirred the trees and sang softly through the frame of the windmill. It moaned about the house and passed inquisitive fingers over Holt Cooper.

The flare of the match came so suddenly that it startled him. First there was inky darkness in the house and then there was the quick yellowish flare of the lucifer. He caught a glimpse of a face and then it disappeared, leaving only the tiny dot of fire which flared up and died away as the cigarette smoke was inhaled.

He eased back and squatted in the brush. His slitted vision passed over the ground, inch by inch. Then he saw a suspicious shadow among the trees near the gate. It was too fat for a natural shadow. Another man.

He looked back over his shoulder. Minutes ticked past. He heard the scuffle of something to his left amongst a jumbled mass of rock. A cold finger seemed to trace the length of his spine. He had passed within a hundred yards of the man hidden there. He lay down and bellied his way out of the brush, taking advantage of every wrinkle on the ground. His elbows and knees were raw when at last he reached a rock ledge on the slope, just below the dark towering butte.

Holt lay flat and rested his chin on his forearms. They figured he was still in the hills. They had taken a chance that he might return to the house for supplies or to see Vivian. Neat, very neat, he thought. But he still needed cartridges. He had used up his own supply and those he had found in the cave. There was just one place to replenish his stock. Rockyhill.

He turned the thought over in his mind and then grinned. It was the last place they would think of looking for him. He looked down at the brooding house, bathed in the soft peaceful light. A house which held death for one Holt Cooper. "Sit there, you bastards," he said softly. "Sit there all night and freeze your rumps off."

He padded through the brush to Panhandle. He led the big dun along the base of the butte, picking his way past talus piles, until he was a mile from the house. Then he mounted and rode east until he reached the creek. He rode the dun into the water and rode toward the bridge.

When he reached the road, clear in the moonlight, he headed for Rockyhill. Just like any peaceful rancher going to town on Saturday night for a high lonesome.

CHAPTER TWENTY-SIX

The road had been as empty as last night's bottle of forty-rod. Holt left the dun in the woods west of the creek. Hipshot ponies dozed at the hitching racks in front of the saloons, and only the saloons showed much light. Holt walked through the alleys until he reached Sloan Minner's house. He stood in the shadows of the small barn for a while, watching the house. Then he tried the back door. It swung open at his touch.

He walked into the dim parlor. Minner's big Bible was placed squarely in the center of the round, marble-topped table, which was placed squarely in the center of the room. Holt wondered if Minner kept it there to ease his conscience about the high prices he charged.

The sound of dry breathing came from the bedroom. Holt walked in and looked down at Minner. Then he placed a cool hand on the old man's forehead. Minner gasped and opened his eyes. "I tell you I don't know where he is," he said. Then he stared at Holt. "*You!* Almighty God! What are you doing here?"

"I've been in the hills, Sloan. I'm running out of supplies, cartridges and patience."

Minner sat up. "Yeah, but there's one thing you ain't run out of, Holt."

"What's that?"

"Pure cussedness. Shooting up the MM. Killing cattle. Killing men. Those who live by the sword shall die by the sword. Remember that!"

Holt stepped back. "I haven't killed any men."

"No? What about Sim Pastor and Lew Manning? What about Link and Perry Owens?"

"Damn you! I said I hadn't killed any men!"

Minner stood up and scratched his lean belly under his nightshirt. "It's your word against that of many."

Holt gripped him by the front of his nightshirt. "Look, Minner. I've been fighting for my home. Have you heard what *they* did? My fences have been cut. I haven't got a single head of stock. My house is all that's left of the ranch. The rest is ashes. Why, even tonight I found men waiting for me at the house. It hasn't been any box supper at the Ladies Aid for me."

Minner loosened Holt's hand. "Take it easy. What do you want?"

"Grub. Cartridges."

"You don't expect me to get them from the store?"

"I've got to have them."

Minner rubbed his forehead. "All right. All right. I'll give you a key. Take what you want but mark it down. Mind now, mark it—"

"You'll get your money."

"How? You're out of business."

"I'm still in business as long as I'm alive."

"What kind of business? Colt and Winchester business, that's what! I wish to God I'd never seen you."

Holt walked to the door. "You'll get paid for your trouble."

Minner pulled on his trousers over his nightshirt. "Yeah. By Drake Manning. Things have changed. Lew was no bargain, but Drake is a hellion."

"Give me the damned key!"

Minner opened a dresser drawer and took out a key. "Be

careful," he said. "I don't want people to think I'm helping an outlaw."

Holt took the key. "I'll be out of there in less than fifteen minutes. Is Ab in town?"

"Yes. He's bunking at the livery stable."

"Where is Vivian Leslie?"

Minner seemed to hesitate. "Around town. You mixed up with her too?"

"You know damned well she was out at my place."

"The whole town knows it now. Why did she come to you?"

"I don't know myself."

"There's a lot of dirty talk going on."

"That could be expected."

"You know Drake Manning is interested in her. What are you trying to do, Cooper?"

"Let me worry about what I'm trying to do. I want the man that killed Niles. I'll go about it in my own way."

"Like a bull in a china shop," Minner said. He came close to Holt. "Look. Let me sell the place. You get out of town. Go to Cheyenne or anywhere you like. Send me your forwarding address. I'll sell the place for a good price. Take the woman with you. For God's sake listen to reason!"

"I'm staying." Holt walked to the back door followed by Minner.

"Anyone see you in town?"

"You think I'm that big a fool?"

"Now that you ask me, I'll say you *are* a fool."

Holt opened the door. "Thanks for everything."

Minner nodded. He watched Holt go past the barn. Then he walked into the living room and lit a lamp. He slewed the big Bible about and opened it. He put on his glasses and peered closely at the page. "Ezekiel, chapter thirty-three," he read. "Son of man, speak to the children of thy people, and say unto them, 'When I bring the sword upon a land, if the people of the land take a man of their coasts, and set him for their watchman:

"'If when he seeth the sword come upon the land, he blow the trumpet, and warn the people;

"'Then whosoever heareth the sound of the trumpet, and taketh not warning; if the sword come, and take him away, his blood shall be upon his own head.

"'He heard the sound of the trumpet, and took not warning; his blood shall be upon him. But he that taketh warning shall deliver his soul.

"'But if the watchman see the sword come, and blow not the trumpet, and the people be not warned; if the sword come, and take *any* person from among them, he is taken away in his iniquity; but his blood I shall require at the watchman's hand.'"

Minner closed his eyes, running his gnarled forefinger up and down the open pages. He stopped his finger and looked at the words. "Say thou thus unto them, Thus saith the Lord GOD: As I live, surely they that *are* in the wastes shall fall by the sword, and him that is in the open field will I give to the beasts to be devoured, and they that be in the forts and in the caves shall die of the pestilence."

Minner felt the cold sweat work down his skinny sides. He closed the Bible and laid his hand upon it. Then he dressed swiftly and left the house. He hurried through the alleyway to Front Street and headed for the Stockmen's Bar. Now and then he looked over his shoulder as if the devil himself were threading the byways after him, and there was an ungodly fear in him.

CHAPTER TWENTY-SEVEN

Holt took a carton of .38/56 cartridges from the glass case. He slid two boxes of six-gun cartridges into his coat pocket. He walked to the grocery department and took a small gunnysack from a pile. He began to fill it with food. Suddenly he stopped and turned. The store was dark, dimly lit by the rays of the moon which poked around the sides of the tattered shades and through the holes.

Shouldering the gunnysack, he walked through the rear office to the door. A subtle warning seemed to come to him from out of the night. He drew his Colt and eased open the door. Silvery light revealed the whole alley.

He stood there like a hunted animal, listening to the night sounds: the distant bark of a dog; the soughing of the wind through the trees on the next street; the thud of a restless pony's hoof from Front Street.

He slung the sack over his left shoulder and stepped out into the alleyway. Something moved between two sheds fifty feet up the street. Holt faded back into the shadows and turned to go the other way. A man looked around the side of a shed. The moonlight shone on metal. Holt cocked his Colt.

"Stay where you are," the man warned. "Drop that six-shooter."

Holt jumped back between two buildings as a pistol roared and flashed up the alleyway. The slug rapped into the corner of the general store, ripping loose a long splinter. Another six-gun spat flame directly across from Holt.

The slug fanned past his head. He jumped behind a rain barrel and fired. A man grunted.

Holt sprinted for Front Street as a hell's delight of shooting rippled out in the alleyway. "He's heading for the main stem!" yelled a man. Boots thudded on the packed earth.

Holt ran the length of the long porch in front of the store. A pistol flashed from across the street, followed by the deeper booming of a shotgun. The double charge whipped past Holt, jerking at his coat tail. Something stung his left side. He gasped as he stepped off the end of the porch. A gun spat flame to his right from the alley behind the store. He ran down the street toward the bridge, cursing the weight of the gunnysack. A man jumped out from behind a wagon and raised a rifle. Holt hurled the sack at him. He went over backwards, dropping the rifle.

Holt jumped behind a building and ripped out two shots. A light went on behind the window in back of him, outlining him. He ran for the bridge as slugs whispered about him. The door of the livery stable opened. A little man jumped out into the street holding a shotgun. He raised it. "Ab!" Holt yelled. "It's me! Cooper!"

"Run, yuh loco bastard!"

Ab threw the shotgun to Holt. The little man opened up with his Colt, spraying the air with slugs. Holt raced for the bridge. He hammered across it and then plunged into the brush as he heard the beat of hoofs on the hard earth of the main street.

"Get the sheriff!" a man yelled.

Holt plowed through the brush. A horseman thundered across the bridge and drew rein. He stood up in his stirrups and looked toward Holt. Holt whirled and touched off both barrels. The shotgun threw its load of slugs over the man's head. He dropped into his saddle and turned his horse, digging in the hooks. Holt threw the shotgun into the creek and ran for his dun. He swung up and reached down to untether the reins. More horses were raising the dust on Front Street.

Holt dug his spurs into the dun's flanks and headed south through the woods, reloading his Colt as he rode. He left the woods and set the dun at a low fence. Panhandle cleared it easily.

The wind carried the sound of shooting to Holt as he crossed a grassy meadow and rode toward the hills behind the town.

Sloan Minner was at the bar when Drake Manning pushed through the batwings and stamped toward him. The saloon was empty. Even the bartender had gone outside to see the fun. Manning stopped beside Minner. "It was him all right. Whyn't you tell me earlier?"

Minner downed his rye. "I told you he come to the house and took the store key. You think I wanted him watching for me when I come out? I had to give him time to get into the store, didn't I?"

"You never did have any guts."

Minner coughed. "I wish I never got mixed up with you, Manning."

"Yeah? Well, you are!"

Minner refilled his glass. "There's one way you might round him up."

"So?"

Minner's pale eyes half closed. "Ab Chisum worked with him. Ab's staying at the livery stable. Get the little sonofabitch and make him talk. He'll know where Cooper's hiding out."

Manning nodded. "Yeah. I never thought of that."

Minner wet his lips. "I tried to get Cooper to leave town. If he does, I'll sell you the Diamond W."

"There's one thing I never figured out about you, Minner. You told me you'd sell me the Diamond W after Niles Williston was killed. That was taken care of. Then you make a deal with Holt Cooper. Why?"

Minner swallowed hard. "I was afraid of him."

Manning gripped Minner by the front of his coat. He cocked a big fist. "Talk, you sanctimonious bastard! Why did you do it?"

Minner placed a hand on Manning's. "All right. Holt Cooper is Williston's half-brother. He come here to find out who killed Williston. Williston left him the Diamond W."

Manning slowly released the trembling storekeeper. "So that's it!"

"Yeah," Minner said shakily. "Now let me alone."

Manning filled a glass. "Why didn't you tell me before this?"

"Like I said, I'm afraid of him. He's hard, Drake. Hard as a diamond. A killer if I ever seen one."

Manning eyed the old man. "You damned liar. You had power of attorney to sell the Diamond W. You figured you'd hold me up for it."

Minner shook his head. "You kill him and then what happens? Maybe he ain't got a will. Then you'll never get your hands on the Diamond W. Leastways for a long time."

"I got ways," Manning said. "Anyone else takes over the place and they'll damned soon find out who runs this country."

Tim Conlon came in. "Goddammit! What's been going on here?"

Manning turned. "It was Cooper. Stealing food from Minner's Emporium. Sloan here found out and tipped me off."

"You taking the law into your own hands again?"

"Yes," Drake Manning said flatly. "If it wasn't for me and Lew, you'd still be a jailkeeper here in Rockyhill instead of sheriff. And don't you ever forget it."

Conlon ripped off his badge. "Take it," he said.

Manning sneered at the badge. "You keep it. You got a job to do. Ten of my men are here in town. Swear them in. We'll comb them damned hills until we find him. Hear?"

"All right," Conlon said quietly, "But we'll do it my way. He comes in for trial. I'm the law here."

Manning grinned. "Have it your own way. But get moving."

"You coming along?"

"No. I've got to protect my interests. I'm going home."

Conlon left. Minner filled his glass. He hiccupped. "God help me," he said.

Manning walked to the door. "You say Ab's at the livery stable?"

"Yes."

"Fine." Manning walked out into the street. Walt Short came up. "He winged Chuck Heeney," Short said.

"Goddammit! You had him boxed in."

"I didn't see you out there, *boss.*"

Manning flushed. "Ab Chisum is staying at the livery stable. Go get him. Take him out the ranch. He makes any commotion, you slap him silly. Hear?"

Short nodded. He walked toward the livery stable. Manning lit a cigar. He looked back at the saloon. So Cooper was Williston's half-brother. Things were getting complicated. But not too complicated for Drake Manning.

CHAPTER TWENTY-EIGHT

Bedloe was awakening as Holt rode down the main street. Storekeepers were washing down their front windows and sluicing down their porches. Kids were on their way to the white-painted school whose bell was ringing steadily, echoing back from the hills.

Holt dismounted in front of the livery stable. A big man looked up from his work. "Mornin'," Holt said. "My dun needs shoes."

"This is the place to get 'em." The blacksmith examined the dun. "You been ridin' a lot."

Holt nodded.

"Where you from?"

"Cheyenne."

"A long ways," the smith said. "You want the dun fed?"

"Yes. Where can I get a good breakfast?"

"Over to the Deluxe. Right across from the post office. Tell Maggie I sent you."

Holt eased his crotch. The dun was beat and so was he. He walked to the Deluxe and sat at the counter. The place was empty except for a fat blonde who sat behind the counter. "Morning," she said.

"Fried eggs, ham, potatoes. The works."

She eyed his dusty clothing. "You come a long way?"

"Cheyenne."

"That *is* a long way." She smiled archly. "Staying long?"

"Long enough to get my horse shoed and fill my belly."

She sighed. "That's the way it always is."

"What do you mean?"

"Bedloe is like living on Mars. Fine looking men come in, eat and have their hosses shod, and then they take off."

"What's the best way to get to the range country north of here?"

She cracked an egg and put it on the grill. "Take the creek road east and then south. You missed your turn three miles back."

"There should be a quicker way."

She nodded as she cracked another egg and placed a slab of ham on the grill. "You can go through the hills. Rough country. Dangerous too."

"How so?"

"Rustlers and suchlike. All kinds of trouble on the range north of here. Killings and rustling. We used to get some of the trouble awhile back. Men would drive cows through here heading for the Colorado line. First thing you know, here would come a posse. They had some shooting just south of here once. Killed two rustlers and wounded one. It was exciting. Don't happen anymore though. Like I said, it's like living on Mars."

She dumped potatoes in the grease. "You looking for someone?"

"Why do you ask?"

"Most strangers that come through here are usually looking for someone—or running away from someone looking for them."

"I'm clean, if that's what you mean."

"Oh, I didn't mean that." She studied him. "You look like a nice fella. You married?"

"No."

She smiled. "There's a dance at the Bijou hall tonight."

"That's nice."

Her face fell. "You're leaving today then?"

"Yes."

"That figures. They come in, eat and get their horses shod and then take off into the hills. Maybe you're an Association man."

"No."

"U.S. Marshal?"

"No."

"Pinkerton then?"

"You're burning the ham, sister."

She served him silently, but she couldn't stay that way.

"Once a woman come through here. Not too long ago either."

Holt looked up quickly, ham pouched in his cheek.

"I knew you'd be interested," she said.

"Why?"

"She was a woman, wasn't she? Best story I got to tell." Maggie touched up her dry hair. She filled two coffee cups and leaned against the counter. "My, you was hungry. More ham? Eggs? Toast?"

"Just toast."

She sliced the bread. "She come in here one evening. Looking for a man, she said. What woman *ain't?* Hawww! Raining like blazes it was. She was tired. I seen her hoss. A fine mare with a sidesaddle. Don't nobody ride sidesaddle around here anymore. She et like she was starved. Fine looking woman. I tell you the boys eyed her up and down like they was thinking of indecent things. Dark hair and eyes. Built, too, if you know what I mean."

"I know what you mean," Holt said.

She smirked. "She was looking for a man."

"Yeah?"

"Blond man. Hair and mustache. Riding a big clay bank. I had seen him."

Holt buttered his toast. "Go on," he said.

"Cold-eyed man he was. I'd seen him quite a few times.

Useta come into Bedloe and get supplies. Said he was a prospector. But he wasn't. I think he was a stock detective or suchlike. Very mysterious. Useta stay at the hotel and sleep through the clock and then he'd be gone without anybody seeing him."

Holt finished his toast and lit a cigar. "Got you curious, eh?"

She nodded. "Well, anyways, this woman asks a lot of questions about him. All I know is, he was working in the hills north of here. Prospecting, he said, although there ain't nothing in them hills but rocks and brush. Anyways, he musta been working hard at it because he always looked like he'd been through hell's back door when he'd show up here. Thin and dusty."

"Owlhooter maybe."

She shrugged. "The sheriff kept an eye on him, I tell you, but never got anything on him. The woman leaves here in a rainstorm. Rides into the hills."

"How along ago?"

She eyed him suspiciously. "You looking for her?"

"No. But I'm interested in the story."

"That's all I know. She come through here a coupla weeks ago or thereabouts. I often wondered where she went."

Holt stood up and paid his bill.

"You ain't staying the night?"

"No."

"That figures," she said, and picked up his dishes. "We ain't even got a newspaper in this town like Rockyhill has. Sometimes we get the Cheyenne papers. You think a girl like me could get by in Cheyenne? I hear there's lots of rich men in Cheyenne."

"There are."

"Maybe I'll sell out and go there. This town's dead. Ain't even got a newspaper to learn the gossip from."

Holt grinned. "You're wrong there. About the newspaper, I mean. Bedloe's got one."

She stared at him. "We have?"

"Yes—*you*. Good morning, Maggie."

She watched him leave the shop. "Someday," she said, "one of these men is gonna like me."

Holt walked back to the smithy. The blacksmith said, "Be ready in fifteen minutes. These shoes was worn so thin you could read through them."

Holt crossed the street to the general store to get his supplies. "Ever see a blond man in here?" he asked the woman behind the counter. "About five feet eight or nine? Thin? Blond hair and mustache? Wearing all black clothes? Riding a clay bank?"

She measured him carefully. "You a lawman?"

Holt nodded solemnly.

"Yeah, I've seen him. Never knowed his name. Used to come in here for supplies. Never talked. Funny thing you should ask about him."

"Why?"

"You *sure* you're a lawman?"

"Yes."

"Well, about a week ago a man comes in here asking for him too. Fellow from the MM Connected, north of here, near Rockyhill. Said he was his brother. I didn't take any stock in that, I tell you. They didn't look no more like each other than you and me do. But the MM man was nervous as all getout. Wanted to know the last time the blond man was in Bedloe. I saw him wandering around town asking everybody. Seems like there was a death in the family and the blond man was wanted."

"He was right about that," Holt said quietly.

"What do you mean?"

"Nothing. Nothing at all."

Holt took his supplies and went back to the livery stable. The dun had been shod. Holt paid his bill with the last of his money. He tied his supplies to the cantle.

"Riding a long ways?" the blacksmith asked.

"Not too far. Toward the Utah line."

"You got enough grub for a long ride."

"I eat a lot."

The blacksmith grunted.

Holt led the dun out into the street and rode west. The blacksmith watched him and then he hurried to the marshal's office and spent ten minutes of his time reading the Wanted posters with no luck whatsoever.

CHAPTER TWENTY-NINE

Rain pattered steadily on the brush and trees as Holt drew rein half a mile from the unknown's cave. From what he had learned from the talkative people of Bedloe, he was sure the blond man was the one he had killed, the one who had kept initialed records. He was sorry now that he had killed the slinking bastard. If he had caught him alive, he could have cleared up the whole mess. Either Drake or Lew Manning, or both of them, had been paying the man to kill. Now Lew Manning was dead, slain by another unknown. But, according to what Holt had learned in Bedloe, someone from the MM Connected had been searching for the killer. Which meant that the searcher didn't know the bushwhacker was dead.

It wasn't an unusual custom in that country to hire rustler-killers. Omniscient and omnipotent men accepted it as their "duty" to put the fear of God into rustlers, brand blotters and those who butchered other people's steers. Some counties in Wyoming had "Regulators" who burned out the smaller cattle ranches to drive them out of competing with bigger interests.

Suddenly the dun shied and blew. Holt whipped out his Colt and eyed the brush. The dun backed off. There was no sound other than the steady drumming of the rain. Holt slid from his saddle and walked toward the brush. There was something in there. Holt parted it and looked down on a body. The hands and head had been gnawed by teeth. A faint sweetish odor drifted up to Holt as he hooked a foot under the corpse and rolled it over. The flesh had been stripped from the head, but he could tell that a bullet had shattered one side of the skull.

Holt knelt by the body and felt inside the rotting coat. There was no wallet. The big belt buckle bore a dented set of initials. "C.K." Holt said. He searched his memory. "Charlie Krico," he said.

Despite his disgust he fingered through the stinking clothing. Something crackled in the lining of the trousers. He took out his case knife and cut through the rotten cloth. A fold of paper fell on the ground. He picked it up and scrutinized it in the dim light. There was a picture of a grim-faced man. The paper was a Pinkerton authorization, naming one, Carl Kreske, as an agent of the famous undercover organization.

Holt rubbed his jaw. The poor bastard had poked his nose in too far. He had paid a high price for his inquisitiveness. Holt cut branches and covered the sad relic of a man. He weighted them down with rocks and then went back to Panhandle, tucking the Pinkerton paper into his inner coat pocket. Another unsolved killing. The .38/56 slugs had been flying in that country, striking down everyone who got too nosy.

He reached the unknown's cave as the heavens let loose with a downpour, lashing the trees and brush. Water began to trickle down from the rock walls in steady sheets. Holt made a fire in the fire-hole and cooked beans and sowbelly. He drank three cups of black coffee and squatted beside the dying fire with his cup in his hand. There was an eerie quality about the place; it had been a den of plotted, cold-blooded death. But someone else must know where it was hidden. The man who paid the death bills. Sometime he would come looking there for the killer. Holt meant to wait for *him*.

He shrugged into his slicker and went outside. He took his tarp and blankets and walked up the crumbling slopes until he found a nest of huge boulders. Patiently he made a small camp, hiding it from the view of anyone below by crossing branches in front of it and covering the top with interwoven branches. He went down to the dun and unsaddled him, leading the horse up the slope and through a rocky chaos until he found a place where a rock wall leaned outward forming a shelter for the tired dun.

There was grass within reach of the horse and water was filling a rock pan. He picketed Panhandle and carried the saddle back to his new hideout. Then he went down to the cave and smothered the fire. He removed all traces of his occupancy and brushed the ground with a branch to hide his boot tracks.

He went back to his new camp and risked lighting a cigar. His side was still stiff where the shotgun slugs had played a devil's tattoo on it. It had been too damned close for comfort.

CHAPTER THIRTY

W hen a man has lived in wild country for many years, he seems to develop a sixth sense, a sense that subtly warns him of danger. So it was with Holt Cooper. He opened his eyes and stared up at the dim canvas roof above him. His blankets were wet from a steady trickle of water which had worked through the aged tarp. He sat up, cursing as the water dribbled down his neck. The light outside was gray. It was almost dawn.

Holt pulled on his boots and crawled to the edge of his shelter. He looked down toward the cave. He placed his hand on his Winchester. Minutes ticked past. The rain pattered steadily on the dripping brush. Then he saw the movement in the brush not far from the cave. He jammed on his hat and worked his way down the slope. The drumming of the rain drowned out his noise. He squatted in the brush a hundred feet from the cave and looked up the rock passageway which led toward his land. He saw an indistinct form in a thicket.

Holt placed his rifle on a rock and worked his way through the soaked brush. Fifty feet from the thicket he drew his Colt. Then he Indianed toward it. Suddenly the figure moved. A gun flashed. Holt threw himself to one side. He jumped forward and closed on the figure. There was a muffled scream as he struck hard with the barrel of his Colt. He looked down on the pale face of Vivian Leslie. Blood trickled slowly from her hairline. He knelt beside her and took the little Colt from her right hand. Then he picked her up and carried her up the slope to his shelter. He bathed her face with water from his canteen and chafed her wrists.

She opened her eyes and stared uncomprehendingly at him. "*You,*" she said. "Thank God I've found you."

Holt sat back on his heels. "How did you know where I was?"

She passed a hand across her tired eyes. "I didn't, Holt."

"You came right here," he said. "Who's with you?"

"No one."

He stood up and walked down to his rifle. He scouted through the brush and walked a quarter of a mile up the passageway. A small gray was tethered to a tree. He led the gray back to join Panhandle. Before he returned to the shelter he probed into the saddlebags and found the picture of the man he had killed. He placed it in his pocket and returned to Vivian. She was eating a piece of bread.

"I'll cook some grub," he said.

"No! This will do! Don't make a fire, Holt!"

"Why?"

She wiped her mouth, then touched her bruised forehead. "I may have been followed."

"What were you doing in here?"

"Looking for you."

"Don't lie to me."

"I'm not, Holt! I'm not!"

He rolled a cigarette and placed it between her lips. He cupped a match and lit the smoke. "It's about time you and I had a long talk," he said.

She leaned back against his saddlebags. "Yes."

"Talk about yourself," he said coldly.

"What do you want to know?"

"Why did you come to the Diamond W after running out on my brother?"

She stared at him. "Your *brother?*"

"Yes. Niles Williston was my half-brother."

"That explains a lot of things."

"Maybe to you, but not to me."

She drew the smoke into her lungs. "I can see now why you were so stubborn about leaving the Diamond W."

"It's my land," he said.

She placed a hand on his. "Why don't you leave this country before they kill you too?"

"Who?"

She looked surprised. "The MM men. There are three posses combing the country. You must get out of here while you have the chance."

Holt took the picture from his pocket and held it out to her. "Who is this?"

She gasped. "You took the picture from my saddlebag."

"I saw it once before. I did some investigating in Bedloe yesterday. You were looking for this man some time ago. Who is he, Vivian?"

She lowered her head. "Phil Allison."

"What is he to you?"

She looked up at him. "My fiancé."

Holt dropped the picture onto her lap. "What's the rest of the story? I want the *truth.*"

"I knew Phil some years ago. We were raised together in Denver. We went to school together. I think I loved him then." She placed her slim hands over her eyes. "Phil got into trouble. Money was all he thought about. He left Denver and went to Arizona. I heard later he got into trouble there. When he came back to Denver, he had changed a great deal. He had been just a wild kid when he left. When he came back, he was a man I didn't even know."

Holt rolled another smoke and lit it. The story seemed to be torn from her. He had never seen her like this before.

"Phil wanted to get married, but I was afraid of him. He gambled a lot and always wanted money. I helped him with the money willed to me by my father, but it was never enough. Then he got into trouble again and left for Cheyenne. I followed him."

"Why?"

"I still loved him." Vivian snubbed out her cigarette. "For a long time, I followed him. He was like a ghost drifting here and there. I suppose I was a fool to follow him, but I was younger then, and led on by some misguided sense of loyalty. He wrote to me now and then, but I never knew where he'd be from one day to the next. Then I heard he was in this country. I came to Rockyhill with the last of my money. Then I met Niles."

"That was good luck for him," Holt said bitterly.

"Let me alone! Niles was so different from Phil. Steady and reliable. My money was almost gone. Niles made a fool of himself over me. I didn't want to go back to Denver and face my friends. My reputation was gone as far as they were concerned. Niles was so persistent, and I hadn't found Phil. Gradually I began to forget about him. Then Drake Manning wanted me. I suppose he thought I was his kind of woman. It did look bad, living alone in Rockyhill. I decided to marry Niles."

Thunder rolled in the hills and the rain slashed down fiercely. Holt handed her his slicker as water dripped from the sodden tarp. She placed it about her shoulders gratefully. "Drake was furious. He warned me he'd do anything to keep Niles from having me. I was afraid for Niles. I left town with the last money I had, hoping Niles would forget me."

"He didn't," Holt said.

She looked away. "Yes, I know he didn't. Ab Chisum told me. Phil showed up in Denver one day. He had plenty of money and he spent it as though he had some inexhaustible source of supply. He was good to me. I thought he'd change but he wouldn't talk when I asked him where he got his money. All he would say was that he was working for a big cattle interest in southern Wyoming. It never occurred to me that he was working around here."

"Killing."

She met his eyes. "Yes. One time when he was drunk, he talked about 'regulating' but I didn't know what he meant. He said he got five hundred dollars every time he did a job and that he had been busy at his work and there was a great deal more money where the rest had come from."

"He was doing all right for himself," Holt said.

"He sent me a letter from Bedloe while he was on one of his trips. I didn't know what to do about him. I knew Bedloe was near Rockyhill but I had no idea of what he was doing. There was a lot of talk among my friends. I decided to follow Phil and went to Bedloe. I couldn't find him. All I knew was that he was in these hills somewhere. I followed him into the hills."

"You loved him a great deal."

She shook her head. "I followed him to tell him I wanted nothing more to do with him."

"So you could run back to Niles."

Her hand cracked across his face. "Damn you!"

Holt touched his stinging face. "Well?"

"I wanted to see Niles."

"You didn't seem much concerned when I told you he was dead."

"Why should I reveal my emotions to *you?*"

"You've got me there, Vivian."

She bent her head. "I'm sorry. You've been more than kind to me."

"You never saw Phil again?"

She shook her head. "I came in these hills looking for <u>him</u>. I found the cave down there. But I had no way of knowing where he was."

"Vivian," he said quietly.

She looked up at him.

Holt jerked his head. "He's dead. He killed Link and Perry Owens and tried to kill me. I killed him. He's buried in the trees not more than a quarter of a mile from here."

She placed a hand at her throat. "Somehow I knew it."

Holt took the leatherbound book from his pocket. "As near as I can figure it out, he was paid by someone to kill anyone he was told to kill. Joe Stroud and Ray Bascomb. Charlie Krico. Oscar Brink, Danny Casner, Norris Hayes, and Niles Williston. Possibly others as well."

"You're sure?"

"Yes."

"Then I'm glad he's dead."

"He paid the butcher's bill. There's one other man who will pay it too. The man who paid this Phil to kill."

"Who is it?"

"I'm willing to bet my life that it's Drake Manning."

"But Lew Manning was killed too!"

Holt nodded. *"After* Phil was killed."

Slowly she placed her hand to her mouth. She put her other hand on his. "They say in town that you killed Sim Pastor, the Owens brothers and Lew Manning. Tim ConIon has warrants made out for you charging you with their murders."

Holt looked into the dark eyes. "Do you think I did?"

"No." She shook her head. "No! Holt, why don't you leave this country? You'll end up being killed. The ranch isn't worth it."

"I came here to find the man who killed Niles. It may have been Phil who did it, but I want the man who paid him to do the job. I'm staying here until I find him."

"Please leave. I'll go with you."

"Why?"

"Don't you know?"

He knew. He had known for a long time. Suddenly he drew her close. She didn't resist. The rain slashed down through the graying sky as they found each other at last.

CHAPTER THIRTY-ONE

She sat at the edge of the tarp watching the rain. Holt lay back on the blankets and watched her watching the rain. Lazily he rolled a smoke and lit it. He eyed the smoke as it drifted about, seeking a way out of the shelter. Damn it, he felt good, even though the mood wouldn't last long enough to make a good memory.

She put her hands out into the rain and then pressed them against her forehead.

"Does it still hurt?" he asked.

She chuckled softly. "I have a hard head, Holt. You should have known that when I stayed on at your house when I thought I wasn't wanted."

"I'm glad you did."

"You shouldn't be. You've no home at all now. Ab always said I was a jinx."

He sat up. "I wonder if Ab is still in Rockyhill."

"Oh!" She clapped a hand across her mouth.

"What is it, Vivian?"

"I forgot to tell you. After you got away from Rockyhill, Walt Short took Ab from the livery stable. Tim Conlon said he saw Short and Manning riding out of town with Ab."

A coldness grew in him. "You forgot? You forgot to tell me *that*?"

She seemed startled. "Why? They won't hurt Ab. Everybody likes him. He's never bothered anyone."

"Not up until I came to the Diamond W. Ab took my side. That's enough to turn Manning against him. But there's more to it than just that. Drake Manning probably thinks Ab knows where I'm hiding out and he won't stop short of murder to force it out of the poor old coot."

Holt buckled on his gun belt and reached for his coat

"You're not going to look for him?" she asked.

"What else would I do?"

He took his rifle and crawled to the edge of the shelter. She gripped him by the arm. "Holt, you *can't* leave! They have men on the roads. The MM men and the sheriff's men both. They'll shoot on sight."

Holt took her hand from his arm. "I'll take that chance." He stood up in the slanting rain and shrugged into his old slicker. "Stay tight," he said. "No fires. I'll be back as soon as I can."

"If they don't kill you."

He whirled. "Shut up! I can do a little killing myself if I have to."

"Isn't there anything I can do?"

"Watch that cave. But if you see anyone nosing around down there, make damned sure they don't see you."

An unholy haste was in him as he rode out of the hills. The rain offered a short-term break for him, but he didn't delude himself into thinking he wouldn't be seen. He stopped now and then and studied the dripping landscape with his glasses. He rode along the side of the hills to the west of the ranch, stopped half a mile from his house and studied it with his glasses. He was about to ride on when something seemed to tell him to ride closer.

He dismounted five hundred yards from the house and scanned it again. A faint trace of smoke struggled up from the chimney, only to be beaten down by the rain.

He took his Winchester and worked his way through the dripping trees. He saw a horse below the benchland, standing in the shelter of a motte. It was Ab's mouse-colored mount. He walked softly across to the house and flattened himself against the wall. He heard a stirring in the kitchen. He eased along until he could look into the window. Ab Chisum sat on the floor beside the stove, with his back against the wall and his face turned toward the smoking stove.

"Ab," he said.

The little man did not move.

"Ab!"

The little man slowly turned his head. Holt's guts churned as he saw Ab's face. The eyes were lost in great bloated blobs of blue-black, bruised flesh. The nose had been smashed to one side and caked blood encrusted Ab's shaggy mustache. His lips were caricatures, swollen and split. Holt stepped through the window and knelt beside him.

"Who did it, Ab?"

Ab put a hand on Holt's arm. "It's you, ain't it, boy? I thought mebbe they mighta killed yuh by now."

"Who did it?"

Ab reached up and touched his swollen mouth. "Hurts like thunder," he lisped. "'Twas Drake Manning and Walt Short. They give me a goin' over like I was a punchin' bag."

Holt went outside and filled a bucket with water. He took it into the house and tore up a towel. Tenderly he bathed the battered face. Ab groaned. "Git me a bottle of the Companion," he said. "I didn't have the strength to rise up, Holt."

Holt got a bottle and opened it. He poured the liquid into a cup and spooned the tonic between puffed lips. Ab sighed. "Better," he said.

"Where are they, Ab?"

"Lookin' for you. They thought I knowed where you was. I thought mebbe yuh had enough sense to take out of this country. Yore muleheaded, Holt."

"I'm staying until I clear up Niles' death—and pay those bastards off for what they did to you."

"Fergit about me! Pound leather outa here, I tell yuh. Before it's too late!"

Holt patted Ab's shoulders. He stoked up the smoldering fire and then went into Ab's bedroom. The place stank of fecal matter and urine. The MM men had acted like pigs in his house. Holt took blankets into the kitchen and made the little man comfortable.

Ab shivered as he crouched down in the blankets. But he had to talk. "Sloan Minner put the finger on yuh, Holt. He told Drake yuh was in the emporium. I heard Drake and Walt talkin' about it. They thought I was out cold. Takes more than them two bastards to lick Ab Chisum."

"Sure, Ab. Sure."

"Get me my old Remington .44 outa my hair trunk."

Holt got the heavy sidearm and checked the loads. "You're coming with me," he said.

"No. I can't travel. I'll stay here. You light a shuck outa here."

Holt thought it over. Ab was right. He was in bad shape.

Ab shivered again. "I'm goin' to talk," he said. "I kept my mouth shut long enough as it is. There's somethin' about me yuh don't know, Holt."

"So?"

Ab felt inside his coat and took out a tobacco pouch. He handed it to Holt. "Open it. Feel down inside the tobacco."

Ab coughed hard. Thick dark blood spewed out on the floor. He slowly wiped his battered lips. "They belted me in the guts," he said. "I ain't never felt like killin' anyone, but I hope I live long enough to get a bead on Walt Short."

"You'll live to be a hundred, Ab."

"Hell with that. Feel down inside the tobacco like I said."

Holt probed down into the tobacco. His fingers touched metal. He took out a badge. "Deputy United States Marshal," he said and swallowed hard. It took a moment for the fact to sink in.

"My commission is in my left boot," Ab said.

"What's the story?" Holt asked and felt humble.

"I was sent in here undercover after the killings got real bad. I was well known around here before I went into government service. So it was easy for me to drift back and take any job that come along. I learned plenty. Wrote it all down. You'll find the report behind that picture on my bedroom wall. Yore eyes will bug out, son."

"Who killed Niles?"

"'Tweren't that man yuh killed in the hills. 'Twas Drake Manning. That's one job he wanted to do hisself. I know it wasn't the hired killer, because I learned later, he was seen in Bedloe the day before the killin' and the day of the killin'. Drake took off his boots to make it look like he was the hired bushwhacker."

Holt knelt beside the little marshal. "You're sure?"

"Yes. Sloan Minner knew. Drake bragged about it to him once when he was drunk. Minner hisself told it to me when he was figgerin' on askin' for the reward. Ole Minner was half full at the time. Sanctimonious, Bible-thumpin', two-faced sonofabitch!"

"What's Minner's angle?"

"Money! What else?" Ab coughed harshly and wiped the blood from his lips. "Minner worked with Drake. Drake was always borrowin' money from Minner 'cause he didn't want Lew to know he was in the hole from gamblin'. Drake always figgered he'd get in solid with Lew if Sloan could get the Diamond W for him. Lew never had much use for Minner."

"Who killed Lew?"

"It weren't the hired dry-gulcher. Yuh know better then anyone else it wasn't *him,* lessn' he come from the grave."

"I'll have to get you to a doctor, Ab."

"No. It kin wait! Yuh got work to do."

"Was Drake paying the man I killed?"

"I think so. Never could prove it. But who else would it be? Wasn't Lew. Lew did his own fightin'. Drake wanted power. The man's loco. He won't let no one stand in his way. He always figgered Lew was too soft for real dirty killin'. He was right there. Holt, get that report I made out. It'll clear yuh of some of the things they said you done."

"Not now," a cold voice said.

Holt whirled, dropping his hand for a draw. Walt Short stood in the kitchen doorway with his Winchester aimed at Holt's belly. Short looked down at Ab. "You shoulda talked before we worked yuh over, Chisum. What do yuh owe this killin' bastard?"

Ab coughed. "Yuh sonofabitch," he gasped. "I'll tell yuh! Friendship! That's what! Somethin' yuh don't know the meanin' of."

"Do tell," Short jeered.

The MM man jerked his head. "Get them hands up, Cooper. How do yuh want it? Belly or—"

Ab raised the old Remington. Short jumped to one side and fired his Winchester. Ab jerked as the slug struck him. Holt rushed Short. The tall MM man whirled, levering in a round. But Ab Chisum wasn't done. The old Remington blasted. Short buckled over and fell heavily. His head rested on Ab's legs. Ab lowered the smoking six-gun. He looked up at Holt and smiled. "Yuh kin have the rest of the Companion," he said quietly. "I won't need it where I'm goin'."

Holt dragged the dead MM man from Ab's legs. He gripped Ab by the shoulders. The little marshal's eyes looked blankly into his.

Holt stepped back. Ab had saved him from a cold-blooded killing. Holt walked into Ab's bedroom and ripped the faded picture from the wall. A fold of papers was tacked to the peeling wallpaper. Holt took it. Then he turned. A man had yelled from down in the valley. Holt ran into the living room and peered through a shattered window. Big Tim Conlon was urging his horse up the soft slope. Four men were pushing up behind him.

Holt dashed through the house and out of the back door. He kept the house between him and the posse as he made heavy going up the soft slope. He darted into the trees. A rifle cracked near the house. The slug thudded into a tree. Holt broke from the woods and headed for Panhandle. He turned and fired four rounds over the house. The posse-men slid from their mounts and broke for cover.

Holt reached the big dun and spurred him to the south. Rifles rattled through the slanting rain as he made the shelter of a shoulder of the big butte. He headed for the dim hills, and Vivian.

CHAPTER THIRTY-TWO

Holt looked back as he rode. Conlon's men would shoot to kill, and they were sure of their target—Holt Cooper.

He left the dun hidden in a small box canyon and worked his way over the rough country, avoiding the passageway which led into the cave area. He didn't want any part of that passageway. Not with Drake Manning still on the loose.

He came out in the area where Vivian's horse was picketed. The horse whinnied loudly when he saw Holt. Holt cursed him for a loudmouth. He walked through the dripping brush and came out on a ledge where he could see the shelter, but he didn't see Vivian. He slid down the greasy slope and padded toward the shelter. He lifted the edge of the tarp. No one there.

Holt crawled into the shelter. Damn her. He had told her to stick tight. He took out the paper he had found behind the picture and folded it inside the leatherbound book. He placed the book in a small canvas bag and tied the top. Then he took the bag up the slope and secreted it beneath an overhanging rock.

The rain poured down, soaking beneath his slicker and making a sodden mass of his battered hat. Where in hell's name was she? He went back to the shelter and crawled in. Beyond the shelter he saw puddled footmarks. Hers. He loaded his Winchester and worked through the jumble of rocks to where he could see the cave. There were more foot-prints in the gravelly earth in front of it.

Holt froze as a man called out something far up the rock passageway. Then he heard the thud of hoofs and the clicking of stones. He faded back into the brush and dropped flat, shoving his rifle forward.

The thudding of hoofs came closer. He heard the creak of saddle leather. A big man, draped in a poncho, hove into Holt's view. It was Tim Conlon, riding with a rifle across his thighs, peering into the dripping brush as he rode. Four men followed him. One of them cursed. "He ain't in here, Tim! He's headed south toward Bedloe!"

"You ain't got the brains God gave a rat!" snapped the big sheriff. "He's in here. And by God we'll stay in here until we find him!"

"I ain't about to feel happy about running into that jasper in here," another man said. "What with the way he handles a long gun."

"Shoot to kill," Conlon said. "Don't take no chances."

"Don't worry, Tim. We will."

They passed the cave and out of Holt's sight. In a little while the noise of their passage was drowned out by the pelting rain.

Holt stood up and walked toward the cave. Something moved. He jumped to one side and raised his rifle. Then he lowered it as Vivian came to the front of the cave. Her face was pale, and her hair hung over her forehead. She stared at Holt, opened her mouth and then closed it

Holt stepped forward.

"Run!" she screamed. "He's here!"

An arm reached out and shoved her aside. Drake Manning stood there with his cocked Colt in his hand, pressing it into her waist. "Drop that Winchester, Cooper," he said.

Holt dropped his rifle.

"Take out your six-gun. Throw it in the brush. No tricks mind, or she'll get it."

Holt slowly unbuttoned his slicker and drew out his Colt. He had no chance. He threw it into the brush.

"Raise your hands," Manning said. "Come on in out of the rain."

Holt raised his hands and rested them atop his soaked hat. He walked toward the cave. Manning shoved Vivian in ahead of him. Holt stopped inside the cave entrance. "Keep coming," Drake said. "Set on that rock." Holt did as he was told, never taking his eyes from the rancher. Drake looked out of the cave. "I hope to God he goes all the way to Bedloe."

"You won't get away with anything," Holt said.

Drake spat. "No? You'll see. I got too much at stake to louse things up now. Where's Allison's tally book?"

"I don't know."

"You're a damned liar."

"You're worried about that book, aren't you? It would hang you, Manning."

"I'm not going to hang. Neither are you. I won't have the county stand that expense."

His meaning was clear. A ball of ice seemed to form in Holt's gut. Vivian had disobeyed orders. She had made a fatal mistake. Fatal for Holt Cooper and maybe for her as well.

Manning glanced at her. "You could have had it made," he said. "You can still have me if you'll keep your mouth shut."

She pushed the hair from her eyes. "No," she said.

"You'd rather die with him then?"

"If I have to."

"How touching," Manning said.

"I wouldn't expect *you* to understand."

"Get up!" he snarled. "Both of you!"

They did as they were told.

"Walk up the slope," Manning ordered.

Holt gave Vivian a hand. She looked up into his face.

"I'm sorry," she said. "I left the shelter just as he came to the cave."

Holt squeezed her arm.

They stopped at the shelter. "Very cosy," Manning said. "What were you waiting for, Cooper?"

"You."

"I figured as much. Walk up the slope."

They slipped on the greasy earth as they climbed up the. slope. Then they walked through the narrow passageway to where Vivian's horse was picketed. Manning stopped to look back. Vivian pressed her hand against Holt's. He opened it and felt cold metal. He didn't have to look down to know that he had her little .41 Colt in his hand. He closed his hand and held it tight against his slicker.

They walked farther up the gloomy canyon. Manning looked back. Holt knew he didn't want Conlon's posse to hear the shooting. He might explain Holt's death, but he'd never convince Westerners of the necessity of killing a woman.

"This is far enough," Drake said finally.

Holt turned toward him.

"Where's Phil Allison?" asked Manning.

"Dead," Holt said.

"Uh-huh. I thought so."

"He did your last dirty job," Holt said evenly. "Killing off the Owens brothers."

Manning grinned evilly. "Didn't cost me anything," he said.

"Then you *were* the payoff man?"

"I didn't say that."

"Who else would it be?"

"You guessed right, Holt. Too bad you didn't guess I was here before you came back."

The rain sluiced down. Thunder boomed in the hills and lightning lanced into a butte high above them. The sound and the odor of electrical discharge filled the air. Holt cocked the little stingy gun. Even he couldn't hear the click.

Manning shrugged down into his slicker. He jerked his head at Vivian. "Get away from him."

She walked ten feet away. There was a set white look to her oval face. She glanced quickly at Holt.

Manning stepped back and raised the Winchester. Holt tilted the Colt and fired. Manning cursed as the slug whipped through the slack of his slicker. The Winchester roared. Holt was already halfway to Manning, running in a crouch. He felt something sting across his back as he ran. Manning jumped back, levering in another round.

Holt fired again and missed. Then he was on Manning, dropping the stingy Colt, wrestling Drake for the rifle. They stood there, swaying back and forth, straining against each other. Holt's left hand was ripped by the rear sight. Manning spat in Holt's face and wrenched the rifle away from him.

Holt went down on one knee. Manning slashed at him with the rifle barrel. The blow fell heavily on Holt's left shoulder. He groveled for the Colt, but it had been tramped into the mud. He came up and belted Manning in the guts, hurting his hand cruelly on the big belt buckle. The Winchester flatted off into the air. Manning swung it hard, but Holt went underneath it. Manning swung again and knocked Holt sprawling.

The rancher ran up a slope, clawing at the bushes with his free hand. Holt snatched up the Colt. It was hopelessly jammed with mud. He hurled it at Manning. It struck him between the shoulder blades. Manning slipped. The Winchester slid down toward Holt. He snatched it up.

"For Christ's sake, don't shoot!" Drake Manning yelled. Then he gripped a rock with his right hand and threw it hard. The rock clicked against the gun barrel. Manning plowed up the greasy slope. Holt cast the rifle aside and went up after him. He caught up with the struggling man and grabbed for a heel. The spur cut his hand to the bone.

Manning was down, slipping and struggling on the slope. Holt held on like grim death and managed to grip Manning's ankle. He pulled Manning down toward him. Manning got to his knees and pawed for one of his Colts. Holt kicked himself upward and gripped Manning about the waist. They clung there for a few seconds and then Drake went headfirst over Holt. Holt hung on and they came rolling down the slope, throwing punches from all angles. Holt hit hard with Manning on top of him. The rancher dug a knee into Holt's groin and hammered at his face.

Holt got to his knees and slammed vicious punches in close, battering at Drake's eyes. Drake broke away and started to run but Vivian threw the rifle in between his churning legs. He hit hard, gasping for breath. Holt landed on top of him. He tore off Manning's hat and gripped his long fine hair. He pulled back his head and hooked his free arm about the straining throat. He closed off Drake Manning's wind and then stood up, dragging him to a shallow rock pool. He released the gasping rancher and hit him in the guts and then on the jaw. Manning sobbed as he went down. He freed a Colt and fired from pointblank range. The slug smashed into Holt's left shoulder, knocking him back.

Manning got up to his knees and cocked the Colt. Holt kicked out desperately. The Colt roared as it moved up. Then Holt was on Manning again, pounding his head. against the rocks. He gripped the weakened rancher by the throat and forced his head under the water. There was a set intentness on Holt's smeared face. Manning's legs flailed weakly.

Something tore at Holt. He looked back over his shoulder and saw Vivian Leslie. "No, Holt!" she screamed. "Let him up. For God's sake don't have a killing on your hands!"

Holt dragged the unconscious man from the roiled water. He stood up and shook his head. Blood flowed from his wound. He pressed a hand against it. "Get Conlon," he said, and fell flat on his face in the trampled mud.

"He'll live," the voice said from a long way off.

Holt opened his eyes. He lay on his back in the cave. The heat of a fire felt good against his body. Tim Conlon wiped his bloody hands. "The slug is out," he said. "No bones smashed."

"Where's Manning?"

Conlon jerked his head. Drake Manning lay tied hand and foot. His eyes were sunk deep in his head.

"Outa his mind," Conlon said. "Maybe he'll cheat the noose after all."

Holt gathered himself. "Help me up, Conlon."

"You can't move, man."

"Help me up!"

Conlon sighed and helped Holt to his feet. He aided Holt from the cave. Holt felt waves of nausea flow over him as he went to the place where he had hidden Ab's report and the tally book. He gripped it tightly as Conlon helped him back into the grateful warmth of the cave.

Holt dropped on the damp blankets. "It's all there. Chisum was a deputy U.S. Marshal. The tally book is a record kept by a man named Phil Allison. He was Manning's paid killer."

"Allison? I've got Wanted posters on him."

"He's dead. I killed him after he killed Link Owens and wounded Perry Owens."

"I knowed you didn't have anything to do with that."

"I killed one man. Phil Allison. I'll stand trial for that in any court in the land."

"You won't have to," Conlon said, and stood up. "She's waiting for you, Cooper. She couldn't stand to see me dig out that slug."

"Get her."

Conlon walked out of the cave. "Kelly!" he yelled. "Tell Miss Leslie to come down. He's all right now."

She came into the cave. Conlon coughed and walked outside. "Get the hosses!" he yelled.

Vivian knelt beside Holt and cradled his head in her arms. "It'll be all right now," he said, and she kissed him. Her face was wet with mingled tears and rain.

TAKE A LOOK AT RIDE A LONE TRAIL AND MASSACRE CREEK

Two Full Length Western Novels

THERE'S CARNAGE IN THE CONCHAS IN THIS CLASSIC WESTERN DOUBLE.

Ride a Lone Trail

When Ken Macklin left the Double H a few years back, he had sworn never to return. But now that his father had been gunned down in ambush, he had no choice. Someone had to pay.

But as he trailed across the Lazy J spread, he learned he was being followed. It looked as if he were to be drygulch victim Number Two. For things were as bad as when he'd left, only now the valley was about to explode into open range war. All it had needed was the fuse, and Ken was it.

Massacre Creek

Tough cavalryman Sabin Shay faced his Cheyenne captors. He knew the price of defeat—and waited for his own destruction. But then he saw the hatred in the Redmen's eyes. If they just killed him plain and simple, he'd be lucky...

"The joy of reading Shirreffs' work is in his mastery of pacing and his tough, gritty prose." **– James Reasoner, author of Outlaw Ranger**

COMING DECEMBER 2021

ABOUT THE AUTHOR

Gordon D. Shirreffs published more than 80 western novels, 20 of them juvenile books, and John Wayne bought his book title, Rio Bravo, during the 1950s for a motion picture, which Shirreffs said constituted *"the most money I ever earned for two words."* Four of his novels were adapted to motion pictures, and he wrote a Playhouse 90 and the Boots and Saddles TV series pilot in 1957.

A former pulp magazine writer, he survived the transition to western novels without undue trauma, earning the admiration of his peers along the way. The novelist saw life a bit cynically from the edge of his funny bone and described himself as looking like a slightly parboiled owl. Despite his multifarious quips, he was dead serious about the writing profession.

Gordon D. Shirreffs was the 1995 recipient of the Owen Wister Award, given by the Western Writers of America for "a living individual who has made an outstanding contribution to the American West."

He passed in 1996.

www.ingramcontent.com/pod-product-compliance
Lightning Source LLC
Chambersburg PA
CBHW011420010726
47494CB00011B/2426